CODENAME: BLACKJACK

Now Available from Ternary Publishing

SAGAS OF THE CINCINNATI

Cincinnatus

Codename: Blackjack

OTHER TITLES

Crosley:
Two Brothers and A Business Empire
That Transformed The Nation

Coral Castle:
The Mystery of Ed Leedskalnin
and his American Stonehenge

www.ternarypublishing.com

CODENAME: BLACKJACK

Rusty McClure & David Stern

TERNARY PUBLISHING

CODENAME: BLACKJACK

Copyright @2024 by Rusty McClure

All rights reserved. No portion of this book may be reproduced in any fashion, print, facsimile, or electronic, or by any method yet to be developed, without express permission of the copyright holder.

Ternary Publishing

Library of Congress Cataloging-in-Publication Data

McClure, Rusty, 1950-
Codename: Blackjack / by Rusty McClure and David Stern
p. cm.
ISBN hardback edition: 979-8-9915240-0-1
ISBN e-book edition: 979-8-9915240-1-8
Stern, David. II. Title.

This book is a work of fiction. Any reference to historical events, real people, or real locales are used fictitiously. Other names, characters, places, and incidents are products of the author's imagination. Any resemblance to actual events or locales or persons, living or dead, is entirely coincidental.

Official government documents that appear in the color section between pages 126 and 127 are all in the public domain.

All photographs appearing within that section are used with permission of the copyright holder(s).

Edited by Heather Shaw
Book and Cover design by Craig Ramsdell, Ramsdell Design
Cover illustration by Tim Parker
Back cover illustration by Nick Stull
Sagas of the Cincinnati logo by Steve Campbell

To Patriotic Courage
We Dedicate Our Saga

CONTENTS

1963
"Three may keep a secret…"
1

PRESENT DAY
"…what a tangled web we weave…"
15

TEN DAYS LATER
"…he wanted to splinter the CIA into a thousand pieces…"
129

THE NEXT MORNING
"It was our country for awhile…"
243

Cast of Characters
508

Acknowledgements
510

1963

Three may keep a secret,
if two of them are dead.

Benjamin Franklin,
Poor Richard's Almanack

PROLOGUE

Apex, Nevada
20 Miles Northeast of Las Vegas
Sunday, October 27, 1963

The hat was a white Stetson.

Over the last six months, Averill had taken to wearing it as a matter of course. Not because he was trying to fit in out here—that would be a waste of time. Averill was as East Coast blueblood as they came (with a name like James Preston Averill, how could he be otherwise?), a product of Choate, Yale (Skull and Bones, of course), then the CIA and a half dozen other acronymed government agencies that had come and gone over the last decade. Before his hair thinned, before he'd let twenty pounds worth of embassy dinners and DC banquets accumulate around his midsection, he'd been the archetypal blond-haired, blue-eyed, square-jawed American prep-school kid. He still was. No sense in trying to pretend otherwise.

No, he wore the hat not to roleplay, but to honor the man who'd given it to him: the late General Kazmir Wachtel, USAF. What had happened to Wachtel was a shame—necessary, but a shame nonetheless. Every time he put on the hat, Averill thought of Kaz.

Your sacrifice was not in vain, General. I promise.

Averill sat behind the wheel of a black Ford Galaxy, heading northeast out of Vegas on the Salt Lake Highway. Windows open to feel the breeze. The cold braced him, refreshed him after the day's heat—close to a hundred degrees. Unseasonably warm.

The road straightened, swooping down from the ridgeline into a vast and empty basin. The full moon poured down enough light to get a sense of scope and distance. The landscape here was immense—most of it desert. A single light shone in the darkness a few miles ahead.

"Is that it? That has to be it, right?" His passenger pointed toward that light with the rolled-up newspaper he held in his right hand, the same newspaper he'd been tapping against his knee throughout their journey.

"I would think so." Averill glanced at the man out of the corner of his eye. "Relax, lieutenant. This is all going to be very straightforward."

The "lieutenant" was an honorific. Stephen Guidry was a geologist, not a military man. Averill had convinced Guidry to leave Saudi Arabia and come to work for his country, use his expertise in service to something other than profit. It had been easier to have him enlist than to run through the paperwork required for the civilian clearance that would have been required to fully brief Guidry on Ararat—so the man understood the necessity, the urgency, of the task facing them.

"Yes, sir. Understood, sir." Guidry stopped fidgeting and sat quietly for a moment … and then went right back to tapping the newspaper on his knee.

Averill sighed inwardly.

Guidry was a good man—a solid citizen, married, beautiful wife, two beautiful kids. Averill had gone to his house for a holiday party last year. Everyone from Ararat had been there; it was all drinks and laughter, the old bonhomie among friends, the shared smiles between men who knew the importance of what they were doing.

That was before the "accident," of course.

Now, good man or not, Guidry was a problem. His nervousness, Averill knew, masked a deep unease. Immense guilt over what they'd done. How much longer could he hold those feelings

PROLOGUE

in? Not much, Averill suspected. He saw a reckoning coming, sooner rather than later.

Not that he wasn't haunted occasionally by the specter of that afternoon himself. The look on General Wachtel's face, on the closed-circuit monitor in the control room.

"Jim," Wachtel had said. "Something's wrong. We can't breathe down here. Jim." There had been desperation in his voice, in his eyes, desperation mirrored by the frantic activity behind him, the other men trapped beneath the surface, trying desperately—fruitlessly—to find a way out of the deathtrap they were in.

Averill pushed those memories away, pushed the brim of the Stetson back, letting the cool breeze hit his forehead. The past was past. What was done was done. What was important now: the future. The promise of a better tomorrow. Not just for him but for the whole country. For the whole world.

The promise of Ararat.

He drove on.

The light in the distance grew closer. It resolved into a single sodium spot fastened high above a wooden sign at the side of the road, two stories high.

American Lime Products Corporation
No Trespassing

Averill turned off the highway and onto a gravel drive. American Lime Products was a huge company, a big supplier to the ongoing construction in and around Las Vegas. The site here was quarry and refinery, plant and offices. The road snaked past a series of huts and trailers, conveyor belts and gravel hoppers, huge piles of rock and sand, until it curved around a mound of earth and there, hidden from sight, a car was waiting.

Averill glanced at the dashboard clock: 2:51.

His man was early. Not a surprise, Averill thought. He and Guidry were early too. Force of habit. What was a surprise: His man was not alone. There was someone else with him. A woman.

Averill had a moment of unease. He felt the weight of the gun in his shoulder holster, the heft of the knife strapped around his ankle. His days in the field were long over, but he'd made a point of keeping up with his training. If things went south, he had full confidence that that training would be more than adequate. And if it wasn't…

The risk was worth taking.

Averill set the parking brake and stepped out of the car.

The man he'd come here to meet stepped forward, giving Averill his first up-close look at Frank Ferrone.

Ferrone was general manager of the Peacock Hotel and Casino, in the heart of the Vegas Strip. Forty-eight years old, unmarried, worked eighteen hours a day. Even now he was dressed for his job: dark suit, white shirt, thin black tie. Thinning black hair. An altogether unremarkable face—an altogether unremarkable man.

Other than a rumored taste for showgirls, Ferrone eschewed flash and Vegas glitz entirely. Made a point of flying under the radar at all times, unlike any other member of La Cosa Nostra, the Mafia, that Averill had ever come across.

Which made him perfect for the job.

The two men stopped six feet apart and regarded each other.

"Colonel Averill. A pleasure."

"Mr. Ferrone. Thank you for coming."

"How could I say no? Your invitation was … intriguing, to say the least."

"I'm glad. But that invitation was for you, Mr. Ferrone. And you alone." Averill put some steel in his voice. "I stressed the importance of keeping this meeting secret, didn't I? And yet, you

PROLOGUE

bring her." He gestured to the woman.

She was taller than Ferrone. Dressed for work as well, a tailored suit for a well-proportioned figure. Dark wavy hair, strong features—handsome, not beautiful. A showgirl? No, he decided. Something else. But what?

"Who is she?" Averill asked. "And why is she here?"

"Miss Falconetti is my right hand," Ferrone said. "She's involved with every aspect of my work. Whatever deal we make, she'll be part of it."

"You don't have to worry. I know how to keep a secret," Miss Falconetti said.

Averill heard a Chicago accent in her voice. Educated guess: She had come here from the Windy City with Ferrone, who'd moved to Vegas a dozen years ago. The man had quickly proven himself so capable that the Committee—the organization that represented the interests of all the families and ruled the Mob everywhere, not just in Vegas but Chicago and New York, Miami, Jersey and Rhode Island, Philly and Cleveland and every place in between—had taken notice of him. Had promoted him up the ladder time and again until Ferrone worked for not just one family … but all of them.

Frank Ferrone managed the Committee's money here in Vegas—greased the wheels that needed greasing, kept the construction unions in line, paid the building inspectors to obtain the necessary permits, handled the cops whose instincts needed massaging, kept the politicians' ambitions in check. An incredibly able man, driven and hardworking. Just the sort of man Averill needed.

"I'll count on your discretion, Miss Falconetti. Your ability to keep secrets. This, by the way, is Lieutenant Guidry. He's an associate of mine in this matter."

"Lieutenant." Ferrone nodded, a greeting and an acknowledgement. "So, what exactly are you up to these days, Colonel?"

"Excuse me?"

"Give me a name, I'm usually pretty good at finding out who the person is. What they do. But in your case…" Ferrone shook his head. "Last thing I found on you is from ten years ago. You were in Korea, with General MacArthur. A special advisor."

"I'm still with the government," Averill said.

"Not the Department of Justice, I hope." Ferrone's face darkened. "Not that cocksucker Bobby Kennedy. Because if that's what all this hush-hush, tell-nobody, three a.m. bullshit is about, you trying to get me to rat out the people I work for, we got a huge problem."

Ferrone shifted position and Averill saw the telltale bulge of a gun under his suit coat. The woman was probably carrying a weapon as well. Averill made a few mental calculations. "No. Rest easy, Mr. Ferrone, I'm not with the Department of Justice. I'm with the Central Intelligence Agency now. And for the record, I'm not a fan of our current attorney general either. Or his brother, for that matter."

Averill had a particular animus for JFK. Part of the reason he was here.

"Good. Because those goddamn Kennedys, they're making life just about impossible for us here. We invented this town, and now they're trying to squeeze us out."

"I'm sure you'll find a way to keep a hand in," Averill said. Even if that hand was largely invisible. As much cash as there was pouring into Vegas, as there always would be—he knew the mob would find a way to stay involved.

"Okay, so you're not with the DOJ. That's good. I still don't know what it is you want with me, though."

"That's simple. I want us to be partners."

PROLOGUE

Ferrone smiled. "You want to go into the casino business?"

"Hardly."

"So?"

"Let me give you a little background first. Lieutenant Guidry?" Averill held out his hand and Guidry handed him the rolled-up newspaper. "This is a copy of the *Las Vegas Journal Review*, from two weeks ago. You may have seen—"

"I'm too busy to read the papers," Ferrone interrupted.

"I read them," Miss Falconetti said.

"Good. Then perhaps you remember this article." He flipped through the paper and held it up so the moonlight shone on the headline he now pointed to. "Here."

"Deadly Desert Disaster." Miss Falconetti nodded. "Yes. I think I did see this. There was an accident of some sort at Nellis Air Force Base. Some equipment that malfunctioned. A number of people were killed."

"Yes. Twenty-six, to be exact."

"Well, that's a shame," Ferrone said. "Friends of yours?"

"Yes," Averill said. "Some of them. Friends and colleagues."

He pictured Wachtel's face again. *Jim. Can you hear us? Jim!*

"But it wasn't an accident," Averill continued. "We just made it look that way. What it was, really, was murder."

"What?"

"Murder." Averill looked Ferrone in the eye. "I killed them."

"Hey. Hold on here." Ferrone shook his head. "You sure you want to be telling me this?"

"Absolutely I'm sure. You need to understand the importance of what we're discussing here. The seriousness of our mutual endeavor."

"I haven't said yes yet."

"You said yes the moment you agreed to this meeting," Averill replied.

The two men stared at each other for a moment. Averill had shifted position slightly, so his sport coat hung a little more loosely on his left side. So the gun handle was a little more accessible.

"So that's how it is," Ferrone said.

Averill nodded. "That's right."

"Okay. So, these twenty-six people. Tell me why you killed them," Ferrone said.

"Ararat."

"Ararat. What's that?"

"Project Ararat. A top-secret program we were all part of."

"That's from the Bible," Miss Falconetti said. "Ararat."

"That's right." Averill nodded. "The mountain where Noah landed after the flood. Where the world began again."

"So what was this top-secret program about?" Ferrone asked.

Averill smiled. "Well. I don't have to tell you these are dangerous times we're living in, Mr. Ferrone," he began. And now he was thinking of JFK again, President John Fitzgerald Kennedy, who had ignored the wisdom of the agency's old hands and bungled the Bay of Pigs invasion, who had caved to the Soviet Union during the Cuban missile crisis barely a year later, who had withdrawn nuclear missiles from the Izmir bases in Turkey, whose misadventures and timidity in Southeast Asia were threatening the stability of an entire continent. But it wasn't just JFK's foreign entanglements that worried Averill. No, Averill's animus for the president sprang from actions closer to home as well. JFK's actions, and his words, and his intentions. Despite the president's own military experience—the PT 109 incident, which had made him a war hero—Averill found the man naïve at the best of times and dangerously misguided at others.

"These are times of crisis," he continued. "Crisis and opportunity. Times that demand bold and decisive action by bold and

PROLOGUE

decisive men."

"Like you," Ferrone said.

"And you. Lieutenant?"

"Sir?"

Averill motioned Guidry forward. "Tell our friends, broad strokes, what Ararat is about."

Guidry cleared his throat and began to speak. Nervously at first, about the project's history, and then with more confidence as he delved into the science. How the project had progressed over the years, and then how it all had changed in one night. With one simple discovery.

Averill watched Ferrone and Falconetti as Guidry talked about the implications of that discovery.

When Guidry was done speaking, there was silence again for a moment.

"Jesus Christ," Ferrone said finally.

Averill smiled. "Yes."

"If what he's saying—what you're saying—if that's true…"

"It is."

"Then these numbers. They're for real?" Ferrone reached into his suit pocket and pulled out a slip of paper. It had been fabricated to look exactly like a slot machine receipt from the Peacock Casino, but the numbers on the paper had nothing to do with slot machines, would be meaningless without the explanation Averill had supplied in the invitation itself. And the dollar figures those numbers translated into.

"Real? They most certainly are. As real and solid as the ground we're standing on."

Averill could see Ferrone's wheels spinning. Could see him doing the math. The man might not be as flashy as his other mafia brethren, but deep down he was motivated by the same thing they all were. Money.

"I think we could have something here, Mr. Averill," Ferrone said.

"This is too dangerous." Miss Falconetti spoke. The way she looked at Ferrone then, Averill could see the two of them were more than just colleagues. Lovers? Maybe. "You're asking us to betray the people we work for. The Committee will never allow it."

"The Committee will never know," Ferrone said. "They'll never find out about this. As long as we keep this secret."

"The Committee always finds out. And they'll kill all of us when they do."

They were both right. The Committee would kill Ferrone if they ever became aware of this arrangement. Of the dollar figures involved. Discretion was a matter of life and death—not just Ferrone's but Averill's.

Averill ignored her, focused his attention on his partner. "This is the one and only time you and I will meet in person, Mr. Ferrone. In the future, we'll communicate in the same way I just reached out to you."

Ferrone held up the slot machine receipt. "This?"

"Exactly. A fabricated receipt from the casino. The numbers on it will relate to the requirements we've just discussed. And they'll vary, of course. As circumstances dictate."

"Of course," Ferrone said. "We want to be smart about this. And percentages…"

"We're partners, as I said." Averill held out his hand. "Fifty-fifty. Equal risk, equal reward."

A broad smile cracked Ferrone's face. "Good. I'm glad to hear that. Then we have a deal, Colonel." He reached out his hand.

"Please," Averill said, "call me Jim."

The two shook hands.

PROLOGUE

"Just one thing," Ferrone said. "One problem."

"Oh? And what might that be?"

Ferrone pointed at Guidry. "Him."

"Excuse me?"

"Look at him," Ferrone said. "Your lieutenant. He's scared to death. I've spent ten minutes with the guy, and I can tell he's not comfortable with any of this. Those men you killed—they were his friends, yes?"

"Yes."

"He's going to talk."

"I won't," Guidry said. "I would never betray—"

"You got that right," Ferrone said, and then—Where it had come from? When had he drawn it?—there was a gun in his hand.

He shot Guidry. Right in the forehead.

Guidry fell backward to the ground.

Averill was too stunned to respond for a second. He looked at Ferrone, who held the gun down at his side, his finger still on the trigger. Ready to shoot again, if necessary.

Averill knelt next to Guidry.

The man had the same perplexed look on his face that Kaz Wachtel had worn in the last few seconds of his life. *Jim. Override the latch. Jim. Please. If you can hear me, you have to hear me, we're dying down here. We're dying.*

He looked back up at Ferrone.

Guidry had a family, Averill was about to say, we could have used them as insurance. But he recognized that thought as sentiment and cast it aside. "I wish you hadn't done that. Mr. Guidry's expertise was invaluable," he said.

"Yeah, well, in my experience … you can always buy expertise. You can't buy trust."

Averill nodded. He could buy expertise like Guidry's. And the man had been a problem. Ferrone was right about that. But there was another problem now.

"I agree," Averill replied. "You can't buy trust."

"I'm glad you feel that way," Ferrone said and relaxed … just a little.

Just enough.

"Something else you can't buy," Averill said, beginning to stand. "Respect."

He drew the knife from his ankle and, in one smooth motion, threw it.

It caught Miss Falconetti square in the right eye, and she fell without a sound.

Ferrone turned, his eyes widening in shock, giving Averill time to draw his own gun.

Ferrone and Averill stood facing each other, arms extended, weapons at the ready. They remained that way for a long moment.

"You…" Ferrone gasped, struggling to master his emotions. "You sonofa…"

"Now we not only understand each other, we respect each other. Don't we, Mr. Ferrone?" Averill asked.

"Respect," Ferrone said slowly, "is not the word I'd use."

"Use whatever word you'd like. Do we have a deal?"

Ferrone took a deep breath and then lowered his weapon. Averill did the same.

"We do," Ferrone said.

"Good. Then I'll leave the bodies to you." Averill holstered his gun. "And I'll be in touch. As discussed."

He climbed back in his car and got back on the road. Far ahead, the lights of Vegas beckoned.

Sin City, they called it.

Las Vegas knew nothing about sin.

PRESENT DAY

Oh what a tangled web we weave
When first we practise to deceive!

Sir Walter Scott,
Marmion: A Tale of Flodden Field

1

It was the look she gave him, a quick once-over as she came up the stairs out of the metro station—the Minnesota Ave. station in Southeast DC. He thought this chica was just checking him out the way he was checking her out, but then her eyes met his, and he realized he was wrong. She was checking him out, yeah, but she wasn't flirting. She was assessing. Interesting.

Show—short for Showtime, what people around here had been calling him for the last six months—pushed off the brick half-wall at the edge of the station and started toward her.

The woman had just come in on the Carrollton line from downtown, heading home after a day's work, was his guess. Way she was dressed, she wasn't any kind of office worker, she was—what? Maybe worked in a restaurant or something, some place where she had to wear a uniform, change in and out of her casual clothes, though—Show couldn't help but notice—these casual clothes of hers didn't look very worn at all. Looked almost brand new, in fact. The kind of thing that he liked to think of as a "disconnect." The kind of thing that didn't quite add up.

The kind of thing that Z—among others—always told him to be on the lookout for.

"Hey, baby," he said as she started across the parking lot. She was drawing attention. Admiring glances. Damn-but-ain't-you-fine glances, and a few catcalls too. "Hold up a minute."

The woman ignored him, kept walking. She was Latina—olive skin, long dark hair, heart-shaped face—though there was some Anglo in her features too. Good-looking mix. Early to mid-thirties, tight jeans and a tight top too, though not as tight as some Latinas liked to wear them. She had a nice shape.

She had something else, too. Something Show didn't see around here very often.

Purpose.

"Don't have a minute," she said, not breaking stride, and there was no Latina in her voice at all.

"What's your name, baby?" Show asked. "You got a name, right?"

"Uh-uh."

"What you mean, uh-uh?"

"I mean not interested."

"Seriously," Show said, "you and me should—"

She stopped and turned to face him. "Leave me alone. I'm not going to say it again. You understand?"

Show stopped too, trying to decide whether or not to laugh. Was she threatening him? Seriously? The woman was what, five two, five three? Her head barely came up to the middle of his chest. And yet, the look in her eye … Girl was serious. Like a heart attack.

"I hear you," he said. "But—"

"Good." She walked off without another word.

Most folks coming off the train here picked up one of a dozen bus lines heading deeper into the city. That's what Show would've bet the woman was going to do, but she surprised him, turned right on Minnesota and started heading south. Heading right into the middle of Z's territory.

He stood there, hands on hips, watching her go. Moving with the crowd. She fit right in, the way she was dressed, and yet the way she had talked to him, the look in her eye … She didn't fit in at all.

So what was she doing here?

Worth a little bit of his time, Show decided, to try and find out.

CHAPTER 1

She felt the man's eyes on her as she walked away. She was tempted to turn around, warn him off again. But no. She'd made her point. She didn't want to waste another second on the guy. Too much else of too much importance lay before her. On his head if he couldn't take a hint.

She reached up and touched her right earlobe, pressed the little button on the earpiece—flesh-colored, all but invisible—in that ear. She heard a tiny chime. Electronics activating.

"Time?" she said under her breath.

"Fifteen minutes. You are right on schedule." The voice in her earpiece came to her from a place called Anderson House, on the other side of the Anacostia River in DC proper. Mission control for the mission she was on right now.

Her name was Esperanza Harper. Espy to her friends, Harper to her colleagues at the Department of Justice. Her day job, as she liked to think about it. There, she ran an investigative task force called ICE-T: Interagency Command for Economic Terrorism. Very occasionally, that work put her in the news. That was why she wore the disguise. The clothes she had on now. If any of those colleagues saw her at this moment, they'd raise an eyebrow. Because what she was doing now had nothing to do with her day job.

What she was doing now was much more important.

Espy quickened her pace. She reached the intersection of Minnesota and Benning. Traffic was gridlocked coming over the bridge into Anacostia. Cars honking. Pedestrians weaving in and out of traffic. She joined the crowd, crossed catty-corner to the other side of the intersection. There were half a dozen street vendors set up on the sidewalk there. She pretended to shop, circling the tables, looking left, right, behind her, checking not just for the guy who'd hassled her coming out of the metro but anyone else who might be following.

No one. Nothing.

She looked up at the traffic light hanging over the intersection. At the surveillance camera positioned above it.

"I see you." The voice in her ear again. A woman's voice—Li's voice, Li who was back at Anderson House, sitting in their communications center behind an array of video monitors, observing Espy's movements.

"See anything else?" Espy asked.

"Such as…"

"Anyone following me?"

A moment's pause. "No."

"Good. I'm moving on."

Espy crossed the street again and continued south, turning right onto a little access road sloping downhill, headed toward the riverfront. She passed a hair salon, then a boarded-up storefront. She was out of range of that camera at Benning and Minnesota now. Of the hundreds of surveillance cameras in the DC area, that was the closest one to the rendezvous point. From this moment forward, she was on her own … more or less.

"Hey sister. Help a man out." A man in a ratty green overcoat huddled on the sidewalk in front of her. He waggled a hand in her direction—a big hand, pretty much all that was visible of the guy, save for a thinning mop of greasy, dirty-blonde hair. His voice wasn't much more than a mumble. Slurred. He sounded drunk.

She took a step closer and nearly gagged. "Good lord, you stink," she said.

"I'll take that as a compliment." The man's voice changed. He brushed the ratty hair back from his face and looked up at her. "That's a terrible wig, by the way."

CHAPTER 1

"Best I could do on short notice. And you're one to talk. Your teeth."

"What about them?"

"They're a little too perfect for a homeless guy."

"Yeah, well. Short notice, like you said."

The man's name was Neil Frederickson. Ex–Special Forces. Current FBI. And a member of the organization Espy and Li also belonged to.

"Keep an eye out," Espy said. "There was a guy. Hassled me when I came out of the metro."

"A guy?"

"Black guy. Light-skinned, white leather jacket, red t-shirt. Five eight, maybe. A hundred sixty pounds or so."

"Yeah, well, you dress like that, you're gonna get hassled."

"No, I mean this guy…" She tried to put into words the feeling she'd gotten from him. "He was suspicious. The way he was looking at me—"

"Five minutes," Li said in her ear.

"I got you covered." Frederickson waved her on, hearing Li through an earpiece of his own. "Go."

She nodded, and continued down the sidewalk. Across the street to her left was a ten-story self-storage building. To her right were sheets of weathered plywood, plastered with graffiti, movie posters, handbills for upcoming and long-past concerts. The plywood gave way to a chain-link fence bordering an empty lot. A hundred feet on, she came to a metal placard:

Active Construction Site
Danger
No Trespassing

She was here.

"Just beyond the *No Trespassing* sign," the man had said. "There will be an opening in the fence. Enter there. I will be waiting."

She saw the opening now, the wire cut and folded back.

She took a deep breath and stepped through.

The woman hadn't fooled him for a minute.

Show had hung back in the shadows on the far side of Minnesota Avenue as she circled the street vendors, pretending to shop. What she was really doing, though, was checking her rear view. Seeing if anybody was watching her. Following her. And the way she was doing it, a look here, a look there—she was a professional. Used to doing this kind of thing.

She was no commuter. No cleaning lady, no waitress, or anything like that. So who was she? And what was she doing here?

"Your job?" Z had leaned closer so Show could hear him over the music at the club, which was pounding so loud that Show could feel the bass in his gut. "You keep an eye out."

Show had nodded. He got it. "For five-oh." The police.

"Five-oh, yeah. Anything that might mess with my business. Anything that seems off. Anyone that don't belong, you let me know."

Z—given name Rondell Zachary—ran the drug trade in this part of Southeast, Minnesota Ave. south from the metro for half a dozen blocks or so, west to the river, east to 38th. Show had first met him a few months back through DeWayne, whose sister, LaCosta, was Z's girlfriend. After a basketball game down at Barry Rec, where he had—no other way to put it—put on a show. Made DeWayne look foolish. Which was how he'd gotten his nickname.

"Showtime," Z had said. "That's what I'm calling you."

Showtime. Soon shortened to Show. Soon too, he and DeWayne got to be friendly, hanging out during the games, sometimes after.

CHAPTER 1

One night Z and a couple other guys showed up to watch, and they all went out afterward; the same thing happened again the next week, and the week after that, and the next thing he knew … Show was on Z's payroll.

Low-level work at first, but he'd climbed the ladder these last few months. Now he was Z's eyes and ears out here on Minnesota Ave. Which was why he was following the woman. Well, partly why, if he was honest. He had reasons all his own to be curious. Still, for the moment, Z's interests and his aligned.

Show watched now as the woman finished pretending to look through a pile of scarves and started moving again. And again he was surprised, because now she turned right, off the avenue, down the little access road toward the waterfront.

Soon as she did that, Show knew where she was going: River Guard. A big abandoned construction site down by the waterfront. There was nothing else down that way. Z used the towers himself sometimes, as a rendezvous point. A place to conduct some of his more important business. And that business had been booming these last few months, Z's territory becoming more and more valuable.

Which was why MS-13 was looking to move in.

At least that was the talk Show had been hearing. MS-13—Mara Salvatrucha, a Salvadoran gang, a big presence up in Prince George County, now looking to move down into the city proper, move Z out of the way and take over the trade here themselves. Watching the woman now, Show wondered if she was with MS-13. A kind of advance scout. Someone who could fly in under the radar. Maybe that was why she was going to the towers. Maybe she was meeting someone. Somebody else in Z's organization? A Somebody who was going to help her help the people she worked for get a leg up here?

CODENAME: BLACKJACK

Hey now, Show thought. If Z had a rat in his organization, and he exposed that…

Another rung up the ladder. Another step closer to the top.

First he had to get the facts. Go to the towers himself, see what the woman was really up to. Then have a little talk with her.

He felt the comforting weight of the gun in the small of his back and smiled.

Little Miss Latina would be a lot more cooperative in their next conversation, he was sure about that.

The call that brought her here had come in early this afternoon. Lunchtime. Espy had been at her desk in the RFK building on Pennsylvania Ave. when the phone rang. Her private number, which she never gave out. *Unknown caller*, the screen read. Robocall, Espy thought. Spam. She ignored it.

But a few seconds later she had an incoming text from the same number.

Answer my call.

She'd raised an eyebrow. That was a new one. A real hard-sell. Spammers. They ticked her off. So when that same number called again—

"Whoever this is," she snapped, "however you got this number, you're in a world of trouble if you don't stop bothering me."

"Who I am does not matter. What is important is the proposition I have for you, Ms. Harper."

She heard her name and sat up a little straighter in her chair.

Maybe this wasn't spam.

The speaker had an accent. Eastern European, it sounded like. Polish, maybe. Ukranian? Russian? That was a clue. Her department had several open investigations involving Russian oligarchs,

CHAPTER 1

the oil-rich robber barons who still managed to avoid all the sanctions, all the financial penalties set in place by the civilized world. Nothing would please her more than nailing one of those bastards.

"A proposition," she said. "Something to do with one of my cases?"

"One of your cases." The man sounded amused. "Yes, you could say that. The case of Garrett Crandall."

Espy froze in her chair. Garrett Crandall. Her friend. Her mentor.

She'd gone to his funeral two weeks ago.

"Garrett Crandall is dead."

"Oh, I know that. I'm the one who murdered him."

It took her a second to find her voice. "That's not funny."

"It's not meant to be."

"Garrett Crandall died in a car accident."

"I made it look that way, yes. But in fact—"

She hung up.

Sonuvabitch.

She took a second to gather her thoughts, heart pounding in her chest. Whoever that was, they had a lot of nerve calling her here—and a complete lack of common sense. Easy for her to trace that number, find that person, and—

Her phone buzzed again. Another text.

Shall I call Mr. Frederickson instead?

The pounding in her chest doubled in intensity.

Because now she knew for certain. This was no spammer. No crank call. This man knew—somehow—about the connection she and Frederickson shared. Which meant that there was a chance he was somehow, actually, impossibly telling the truth.

Garrett Crandall, murdered?

"Problem." Li's voice snapped Espy back to the here and now.

Back to the abandoned construction site and the waist-high wall of weeds in front of her.

"I'm listening." Espy pushed through those weeds toward the three steel-framed towers looming in the distance. The path was littered with debris—broken bricks, snapped steel reinforcing rods, remnants of construction supplies left behind when the work on the project had stopped. Silly of the builders to think they could leave those sorts of things lying around for more than a day or two before they got stolen. "And speak up, please," Espy continued. "I'm having a hard time hearing you."

"And I you. Something is interfering with your signal."

"What?"

"Yes. Broadband interference. All up and down the spectrum. Jamming our communications. Including—"

"The drone."

"Yes," Li said. "Attempting to compensate."

Espy stopped walking and looked up.

The drone. Her guardian angel.

Li sent the machine up after Espy had decided to meet with her mystery caller. A drone with full audiovisual monitoring capabilities to supplement the closed-circuit feeds they were also monitoring.

"I don't like any of this." Frederickson's voice was in her ear now too. "We should abort."

Espy shook her head. As if either of them could see her. "No. I want to find out who this guy is. How he knows what he knows."

"Espy." There was a note of warning in his voice. "Listen to the old hand here. This is all happening too quickly. Pull back. We can always—"

"Your objections are noted," she said. At that precise moment, a figure stepped out from the shadow of one of those half-finished

CHAPTER 1

towers. A tall, thin man in stovepipe black jeans, plain white t-shirt, and a navy blue coat. Pale skin, shaved head. Made it hard to guess his age. He could be thirty. He could be sixty.

He stopped, folded his arms across his chest, and waited for her.

"Stay alert. Wait for my signal," Espy said.

"Espy," Frederickson began, but as she stepped forward his voice turned to static and was gone. Now she really was on her own.

The pale man smiled as she approached.

"Esperanza Harper. Thank you for coming on such short notice. We have not very much time. The people who hired me, they are suspicious already." As he spoke, she saw something in his right hand; a little black box with a blinking red light.

A jamming device, she guessed. The source of the interference Li was encountering.

The man smiled at her, as if he could read her thoughts.

"Let us conduct our business quickly," he said, "and then be gone."

❖ ❖ ❖ ❖ ❖

This had nothing to do with MS-13.

Show realized that right away. Nothing to do with any other gang; nothing to do with someone trying to cut in on Z's business, or with drugs at all. It wasn't a lover's lane meetup either. Just the way they were talking, even though he wasn't close enough to hear—their body language, the way they positioned themselves in relation to each other, to their surroundings…

This was something else entirely. Some kind of hush-hush, top-secret, James Bond, Ethan Hunt, if-people-knew-I-was-here-I'd-be-dead kind of thing. The kind of thing his dad had done in

Iraq, during the war. Talking with informers, insurgents, whoever he could, to try and save the country from falling into chaos. His dad. The master sergeant.

For a second—and not for the first time—Show wondered what his father would make of the life his son had chosen. Probably wouldn't be happy about it. Worry about that later. Right now his job was simple.

Figure out who this woman was and what she was doing here.

Show had come via the highway underpass, through a homeless encampment. He'd had to bulldoze his way through a sea of raggedy tents and makeshift cardboard houses, getting a particularly evil eye from a scrawny little woman with a big tuft of spikey white hair. He thought she was actually going to try and stop him from getting through for a minute. Then she'd smiled and stepped aside, and Show had made his way into the site.

Now he had to get closer.

He ducked down and half-crawled, half-crabbed his way to the support beam closest to the man and woman. The beam was wide enough, barely, for him to hide behind. He straightened up slowly, then carefully peered around the beam, got the two of them in profile. Got his first good look at the guy, too. He was tall, six two, six three. Shaved head. Thin, angular face.

Show was close enough now to pick up what they were saying.

"The account is numbered. You will not need a name," the man said.

"I like to know who I'm dealing with," the woman shot back.

"Very well. Then you may call me Nemkov. Yuri Nemkov." The guy's voice had a touch of contempt in it. He had an accent, too. Russian, to Show's ears. Maybe this was a mob thing? Russians were big up in Baltimore, not so much down here. Were they trying to cut in on Z's territory?

CHAPTER 1

"Yuri Nemkov. Is that your real name?" The woman shook her head in disgust. "Never mind. I want specifics, Mr. Nemkov. Who hired you and why."

"Of course. That is information I will be happy to share—once the $10 million is in my account."

Show blinked. *$10 million?*

"You don't see a penny of that money," the woman snapped, "until I see some proof."

"Proof?" Nemkov shook his head. "There is no proof, I'm afraid."

"I don't like the sound of that," she said. "If this is some kind of trick—"

"Ms. Harper, my job was to leave no proof," he snapped. And now Show had a name for her too: Harper. Interesting. Not Latina at all. "That is what they paid me for. These people, they leave no trails."

"Everyone leaves trails," Espy shot back.

Nemkov laughed. "No. Not everyone. You have no idea who you are dealing with here. What they are capable of."

"I don't see what's so funny," Espy said.

"Forgive me," he replied. "But it is an amusing situation."

"And why is that?"

"Because, Ms. Harper, you already have all the proof you need in your possession. Right under your nose, in fact."

"I don't know what you're talking about."

"I'm talking about Blackjack, Ms. Harper. Blackjack." The man said the word slowly, in his thick accent, emphasizing both syllables.

"What's that mean?" Espy asked.

Nemkov smiled. He reached into the pocket of his jacket…

And Espy pulled out a gun—from where, Show had no idea.

"Easy," she said. "No sudden moves. What are you doing?"

"Chewing gum," Nemkov said and held out the pack for her to see. "May I?"

Espy nodded, but didn't lower her weapon. Nemkov popped the gum into his mouth, tossed the foil wrapper onto the ground.

And at that second, out of the corner of his eye, Show saw a flash of light high up in the tower opposite him. Light glinting off metal. Reflected sunlight? Something else? He squinted into the distance but couldn't make out any details.

"Now. Where was I?" Nemkov asked.

"Blackjack," Espy said. "Evidence you said we already have in our possession. What's that mean?"

"Blackjack?" Nemkov smiled. "Why that, Ms. Harper, is the secret I was hired to protect. The reason your senator was murdered."

Show's hand slipped on the beam. If he hadn't been quicker, he would have actually fallen. Senator? As in US senator? Murdered? What the hell had he stumbled into here?

As he took a moment to steady himself, Show saw another flash of light, high up, movement too this time. Somebody was up there on one of the high beams.

It was a trap, he thought. The woman had walked into a trap.

And then, before he could think what to do or say, whether he should step forward and reveal himself, he heard a muffled pop. The sound of air being displaced. A gunshot.

A patch of red blossomed on the front of Nemkov's windbreaker, and he staggered backward, eyes wide with surprise.

A second shot sounded. The man fell backward onto a tarp. Blood pooled around him.

And then all hell broke loose.

2

More gunshots came, faster than he could keep track of, kicking up the dirt in front of the woman, who was running back the way she had come, gun held out in front of her, firing silenced shots as well, laying down cover for her retreat. Only it wasn't working. Whoever was up there just kept firing, and Show realized he needed to clear out too, because sooner rather than later the shooter would be coming down from that tower, and he did not want to get in the middle of this thing, not any more than he was already. He turned and took a step forward.

A spray of bullets pinged off the beam in front of him.

Shit. Show started running full speed toward the little access road, the closest exit, not giving a damn anymore about how much noise he made or trying to stay hidden, just trying to stay alive, moving as fast as he could, expecting at any second to catch a bullet. He put his head down and plowed forward.

He was almost to the fence when a guy stepped right in front him. A homeless guy, was his first thought. A big one. Scraggly hair, ratty overcoat, beat-up combat boots. And carrying what looked like a hunting rifle.

"Well look who it is," the guy said, and slugged him right across the mouth with the gun butt.

Show staggered and fell back.

The woman burst through the weeds, wild-eyed, breathing heavily.

"Somebody shot…" she began, and then saw Show on the ground. Her eyes widened.

"Damn it," she said. "That's him."

"So I guessed," the guy with the rifle said.

She glared at Show. "You followed me. You're part of this."

"Lady, I don't even know what this is," Show said. "I followed you, yeah, but I ain't—"

"Shut up," the woman snapped. Show could hear sirens in the distance. She turned to the big guy. "We need to get out of here. Now."

"And him?" the guy asked.

A look passed between the two of them.

"Do it," she said.

Show's stomach lurched. "Whoa," he said. "Whoa, whoa, whoa. Hold on, you got the wrong idea. I—"

The big guy swung the rifle around.

One second, Show was staring down the gun barrel. The next, he heard a faint popping sound. A silencer? On a rifle? That was his last thought before something struck him hard in the chest, and the world faded to black.

❖ ❖ ❖ ❖ ❖

"Li," Espy said, heart racing as she came up the stairs a step behind Frederickson, ten minutes removed from the chaos at the towers. "We have anything yet?"

"At the site? No. The drone remains nonfunctional."

"How is that possible?"

"Working on it."

Work faster, Espy almost said, but tempered her impatience.

Frederickson yanked the door at the top of the stairs open. Set down what he was carrying and turned to Espy.

"Don't say it," she said.

"What?"

CHAPTER 2

"I told you so."

"Not going to say anything. Still catching my breath." He smiled. But she knew what he was thinking.

Listen to the old hand, Espy.

But she hadn't. And now…

"You think Nemkov's dead?" Frederickson asked.

"Sure looked that way," Espy said.

"Police have responded to reports of gunfire at the construction site. Nothing else yet on scanners," Li added.

Espy nodded. Looked around. They were in an abandoned factory just over the Maryland line. They had a half-dozen such sites scattered around the DC area, raw space they could reconfigure at the drop of a hat. This one had a long row of overhead fluorescent lights and some heavy-duty tables and chairs.

"Do we believe what he told you?" Frederickson looked her in the eye. "Garrett was murdered?"

"I don't know." She sighed. "We need more information. Who do we have down at the medical examiner's office?" The authorities would ID Nemkov off his fingerprints, his dental work. She wanted to have that information in hand, soon as possible.

"Nights, not sure. Day shift, I have a guy," Frederickson said, pulling out a roll of duct tape from his overcoat. "A woman, actually. Denise. She—"

"There is no body," Li said.

"What?" Espy and Frederickson spoke at the same time.

"Authorities are on scene now. There is no body."

"How is that possible?" All those gunshots, all that blood … "Where did it go?"

"They took it," Frederickson said. "The people who shot him."

"I concur," Li said. "That seems the most likely explanation. Mr. Nemkov's employers wished to prevent him from revealing any information whatsoever."

"Him or his corpse," Frederickson said.

"I have identified the man who followed you from the metro station," Li said. "Coming in to your devices."

Espy pulled out her phone. "Michael Cochrane. Drug dealer. In and out of jail half a dozen times. Hell." She looked over at Frederickson. "He wasn't part of this at all."

"We don't know that for sure," Frederickson said.

"Dammit." Espy started pacing. "I warned him. I told him to leave me alone."

"Hey. Don't feel guilty. Wrong side of the fence, guy got what he deserved," Frederickson said.

"I suppose."

"But if he was not with Nemkov, or the people who killed him," Li said, "then why was he following you?"

A groan issued from the chair behind Frederickson—from the man he'd carried up the stairs and dropped there.

Showtime blinked and opened his eyes.

"I don't know," Frederickson said. "Let's ask him."

❖ ❖ ❖ ❖ ❖

The world was a little blurry at first. Things took a minute to come into focus.

When they did, Show saw the woman from the construction site, Harper, sitting opposite him. Staring him straight in the eye. The big guy from the construction site was there too, standing behind her.

Show tried to move. He couldn't.

He was duct-taped to a chair.

The tape was wrapped around his chest, binding his arms close to his sides, his ankles to the chair legs, his wrists behind him.

CHAPTER 2

He was in a big empty room with a low ceiling, fifteen feet wide, twice as long. Gray concrete walls, floor, ceiling, a single row of overhead fluorescent lights. A metal door at the far end. No windows.

"White 17," Harper said. "That's what we call it."

"What?"

"White 17. What you were shot with. Tranquilizer. Your body metabolizes the chemicals very fast. So it doesn't leave any trace. No aftereffects to worry about. You feeling okay?"

"Yeah." Show nodded. "Yeah. I guess so."

"Good. Because we need to have a conversation here. Get a few things straight."

"Hey. I'm all for that. Cut me loose, let's talk."

The big guy laughed. "Yeah. Right."

That big guy. He'd hit Show with the rifle before shooting him. That's why his lip felt swollen—why his head ached. He remembered now. He remembered other things too. The guy with the Russian accent. The $10 million.

And the dead senator. The murdered senator?

"Simple question to start with, Michael." Harper slid her chair closer. "Why were you following me?"

Michael? His heart leapt into his chest. "How do you know my name?"

She held up his wallet. "Not rocket science. Now. Let's talk about—"

"Show," he said. "That's what they call me around here. And I got nothing to do with that guy that got shot. Nothing. You let me go, I'm on my way, I—"

"This'll go much quicker if you don't interrupt. Understand?"

Show nodded, trying to calm himself. "Yeah, okay. Sure."

"Good. So. Show. Why were you following me?"

"On account of it's my job." Show told her about Z. Who he was, what Show did for him. Then he told her how he'd seen her come out of the metro, how something didn't seem to fit. How he thought maybe she was with MS-13, which got a laugh out of the big guy, who shook his head and left the room. How he'd realized where she was going and decided to follow her to the construction site himself. Gave her his thinking, his movements, all of it 100 percent true. Right up until the part where he'd started eavesdropping.

Then he lied.

"So you couldn't hear what we were saying?" she asked.

"No. Like I told you." Show tried to sound casual. "I was trying to get closer, but—"

"How far away were you? Twenty, thirty feet?"

"Man, I don't know. Didn't have no damn tape measure with me."

"That's pretty close, twenty, thirty feet," she said, as if he hadn't answered, as if she was talking to herself. "About the length of this room. That seem right to you?"

"I guess," he said. "Maybe a little further away. I don't know."

Harper looked him in the eye. Show looked right back.

He didn't know who she was, who that guy Nemkov had been. All he knew for certain—a homeless-looking guy with a tranquilizer dart rifle, $10 million, dead senators—this was serious business. Life or death business. He was better off playing dumb until he could find out more.

"You didn't hear anything. Okay." She leaned back in her chair. "What about the shots? Did you see where they came from?"

He shrugged. No harm telling the truth here. "Up high. Way up in the tower."

"Did you see anybody up there?"

CHAPTER 2

"No. But—"

The door at the end of the room slammed open. The big guy stood there. He looked angry. A look he transferred to Show.

"What?" Show asked.

The big guy ignored him. "Gotta talk to you," he said to Harper.

"Not now." She spoke without turning.

"Now," he snapped. "Right now. It's important."

Harper glared and got to her feet. The guy held the door open for her and followed her out. The door shut behind them. Not ten seconds later, it slammed open again.

Harper strode back through, holding a computer tablet in one hand. The big guy was a step behind her. Now they both looked angry.

The big guy drew a knife from his belt. A big knife. He walked straight toward Show.

"Wait," Show said, bracing himself. "Wait. Hold up. Don't—"

Harper held the tablet up in front of Show's face.

The screen had a picture of his face on it. Underneath that was his name—his real name, Michael Cockerell III—and a series of numbers and letters. DC4-807C.

"Shit," he said.

"Shit is right," Harper said. "Why the hell didn't you tell me you were a cop?"

3

An undercover cop.

Espy stared at Show—Detective Cockerell. He gave her a small, tight smile.

"Didn't seem like the time for true confessions," he said.

Frederickson went around behind Show's chair, bent down, and started cutting through the duct tape.

"Thanks." Cockerell looked up at her. "Why don't we start over? What's going on here? Who are you two? What was that guy at the construction site talking about back there? Killing a senator?"

Espy and Frederickson exchanged a look.

"I thought you couldn't hear our conversation," she said.

"That was then," Cockerell said.

"When you were lying."

"When I was undercover."

"Well, we're undercover too," she said. "So let's just say our operations crossed paths, and leave it at that."

There was a loud snap as Frederickson finished sawing through the duct tape at Cockerell's back. The detective yanked his arms forward. Strands of duct tape still hung from his jacket, and he started ripping them off.

"I'd like to oblige you. Really I would," Cockerell said. "But there's one small problem. A man just got shot and killed, right in front of me."

"We'll handle it."

"Not your call."

CHAPTER 3

"But it is. This is our case. Our territory. Best thing for you to do is go back to work."

"Not going to happen."

"Listen, chief." Frederickson knelt down and slid the knife back into his ankle holster. "We're on the same side here."

"Is that so?"

"Yeah. That's so. How do you think we got your information so quickly?"

Espy saw the certainty in Cockerell's eyes waver.

"Okay. Fair point." He gestured to his legs, which were still bound to the chair. "Finish cutting me loose, and we'll talk."

"Sorry. But there's nothing else to talk about," Espy said. "Shouldn't take you too long to get yourself free. We'll leave your phone and your shoes outside the door."

"Hey. You don't want to do this." Cockerell looked up at her. "You'll be making a bad situation worse. Assaulting and kidnapping a police officer, you're looking at serious jail time."

"Kidnapping." She shook her head. "Seriously?"

"Word to the wise, chief." Frederickson said. "You just fell down the rabbit hole. We pulled you out. Start asking questions, making noise, you could fall right back in again."

"Is that a threat?"

"No. Just a fact. You're in over your head here."

"Thanks for your concern. I can take care of myself."

"Which is how you ended up duct-taped to a chair, right? Your funeral." Frederickson shrugged, and headed for the door.

Espy started to follow … and then turned back.

"Look. Detective." Espy met Cockerell's gaze. "I understand your position. I sympathize, believe me. But this is for your own good. Go back to your work. Forget all this ever happened."

The man took a moment before responding.

39

"I'll be seeing you—the both of you—again. Soon. Because this is not over."

There was a certainty in his voice, in his eyes, that gave her pause. Made her think, for a split-second, about telling him—not the whole story, but enough to satisfy him, to send him on his own undercover way.

But that would be stupid.

That would be breaking protocol.

That would be betraying a secret over two hundred years in the making.

"Goodbye, Detective," she said instead. "And good luck."

She followed Frederickson out the door. Cockerell watched it slam shut…

And let a little smile creep up on his face.

Good luck? I don't need luck, he thought.

Because I know your name, Harper. And soon enough … I'll find out who you really are. And then we'll continue this conversation.

He bent down and started ripping at the tape around his legs.

❖ ❖ ❖ ❖ ❖

"What a shitshow." Espy ripped off her wig and tossed it in the back seat.

"Language." Frederickson looked over at her. "What would your mom say if she heard you talking like that?"

"She'd tell me it was about time I loosened up."

"Yeah." Frederickson snorted. "She would at that."

They were on the 11th Street Bridge, crossing back into DC proper. Espy saw the Capitol dome in the distance. Behind it was the Russell Senate Office Building. Where Garrett's office had been these last ten years.

"Blackjack." Frederickson frowned. "Like the card game, right?

CHAPTER 3

I mean, what else could it be?"

"Any number of things." Li's voice came in over the car's speaker system. Espy deactivated her earpiece to prevent an echo. "The weapon. The chewing gum. And depending on context—"

"It's not chewing gum. I guarantee that," Frederickson said. "Did Garrett have anything to do with gambling? Casinos maybe?"

"Don't think so. His first term, he was on one of the banking subcommittees. Consumer protection." *Not my cup of tea*, he'd told Espy. More than once, he'd asked her to explain some esoteric testimony from one financial industry specialist or another. She recalled nothing to do with casinos, online gambling, or card games.

"Maybe there was some legislation he was involved with," Frederickson said. "Something he was sponsoring. Something that pissed off the wrong people."

"Maybe. We'll check, obviously." She thought back for a moment. "No proof of the murder, Nemkov told me. But all the proof we needed about why Garrett was killed, that was right under our noses. What does that mean?"

"Under our noses." Frederickson flipped on a turn signal, changed lanes. "You think he was talking about Anderson House?"

"Yeah. I'm afraid I do."

"Well that's a problem."

"It sure as hell is." Because if Nemkov knew about Anderson House, then the people who hired him did too, and that was not good. Not good at all.

"Dammit." She slapped the dashboard in front of her.

"Hey." Frederickson's head swiveled. "Don't take it out on the car."

"Sorry," Espy said. "It's just been a day."

She should have known better. The car was Frederickson's

pride and joy. A thirty-year-old Range Rover. He'd had it rebuilt from the ground up: new engine, transmission, electrical system, reinforced steel chassis, bulletproof glass…

Boys and their toys, Espy thought. Boys and their toys.

She flashed back to the smile on Matt's face after he'd opened his birthday present last year.

"The Blast Swing and Stroke Analyzer. Cool."

"Yeah." She'd pointed to the illustration on the box. "You attach it to your club, and then the data comes in to an app on your phone."

"Great." He turned the box over in his hands, studied the other side. "I can totally use this for my students."

"No, dummy. It's not for your students." She took the box from him, set it down on the coffee table behind her. Put her hands on his shoulders. "It's for you."

"Me?"

"Yeah." She brushed his hair back from his forehead. "Get your game back on track. Get you back on the tour."

"Back on the tour." He put his hands on her waist, drew her close. They kissed. "I like the sound of that."

Focus, Espy told herself. Focus.

The car came to a stop. She looked up. They were on Massachusetts Avenue, right in front of the Indian Embassy.

"Letting you off here," he said. "I gotta go home and shower."

"That you do." Espy climbed out. "See you soon."

"That you will."

He pulled away. She turned and looked across the street. Anderson House loomed in front of her.

Anderson House. A fifty-room, Beaux Arts marble and steel structure built in the early 1900s by a diplomat named Larz Anderson, who'd served as a minister to Belgium and ambassador

CHAPTER 3

to Japan. Anderson had also been a member of the Society of the Cincinnati, a patriotic organization formed by officers of the American Revolution, whose purpose was to preserve, protect, and defend the revolution's ideals.

On his death, Anderson had deeded the mansion to the Society. It now served as the group's headquarters. They used it for events throughout the year: concerts, author talks, guest lectures, luncheons, holiday celebrations, etc. It was also a museum, one that displayed not only the Society's history, but also Anderson's own massive art collection. There was a library too, one that held rare books and manuscripts, many related to the Society's extensive history.

But there was another part to the mansion that was not on public display, a part that used Anderson House for its own purposes.

A clandestine intelligence network, a chapter of which was called Woodhull.

A chapter that Espy, after Garrett's death, now ran.

❖ ❖ ❖ ❖ ❖

This time of night, the mansion was dark.

The tourists and docents, museum and gift shop employees had all gone home for the day. Espy strode to the front door, punched in the keypad code, then headed straight for the back of the mansion, glancing quickly at the freestanding easel behind the reception desk.

1787
The Year America Was Born
Starring
Doug Rivers, Ayesha Vatril, and Penelope Harper
World Premiere Benefit and Reception Friday Night

Up until Nemkov's call this afternoon, that benefit had been uppermost in her mind. Now it took second place.

She strode on, pushing through the swinging doors at the back of the storeroom and into a little-used corridor. Toward the service elevator. She punched the call button and heard the ancient machinery grind to life.

The door slid open with an audible thunk, and Espy stepped inside. The elevator was small by modern standards. The interior was draped with moving blankets to protect the wood paneling, making it feel cramped, claustrophobic.

The official blueprints for Anderson House showed four floors, as well as a basement and subbasement. The elevator control panel had buttons to match.

Espy pressed not one but two of those buttons simultaneously, then a third and fourth button. Entering not a destination, but a code. Activating a second set of quieter, more modern machinery.

The doors shut. The car headed down. The *B* above the door lit up. Then the *SB*.

The elevator kept moving. Kept going down.

Blackjack. The secret I was hired to protect.

The reason your senator was murdered.

In her mind's eye, Espy flashed back to that horrible night two weeks ago.

❖ ❖ ❖ ❖ ❖

There had been a snowstorm. A freak confluence of atmospheric disturbances—an unexpected near-blizzard that had paralyzed the city.

Garrett had been at a party out in Virginia. Pressing the congressional flesh. When the storm hit, he'd been advised to spend the evening at his host's house. He had gently but firmly

CHAPTER 3

refused. "Work," he'd said, according to witnesses.

He left Virginia at 9:07 p.m. His drive back should have taken forty minutes, but the weather had closed roads. Had caused accidents. Espy had been at Woodhull.

"GPS is sending us onto Dalecarlia," he'd told her. "We'll be another hour or so."

"Hour and a half," a voice in the background added. Espy recognized it: Karl Royko, Garrett's driver. Bodyguard. Ex–Columbus cop. The two men had been friends for decades.

"Okay. Maybe longer," Garrett added.

"Understood. I'll be waiting," she'd said, and hung up. The last words she'd ever spoken to him.

Ten minutes later, on Dalecarlia, the car had spun out on a downhill slope. Crashed into a curb, got a dented fender and two flat tires. Garrett and Karl both tried calling for help, but the weather was playing havoc with cell service.

Karl had seen houses, lights on, through the curtain of trees lining the parkway. He went for help. He left the engine running, Garrett in the back seat, briefcase open, papers scattered everywhere. Karl returned forty-five minutes later, having called both a tow truck and the secret service. He'd opened the car door, looked into the back seat.

"First I thought he was asleep. But then I saw—there was something wrong. His face—the color of his skin—"

The last time she'd talked to Karl. He was sitting at a bar, a half-empty glass in front of him, the two of them a couple among dozens of Garrett's friends and colleagues, gathered at a restaurant near the Crandalls' brownstone after Garrett's wake. She'd seen him alone, brooding. Went over to talk to him. Boost his spirits.

"Not your fault," she'd said. "An accident."

Carbon monoxide poisoning. Except now—

They wanted me to make it look like an accident.

The elevator door opened. Espy took a step forward and almost jumped out of her skin.

Li was standing right in front of her.

She looked the same as always—like an unkempt teenager. Five feet tall and ninety-five pounds. Short dark hair whose color seemed to change every other week. Wearing a Cincinnati Reds sweatshirt and gray sweatpants. Espy still had a hard time reconciling Li's physical appearance with the person she'd read about long before they'd met. Li Min-Jing, head of Persistent Typhoon—the infamous all-female Chinese computer-hacking group.

Several years ago, Garrett had saved Li's life. Helped her defect hours before she was about to be "disappeared" by the Chinese state. He'd brought her into the Society. Made her part of Woodhull. Garrett's death had nearly shattered Li. She'd barely left the operations center during the last couple weeks.

Espy could only imagine what she was feeling now.

"You startled me."

Li bowed her head. "My apologies, Ms. Harper. I have been trying to reach you."

"Sorry. My bad." Espy realized she hadn't reactivated her earpiece after turning it off in the car. "What's happening? Any news on the scanners? Nemkov's body?"

She stepped past Li into a long, sleek corridor with dark-gray carpet and hardwood walls, sound absorption paneling every few feet. *W3* carved into the wall: Woodhull, Level 3. Operations.

"No. But that is not what I wished to discuss," Li began. "I wanted to let you know—"

"We're going to need to look at the circumstances of that car accident all over again. Look at what happened, exactly. Talk to

CHAPTER 3

people from the party too—see if anyone matching Nemkov's description was there. People at the scene of the crash as well. We—"

"Yes, of course. I understand." Li followed Espy down the corridor. "But, Ms. Harper—"

"And footage from the construction site. Our drone, before it stopped working."

"Yes. But first, I do have something important to tell you."

"Sorry." She spun on her heel to face Li. "Go on. What is it?"

"I wanted to tell you that—"

A door behind them opened, and a man stepped out into the hall. An older man, a big man, with a big white beard and a shock of bushy white hair.

"My niece keeps telling me I ought to shave," he had told her at Garrett's funeral. "That I look more and more like Santa Claus every day."

There was some truth to that statement. A resemblance, especially when he was smiling. But he wasn't smiling now.

"Mr. Crane has arrived," Li finished.

"Yes. I can see that," Espy said.

Stuart Crane. After Garrett's death, he'd put her in provisional charge of Woodhull. But Woodhull wasn't the Society's only chapter. There were multiple others, in multiple states.

And Stuart ran them all.

"I got here as quickly as I could." Stuart gestured to the room behind him. "Please. Come inside and fill me in."

4

Z glared. "You should've called me right off."

"Maybe. But what I was thinking—"

"You ain't getting paid to think," Z snapped.

"Yeah. You're right. Sorry." Cockerell nodded. He, Z, DeWayne, and Z's number two, Wallet, were crammed into a booth at Red House, an all-night Chinese restaurant a block off Minnesota. Cockerell was telling Z and the others where he'd been the last few hours. A story that he'd kept pretty close to the truth, right up until he'd reached the construction site. Then he'd changed details—changed the tall thin guy, Nemkov, to another Latino, told Z that he got caught eavesdropping on the meeting and taken for a ride to that abandoned factory.

"MS-13. We gonna have to check this out." Z shook his head, leaned back in his seat. Z was short, maybe five six, built like a fireplug. Solid muscle. Smart, too. Instinctual. Had a nose for bullshit.

Cockerell had a feeling he was smelling it now.

He was getting that same feeling off of Wallet, who sat stone-faced next to Z, not saying a word. He'd taken out his knife halfway through Cockerell's story and started carving something into the table. Cockerell had seen Wallet use that knife way too many times these last few months. Seen him slice a girl's nose because she told Wallet he smelled bad. Seen him stab a man in the stomach for screwing up a fifty dollar transaction and leave him to bleed to death in Fort Mahan.

You did not—he did not—want to get on the wrong side of that weapon.

CHAPTER 4

Six months he'd been on this assignment. As deep undercover as he'd ever gone. Not just slipping on a different set of clothes and going to work each day, but living like a different person. If Z went poking around, asking about MS-13, if he found out something, anything that put the lie to what Cockerell had just told him ... the whole operation could go south in a hurry. He couldn't let that happen.

Thankfully, the food arrived before Z could press him any further. Wallet put away his knife. They started eating. DeWayne started going on about a tryout with the DC Defenders, a semi-pro team out of Southeast; Wallet told DeWayne he better slow down on the chicken if he didn't want to have a heart attack on the court; Z laughing, and then saying the hell with MS-13 moving in on him, he was going to move in on them; and Cockerell, as always, not saying anything at all. Keeping his ears open. Staying focused. But...

Harper. Nemkov. Blackjack.

It was two in the morning before he could safely excuse himself from the group, two thirty by the time he got back to his apartment and got himself into bed. But his brain wouldn't shut off.

The secret your senator was killed to protect.

He dozed on and off for a few hours. Finally got up, took a shower, and got dressed. Then he went to the electrical panel in the kitchen and opened it. There were four breakers. He flipped the bottom one on the right, and it popped out of the panel and into his hand. False front. He reached into the hole and pulled out a cell phone. A burner. He sat at the kitchen table and dialed a number he knew by heart.

"Colitti," a voice answered.

"Lieutenant," Cockerell said, "bring me in."

CODENAME: BLACKJACK

❖ ❖ ❖ ❖ ❖

An hour later he was in Interview Room E4, in the basement of the 12th precinct, having been grabbed up by two detectives (lights flashing, car doors opening, we got some questions for you, punk let's go, that sort of thing) while he was standing, as arranged, at the corner of Minnesota and Clay.

E4 was painted light green, not gray, but the walls were the same low-grade concrete as the room last night. Same cheap fluorescent lights, same cheap metal chairs. Déjà vu all over again.

Harper. Nemkov. Blackjack.

The interview room door swung open.

"The prodigal son returns. Good to see you, Mikey." Colitti was in his late thirties, about five six, and built like a tank. Guy was a walking stereotype: donut in one hand, cup of coffee in the other. "What's up, you missed me? Needed to see my smiling face?"

"No other reason."

Colitti put his coffee down on the table, which was bolted to the floor, sat down across from Cockerell, and frowned. "What happened to you?"

"What?"

"Your lip there."

"Yeah. Right." Cockerell had almost forgotten about that. "That's why I'm here. Something really strange went down last night."

"What, you got laid?"

"No." Cockerell smiled. "But there was a girl involved."

Colitti took a bite out of his donut. Powdered sugar exploded all over his shirt. He didn't notice. "Do tell."

"That shooting. At the construction site." Cockerell leaned forward. "Tell me what you got on it."

CHAPTER 4

"Come again?"

"The guy that got shot? At River Guard?"

"When was this?" Now Colitti saw the sugar; he brushed it off his shirt, onto the floor.

"Rush hour. Five thirty or so."

"I didn't hear anything about it. This something your buddy Z was involved in?"

"No," Cockerell said, and the door opened again. Captain Becky Jorgensen. Squad commander. She looked stressed, harassed, aggravated. Same as always.

"Mike. Good to see you."

"Yeah, Captain. Good to see you too." He stood up, and they shook hands.

"So what do we have?" she asked.

"We're just getting started," Colitti said. "Mikey was telling me about this shooting he saw."

"Shooting?" Jorgensen looked puzzled. "What shooting?"

"The towers. Minnesota and Benning," Cockerell said.

"When was this?" she asked.

"Five thirty or so. Yesterday afternoon," Colitti said. "That right?"

The two of them turned and looked at Cockerell.

You fell down the rabbit hole, chief.

"That's right," he said. "Five thirty or so."

"Somebody must have details," Jorgensen said. "Find out. Later. I'm here to talk about what happened at Red House. You were there last night, right?"

"Yeah," Cockerell said. "Left about two a.m. But—"

"Hell. You just missed 'em."

"Missed who?"

"Koppelman's son. And his girlfriend."

"Koppelman? As in Chief of Police Koppelman? His son was at Red House? At two in the morning?"

"Two thirty, more like. The kid and his girlfriend wanted wings, so…"

"Best wings in the city," Cockerell said. "But at two thirty in the morning? What a moron."

"Spoiled brat is what he is," Colitti said.

"Easy." Jorgensen held up a hand. "The walls have ears. Anyway, Z makes some comments to the girlfriend, she makes some comments back, and then they leave. But Z goes after them. He's pissed off about something."

"Shit," Cockerell said.

"Yeah. They're both cut up pretty bad. Your psycho friend, what's his name … ?"

"Wallet."

"Yeah. He really went to town on them." Jorgensen sighed. "It's a shitstorm. And it's only going to get worse. It's all the news this morning. The stuff they're saying—"

Jorgensen's phone buzzed. She looked at the screen and exhaled in disgust. "Gotta go." She turned back to Cockerell. "Keep your ears open when you get back out there, all right?"

And then she was gone.

"All right. Do me a favor. Ask around." Colitti said. "See if you can find anybody who saw anything at Red House. A reliable witness."

"A reliable witness?" Cockerell shook his head. "Come on. Nobody's going to stand up against Z."

"Don't shit on my dreams this early in the morning. Just see what you can do." Colitti got on his feet. "I'll see what I can find out on that River Guard thing for you."

Cockerell hesitated.

CHAPTER 4

You start asking questions, you could fall right back in.

"That's all right," he said. "I'll check it out myself."

"Not sure that's a good idea." Colitti looked troubled. Cockerell knew why. The man didn't want him to break cover, even in the precinct house. There were a lot of comings and goings upstairs. A lot of people might see him there. Loose lips, sinking ships, that sort of thing.

"Relax," Cockerell said. "I'll be in and out, half an hour."

"Relax." Colitti picked up his coffee. Patted his belly. "Mikey. Come on, look at me. Do I look like the kind of guy who relaxes?"

❖ ❖ ❖ ❖ ❖

Colitti brought him up the back stairs. Through the break room, where Cockerell grabbed a coffee and a donut himself—hey, when in Rome—before going to his desk and booting up his computer.

First thing he did was check the log sheets from last night.

He found a report of gunshots at River Guard. A car had been called to the scene, yes. Shell casings recovered. But that was all. There was no body. So, Harper and her friend had gone back for it. Or whoever shot Nemkov had taken the body with them. Or maybe … Nemkov wasn't dead. Maybe he'd gotten up and walked away.

Cockerell found that difficult to believe. Gunshot to the chest, all that blood. He did some checking anyway: ambulance logs, hospital admittance records. A lot of gunshot wounds, nobody that matched Nemkov's description.

He did find Koppelman. The chief's son. And his girlfriend. Reading the report on what happened to them, on the kind and extent of cutting Wallet had done, made his stomach churn. Made him want those guys off the street and in a cell, sooner rather than later.

He widened the hospital search to Prince George County. Found a report on a John Doe who'd bled out from a chest wound, but the picture, when he finally found it, didn't match. What the hell? He hadn't hallucinated the whole thing, that was for sure. So what happened? Why was there no corpse?

He started the search again, adding the guy's name, Yuri Nemkov, into his query. The first result was a picture. Not a photo, but a cartoon, a guy dressed all in black, wearing black sunglasses, a rifle in one hand and a pistol in the other. *Yuri Nemkov*, the caption read, *the world's most dangerous assassin.*

Cockerell clicked on the picture. Got a slick-looking web page for something called Game of Spies, which turned out to be a video game. Yuri Nemkov was one of the main characters.

A video game character. Nemkov was an alias? Was that possible?

And what about Harper? Was that name a fake too?

He put it in the search box now, got a bunch of completely irrelevant results. He ran his hands through his hair, checked his watch. Time for another approach. Get off the computer, get out into the real world. Maybe go back to River Guard and see what, if anything, he could find there. Hit the mean streets of the nation's capital.

Then he heard a voice in his head. Harper's.

This is our case. Our territory.

He added Washington, DC, to his search terms, and his eyes widened. Because there she was.

5

Espy gave the big globe a spin. "Say that again."

"Pirates." Li was sitting in Garrett's desk chair, her face nearly hidden by the pile of paper in front of her. She held up a laminated image of a skull and crossbones. "Indonesian pirates, to be more precise. Some of them have adopted this symbol as their flag. A flag commonly known as the Jolly Roger, but also sometimes called—"

"Let me guess. Blackjack."

"Yes," Li said. "Precisely."

They were in Garrett's home office, in his DC townhouse, a circular room with fifteen-foot ceilings, a brick fireplace, walls covered with bookshelves, a huge old wooden desk and an antique globe. A globe of the world around the time of the American Revolution—a gift to Garrett from Stuart Crane, long ago.

Pirates?

"No. I don't think so," Espy said. "Garrett's interest in international law was strictly related to climate change. I'm sure of that." Garrett had, in fact, become laser-focused on that issue these last few years. He'd chaired a special Senate subcommittee on the long-term effects of global warming on the US economy and infrastructure, had even crossed party lines to show his support for national standards related to the issue.

Li nodded. "Yes. Agreed." And without another word, she turned back to the stack of paper in front of her.

Two days had passed since the shooting at River Guard, and they were still at square one. Still trying to figure out what the man calling himself Nemkov had meant. "Right under your nose." "The secret your senator was killed to protect."

Blackjack.

Li had spent hours combing through the archives, searching records of missions undertaken by Woodhull and other chapters of their hidden Society. Looking for anything to do with the term. She had come up with interesting but irrelevant results. Espy had gone to Garrett's Senate office and, with Alice's permission, engaged in a similarly unproductive search there. Today they had moved on to Garrett's brownstone.

So far nothing.

Espy sat down in a red leather chair next to the fireplace. It had been Garrett's favorite. On the table was a folder of material from Frederickson's connection at the medical examiner's office, records related to Garrett's death. She'd glanced at it quickly last night; she decided to give it a second look now.

First up was the official police accident report: sketches and photos from the scene. None of those documents told her anything she didn't already know. Told her anything new. Especially the picture of Karl Royko—Garrett's driver—sitting on the curb, face buried in his hands, snow covering the lapels of his overcoat. That poor man. He was going to carry his guilt with him to the grave.

She set that cheery thought aside and moved on.

Next up was a report from the DMV, whose investigators had thoroughly gone over the senator's car and found no mechanical defects in either the body construction or the exhaust mechanism. After that was a letter from Great American, Crandall's insurance company, that said much the same thing in far fewer words. After that, a printout of an email from the chief legal counsel to Crandall's (and Royko's) cellular provider, stating that the unusual amounts of precipitation associated with the storm that

CHAPTER 5

night "could possibly" have affected signal strength in the area, though the memo was couched in such legalese that it read less like an apology and more like an advertisement for the company's services.

Next up was the autopsy report. More photos, along with extensive notes about the "condition of the decedent" Espy had no need to linger over. She did pause to scan the page of supplemental notes that followed, which detailed the contents of Garrett's pockets at the time of death (business cards, a money clip containing $146, a valet ticket from the Braddock Farms Country Club) and a description of the clothes he'd been wearing (a Canali topcoat, Paul Reid Smith suit, Allen Edmonds boots, down gloves, hat).

A Paul Reid Smith suit.

The same suit, Espy realized, he'd been buried in.

She flashed back to the funeral itself. Remembered standing in front of the casket with Frederickson, looking down on Garrett's still, artificially composed face. She'd been to only one other open-casket funeral in her life, an agent her dad had worked with. She was maybe fifteen, sixteen years old, and hadn't gotten closer than twenty feet from the casket. She was a lot closer here. Only a rope line between her and Garrett's body.

"This is strange to say, but ... he looks good." She had one hand resting on the rope line.

Frederickson leaned closer to whisper. "You're a sick puppy, Espy. You know that, right?"

She looked over at him, started to smile—and then saw the line of people behind waiting to view the body, the closest half-dozen of whom were staring daggers into her back.

There was Gene Carter from the NGA, Jenn Woodring from the CIA, Perrin Talbot from Defense—upper-level members of the intelligence community who she'd crossed swords with during her first assignment for Woodhull. Crossed swords over a program called CASHIER—a top-secret surveillance network the intelligence community had spent years designing and preparing to implement.

But CASHIER had been more than that. It had also been a plan for mass murder on an unprecedented scale. A Holocaust-level event that she, and Woodhull—and yes, Matt, couldn't forget Matt's role—had thwarted.

None of the people standing behind her had known the truth about that program. And they never would.

But they would never forgive her for what she'd done, either.

"You're right," she'd told Frederickson. "Let's move on."

❖ ❖ ❖ ❖ ❖

She left Li, went to the townhouse kitchen to make herself some tea. Picked up messages, checked in with her assistant, Greg. On her way back upstairs, she paused a moment in the hallway outside Garrett's office, which was lined with framed photos: Garrett and his wife, Alice; Garrett and his daughter Stephanie. Garrett posing with the president in the Oval Office; on the set of the film *Aurora*, standing between (of course) Doug Rivers and Jennifer Lawrence; posing on a sailboat, with Ted Kennedy handling the tiller.

The inscription on that photo read: *Garrett. To many more voyages together. Ted.*

Just then the front door opened. Frederickson came bolting up the stairs. He stopped short when he saw her. Stopped short, and smiled.

"You found something," she said.

"In a way."

"In a way?" She frowned. "What's that mean?"

"Was just with a friend of mine. The guy I told you

CHAPTER 5

about—works at the JOCC?"

Espy felt a little spark of excitement. The Joint Operations Command Center, in the Daly building on Indiana Ave. Where the video feeds from every camera in the DC area were piped in and recorded. Maybe, she thought, they had something from the day of the shooting at River Guard. Something on Nemkov, or his killers.

"Go on," she said.

"He doesn't work at the JOCC anymore."

"Well, that's not good news," Espy said.

"No, it's not." But he was still smiling.

"You found something, though?"

"Something … not exactly. More like … someone."

6

DeWayne was in his usual spot on one of the big concrete barriers between the Tasty King and the liquor store, eating a burger.

"Show." DeWayne smiled, gave him a fist bump without getting up. "What's up? Where you been? You all right?"

"All right," Cockerell responded, answering the last question, ignoring the others.

"You oughta get with him," DeWayne said. "He's been trying to reach you."

Meaning Z, of course. He and Wallet were laying low after what had happened with the Koppelman kid. Laying low, but still conducting their business. Cockerell was doing the same, only his business these last couple days had been more about River Guard than standing lookout on Minnesota Ave. More about Nemkov, less about Z … and much more about Harper.

Esperanza Marcelina Harper. Department of Justice lawyer. Office in the Federal Triangle, at the RFK building. She'd moved to DC a dozen or so years ago from Cincinnati, had risen through the ranks till she now headed up an interagency task force on international financial crimes. At first, he'd had a hard time believing she was the same woman who he'd trailed from the metro. The way she'd checked to see if she was being trailed coming out of the metro, how she'd handled that gun … and the dead senator? She was more than just a lawyer, that was for sure.

And that wasn't the only surprise he'd uncovered. Harper's father, it turned out, was Sam Hernandez.

Sam Hernandez, FBI agent, American hero. A decade earlier,

CHAPTER 6

a high school out in Long Beach had been attacked by terrorists; Hernandez led the FBI assault team that took out the killers before they could shoot up the whole school. Eight months later he was dead, assassinated by the remnants of that same terrorist group. Al-Hasra. The unconquerable.

Harper (she'd taken her mom's name, not her dad's; the parents were divorced) seemed to be following in his footsteps.

DeWayne was still talking. "Anyway, they ain't got the whole story. Z, he was provoked, man."

"Provoked?"

"Yeah. Them kids." DeWayne went on to give him a version of what had happened at Red House the other night, a version that played up the "mouthy bitch" that Wallet had cut and played down any role Z might have had in the whole thing. "Mouthy bitch" made Cockerell think of Rhonda Kruck, a friend (okay, maybe a little more than a friend) who had gotten fired from the FBI last year for mouthing off to her boss. Rhonda was now working at the DOJ. She could maybe find out some things for him about Harper. Maybe. Worth a shot.

He left DeWayne, walked a couple blocks before taking out his phone to call Rhonda. She was in a bad mood, which she always seemed to be whenever he called, but after some pussyfooting around he got down to it. Asked if she could do him the favor. He heard the "why" in her voice, but to Rhonda's credit, she didn't ask the question, said she'd see what she could find out. Cockerell thanked her and hung up.

Harper. Nemkov. Blackjack.

The secret your senator was killed to protect.

Had he heard that right? Had Nemkov really been confessing to the murder of a senator? Cockerell had done a little research. Three senators had died in the last two years: one from lung cancer, one from a heart attack, the last and most recent from carbon monoxide poisoning.

They wanted me to make it look like an accident.

That ruled out lung cancer. The heart attack? Maybe. He knew there were drugs that could trigger cardiac arrest, make a murder look like natural causes. That was James Bond territory too. Not his field of expertise. And the carbon monoxide poisoning? Looking at the details there—car crash during a snowstorm, driver went to get help, senator fell asleep in the back seat—how could you plan something like that?

So maybe he'd heard wrong.

Maybe it wasn't a United States senator Nemkov had been talking about. Maybe a state senator. Or maybe … what? He didn't know. All he knew for sure: Harper was the only solid lead he had.

He went back home, to the dump that was posing as his home for now, anyway. Last week there had been something wrong with the lock on the front door, and now it looked like something was up with the plumbing. There was a green van parked out front, with the words *AM/PM Plumbing, We Never Close!!* painted in bright yellow across the sides. Great. Thankfully, whatever the problem was, it didn't seem to be affecting his apartment. Water was running just fine, hot and cold, toilet flushing all right.

He grabbed a few hours of sleep and went back to work on Minnesota Ave. around ten p.m., keeping an eye out for Z's regular customers, for cops, for anything out of the ordinary. At three a.m. he was back at Red House, just him and DeWayne, five thirty he was in bed, nine forty his phone rang. Rhonda Kruck.

"Got a little information on that woman for you," Rhonda said. "Harper."

"Yeah, yeah." He sat up in bed and rubbed his eyes. "Gimme a second here, find a pen, write things down."

CHAPTER 6

"Don't know that you'll need it," Rhonda said. "There's not much to tell."

Esperanza Harper. Espy to her friends. Rhonda confirmed the information he'd gathered before—the move from Cincinnati, the task force she worked for, ICE-T, short for Interagency Command for Economic Terrorism. They did the kind of work that required heavy brainpower, which Harper, the consensus was, had to spare.

"Any gossip?" Cockerell asked. "Dirty laundry?"

"What are you looking for?" Rhonda asked. "You think she's on the take or something?"

"No, no. Not at all. Just curious."

"Right." She snorted. "Don't tell me. But there's nothing on her."

"Nothing?"

"Nothing. And I mean nothing. Woman's a cypher, doesn't have friends, or enemies, or socialize even, as far as my contacts can figure out. There's a rumor floating around that she had an affair with some guy in the Philadelphia office a year or so ago, but that's just a rumor."

"Philadelphia."

"Yeah. She was sent out there to make sure the locals played nice on this case she was part of. Oh wait. One thing. Not dirt. It's just interesting."

"What?"

"Three times in the last two years she's taken leaves of absence. Extended leaves. Away for like a month each time."

"Huh." Cockerell frowned. That was interesting. "Why?"

"How the hell would I know? Does it matter?"

"No," he replied, although something in his gut told him otherwise. Because that was odd, right? A month-long leave of absence? Three times in two years? Who got to do that and keep their job?

It didn't add up. Which told him what his next move had to be.

Surveillance.

He thanked Rhonda, they made noises about getting together for lunch soon, real soon, and then he hung up, grabbed a shower, and headed out. Took the Orange Line into the city, transferred at Metro to the Red, and got off at Dupont. Came up on Mass. Avenue with a smile on his face, giving the "hey, how's it going" to folks as he strolled along. He took a right on 21st Street, still wearing that smile as he passed Hillyer and came to number 1616.

Harper's townhouse. Looked a little run down. In need of a fresh coat of paint. Might be worth taking a look at her mailbox, he decided, and started up the half-flight of concrete steps just as the front door opened and a woman stepped out.

He recognized her right off. Harper's mom.

"Hello." She smiled. "Can I help you with something?"

❖ ❖ ❖ ❖ ❖

Penelope Harper. She'd moved to DC half a dozen years ago to be near her daughter. She might not have had Sam Hernandez's notoriety, but there was plenty out there on the internet about her. Some of it due to her ex, some to the career she'd had before she and Sam Hernandez divorced. Not all of it favorable, which Cockerell supposed went with the territory. She had been an actress, and she still looked the part: long white leather jacket, black jeans, black boots. Five nine, blond, blue eyes. Drop-dead gorgeous.

"Well, I hope so," Cockerell said smoothly. "Are you Erica?"

"Erica?" She shook her head. "No."

"Oh. Then..." Cockerell looked behind her, at the apartment, then made a show of taking out his phone, tapping the screen. "Sorry. My bad." He looked up and smiled. "2616. That's what I

CHAPTER 6

want. Sorry."

She gave him the smile right back, but there was a trace of suspicion in her eyes. "Of course. Have a nice day."

"Thanks. You too." There was nothing to do then but put his phone back in his pocket, nod, and turn back onto the sidewalk. Keep heading north. He didn't even bother turning around. That suspicion in her eyes—it would be stupid to try anything now. Who knows how long she'd be in the neighborhood. He'd have to come back another day.

He walked north a few blocks, cut over to 22nd, and headed back down to the avenue ... just in time to see Harper's mom on the other side of the street, walking down the drive of what looked like a museum. Or a mansion of some sort. Past a little statue on the front lawn, headed for the main entrance.

There was a statue out front. After she entered, he crossed to get a closer look.

George Washington. Anderson House. Headquarters of a group called the Society of the Cincinnati.

What was Harper's mom doing in there?

No way of knowing, he decided, and headed back across the river. He had a couple hours before he was due out on the avenue; he'd change clothes, get a little sleep before starting his Showtime workday.

When he got back to his place, though, not only was the big green plumbing van still there, there were nonstop banging noises coming from the basement. Terrific. And the lock on the front door was busted again—the interior door stood wide open.

Those things distracted him a little as he climbed the stairs to his apartment, so he wasn't really paying attention as he reached for his key, didn't grasp the significance of the scratches around the lock right away, not until the door moved, started to swing open at his touch.

It only took him a second then to realize something was wrong, but that was one second too many.

Z was sitting at the kitchen table. DeWayne stood next to him, filling the doorway to the bedroom.

He felt a knife at the back of his neck. "You all dressed up, brother," Wallet breathed.

"Yeah." Z rose from the table. "Tell me about that."

Wallet shoved Cockerell forward, into the apartment.

7

The door slammed shut behind him.

Wallet looked angry. And Z, the look on his face—whatever was happening, whatever had brought these guys here right now—it wasn't good.

Best defense here, he decided, was a good offense.

"Yo, what the hell? Did you guys—" He made a show of looking at the ruined lock plate. "Damn, man. You busted up my door? Why?"

"Hell with your door." Z shoved him backward, slamming him against the wall. "Where you been?"

"In the city, man," Cockerell said. "I went into DC. I—"

"You supposed to be working for me," Z said. "You supposed to be taking care of my business. Not yours."

"Hey, I been doing that." Cockerell gestured toward DeWayne. "You ask him, I been out there every day."

"Yeah, but you been late," DeWayne said. "Every day you been late."

Cockerell looked DeWayne in the eye. Just being late, that wouldn't have Z so worked up, and DeWayne wasn't the type of guy would go running to Z just because of that. It must have worked the other way around—something made Z suspicious so he went to DeWayne with questions. The question was what.

Cockerell had to find out. Fast.

"Listen, yeah, I been late, but I been making it up on the other end. Ask DeWayne, he could tell you I been staying till—"

"Stop lying to me."

"I'm not lying," Cockerell said, and Z's eyes flickered then, his head inclined just a little bit, the slightest of nods.

Wallet drew his knife, and took a step forward.

"Whoa. Take it easy." Cockerell glanced over at Z and then right back at Wallet, who was circling. Coming toward him. "Don't know what you think is going on, but—"

Wallet lunged.

Cockerell saw the move coming, and rather than dodge, he moved forward. Wallet wasn't expecting that. Cockerell chopped down, and the knife hit the ground.

"Come on, guys," Cockerell said, continuing to circle. "Let's talk—"

Something slammed into his back, and he found himself lying on the ground, face first, pinned down.

"Yeah. Let's talk." Z hissed in his ear. Pressed a gun up against his head. "Why don't you start by telling me the truth."

Footsteps sounded on the floor above. Someone in the apartment upstairs.

"Not a sound. You understand?" Z breathed.

Cockerell couldn't do anything but nod. The footsteps above him stopped.

"Now." Z got to his feet, let Cockerell stand. "The truth. Let's have it."

"The truth about what?"

"That MS-13 bullshit. That woman," Z said, and in that instant Cockerell knew exactly what was going on here. Somebody had followed him at some point over the last couple days. Tracked him while he was tracking Harper.

"Yeah, that's why I went to the city," Cockerell said. "I saw her again and I was following her. Trying to figure out—"

"You didn't say nothing about that." Z's eyes narrowed.

CHAPTER 7

"I wasn't sure," Cockerell said. "Who she was, what was going on. That's why."

"She ain't MS-13," Z said.

"No, man. She's some kind of Fed. I found that out."

"Yeah," Z said. "Yeah. Okay."

Only looking into the man's eyes, Cockerell saw it wasn't okay. Not at all.

Z was going to kill him. Right here, right now.

Footsteps sounded on the upstairs floor again. Loud footsteps. Z looked up. They all did.

The footsteps changed in character, got even louder, which was when Cockerell realized they weren't footsteps at all. The sound was metal on metal. Somebody hammering on the floor upstairs.

There was a loud crash nearby. The bathroom.

"Damn it!" A voice called out from upstairs. "Hey, anybody down there?"

Cockerell heard another noise then, a sound it took him a second to place. The sound of water running.

DeWayne peered around the corner, came back shaking his head. "There's plaster and shit on the floor. Water coming through the ceiling."

"Somebody there? Hang on!" the voice yelled again. "I'll be right down."

Cockerell heard the sound of things being dragged, heavy things clanking together. Tools.

"The plumber," he said. "Guy's been here all week."

The footsteps started again, right over their heads. A door opened and closed, and the footsteps continued down the stairs.

Cockerell tried to keep the relief he felt off his face; not much cause for it anyway. They were still going to kill him, kill the plumber too, if he got in the way. Another body wouldn't matter at all to these guys.

There was a knock at the door.

"Yo!" The same voice called out. "2B! You in there?"

Z and Wallet looked at each other. Z motioned, and Wallet nodded and got behind the door. Z waved his gun, pointed it right at Cockerell's forehead.

"You tell the guy to come back later," he said. "Understand?"

Cockerell nodded. "Yeah man. Absolutely."

The knocking got louder. "2B! It's the plumber. Open up, man. I gotta fix—"

Cockerell cracked the door open.

It was Harper's friend.

The big guy from River Guard. The guy who had shot him, drugged him, duct-taped him, and then cut him loose.

The long hair was gone, the ratty overcoat along with it. Disguises, both of them. Now he was in loose-fitting jeans and a light-blue button-down shirt with an *AM/PM Plumbing* patch sewn on the front pocket. He had a crewcut, salt-and-pepper hair, lines on his brow. He was older than Cockerell had first thought—forties, not thirties. Maybe even fifties.

"2B. What took you so long? I was worried, man. Thought I might've hit you on the head by accident." The guy had the balls to actually smile. "You all right? Something the matter?"

Cockerell tried to find his voice. Tried to figure out what was going on. It didn't make sense. How—

He felt something prick his side then.

Wallet's knife.

"I'm good. But now's a bad time," Cockerell said. "You gotta come back later."

"Bad time?" The guy kept smiling. "No shit, Sherlock. I cracked the cold water feed upstairs. I gotta clamp it off in there."

CHAPTER 7

He nodded towards the bathroom.

Cockerell shook his head. "Now's not good."

"Gonna be a whole lot worse in another couple minutes. Water keeps going like that, it's gonna flood the whole building. Now let me just—"

"Just shut it all down." Cockerell turned and saw Z, gun nowhere in sight, stepping forward, holding out something in his hand. "Shut the whole damn thing off."

"Shut the main?" The man looked incredulous. He took a step closer; Cockerell let the door open a crack wider. "What, are you serious? I can't..." His voice trailed off as he saw what Z was holding out. A wad of bills. The man smiled. A big, toothy smile. "That's for me?" he asked, extending his hand forward.

Z nodded. "Absolutely."

"All right then." He took the money, shoved it in his pocket, and then reached down to his toolbelt. "And this is for you."

He came up with a gun.

He shot Z—*phhtt*, a silencer—who gasped, grabbed the side of his neck, and stumbled backward.

Wallet was shoving Cockerell out of the way, coming from behind the door, knife hand coming forward. But the man was moving too, bracing himself in the doorframe, using his leg to kick the door backward again, right into Wallet's chest, slamming him back against the wall. Wallet grunted and dropped his knife, and the man raised the gun again and shot him too.

Wallet grimaced, tried to shove the door back the other way. The man backhanded him across the forehead with the gun barrel. Wallet went limp.

The man shot him again.

He turned and pointed the gun at DeWayne, who was just standing there, eyes wide, not having moved a muscle since

Cockerell first answered the knock.

"Don't—" he began, and the man shot him too. DeWayne went to his knees. The man took a couple steps forward, raised the gun, and shot him a second time. DeWayne fell over and lay still.

Cockerell stood there, stunned.

"Right back," the man said and disappeared into the bathroom. Cockerell heard a high-pitched squeak. A few seconds later, the water stopped running.

The man walked back in the room. "You all right? They hurt you?"

"I'm fine. But…" Cockerell shook his head, looking around at the bodies, the busted door. "What the hell? What did you do?"

"Shut off the cold water feed. And saved your life." The guy smiled. "Here, by the way, is where you say thank you."

Cockerell couldn't find his voice for a second. "Thank you? Are you kidding? You … you killed them, man. Why…"

The guy knelt down next to DeWayne, pulled a dart out of the big man's leg.

"White 17, detective."

The voice came from behind him. A woman's voice.

He looked up and saw Harper standing in the doorway.

"Or don't you remember?"

8

Harper guided him downstairs and outside, to the green van parked at the curb, the *AM/PM Plumbing* van. She opened the back door, revealing an interior filled with not plumbing supplies but surveillance equipment. A workstation, LCD screens, computer components, a couple of chairs. One of the screens showed a view of his apartment: the kitchen and the little entryway, with Wallet, Z, and DeWayne all sprawled out on the floor.

"You were watching me," he said.

"And you've been watching me. Ever since River Guard." She met his gaze. "You lied before. What you heard when Nemkov got shot. You heard my name."

"That's right. Department of Justice, huh?"

"Among other things. That's what I want to talk to you about."

"I'm all ears. But first I gotta call my lieutenant," Cockerell said. "Figure out what how we're gonna play this when those guys wake up."

"They're on their way. Fifteen minutes max." The plumber, Harper's friend, was walking down the apartment building steps.

"Who's on their way?" Cockerell asked. "What are you talking about?"

"The FBI."

"What?"

"Your three buddies up there got in the way of an FBI operation. A drug-smuggling thing. My thing." The guy took off his toolbelt and slid it into the van. "So did you. That's how this all went down."

"You're FBI?" Cockerell asked.

The guy smiled. "Your lieutenant's getting a call right now. Getting a more detailed version of what I just told you. We'll get you the report, so you can study it. Make sure we're all on the same page so we tie this off nice and neat."

"Tie this off? Now? No." Cockerell shook his head. "That's not your call. We're not walking away from this just because—"

"Hey. They made you, chief. You're lucky we were watching or you'd be dead right now."

"You don't know that."

"Face the facts, detective. Your cover was blown. Your operation's over," Harper said.

Cockerell stared at her. Looked up at the apartment he'd been calling home these last six months. And now…

Done?

"Hey." The big guy offered a sympathetic smile. "If it's any consolation, federal involvement means these guys are going away for a long time."

"It's not," he said.

The big guy shrugged. "Well, I gotta move the van before the bureau shows up."

"And we have to clear out," Harper said. "You got a few minutes to talk?"

"A few minutes?" Cockerell shook his head in disgust. "Looks like I got all the time in the world."

❖ ❖ ❖ ❖ ❖

They took a car across the river to Harper's townhouse. It might have looked worn from the outside, but inside was an entirely different story. The lock on the vestibule door was a keypad, a kind he'd never seen before. There were cameras that turned to follow him

CHAPTER 8

as he followed Harper up the stairs; another set that took over as they reached the second floor swiveled as they stopped in front of her apartment door. Another keypad. A fingerprint sensor? Maybe, judging from how quickly the door opened. And the slow, ponderous way that door moved—it was heavy. Well-balanced. Expensive.

Made him wonder just what was so valuable that it required all that security.

The lights flickered on as Harper stepped inside her apartment. He followed her in, and stopped dead in his tracks.

The entire wall in front of him was an aquarium. A wall of glass that started at the floor and rose to the top of a vaulted ceiling. Had to be at least twelve feet high, maybe even more than that across. Behind the glass was a coral reef filled with schools of brightly colored tropical fish of all sizes and shapes.

He shook his head. "That's the biggest fish tank I've ever seen in my life."

"Habitat," Harper said.

"What?"

"Tropical habitat. Not fish tank. Custom built. Leaded glass. Took a year and a half to design, build, and then rebuild. Lot of weight, all that water. Had to reinforce a couple of the support beams. Worth it though." She nodded toward a kitchen, behind her. "I'm going to make tea. You want a cup?"

"Tea? I don't want any tea." He couldn't stop looking at the fish tank. The habitat. He walked closer. One fish swam up to the glass, stared right at him. A little orange and white fish. Looked like the one from that movie. *Finding Nemo*.

He stared into its eyes. The fish blinked.

Hey buddy. What the hell is going on here?

He turned away, saw the fish in the habitat weren't the only ones in the apartment. The walls were covered with pictures of them. Big poster-size photos: close-ups of individual fish, fish in schools, colorful fish, oddly shaped fish…

"You sure you don't want tea?" Harper called out.

"Tea … no. Maybe something stronger, though?"

"I have orange juice."

He turned to look at her. She stood in the kitchen, staring at him. Waiting for a response. Orange juice?

"Never mind," he said. "I'm good."

To his right was a sunken living room with a long glass coffee table in the center. Black leather couch, black leather armchairs. The furniture, the fish tank—this was expensive stuff. Harper had money. He filed the fact away for future reference.

"Come. Let's sit." Harper came up behind him, carrying a mug of tea. Stepped down into the living room, took one of the armchairs, and gestured to him to take the other. He did.

There were a handful of framed pictures on the coffee table: Harper and her dad, smiling at what Cockerell guessed was her college graduation; Harper and her mom, cheek-to-cheek on a beach somewhere; a portrait of a little girl wearing glasses and a very serious expression.

"My niece," Harper said, noticing his gaze. She took a seat on the couch. "She lives in LA."

"Cute kid."

"Yeah. I don't get to see her nearly enough."

"So." He locked eyes with her. "What's this all about? Why—"

"Listen." Harper shook her head. "To begin with, there's some things I can't tell you."

"I don't see the point of keeping secrets, Ms. Harper."

"Espy. Please."

"Okay. Espy. I know your name. I know you work for the DOJ—"

CHAPTER 8

"You don't know anything, Detective. Believe me."

"Mike."

"Okay. Mike." She took a sip of her tea. "You have no idea what's really going on here."

"So what did you want to talk about? You gonna threaten me? Tell me what's gonna happen if I don't keep quiet?"

"No. Not at all." She set her tea down. "You're here because we'd like your help."

"My help?" Cockerell frowned. That was about the last thing he'd expected to hear. "Okay. Then tell me what's going on. Who Nemkov was, who that plumber friend of yours is."

"Nemkov, that's an alias. There's a video game, an assassin who—"

"I know that. But the body. You must have gotten fingerprints off his body, right? So who…" He stopped talking, because Harper was shaking her head again.

"We don't have Nemkov's body."

Cockerell frowned. "Somebody cleaned up the site. That wasn't you?"

"No."

"Then who?"

"Whoever shot him, is my guess."

"Why would they do that?" He realized he knew the answer to that even as he asked the question.

They do not leave trails, you see.

"Okay," Cockerell said. "And your plumber friend?"

"Frederickson. That's what I call him." She shrugged. "You could call him that if you want. I know he's got a couple other names he uses."

"He works for the FBI."

"He does indeed."

"Same way you work for the DOJ, I'm guessing."

"Listen, Detective Cockerell, I—"

"Mike, remember?"

"Right. Mike. I'm not trying to be mysterious here. I'm telling you what I can. My hands are tied to a certain extent."

"So you don't trust me."

"It's not that at all. It's just—"

"Just what?" Suddenly it hit him. Suddenly he was pissed. The last six months of work, the last six months of his life, the entire operation with Z … all down the drain? Because of this woman? "You want my help but you won't tell me a damn thing. I don't need this." He got to his feet.

"Hey." Harper snapped. "I'd ask you to keep in mind that we just saved your life back there."

"What I'm keeping in mind is that you and your Frederickson friend just ruined an operation I spent six months working on."

"You'd rather we let your buddies cut you up?"

"I'd rather none of this had happened."

"You and me both. But here we are."

They glared at each other.

"Listen," she said. "We're on the same side."

"So you guys keep telling me. But I don't see it."

"That's a shame. Because it should be obvious." She looked him in the eye. "Your father would've gotten it right off."

"And what in the hell is that supposed to mean?"

"I mean it's in your blood. Same as mine."

"What is? What are you talking about?"

"Service to your country."

"Seriously?" He rolled his eyes. "That's the card you're going to play?"

"Absolutely it is. It's what this is all about. It's what your father

CHAPTER 8

gave his life for. It's why you followed in his footsteps. Went to West Point."

"News flash. I quit the service."

"And yet here you are. A cop. Still serving."

"That's a different thing."

"Is it?"

"This is my city. I grew up here."

"It's your country too."

"I'm happy right where I am."

"What would your father think?"

"I guess," Cockerell began, and gritted his teeth to keep hold of himself, "I guess we'll never know, will we? Because my father died in some stupid war we spent twenty years fighting for no good reason."

"Wrong." She shook her head. "There was a reason we were in that fight. And a good one. Not to excuse the way that war was conducted, but—"

"I'm done," he said, heading for the door.

"Hey." Harper stood too, started after him. "Hold up. I know how you feel."

"Bullshit. You don't know anything about how I feel."

"On the contrary. I know exactly how you feel. And I'm guessing if you calm down and think for a second, you'll see that."

He stopped and turned back. "Sorry. I don't see that. Not at…" All, he was about to say, and then he saw, over Harper's shoulder, the college graduation photo of her and her father. Sam Hernandez.

And just like that, his anger was gone.

"Yeah," she said, following his gaze. "That's right. Now come sit. Please." She didn't wait for him to respond. Just went back to her chair and picked up her tea again.

It took him a minute, but he followed.

"Okay." He sat back down. "Okay. You want my help. With what?"

She smiled. First smile he'd ever seen from her. It transformed her face. Suddenly he could see that there was, in fact, a little resemblance to her mother there after all. A little bit of movie star.

"Thank you," she said. "I appreciate it. *We* appreciate it."

"Don't thank me yet. I haven't done anything."

She nodded, and the smile disappeared, just as fast as it had come. "Understood. So let me start at the beginning." She took a sip of her tea. "A couple weeks ago, there was an incident. A car crash. A man died. At the time, we thought—"

"Holy shit." A chill went down Cockerell's spine.

They killed a United States senator.

Cockerell got right back on his feet. "Holy shit. You're talking about Crandall. The senator from Ohio. I read about this." He started pacing. "He was coming home from a party. It was snowing. The car skidded, got a couple flat tires, the driver went for help, Crandall stayed in the car. Fell asleep. Died of carbon monoxide poisoning."

"The tailpipe was blocked," Harper said.

"That's right. The tailpipe was blocked." The details were coming back to him. "There was a stand of trees hanging over the road. Some branches cracked, dumped a ton of snow in the wrong place. They proved—"

"They couldn't prove anything," Harper said. "Falling snow was the best explanation they could come up with. Nemkov gave me a different one."

They wanted me to make it look like an accident.

"He did it." Cockerell stopped pacing, looked down at her. "Nemkov. He killed him. That's why you were meeting him at

CHAPTER 8

River Guard."

Harper nodded. "That's right."

"But how?" Cockerell shook his head. He sat back down, his mind racing. "No. That doesn't make sense. He just happened to be driving by when they crashed?"

"He was there. At the party. He was following Crandall. When the accident happened … when the driver left … he saw his chance. He took it."

"Jesus." Cockerell shook his head. "Jesus Christ. This is unbelievable."

"That's what I thought, at first. But now…"

"Okay. But why do you need me? You work for the DOJ, you have the FBI at your disposal…"

"We need you because you're a DC cop. A detective. You can go places we can't. Get answers to questions we don't even get to ask."

"You keep saying 'we.' Who is 'we,' exactly? Your interagency task force, what's it called again?"

"ICE-T. No, it's not that. This is something completely different."

"Yeah. I had a feeling. Something you can't tell me about, am I right?"

"That's right." She leaned closer. "But we're the good guys here, Detective. And we could use your help."

"Mike, remember?"

"Right. Mike." She smiled. He returned it.

"Okay. What is it you need me to do?"

"There's a lot. It's going to take a few minutes." She stood up, held out her mug. "I'm getting a fresh cup. You sure you don't want—"

"Fine," he said. "I'll have some tea."

9

"Hey. That's you." Trina Morales sat before a wall of screens, pointing at one of them. A screen showing the scene at the intersection of Minnesota and Benning—showing him in his Showtime persona, standing in the shadows, eyes fixed on Harper as she'd headed to her rendezvous with Nemkov.

"Sure is," he said.

"Nice jacket," Morales said.

"Hey. Don't make fun."

She smiled. "No, I get it. You're in character."

"Yeah well … that's all over and done with."

"So I heard."

Cockerell smiled faintly, pictured the veins popping on Colitti's neck as he yelled into the phone this morning. He wouldn't be surprised if everyone in DC had heard. He wondered if the guy on the other end, the guy explaining the crossed wires on the operation, was Harper's friend, Frederickson. He hoped so. He wouldn't wish that kind of verbal abuse on a complete stranger.

"Rolling," Morales said, and the video resumed playing.

Cockerell was at the JOCC—the Joint Operations Command Center, a centralized surveillance command post on the fifth floor of the Henry J. Daly Building (a.k.a. police headquarters) on Indiana Ave. The main part of the command center was a long glassed-in area that ran the length of the west corridor. It was actually two rooms. The larger had a couple dozen workstations and several large LCD screens affixed to the wall; the smaller, where he and Morales were, was the only room accessible from

CHAPTER 9

the main hallway. It had four large workstations and displays of its own, along with an entrance to the larger room—a glass door with a metal keypad next to it.

The JOCC received feeds from every camera in the city: Metro, DHS, Capitol Shield, Secret Service, even private. This was the first job Harper had tasked Cockerell with.

"We've seen some of those feeds," she'd told him. "But not all of them."

What she wanted him to do was look for something, anything, that might be a clue not just to Nemkov's movements but to the movements of the people who had shot him. Before, and after, the fusillade of gunfire they'd all run from.

Cockerell continued to watch now as Harper headed down the little side street, toward the towers. Moving out of range of the camera and finally disappearing. "Okay. What else you got, near there?" he asked.

He'd told Morales he was looking for drug sales, not so much evidence of the transactions that he could use in court, but clues to follow up on. That he wanted anything in the vicinity of the Minnesota Ave. metro station.

"Try this one," she said, and the view switched to the underpass by the homeless encampment, the tent city he'd passed through the other day. And there was that white-haired woman, back pressed against the gate leading to the River Guard site. Three guys were coming at her. That didn't look good … for her.

The screen, all of a sudden, went dark.

"Hey. What happened?" he asked.

"Not sure." Morales leaned over her workstation, keyed in a few commands. Keyed in a few more, then sat up straight.

"Horace?" she called out.

A guy across the room looked up. "Yeah?"

"Come take a look at this."

He rolled his chair over.

"We were watching this recording here, and all of a sudden—the monitor went black. I think it's busted."

"Huh. Let me take a look." Horace pushed his chair over to the terminal next to Morales, started keying in commands himself. Looked up at the screen, shook his head, and typed in a few more instructions.

"It's not the monitor," he said. "It's the recording."

"What?"

"There's no signal. Nothing on the drive. Just dead air." He pointed at the screen. "See?"

Cockerell didn't. Couldn't make heads or tails of the symbols on the screen. But Morales nodded.

"Shit," she said. "What happened?"

"Don't know. But whatever it is, it doesn't last too long. Only about half an hour before the recording starts up again."

"Yeah. I see. From five fifteen or so on. Weird."

"Yeah," Cockerell said. "Weird."

Only it was more than that. Half an hour or so, from five fifteen on: exactly the timeframe he was interested in. Exactly when Nemkov and Harper had rendezvoused. When the shooting had taken place.

Horace went back to his desk. Morales and Cockerell switched to another recording, from another camera.

It had the exact same "malfunction," at the exact same time, as the first feed.

That same malfunction showed up in three more sets of recordings—from three more cameras.

"This is really weird," Morales said.

Cockerell nodded, though he knew it was well beyond weird.

CHAPTER 9

These are dangerous people, he thought. *They do not leave trails.*

❖ ❖ ❖ ❖ ❖

He thanked Morales for her time, left the JOCC, and stood outside the front door of the Daly Building for a moment. Coming here had been task number one; task number two on his list was to talk to people who'd been at the party Crandall had been coming from, see if they remembered anybody matching Nemkov's description. Harper had given him the host's name, and contact information.

"But be careful," she'd told him. "Diplomatic. Discreet. There were a lot of movers and shakers there. A lot of important government people."

And at that second, as if on cue, a breeze came up. The American flag hanging over the entrance to the Daly Building fluttered in the wind. The Stars and Stripes.

Important government people.

Service to your country.

It's in your blood, same as mine.

His father, and hers. Sam Hernandez. FBI agent. American hero.

But at that second, it wasn't Harper's dad's face that came to mind.

It was her mother's. Penelope Harper. The actress. Cockerell remembered her walking into that mansion over on Massachusetts Avenue. The one with the statue of George Washington out front. Anderson House. He'd checked into it, found it was home to some kind of patriotic society. What was that name again?

It took him a second, but then he remembered.

10

"The Society of the Cincinnati?" The woman shook her head. "Why Cincinnati, when it's here in Washington, DC?"

"I think it was because he was from Cincinnati," a second woman said. The two of them stood underneath the portrait of George Washington in the main hall of Anderson House. Espy—right behind them, in the crowd jammed into the ballroom for the movie premiere—sighed. She couldn't let that one go.

"Actually…" She cleared her throat. "The 'Cincinnati' comes from Cincinnatus. Lucius Quinctius Cincinnatus. He was a Roman general and statesman. The Society is named after him."

The women both turned. "Excuse me?" one said.

They were younger than she'd thought at first, just girls really, but so made-up, so dressed-up (designer gowns, heels—and could those be real diamonds?) that it was hard to tell their exact age, though she suspected they weren't much out of their teens. Well. Here was an opportunity for education. One of the Society's main missions.

"Sorry. Didn't mean to eavesdrop." She smiled. "I overheard what you were saying. Cincinnatus was Washington's hero. His role model, you might say." Espy pointed at the portrait, in case there was any confusion about who Washington was.

"Ah." Girl number one nodded. "I guess that makes sense. I mean the Romans had slaves too. Just like Washington. Peas in a pod and all."

"Well. Washington was a lot more than a slave owner," Espy said. "He's the reason we have a republic today. He could have

CHAPTER 10

been king. He was a product of his time, yes, but—"

"We did some reading about him in our American History seminar. That man"—she pointed—"he was not the hero people think he was. Not at all."

Espy bit her tongue. "He wasn't perfect, no. But the fact is—"

"Wait a second. Do you work here or something?"

"In a way," Espy said. "Sometimes."

"You don't know Doug Rivers, do you?" The girl moved closer to Espy and lowered her voice. "I mean I can't believe he's really going to be here tonight. This is just crazy. I thought I'd never get a chance to meet him, and then this"—she held up the program—"happens. Right around the corner from us. It's just crazy."

"Yeah. That's crazy," girl number two said.

"But if you know him … maybe you could introduce us?"

They both looked at Espy expectantly.

"Um…" Espy said, because of course she knew Doug Rivers, had probably spent more time with him over the last few years than all but a half-dozen people. And one thing she had learned about him: He was deeply conflicted about being a movie star. About receiving so much adulation, so much money, just because of the way he looked.

"We won't take up too much of his time," girl one said. "We just want to say hi."

"Of course," Espy said. "I understand."

She didn't want to lie, but she didn't want to make promises she couldn't keep. Doug was scheduled to spend most of the evening with his VIP ticket holders, the ones who had paid $1,500 to spend time with him.

But just then, the problem was taken out of her hands.

"Well, look," she said. "Here he is now. Hi, Doug."

"Esperanza Harper." Doug smiled. "Good to see you. You look wonderful. Your hair." He gestured. "Never seen you wear it down before."

"Oh my god," girl one said. "Oh my god."

Girl two opened her mouth, but no words came out.

Doug Rivers had that effect on people. His presence could be unnerving, though not to Espy, a fact that amused Doug no end. Espy suspected it was because she'd grown up around someone else with a breathtaking physical presence.

Doug had told her as much, more than once. "You, my dear," he'd said, "have mommy issues."

Tonight he was dressed in a gray tuxedo jacket with black piping, black pocket square, black tie. His hair, which he'd grown out and had powdered white for the film (just like Washington, who had refused to wear the wig the British and their Tory sympathizers favored) was still long and pulled back from his face. Doug was shorter than Washington had been – five eight, as opposed to the general's six two – but that did nothing to detract from his physical presence. "Hi there." He focused his attention—what the papers called his 10,000-watt smile—on the girls. "I'm Doug."

"Oh my god," girl one said again.

Girl two still couldn't find her voice.

"I could sign those for you if you want." He gestured toward their programs.

Girl one nodded and thrust out her program. The cover was a montage of Doug dressed as George Washington and Ayesha Vatril as Elizabeth Powel, with the movie's title, *1787*, in bold above.

Doug produced a pen from his pocket. "And what's your name?" he asked.

"Natalie. I'm Natalie," girl one said. "This is my friend Suzanne."

"Well, thanks so much for coming tonight, Natalie, Suzanne,

CHAPTER 10

for helping support the Society." He handed Natalie back her program and took Suzanne's from her unresisting hand. Signed that as well. "I really hope you enjoy the film."

"Selfie," Suzanne said.

"Sure," Doug said, and stepped between them, putting an arm around each.

Natalie held her cell phone out to Espy. "Could you?"

"Of course," Espy said, and obliged. Three snaps on each girl's phone.

Doug disengaged from the girls. "Now, would you give me a minute here? To talk to Esperanza alone?"

He took Espy's arm without waiting for an answer and guided her to an adjacent room. The conversational buzz doubled in volume as they entered.

"Shouldn't you be with the VIPs?" Espy asked.

"I thought I'd take a minute to talk to the hoi polloi."

"I'll try not to take that personally."

"Li filled me in. About Garrett. About what's been going on." His expression turned serious. "You should have called. I could have been here earlier."

"We'll talk later. Downstairs. For now, let's just enjoy the evening."

"Understood." Doug looked around the room. "Seen your mom yet?"

"No. Why?"

"You should find her. Talk to her."

"Why? She's not still upset about her part getting cut down, is she?" Her mom was playing Mercy Otis Warren in the film, a Massachusetts woman who'd had a significant role in the composition of the Bill of Rights. It had been a very prominent part in the script, but got considerably less so during filming and then in the editing room. These things happen, Doug had told them separately and together. Her mom had seemed fine with that at the time.

"No. At least, I don't think so," he said.

"Then what?"

"That's for her to tell you," he said.

"Doug…"

He smiled then. Not the 10,000-watt smile. The 'I have a secret' smile. The bedroom smile. Espy was immune to that one too.

More or less.

"Doug!" someone shouted.

Espy turned and saw Casey Bannister, the film's director, walking toward them, a group of older people in tow. VIP ticket holders, no doubt.

Doug sighed. "Back to the salt mines. Talk to you later." He turned on his 10,000-watt smile, leaving Espy alone once more.

Though not really alone at all, of course.

She squeezed her way through the crowd back into the ballroom, picking up a glass of champagne along the way. Found her way to a quiet spot by the stairs, just under a portrait of Alexander Hamilton, the Society's second president general after Washington. She leaned back against the wall and took a deep breath.

The premiere had been scheduled months in advance. She'd bought a new dress, made an appointment at the salon her mother was always begging her to go to, rearranged her work calendar. She'd been looking forward to the event in a way she rarely looked forward to these sorts of things.

Now all she wanted to do was get back downstairs. Get back to work.

"Ma'am?"

She looked up. A waitress was holding out a tray filled with hors d'oeuvres. "No thanks," Espy said.

CHAPTER 10

"I'll take one." A man stepped in front of her and took a dumpling from the tray.

Espy tried to move out of the way, and then another man stepped around on her on the other side, bumping her in the process.

"Are these the pork?" he asked. "Those were delicious."

"Yes sir," the waitress said.

"Great. John?" he called out. "These are the ones. You have to try these."

Espy felt someone else coming up behind her and tried to move back against the wall. Someone else stepped squarely on her foot.

"Hey!" she said.

"Sorry," they said. "You're in the line of fire here."

Espy glared, turned to move, and saw the conversational partner who the men, in their rush to get to the food, had left behind.

"Esperanza," her mother said. "There you are."

❖ ❖ ❖ ❖ ❖

Her mom was wearing a knee-length dress in a close-fitting tan fabric that clung and sparkled as she moved, along with a pearl choker and pearl earrings. Her hair was pulled back in a tight bun. The Grace Kelly look, Espy thought but didn't say, considering her mom's ambivalent feelings about the late Princess of Monaco.

"You look nice," Espy said.

"You look beautiful. I love your hair like that."

"Not exactly—"

"Professional, I know. Still." Her mom smiled. "Thanks for coming. I know you have a lot going on."

You don't know the half of it, Espy thought. "I'm excited to see the film. I've heard great things about it. You have a few scene-stealing turns, I'm told."

"Well," her mom said, sipping absently at her champagne. "I suppose."

Doug was right. Something was up here. "Mom … something the matter?"

"This is not the time or place for that conversation."

"Well, come on then." Espy took her mother's arm and guided her away from the crowd, through the glass doors to the back patio and into the garden.

"It's raining," her mother said, holding out a hand. "My hair…"

"Drizzling," Espy said. "Barely. So you want to talk about it?"

"Talk about what?"

"You know," Espy said. "What happened with the film."

"The film?" Her mom looked puzzled. "What do you mean?"

"Mom. I know you're upset that they cut your part, but—"

"My part?" Her mom laughed. "Esperanza, I'm not upset about my part. The shoot, the people—that was one of the best experiences of my life."

"Okay," Espy said. "If it's not the film, what is it then?"

"The Family J," she said. "They called and offered me the role."

"Why are you sad about that?" Espy clasped her mother's hands. "That's great news." The character her mom was going to play was Clarice, the grande dame of the show, the head of the dysfunctional Family J. Not top-billed, but the emotional center of the program. "When do you start? Where are they filming?"

"I don't know." Her mom looked her in the eye. "I turned it down."

"What?"

"I turned it down. I decided not to do it."

Espy was stunned. "I don't understand."

"I've just … it's not for me, I decided."

CHAPTER 10

"Not for you? Mom, it's the perfect part. Not to mention that Doug went well out of his way to get you the audition."

"I know that. I've talked with him. Thanked him. Told him what I did. He agreed with me. With my reasons."

"Which are what?" Espy snapped. "You still haven't told me."

"It's just not the kind of work I want to do right now."

Oh boy, Espy thought. Here we go again. The last time her mom had worked in the business, she was in her twenties. She'd been the love interest, the eye candy, the half-dressed girl in all the trailers. It had taken Espy and Doug a good long time to convince her of how far past that girl she was, especially considering how men of all ages still reacted to her. But the movies were not real life. Espy thought that lesson had taken. Apparently not.

"Mom," she began. "It's work, right? You've been out of the business for—"

"Exactly," her mom interrupted. "I'm too old for this, Esperanza. I don't want to hustle for parts anymore. What few parts there are for women my age."

"Wait." She looked at her mom. "Are you saying…"

"I've decided I'm done with acting. I'm really done this time."

Espy didn't know how to respond to that.

Penny Harper's whole mantra while Espy was growing up, from high school on up through college and law school, had been that of the aggrieved parent. The single mom who gave up on her own dreams, who sacrificed so her daughter could achieve. These last few years, she'd started to rekindle that career—local theater, commercial work, a handful of TV pilots that hadn't been picked up, and then this. *1787*. Her first film work in a quarter century.

Give up acting?

"Well okay," Espy said. "Then what is it you do want, Mom?"

And if you say grandchildren, Espy added silently to herself, I will stab you with the nearest fork.

"To be honest, I want to take a page from your book."

Espy blinked. "What?"

"By which I mean I want to do something meaningful with my life," she said.

"Oh," Espy said, and then struggled to put different words in her mouth than the ones she had been preparing to say.

Her mom sighed. "I'm so proud of what you do, you know. At the DOJ, and here, which I know I'm not supposed to know about, or talk about, but still. You're making a difference in the world, Esperanza. You really are."

Espy found herself smiling. "I don't know what to say, except thank you."

"You're welcome."

"I mean for everything, Mom. I really … I mean obviously, well, you know." She cleared her throat. "I couldn't have done any of it if you hadn't—"

"Please." Her mom held up a hand. "I was a horrible mother. Let's not—"

"You were not."

"Let's not do this now. Talk about the past."

"Fair enough. So what about the future, then? What are you going to do now?"

"That's another thing I'm sad about. Another thing I've decided." Her mom took a deep breath. "I'm leaving DC."

Espy's heart tightened in her chest. "Leaving?" she said. "What? Where are you going?"

"I'm moving back to Cincinnati."

"But…" Espy struggled for words. "What are you going to do there?"

CHAPTER 10

"I'm not sure just yet, to tell you the truth."

"Well, do you want me to put you in touch with Leonard and Tunde?" Her old boss in Cincinnati and his wife, both of whom were very active in political and charitable causes.

"I already have. In fact, I'm going to be helping Tunde out right away."

"That's great. Doing what?"

"To start with, watching her grandchildren."

"Mom…"

"Well, you asked." She held up her glass. "I could use another drink."

"Absolutely," Espy said. "Another drink."

❖ ❖ ❖ ❖ ❖

They wandered back into the ballroom, which somehow seemed even more tightly packed than before. A huge screen now hung from the second-floor balcony. In front of that was a podium and three rows of folding chairs, with attendants busily setting up more rows behind them.

Her mom headed toward the bar; Espy changed her mind, begged off that second glass of wine. She needed a minute to think here. Done with acting? Moving back to Cincinnati? On top of everything else right now…

She spied Frederickson and Li in intense conversation. She joined them.

"Anything new?" Espy asked.

"She wants to work on the sketch," Frederickson said, gesturing at Li.

"Again?"

They'd already generated an AI composite image of Nemkov, as best as Espy could remember him. They'd run it through multiple databases, hoping (unsuccessfully) for a match.

"Yes. I wish to suggest a new approach," Li said.

"It's not a good idea," Frederickson said.

"It is a new idea. We are in need of new ideas."

Espy couldn't argue with that. "What is it you want to try?"

Li leaned forward, lowered her voice. "Hypnosis."

"Hypnosis."

"Yes," Li said. "I believe your subconscious mind may contain more details about Mr. Nemkov's appearance than your conscious one can access."

"Okay. Maybe. But … we're going to bring in a hypnotist on this?"

"Obviously not," Li said. "Security concerns. I will do it myself."

Frederickson rolled his eyes.

"Hello, everyone. If I could have your attention, please?" A woman Espy didn't recognize was standing at the podium, leaning into the microphone. Doug and the director were standing next to her. "Hello," she said again, louder. "Good evening. We're about ready to get started here, so if you could all find seats…"

No one moved.

Doug leaned in front of her and took the microphone. "Hi, everyone. Hi. If I could have your attention."

People's heads turned. All at once the room quieted.

"Thank you," Doug said. "We're all looking forward to showing you the results of our hard work here. The movie we've spent so much time on. The reason why our country is so important, now more than ever. If you could all find a seat, we can get started here. Thanks again."

He handed back the microphone as the crowd began scrambling for chairs.

Frederickson laughed. "Now there's some hypnosis for you," he

CHAPTER 10

said to Li. "Notice how all the women in the room have congregated in the first two rows."

The first dozen or so rows, in fact, had filled up already. Espy found a group of chairs toward the back; she caught her mother's eye and waved her over. The four of them sat.

The film started. Espy watched as George Washington—Doug Rivers—took counsel from an aged Ben Franklin, argued with a dandified Thomas Jefferson, and flirted with Elizabeth Powel, played by the actress Ayesha Vatril. About forty minutes into the film her mom—playing Mercy Otis Warren—appeared, a lone voice fighting against the ratification of the United State Constitution.

Espy took her mom's hand in hers and squeezed.

A late arrival, a man, sat down on the other side of her mother. On-screen, compromises were made. The constitution was signed, the convention ended. Washington/Rivers rode off triumphantly into the sunset.

The crowd applauded. Espy put a hand on her mom's shoulder.

"You were good, Mom," she said. "So good."

Her mom smiled. "I think I did all right, yes."

The man who'd sat down on her mom's other side leaned forward then and spoke. "Absolutely. You were fantastic," he said.

"Thank you," Espy's mom replied, turning.

Espy turned herself then. Her eyes widened.

"Detective … how … ?"

Cockerell smiled. "Mike, remember?"

11

The expression on Harper's face was priceless. Worth the outrageous price of his $225 admission ticket.

Just wait, he thought. The real surprise was yet to come.

"What are you doing here?" she asked.

"Looking for you."

"Well, you found me." She glared. "What is it you want?"

"Society of the Cincinnati, huh? I thought women couldn't be members."

The big guy, Frederickson, was suddenly standing over him. "Come on, chief. Let's you and me take a little walk."

"I'm not opposed." Cockerell looked at Harper. "But you should come too. I have something to tell you. Something important."

"Wait. I know you, don't I?" Harper's mom was looking at him.

"Not really."

"Yes. Yes. I do." She snapped her fingers. "On the street. You were there outside Esperanza's apartment." She looked from him to her daughter. "But I thought—"

"Long story," Cockerell said.

"For another time," Harper stood too then. She put a hand on Frederickson's arm. "I got this." Then turned back to Cockerell. "Okay. You have something important to tell me? Let's go."

Without waiting for an answer, she began walking toward the back of the ballroom.

Cockerell followed. He caught up to her at the bottom of a huge set of stairs blocked by a security barrier, two posts connected by a waist-high band of cloth, and a gray-haired guard in a white

CHAPTER 11

shirt and tie.

"Evening Ms. Harper," the guard said. "Good to see you again."

"And you, Dutch. Can you give us a minute in private here?"

"Sure thing." The man nodded and left. Harper turned to face Cockerell. "I do not appreciate you busting in here like this."

"I didn't bust in. I bought a ticket. Not cheap. I'm hoping you can reimburse me."

"That's not funny."

"I'm not trying to be funny. That was a $225 ticket."

"Okay. You found me. Congratulations."

"You and your mysterious 'we.' The Society of the Cincinnati."

"What are you talking about?"

"Harper. Espy." He shook his head. "You're a terrible liar."

"I'm not—"

"Come on. It all fits. Patriotic organization, service to your country, your father, mine."

"You didn't need to come here to tell me all that," she said.

"You're right. I came here to tell you something a lot more important."

"Well, don't keep me in suspense."

"Blackjack." He smiled. "I figured it out."

❖ ❖ ❖ ❖ ❖

Instinct had gotten him here, kicked in as he'd stood underneath the Stars and Stripes at the Daly Building, thinking about Harper's mom. A little tingle at the base of his spine. Patriotic organization, Society of the Cincinnati. Research had born out his guess, and more. He'd come to Anderson House, expecting to find what, he wasn't sure. Harper? Frederickson? A bunch of guys in Revolutionary War outfits? What he got instead was an older woman behind the front desk who told him they were done with tours for the day because they were setting up for the movie premiere. And then she'd pointed to the easel behind her.

1787
GALA BENEFIT AND PREMIERE
TONIGHT!
Come meet Doug Rivers, Ayesha Vatril, Penelope Harper, and other stars of the forthcoming motion picture

He'd felt another little tingle. An even stronger one.

By the look on her face, he guessed Harper was feeling something pretty strong right that second too.

"Are you serious? You know what blackjack means?"

"I do."

She looked at him expectantly. "Go on."

"I will. But first, tell me what this is all about." He gestured. "What this place, this party, has to do with Garrett Crandall's murder."

"That's not your concern."

"It is now. I want to know exactly who it is I'm helping here."

"Listen. A good man is dead." Her expression tightened. "A United States senator. Murdered. I would hope that you felt some sense of obligation here. Some sense of—"

"Patriotism? Duty to my country? Oh I feel that, believe me." Cockerell met her gaze without blinking. "But I want to know more."

She set her jaw. Glared. Started to say something, then stopped. Shook her head and began again. "I told you before. My hands are tied. I'm sorry."

"So am I. You know where to find me if you change your mind." He started back toward the ballroom.

"Wait." Harper stepped in front of him, blocking his way.

CHAPTER 11

"Wait? For what?"

"I need a few minutes. I have to talk to some people."

"A few minutes. Okay." He nodded. "I can do that."

"Good." She sighed. "Be right back."

❖ ❖ ❖ ❖ ❖

It took longer than a few minutes, though.

She'd seen Stuart Crane at the screening, but by the time she got back to the ballroom he was gone. She finally found him upstairs, talking to some VIP ticket holders about Anderson House and its history, and the importance of donating generously to the Society. Espy had to wait for a break in that conversation before pulling him off to the side. Before telling him the problem they now faced.

They went downstairs to Woodhull. Stuart faced the far wall of the conference room, hands clasped behind his back as Espy spoke.

"Last bit of background. He's a West Point graduate," she continued. "His father was killed in Afghanistan. He resigned his commission—made a pretty public show of it. Then he joined the police."

"Serving still. I can see why you thought he would help," Stuart replied. "But he won't tell you what he found?"

"No. Not unless I explain to him exactly who we are, what we stand for."

"I thought you went through all that already."

"Some of it. Not enough, apparently." She took a deep breath. "I trust him. But I know it's not my call to make. That's why—"

"There's no call to make here." Stuart turned around. He didn't look angry, as she'd expected. Just resigned. Matter of fact. He spread his hands. "He's here. He says he has the information we've been looking for all week. And we're no closer to finding it ourselves, are we?"

Espy looked over at Frederickson, who shook his head, and then at Li, who did the same.

"No," she said. "We're not."

"All right. It's simple then. We bring him down."

"And tell him what? Everything?" Frederickson asked.

"Broad strokes, yes," Stuart said. "Enough to satisfy his curiosity."

Espy got to her feet. "I'll go get him. And I'm sorry. I didn't think—"

"Please. I told you I wasn't going to micromanage. What's done is done. The only thing I will say." Stuart raised an eyebrow. "Counting on a detective to mind his own business might have been a little shortsighted."

"Yeah." Frederickson cleared his throat. "I would say 'told you so,' but…"

"You don't want to pile on," Espy said.

"Heaven forbid."

"Thank you so much. Appreciated."

She found Cockerell exactly where she'd left him, at the base of the big stairway, talking to Dutch. The ballroom had emptied out; staff members were folding up chairs and packing up the sound system. The big movie screen had been taken down.

"Ms. Harper!" Dutch caught sight of her now and waved her over. "I was just telling Detective Cockerell here, I've never seen so many people in this place before. That Mr. Rivers, he can sure pack them in."

"He sure can," Espy nodded. "Mike, if you're ready—"

"At least those people tonight behaved themselves," Dutch continued. "You remember last weekend? The wedding they had here? That was a scene, wasn't it, Ms. Harper? The mess they made in the Connecticut Room?"

CHAPTER 11

"Yes, it certainly was." She took Cockerell's arm. "Dutch, we'll see you later."

"Sure will. Good night, Ms. Harper." The guard bowed his head to Espy, then to Cockerell. "Nice meeting you, detective."

"You too," Cockerell said.

Espy led him back the way she'd come: through the foyer, down the hall, and into the service elevator.

"Okay," he said as the door closed behind them. "What now?"

"Now you get your questions answered. As promised. And then you tell us what it means. Blackjack. Yes?"

"Yes."

"Good." She pressed elevator buttons. Entered the sequence. The door closed. The elevator started down. The *B* lit up. Then the *SB*.

"Hey," Cockerell said.

She smiled.

"Here we go, Alice. Next stop—Wonderland."

12

Cockerell felt the machinery thrumming beneath his feet. Silent, smooth, powerful. They were going down. Way down. Where to, was the question.

He suddenly realized no one had any idea where he was. What he was doing. He trusted Harper, yes, but if something happened to him…

His mom. She'd never recover.

The doors opened, and he forced those thoughts away. Harper stepped out. He followed, and found himself in a sleek, modern hallway, like the offices of some tech company: thick gray carpet, hardwood walls, treated with sound absorption paneling every few feet. The letters W2 were carved into that hardwood to the left and right.

He looked at Harper and shook his head. "You have got to be kidding."

"Welcome to Woodhull," she said. "This way."

She led him into a conference room. A round room, with a round table maybe twenty feet across—a table made of something black and shiny, very shiny, he couldn't tell if it was metal or wood. There were LCD screens set into it, about the size of a placemat, one in front of each chair.

There were three people seated around that table. He recognized one of them.

"You know Frederickson. And this is Li." Harper gestured to the Asian woman seated next to Frederickson. She looked about fifteen years old to him. "And this"—Harper gestured to an older

CHAPTER 12

man with a shock of white hair and a white beard—"is Stuart Crane."

"Detective Cockerell." The man nodded. "I'm pleased to meet you."

"You're in charge," Cockerell said.

"I am," Crane replied. "And you have questions, I understand."

"I do." Harper pulled out a chair for him, then sat beside him, opposite Crane and the others. "For starters—what is this place? And who are you people, anyway?"

"This is Anderson House. We're part of the Society of the Cincinnati."

Cockerell shook his head. "Not any part I read about."

"You wouldn't have," Crane replied. "The *W* out in the hall? That stands for Abraham Woodhull. He was one of Washington's spies."

"Washington. You mean George Washington?"

"That's right. Washington's the one who started all this."

"The Society of the Cincinnati?"

"Essentially ... yes." Crane leaned forward. "You were at the premiere upstairs. You saw the movie."

"I did."

"You recall the scene where Washington arrives in Philadelphia? His dinner with Knox and Hamilton? That dinner was a fictionalized version of where all this"—Crane gestured, taking in the room and, by implication, the entire underground complex—"was born. You see, Washington attended that dinner reluctantly, because—"

The conference room door opened, and Doug Rivers walked in.

"Sorry. Had trouble getting away." He took a seat on the other side of Harper, then turned his gaze on Cockerell. "So. You figured it out. Blackjack?"

"Uh, yes, I think so," he managed. *Doug Rivers*?

"No need to be starstruck," Frederickson said. "Dougie here puts his pants on one leg at time, just like the rest of us."

Rivers glared. "I have asked you not to call me—"

"To continue," Crane interrupted. "That dinner, with Hamilton and Knox. In real life, it was a meeting of the Society's brain trust—its leadership. Washington went there with the intent leaving the organization—in fact, he wanted the Society dissolved entirely. It smacked of old Europe to him. Primogeniture. Officers only. Aristocracy. And that was not what America was about."

"I'm guessing he changed his mind," Cockerell said.

"He did."

"Why?"

"There's not a simple answer to that. But in large part, it was because of the war. Lessons he learned from winning the revolution," Crane continued. "In particular, lessons based on his wartime experiences with the Culper Ring, a group of patriots who worked under his direction."

"A group of spies, actually," Frederickson said. "People willing to get their hands dirty for the cause."

"That's right," Crane said. "The Culper Ring was the country's first spy network. The role the people in it played in winning the war—that taught Washington the value of espionage. The necessity of keeping some things secret. At that dinner we're talking about, Washington and some of the other attendees—Alexander Hamilton, Henry Knox among them—they realized that it might make sense to keep the Society of the Cincinnati alive. So they could use it as cover. So they could continue to do that kind of work, for the benefit of the country, as needed."

"So that's what this place is. That's who you are." Cockerell

CHAPTER 12

looked around the table as he spoke.

"Exactly." Harper nodded. "Our goals are the same as Washington's. The same goals as they have upstairs. To preserve, protect, and defend the principles of the American Revolution. It's just that upstairs, they give scholarships, fund research, have book signings and movie premieres. And in the meantime, down here—"

"We do the dirty work," Frederickson put in. "Like I said."

"We do what's necessary," Crane said. "When circumstances require it, we act in the national interest—with moral purpose."

"And who decides when circumstances require it?"

Crane smiled. "You're asking if the government knows about us."

"That's right," Cockerell said.

"A few people, yes. But very few."

"And they authorize what you do?"

"It's a gray area, admittedly. Real life is full of them, isn't it?"

"I suppose. But—"

"Detective. I share your concerns. Believe me. All I can tell you is that we act when the gray turns to black and white. When an egregious wrong has been done." He leaned forward, adding intensity to his voice. "When a US senator is murdered in cold blood."

"The point is," Frederickson added, "we're the good guys, chief. You either believe that or you don't."

"And if you do," Espy added, "then let's stop wasting time and get to it. Tell us what you found out. Tell us what Blackjack means."

Cockerell looked from Frederickson, to Crane, to Espy, to Li … and Doug Rivers?

We're on the same side here.

I'm asking you to serve your country.

"Okay." He nodded. "Fair enough. My turn then. And I have to say, it's funny you talking about the film. About all that history."

"And why is that?" Crane asked.

"Because that's how I figured it out." He started from that moment at the JOCC, when he'd made the connection between Harper's mom and Anderson House. "I went back online. Started doing some research, reading about the Society's history, about the officers who founded it and their descendants. And all the famous people who joined afterward. And that's when it hit me."

"What Blackjack was," Espy supplied.

"No. Not what," Cockerell said. "Who."

"Say that again," Frederickson prompted.

"Black Jack. Two words, not one. Nothing to do with gambling at all." He looked around the table again, making eye contact with each of them in turn. "I think Black Jack is a person. Black Jack Bouvier. Not his given name. His nickname. He—"

"Good god," Crane said, and his face went two shades paler.

Frederickson exhaled, a long, slow whistle. Rivers's eyes widened. Li looked confused.

Espy, for some reason, looked angry.

"Black Jack. A person. Not a thing. Fascinating." Li shook her head. "I should have broadened the AI's search parameters. Although I still do not understand. Who is this Bouvier, and why are you so sure he is the Black Jack we are looking for?"

Crane shook his head. "It's not so much about him as his daughter."

"His daughter?" Li asked.

"Jackie," Espy said. Cockerell was pretty sure he knew what was going through her head right that second. The same thoughts that had gone through his earlier that afternoon.

"Jackie. Jacqueline Bouvier. Jesus." Rivers ran a hand through

CHAPTER 12

his hair. From the look on his face, he had just gotten it too. "Are you kidding me?"

Li was still frowning. "Who is Jackie Bouvier, and why is she important?"

"Here," Crane said, tapping the LCD in front of him. The big screen at the end of the room came to life, filling with an image. A photograph of Jacqueline Bouvier posed with the man she married and their two children.

The White House presidential portrait, with the date the shot had been taken.

August 14, 1963.

"Shit on a shingle," Frederickson said. "Jacqueline Bouvier. Jackie Kennedy."

Cockerell looked over at Espy. Their eyes locked.

You have no idea who you are dealing with. What they are capable of.

13

John Bouvier.

A picture flashed across Espy's mind from one of those gossip magazines her mother had kept lying around her Cincinnati apartment. Bouvier in a suit and tie, arms linked with his daughter, looking every bit the handsome rogue that he had been. The article discussed the demons that had eventually killed him—drinking, gambling, an addiction to the high life—and also mentioned the source of his nickname. Nothing to do with gambling at all; it was his tan, how dark his skin had gotten (and stayed) from all those hours on the beach. Maybe from liver disease, too, Espy recalled pointing out to her mother, which had kicked off another fight about her mom's own drinking problem.

Black Jack Bouvier.

How had she missed that?

"Wait," Frederickson said. "Are we suggesting that the people who killed Garrett also killed—"

"Let's not get ahead of ourselves," Stuart said. "Li, can you confirm that Bouvier was a member of the Society?"

Li leaned forward, reading off the inset screen in front of her. "Yes. Confirmed."

"Okay. Nemkov told me the proof we wanted was already in our possession. So what do we have here related to Bouvier?"

"Checking. One moment." Li's hands darted across the screen. "Three items. All in the library upstairs. Two pamphlets on economic matters, credited to John Bouvier—a different John Bouvier, I believe. And one file folder. A dossier containing

CHAPTER 13

miscellaneous documents. Given to the Society in July of 2009."

"Given by who?" Espy asked.

"Apparently," Li replied, frowning, "Senator Garrett Crandall."

"What?" Espy said.

"What?" Stuart's eyes widened. He looked as surprised as Espy had ever seen him. "Are you sure?"

She nodded, eyes focused on the screen. "Yes. Quite sure."

"Well, what are these documents?" Espy asked. "What's in that dossier?"

"Unknown. Most of the data fields here are blank."

"July 2009?" Stuart repeated.

"You said it was in the library upstairs?" Frederickson stood. "I'll go get it."

"You cannot do that, I am afraid," Li said.

"And why not?"

"Because Garrett removed it from the library on February 16."

The room fell silent.

"February 16," Stuart said. "And Garrett died when, Esperanza?"

"Three days later. But that doesn't make sense," Espy said. "The dossier was in the library upstairs? Open to the public?"

"It makes some sense," Frederickson said. "Hidden in plain sight."

"Maybe," she said. "But if this dossier was so important, why didn't Garrett tell anyone about it? Why didn't he tell *you*, Stuart?"

"I'm wondering the same thing myself," Stuart said, and Espy knew that there was more going on inside his head than Stuart was letting on.

He and Garrett had been friends—maybe even best friends—for almost forty years. That Garrett would have withheld something like this from him…

Espy looked up. The picture of Black Jack's daughter and her husband—President Kennedy and the First Lady, circa August 1963—was still up on the screen.

"The secret your senator was killed to protect," Cockerell said. "Looks like you got your work cut out for you."

❖ ❖ ❖ ❖ ❖

"So explains why all those leaves of absence," Cockerell said. "From your job."

Espy gave him a look.

"Sorry." He smiled. "Just thinking out loud."

They were heading in the direction of her townhouse, just passing the big statue of Gandhi on the triangle between Massachusetts Ave. and Q—a statue more than twice as big as the one of Washington in front of Anderson House. Espy always found the comparison striking—and more than a little ironic. Considering.

"No. You're exactly right," she said. "That's why. Two jobs at once. Sometimes you can handle it, sometimes…"

"Yeah. That must be tough. The federal bureaucracy, not to mention your boss. Bosses."

"We make it work," she said, though he was right, it was tough. Mike Pritchett, her immediate superior, was a godsend in that regard, unlike his predecessor, who had made Espy fill out form after form after form each time she'd been called away.

"So you really don't bring the government in on something like this?" Cockerell asked.

"I don't think so. At least, not just yet. We need to find that dossier first. See what's in it, go from there."

"Understood." They'd reached her townhouse now. Espy turned to face him. "Well. Goodnight, Detective."

"Mike, remember?"

CHAPTER 13

"Right. Mike." She smiled. "And thank you, again. I think we would have gotten there eventually, but now … "

"Black Jack Bouvier." Cockerell shook his head. "It's unbelievable. Do you really think that—"

"Hey." She held up a hand. "One step at a time. Find the dossier. That's number one on our list. Then we'll move forward."

"Right." He cleared his throat. "You know … I have time. If you still need a hand."

She frowned. "Come again?"

"I have time now. Since you guys blew up my operation." He shrugged. "I was thinking—I could follow up on Nemkov, check that party Crandall was coming from…"

"You're saying you want to help?"

Cockerell nodded. "I am."

She studied him for a moment. She'd have to talk to Stuart, of course, but…

At that second, the townhouse door opened and her mom emerged.

"I thought I heard voices." She looked at Espy. "I was wondering where you'd gotten to. I thought we were going to meet after the movie. Celebrate. Get something to drink."

"Sorry," Espy said. "Something else came up."

"I can see that." She looked at Cockerell. "You again."

"Me again."

"Well, I can see I'm in the way here."

"No, no," Espy said quickly. "It's not like that at all. Mike here was just—"

"I wouldn't mind a drink," Cockerell said. "And maybe some food. I didn't have a chance to eat before the film."

"Well then, what are we waiting for?" Espy's mom stepped out of the entryway, letting the door shut behind her. "This way."

She took them to a place right around the corner. A restaurant full of young, loud, attractive professionals, twenty- and thirty-somethings laughing and falling all over each other. They found a spot in an alcove near the door. Cockerell ordered a burger and a beer; she and her mom got seltzers.

"Cheers," Cockerell said, and the three of them clinked glasses. He turned to Espy's mom. "I meant what I said before. You were great in the movie tonight."

"That's very nice of you to say. So how do you know Esperanza? Through the Society?"

"DOJ work," Espy said quickly. "Mike is a detective."

"Really?"

He nodded. "Metro police."

"That's dangerous work, I imagine."

"Sometimes."

"Tell me."

And they were off to the races.

Espy tuned out their conversation—easy enough to do, considering the ambient noise level—and turned her focus onto something a little more important.

The dossier.

The fact that Garrett hadn't told any of them about it, that meant he knew how dangerous it was. That was why he'd taken it out of the library, hidden it somewhere. So where was it now?

They'd gone through almost every scrap of paper at Garrett's townhouse, at his Senate office, at Woodhull, and yet, she realized now, they were going to have to do it all over again. A dossier of "miscellaneous papers"? It could be anywhere. Hidden in plain sight. Hidden in a file that had nothing to do with Bouvier, at

CHAPTER 13

Garrett's house in Ohio, or the offices he kept out there. He could have mailed it anywhere in the world, to anyone at all.

"Be right back." Cockerell got to his feet, smiled down at her. "Then you can tell me your side of that story."

He walked off. Espy leaned closer to her mom. "My side of what story?"

"Freshman year," her mom replied. "That ski instructor."

"Mom!" Espy's eyes widened. "You told him *that* story?"

"No reason to be upset. It's a funny story. Unless … there's something going on between the two of you?"

"No," Espy said. "There's not."

"A shame. He's a step up from the golfer, if you want my opinion."

"Matt," Espy said. "In case you've forgotten, the golfer's name is Matt."

"I didn't forget. I just choose not to say his name, that's all."

Golfer.

A little tumbler suddenly clicked in Espy's brain.

Golfer.

"Sorry. I know I promised I wouldn't say bad things about him, but the way he treated you … Esperanza? Are you all right?"

"Fine," Espy said.

"You know, you really have to get over it. You haven't heard from him in close to two years—"

"I'm not thinking about Matt," she snapped, although at that second his face did indeed flash across her mind. Where he was now, god only knew; last Espy heard he was at a fancy country club out in Northern California, teaching young tech entrepreneurs how to putt.

But the golfer she was thinking of at that second wasn't Matt, it was Garrett. And the country club on her mind was a lot closer than California. The country club on her mind was Braddock Farms, Garrett's golf club in Virginia. She was thinking about it—and the slip of paper found in Garrett's pocket the night he died. The valet ticket mentioned in the coroner's supplemental notes.

That ticket had been stamped February 17. The day after he'd taken the dossier from the Society library. Two days before he was murdered.

For him to go to the club in the dead of winter made absolutely no sense. Why would he do that? To visit the gym there? It was probably a nice one, probably open year-round. But there was no need for him to travel forty miles outside the city for a workout. The club no doubt had a restaurant too, a good one, but there were plenty of good restaurants right in DC.

So why had he gone there, two days before he died?

Espy was pretty sure she knew the answer to that question.

"Esperanza? What is it?"

She looked down at her mom and realized that, at some point during her reverie, she had stood up.

"I have to go," she said. "Make my apologies."

"Go?" her mom called after her. "Go where?"

14

Braddock Farms was deep in Virginia horse country at the end of a long and unlit winding road. Espy had the driver pull right up to the clubhouse, alongside a bunch of construction vehicles, right behind a beat-up Subaru with Maryland plates and a *Go Terrapins* bumper sticker. The security guard's car, she guessed.

She gave the driver $50 cash and told him to wait.

He frowned. "How long you gonna be?"

She put another $50 in his palm. "Does it matter? Wait." And she hopped out of the car without waiting for an answer. The clubhouse doors were locked. No surprise. She stepped back, looking for a bell to ring. Nothing. She pressed her nose to the glass; inside she saw a dimly lit hallway lined with trophy cases, oil paintings of landscapes, and a reception desk.

She started pulling on the handles. Hard. The glass rattled.

The lights inside switched on. A middle-aged man in a rent-a-cop uniform came around the corner. Walkie-talkie, name tag, gut pushing his untucked shirt a few inches over his belt. He stood at the glass doors with a dazed expression, trying to wake up, probably, figure out what was going on.

"Esperanza Harper, Department of Justice," Espy said. "I need to enter this facility."

"What?"

"Department of Justice," she said again, louder. "I need to enter this building."

"Department of Justice?" The guy blinked. "You don't look like Department of Justice."

Espy looked down and realized she was still wearing her

banquet dress. She pulled out her badge and slapped it up against the glass. "Open. This. Door."

The guard looked at the badge. Looked at her, nodded, and did as he'd been told.

"Thank you," Espy said, stepping inside.

The guard nodded. "Yeah. But what's this—"

"What's your name, please?"

"Uh, Jeremiah. Jeremiah Thompson."

"Okay. Listen to me, Jeremiah Thompson. I'm here investigating a matter of national security. Which means everything I say to you, everything you say to me, is classified. Any breach of that confidence is an actionable offense. One that can—and I assure you, will—be prosecuted to the fullest extent of the law." She gave the man her best hard-ass look.

"Uh…" Thompson looked stunned.

"You're not in any trouble personally, Mr. Thompson. Jeremiah." Espy offered an encouraging smile. "I just need to look around a little. Ask you a couple questions. Fairly routine. No need to worry."

"Routine?" the guard asked. "At twelve thirty at night?"

"Routine for me." Espy smiled. "Not you."

❖ ❖ ❖ ❖ ❖

"Garrett Crandall? The senator, you mean?"

"Yes. He was a member of this club."

"Yeah. He was. But he's dead."

"I know that. I need to see his locker."

"His locker?" Thompson stopped walking. Shook his head. "Can't do that, sorry."

Espy glared. "Do I need to show you my credentials again?"

"Hey, it's not that I don't want to show you, it's just that the locker room is under construction. Sealed off. We can't get in."

CHAPTER 14

She held up her badge again. "This says we can."

"Fine." Thompson threw up his arms. "Follow me, then."

He led her down a long, narrow hallway. They stopped in front of a dark wood–paneled door sealed off with yellow tape. Above that door was a sign that said MEMBERS LOCKER ROOM.

"This is what I was trying to tell you," Thompson began. "It's off-limits because—"

She stepped past him and ripped the tape off the door.

"Hey!" he said as she stepped forward and flipped on a light switch.

Then she saw what Thompson had meant. Under construction? More like under demolition. The carpet had been ripped up, revealing a cement floor pitted with large holes. Ductwork hung from the ceiling. The walls were splotched with various colors of paint. There were stepladders and wheelbarrows and toolboxes everywhere she looked.

She cursed under her breath and turned to face Thompson. "How long has it been like this?"

"Close to a month, I think. Why?"

She shook her head. Why? Because this was the perfect hiding place. A golf course? In the middle of winter? No one would ever think to look here. But if the locker room had been in this kind of shape two weeks ago...

Where did he put it?

"What?" Thompson asked, which was when she realized she'd spoken out loud.

"Nothing. Garrett Crandall came here two weeks ago. So if the locker room was like this ... where else would he have gone?"

They tried the dining room, where Espy looked about for a spot where Garrett might have hidden the dossier. Nothing jumped out at her. Next up was the member's lounge. Again, nothing, except for a picture of Garrett and a group of other golfers from a celebrity pro-am tournament hanging above a card table. His playing partner that day had been Michael Jordan.

Stuart was in the photo as well.

"That was a great day," Thompson said, looking over her shoulder. "Great tournament. Doing it again in a couple months."

Espy nodded reflexively. The dossier was here, she was as sure of that as she'd ever been of anything in her entire life. But where?

"Some of the members have been coming in all winter. Using the simulator room to practice up," Thompson continued.

Simulator room. Matt had shown her a similar room back at the Pines a while back. Reminded her of a video game. Virtual reality. Real swings, virtual golf course.

Let's go have a look there, she was about to say, and then realized something.

"Wait a second. The simulator room is open."

Thompson nodded. "That's right."

"And members are coming in."

"That they are."

"So … say one of them wants to take a shower after working out, wants to change. Where do they do that?"

"They have to use the guest locker room."

"Guest locker room." She smiled. "Lead on."

The guest locker room had thick hunter and navy carpet, overstuffed chairs, lockers as large as wardrobes, each one identical to the next. The lockers had no names on them. Just numbers.

She opened and closed a few at random. Empty. Empty. Empty.

She stood there a minute, looking around the room.

She wasn't wrong. She couldn't be wrong. It was here. Somewhere. It had to be.

Thompson cleared his throat. "You're welcome to keep, um, looking I guess. But I should get back out front, just in case anyone else shows up."

CHAPTER 14

She started to wave him off, and then sighed.

It had been a long day. Best thing to do was get a fresh start tomorrow. Do a thorough search of the townhouse. Garrett's Senate office. There was the possibility he'd mailed it to Ohio, to his house or office there. Really, there were a million possibilities. A million places it could be.

But it seemed like here wasn't one of them.

"Let's go," she said, striding quickly out of the room.

Thompson led her back to the main entrance, held the door open for her. The car was still idling in the lot.

"Sorry we didn't find what you were looking for, ma'am," Thompson said. "You want to come back tomorrow, there'll be guys on duty who knew the senator. Maybe they can help."

"Maybe," she replied as she stepped out into the parking lot, her eyes falling on the numbers painted on each of the closest spaces, ten and eleven closest to the door for some reason. Ten and eleven. That equalled twenty-one.

Blackjack.

Garrett wasn't a gambling man, but he was a clever one.

"Wait," she said and spun on her heel, heading past an open-mouthed Thompson, back the way she came. Right back to the guest locker room, straight to locker number 21.

She grabbed hold of the latch and lifted. It didn't move.

Espy leaned closer, squinted in the dim light, and saw why. The handle was slightly bent. Anybody coming in here would have tried the handle and found it stuck. Would have moved on to another.

She smiled to herself.

Garrett wouldn't have been happy, having to hide the dossier in a place like this. But he might have felt he didn't have a choice. He probably didn't expect to leave it here long. Still, he would not have wanted to take a chance on anyone stumbling across it. He would have done something just like this. Bent the latch, so it was just a little difficult to open.

She heard the door to the corridor open. Thompson coming to check on her.

"Leave," she snapped and a split-second later heard the guard's footsteps retreating.

She reached up and unbent the latch holding locker 21 shut.

Now it swung open easily at her touch.

The interior was huge: large enough to hang a suit coat or three, fit a briefcase, several pairs of shoes. But there were no shoes inside—no coat, gloves, briefcase, golf balls, or towels.

What there was: an oversize manila envelope.

Heart hammering in her chest, Espy reached in and pulled that envelope out.

The Seal of the United States Senate was embossed on the front, the word *Confidential* stamped across it. Underneath were the words

```
Property of Sen. Garrett Crandall
Please return to I-321
Russell Senate Office Building
```

She turned the packet over. The flap was glued down. She tore it open.

Inside was another envelope.

This one was light blue, with another, familiar seal stamped in the top left corner—an American eagle looking fiercely into the distance. Underneath it, seven words were stenciled in black ink: *PROPERTY OF THE SOCIETY OF THE CINCINNATI*. The envelope label read

```
Author: Bouvier, John
Subject: Unknown
Call #: 387.72B
Contains: 1 Folder: Misc Documents
```

CHAPTER 14

Little doubt about what she had here now, was there?

Espy sat down on the locker room bench and pinched the envelope between her thumb and forefinger. A stack of paper, maybe a quarter-inch thick. She took hold of the red string fastener on the envelope and unwound it, opened the flap, took a deep breath, and reached inside.

Another envelope.

Good god, she thought, and laughed involuntarily.

This was like one of those Russian dolls that come apart to reveal a smaller doll inside the bigger one. And an even smaller one inside that. *Matroyshka*, that's what they were called. Her dad used to have one of Elvis Presley, back in his apartment in Santa Monica. Fat Elvis in a white jumpsuit on the outside, Elvis in black leather inside that, then Elvis in his GI uniform, then a cowboy outfit…

The outermost envelope had been like new, the paper stiff and uncreased. The Society envelope labeled with Bouvier's name— that had a few smudges on it, a few creases. This one was older. Heavily used. One edge was wrinkled and slightly discolored, as if it had been soaked through. It wasn't sealed, either; hadn't even been tucked back into place, she saw, realizing she'd pulled it out upside down.

She turned it over and saw the letter paper-clipped to the front. A typewritten letter on official government stationery.

From the desk of Senator Edward Kennedy.

Garrett: it began. *One last voyage together, old friend.*

Espy felt a chill run down her back.

The picture, in the hallway of Garrett's brownstone. Garrett and Ted Kennedy.

Black Jack Bouvier and his daughter.

The reason your senator was killed.

Edward M. Kennedy

June 11, 2009

Garrett:

    One last voyage together, old friend.

    The documents you now hold in your hand came to me from my nephew's landlord on Martha's Vineyard after his death. For these last ten years I have agonized over what to do with the secrets they contain.

    But now my time as the guardian of these papers is ending. And after our visit, it became clear to me that you - that Woodhull - were the proper ones to succeed me as their custodian. Fitting, in a way, since John's own grandfather was a member of the Society. Since John would have been eligible for membership as well. But now this burden is yours.

    I cannot excuse my own failure to take action over the years, Garrett - my own fear - but over these last few months I have come to believe my nephew was right. These people must be stopped. But if you do decide to proceed against them - know that they will be watching. They fear nothing and no one. They will not hesitate to kill again.

    My best to you and Alice.

        Your friend - now and always,

CHAPTER 14

Espy heard noise in the hall and glanced up. Thompson, pacing, she realized. Let him pace all he wanted. He wouldn't come in here again. He wouldn't dare.

She looked back down at the note. Ran a finger over the embossed surface of the stationery. The raised ink of the Senate emblem. Stared at the date atop the letter.

June 11, 2009.

Ted Kennedy had died in office. Died of brain cancer, if she was remembering right ... she'd seen the funeral on TV, she heard the eulogies in her mind now, the dignitaries who had been there, the presidents, the foreign leaders, the relatives, and realized that, yes, the dates worked, this stack of paper in her hand was a deathbed bequest from Kennedy to Garrett ... to the Society. Only...

The documents you now hold in your hand.

For these last ten years, I have agonized over what to do with the secrets they contain.

Ten years. 1999.

And then the last piece of the puzzle clicked into place.

My nephew.

John's own grandfather was a member of the Society.

John's grandfather. Black Jack Bouvier.

Oh my god, she thought. Oh my god.

Ted Kennedy was talking about JFK Jr.

1999 was the year the heir to Camelot had died.

She remembered that day. Remembered her mom, sobbing. The pictures of JFK Jr. and his wife all over the news. How ridiculously beautiful they'd both been. Cut down in the prime of life. A stupid plane crash.

A stupid accident.

These people must be stopped. They fear nothing and no one.

Are we suggesting that the people who killed Garrett also killed—

"No," she said aloud, and sat up straight. "No."

John would have been eligible for membership.

John—JFK Jr. He could have been part of Woodhull. She could have been working with him. They could have been working together. Her, and him ... and Garrett.

But now this burden is yours, Ted Kennedy had written.

No. Now it was hers. The secret Garrett had hidden from them for so long.

The secret your Senator was killed to protect.

The secret within this envelope.

She unclipped Kennedy's letter, revealing the writing on the front of the envelope:

Via Courier
Personal and Confidential
Hand-Deliver Only
Attention: John F. Kennedy Jr.
President and Publisher: George Magazine

George. A magazine about politics. She remembered it ... vaguely. JFK Jr.'s magazine. Really before her time. But ... *George* magazine? What did that have to do with anything here?

She hefted the envelope in her hand. Felt the stack of paper within.

Enough questions, she thought, and reached inside and gingerly—carefully—slid out the contents.

It was paper. A stack of it, all different kinds of paper, all different sizes, some of it old, and yellowing, the edges of the pages crinkled with age, some newer documents as well...

Like the sheet of paper at the top of the stack.

She looked at the words on that page and gasped.

"Oh," was all she could manage.

Up to that second, it had all been innuendo. Suggestion.

Now it was right there in front of her. In big, bold letters, outlined in stark black and red.

SPECIAL EDITION

George

SEVEN DAYS TO DALLAS
THE MEN WHO MURDERED MY FATHER

BY JOHN F. KENNEDY, JR.

missile assembly building

NASA LAND ACQUISITION

JRA | JAXON RESEARCH ASSOCIATES

John —
Latest round of research.
Focus on Florida — NASA trip,
Cuba/CIA/Mob,
de Mohrenschildt
— Nan

SECURITY PLAN

...ty will land and depart from the CCMTA

...re comprised of representatives from t
...rvice detail; the NASA Security Office
...Enforcement Division, assisted by the
...curity Police Force. The Air Police
...ange) will provide necessary security
...aft and security for logistical matter
...ey will provide a security vehicle fo
...esidential aircraft.

...will be placed in the motorcade as
...g arrangements.

...oute, sufficient security forces will
...n control and any emergencies which m

...pes of special badges have been deve

...of the official Presidential party,
...members of the official motorcade
...ing party.

Blue - Presidential Tour/Press To Be Escorted
Green - Presidential Tour/Press Pool

INCLEMENT WEATHER PLAN

The Presidential Party will arrive and depart from Patrick Air Force Base.

1. Security forces at Patrick Air Force Base will be White Hous Secret Service detail; security and law enforcement division, AFMTC, and OSI; and NASA Security Office. The Air Police 6550th Wing will provide security guards, honors, traffic control and coordinate with local law enforcement agencies regarding escort of motorcade to CCMTA.

2. Security at CCMTA will be the same as basic plan.

3. See attached figures for routings.

Mr. Kurt Debus
Director of the Cape Canaveral Space Center

And

Dr. Werner Von Braun
Director of the Marshall Space Flight Center

Request the Honor of Your Presence
At a Luncheon Honoring

The President of The United States
The Honorable John Fitzgerald Kennedy

Saturday November 16, 1963
At 12:30 in the Afternoon

PROPOSED PRESIDENTIAL ITINERARY -- NOV. 16, 1963

10:05 AM EST - President arrives skid strip - greeted by Mr. Webb, Dr. Seamans, **Dr. Debus** and Gen. Davis. Mr. Webb will... the President.

10:08 AM - Motorcade crosses skid strip, passing by LC 36 on the... LC 19. (Webb briefs President on Centaur as they pas...

10:18 AM - Motorcade arrives at Pad 19. (President greeted by D... who introduces Mr. Low and Astronaut Shepard)

10:30 AM - Motorcade departs for Complex 37

10:35 AM - Motorcade arrives at LC 37 Launch Control Center. (We... President to Dr. Mueller **and Dr. von Braun**.

- MLLP briefing by Dr. Mueller

10:53 AM - Motorcade...

working on list of luncheon attendees

PRESIDENTIAL VISIT

NASA — DOD

Cape Canaveral
November 16, 1963

Commission; and
involvement in

Seven Days To Dallas

Evening Independent

Mild

CITY EDITION

57TH YEAR — NO. 13   PHONE 894-1111   ST. PETERSBURG, FLORIDA, MONDAY, NOVEMBER 18, 1963   PRICE 5 CENTS   34 PAGES

Arrives At Tampa For Speeches

JFK Gets Noisy Welcome

25 Persons Mis...
In N.J. Hotel F...

ATLANTIC CITY, N.J. (AP) — Fire swept through a block...

Sat. Nov. 16th

The Cuban Commandoes have the BOMBS ready for killing JFK and Mayor KING HIGH either at the AIRPORT at the Convention Hall.

...c PADRE is going to give... the Cuban Womens Broadcas... by "RELOJ RADIO" and then... to Dance at Bayfront Park... take along a BOTTLE of wi... ecide who will throw the... igh because he did sign th... druivers being only Americ... nding refugees away, Etc. M...

Cuban involvement ↑

MIAMI BEACH, FLA.   8 30 PM   16 NOV 1963

THIS SIDE OF CARD IS FOR ADDRESS

The Chief of Police
Miami, Florida

4¢   U.S. POS...

DRAFT

Cuban-American

In Book V of the fi...
Committee to Study Governm...
of the intelligence agenci...
assassination, the FBI and...
apparent failure to fully pu...
assassination of President Ke...
to the Warren Commission the...
they did undertake. One suc...
from Texas to Mexico City of...
American on November 23, 196...
November 27. 1/ The lead wa...
the fact that the Cuban-American reportedly attended a
meeting of the Tampa chapter of the Fair Play for Cuba
Committee on November 17, 1963. 2/ The House Select
Committee on Assassinations examined the documents connected
to that lead to determine: (a) whether the facts which were
known by the FBI and CIA about that individual warranted
further investigation and what investigation was undertaken;
(b) whether any of that information was reported to the Warren
Commission; and (c) whether the known facts suggest any
involvement in the assassination of President Kennedy.

DO NOT REPRODUCE
RETURN TO CIA

180-10141-10498

TOP SECRET

    b. Undertaking all other political, economic, and covert actions, short of inspiring a revolt in Cuba or developing the need for U.S. armed intervention.

    c. Be consistent with U.S. overt policy, and remain in position to disengage with minimum loss in assets and U.S. prestige.

    d. Continue JCS planning and essential preliminary actions for a decisive U.S. capability for intervention.

ACCOMPLISHMENT

[text obscured by sticky note: *CIA Reaction* →]

...were organized to reach the ...of where we are on each ...ub-headings below. In general, ...ation, well within the "noise"...

...nformed of progress through ...quent reports. The Special ...s required, in Phase I.

...rdinated the efforts of participa- ...n meetings of the Operational ...w of progress. The Operational ...rticipant in Operation Mongoose ...witch (State), Brig. Gen. Benjamin...

My assessment of the organization, planning, and actions to reach the goals in Phase I:

    Intelligence. CIA had the main assignment to acquire the "hard-intelligence" desired. The headquarters and field staff of CIA are now well organized for a major effort for this aspect of Operation Mongoose, being strengthened by a number of CIA officers experienced in "denied area" operations elsewhere in the world. Planning and actions rate superior, in a professional sense of intelligence collection.

    CIA established the Caribbean Admission Center at Opa-Locka, Florida and an interrogation activity in Spain. It undertook a priority

TOP SECRET

MEMORANDUM FOR THE SECRETARY OF DEFENSE

    Subject: Justification for US Military Intervention in Cuba (TS)

    1. The Joint Chiefs of Staff have considered the attached Memorandum for the Chief of Operations, Cuba Project, which responds to a request of that office for brief but precise description of pretexts which would provide justification for US military intervention in Cuba.

    2. The Joint Chiefs of Staff recommend that the proposed memorandum be forwarded as a preliminary submission suitable for planning purposes. It is assumed that there will be similar submissions from other agencies and that these inputs will be used as a basis for developing a time-phased plan. Individual projects can then be considered on a case-by-case basis.

    3. Further, it is assumed that a single agency will be given the primary responsibility for developing military and para-military aspects of the basic plan. It is recommended that this responsibility for both overt and covert military operations be assigned the Joint Chiefs of Staff.

                          For the Joint Chiefs of Staff:

                                L. L. Lemnitzer
                                L. L. LEMNITZER
                                Chairman
                        Joint Chiefs of Staff

1 Enclosure
  Memo for Chief of Operations, Cuba Project   EXCLUDED FROM GDS

...non-scheduled flight.

...at Eglin AFB would be painted and ...t duplicate for a civil registered ...g to a CIA proprietary organization ...designated time the duplicate would ...he actual civil aircraft and would ...elected passengers, all boarded und... ...d aliases. The actual registered ...converted to a drone.

...mes of the drone aircraft and the ...scheduled to allow a rendezvous so... ...e rendezvous point the passenger-o... ...scend to minimum altitude and go di... ...field at Eglin AFB where arrangem... ...o evacuate the passengers and retu... ...original status. The drone aircra... ...ontinue to fly the filed flight pl... ...one will being transmitting on the ...a frequency a "MAY DAY" message s... ...by Cuban MIG aircraft. The trans... ...ted by destruction of the aircraf... ...radio signal. This will allow IC...

RECONNAISSANCE OBJECTIVES IN CUBA

Legend:
- CRUISE MISSILE SITES
- UNIDENTIFIED - MISSILES
- SURFACE-TO-AIR MISSILE SITES
- JET FIGHTER FIELDS
- NAVAL OPERATING BASES
- NAVAL PORTS
- MILITARY INSTALLATIONS
- SPECIAL AREAS
- BEACHES
- UNIDENTIFIED INSTALLATIONS

Sticky note: "NASA missile targets in Cuba?"

LAUNCH SITES — SAN CRISTOBAL, CUBA — 27 JANUARY 1963

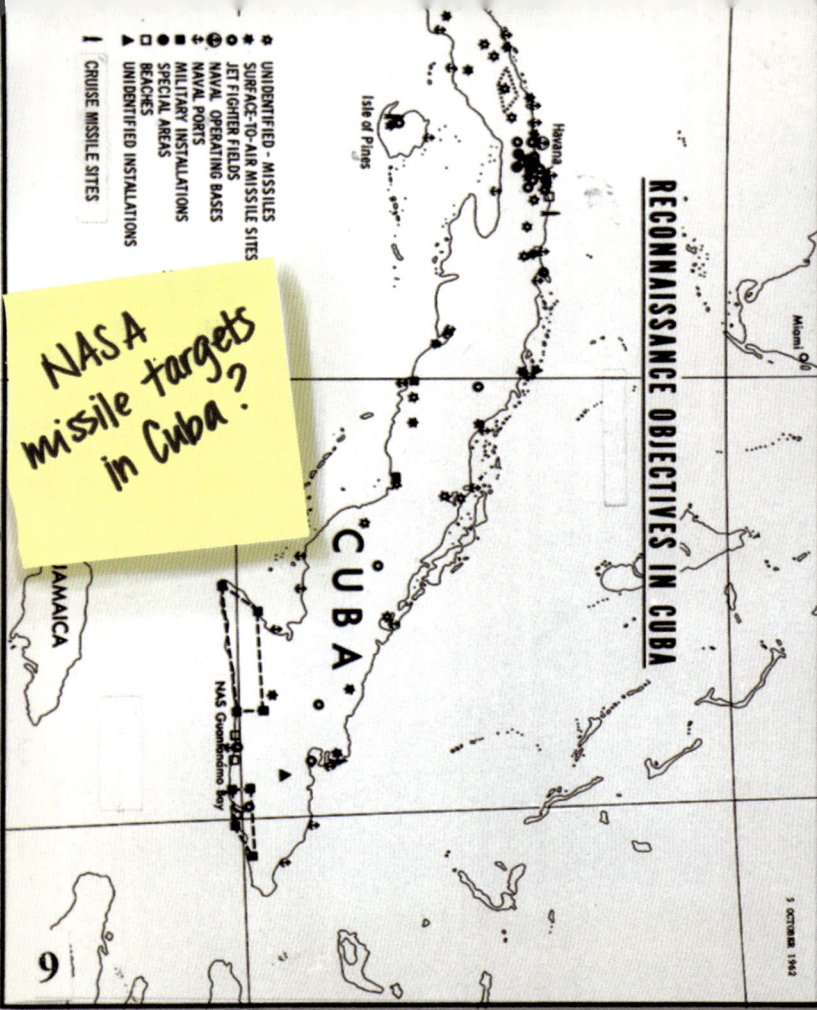

b. United States would respond by executing offensive operations to secure water and power supplies, destroying artillery and mortar emplacements which threaten the base

c. Commence large scale United States military operati

3. A "Remember the Maine" incident could be arranged in eral forms:

a. We could blow up a US ship in Guantanamo Bay and blame Cuba.

b. We could blow up a drone (unmanned) vessel anywhere in the Cuban waters. We could arrange to cause such incide in the vicinity of Havana or Santiago as a spectacular resu Cuban attack from the air or sea, or both. The presence Cuban planes or ships merely investigating the intent of vessel could be fairly compelling evidence that the ship s taken under attack. The nearness to Havana or Santiago uld add credibility especially to those people that might ve heard the blast or have seen the fire. The US could llow up with an air/sea rescue operation covered by US hters to "evacuate" remaining members of the non-existent w. Casualty lists in US newspapers would cause a helpful of national indignation.

---

civil air and surface craft assing measures condoned by ly, genuine defections of Cub ce craft should be encourage an incident which will demons ft has attacked and shot dow ute from the United States t enezuela. The destination w ght plan route to cross Cu of college students off on holiday or any grouping of persons with a common interest t support chartering a non-scheduled flight.

a. An aircraft at Eglin AFB would be painted and numbered as an exact duplicate for a civil registered aircraft belonging to a CIA proprietary organization in Miami area. At a designated time the duplicate would be substituted for the actual civil aircraft and would be loaded with the selected passengers, all boarded under carefully prepared aliases. The actual registered aircraft would be converted to a drone.

b. Take off times of the drone aircraft and the actu aircraft will be scheduled to allow a rendezvous south Florida. From the rendezvous point the passenger-carry aircraft will descend to minimum altitude and go direct into an auxiliary field at Eglin AFB where arrangements have been made to evacuate the passengers and return th aircraft to its original status. The drone aircraft meanwhile will continue to fly the filed flight plan. over Cuba the drone will being transmitting on the inte national distress frequency a "MAY DAY" message statin is under attack by Cuban MIG aircraft. The transmissi will be interrupted by destruction of the aircraft whi be triggered by radio signal. This will allow ICAO re

CAME OUT OF AZCUE OFFICE INTO PATIO. DESCRIBED AS TALL, SOLIDLY
BUILT MULATTO, CURLY HAIR, BROWN SUIT, RED STRIPED TIE, ABOUT
37 YEARS OLD. SUBJ NEVER SAW THIS MAN AFTER 18 SEP.

10. SUBJ OVERHEARD FOLLOWING CONVERSATION BETWEEN NEGRO AND
OSWALD: NEGRO: (IN ENGLISH) I WANT TO KILL THE MAN.
OSWALD: YOU'RE NOT MAN ENOUGH. I CAN DO IT.
NEGRO: (IN SPANISH) I CAN'T GO WITH YOU. I HAVE A LOT TO DO.
OSWALD: THE PEOPLE ARE WAITING FOR ME BACK THERE.

11. NEGRO GAVE OSWALD SIX THOUSAND
IN LARGE DENOMINATION US BILLS SAYING
NE THOUSAND FIVE HUNDRED WAS FOR EXTRA
BOUT 200 MEXICAN PESOS.

12. LATER, SUBJ SAW PRETTY GIRL, BE
ONSULATE, GIVE OSWALD EMBRACE AND TELL
UAREZ NUMBER 407 WHERE HE COULD FIND H
OUT 20 YEARS OLD, MANNERS REMINDED SU
GRO, AND CANADIAN THEN WENT UPSTAIRS.

13. SUBJ LEFT BUILDING MOMENTARILY T
W THREE PERSONS OF PARAGRAPH 7 LEAVE B
RNER OF TACUBAYA WHERE THEY ENTERED PA
EVROLET. SUBJECT RE-ENTERED CONSULATE
S APPROACHED BY TALL CUBAN OF PARAGRAPH

SECRET

---

use of Representatives,
committee on the Assassination
John F. Kennedy of the
lect Committee on Assassination
D. C.

Classification: _____

(This form is to be used for material extracted from CIA—controlled documents.)

been recruited as a CIA agent when he was in Japan.

These persons expressed the opinion that, had Oswald been recruited without their knowledge, it would have been a rare exception contrary to the working policy and guidelines of the [13]

3. <u>Lee Harvey Oswald's CIA File</u>

The CIA has long acknowledged that, prior to the President's assassination, it had a personality file on Lee Harvey Oswald. This f
is referred to as a 201 fi
The Agency has explained t
opened when a person is co
intelligence or counterinte
opening of such a file is de
bringing all of the CIA's in

Classification

> Oswald in Cuba
>
> more when we talk about de Mohrenschildt

---

erning, K. Klein.

Mr. Preyer. The Committee
air recognizes Miss Berning,

| 1 Oct. | 1031 | MO (American) to M |
| 1 Oct. | 1045 | MO (American) to OB Soviet Embassy |

But I don't remember the name
KOSTIKOV. He is dark (hair or
is OSWALD. OBYEDKOV says Just
say that they haven't received
they done anything? OBYEDKOV says Yes, OSWALD says Have
has been sent out, but they say that a request
OSWALD says And what...? OBYEDKOV hangs up.

Oct. 1539 MO OSWALD to MI at Sov. Emb.
                  15-69-87, the Sov MA

OSWALD speaks in broken Spanish then in English to MI. He says
Hello. Visa for Russia. MI says Call on the other phone.
MO says I'm looking for a visa to go to Russia. MI says Please,
call on the telephone of the consul, 15-60-55, one
moment please, I'll have to get a pencil to write the number
down. They issue the visa there! MI That depends on your
conversation. I don't know about this business. Please call
the office of the consul and ask your question. MO asks for the
number again. MI gives him the number and tells him to ask for
the Consul of the Soviet Embassy in Mexico. MO says Thanks.

Photos of unidentified person on entering Soviet Embassy, and
who entered Cuban Embassy on 15 Oct 1963.

MEXICO CITY 6453 reported According LIENVOY 1 Oct 63, American male
who spoke broken Russian said his name Lee OSWALD stated he at SOVEM
28 Sept when spoke with Consul whom he believed to be Valeriy Vladimiro
KOSTIKOV. Subj asked Sov guard Ivan OBYEDKOV who answered, if there
anything new re telegram to Washington. OBYEDKOV upon checking said
nothing received yet, but request had been sent. Have photos male an
be American entering Sovemb 1216 hours leaving

House of Representatives,
Subcommittee on the Assassin
of John F. Kennedy of the
Select Committee on Assassin
Washington, D. C.

pursuant to notice,
, Honorable Rich
ding.
es, Fauntroy, Do
thews, R. Morris
, J. Wolf, A. Pu
Hornbeck, E.

Gangland figure Santo Trafficante today told the House Assassinations Committee he decided to go along with a CIA plot to try to kill Fidel Castro because he thought it was "the same thing as a war and because the U.S. government wanted it done."

He said he knew nothing about attempt

The 63 testified Preyer. U.S. Dist issued at Trafficant his testim Traffic first time in Miami after he several ti

Mob Figure Testifies On Anti-Castro Plots

my total involvement prefer between Maheu and the Cuban people see."

TE said he was taken Havana several times k control of the government ary 1959 and was ort of immigration isconsin along with ino operators. as Fidel's brother.

TRAFFICANTE, however, acknowledged that he might have said that Kennedy wasn't going to get reelected. "How did you know he wouldn't be re-elected?" Stokes asked. "I thought he wouldn't," Trafficante responded. "They had the Bay of Pigs, the Cuban question, a lot of people were criticizing Kennedy. I might have said there'd be no reelection, but I didn't say he's gonna

↑ the mob's main guy in Cuba

Mr. Preyer. The Committee will come to order. The
r recognizes Miss Berning, the Clerk of the Committee,
ead for the record those members who officially are
designated to be on the Subcommittee today pursuant to

between Mr. Alamon --

Mr. Trafficante. There may have been.

Mr. Hornbeck. And you were not present?

Mr. Trafficante. I was not present. The only thing I remember was about the milk.

Mr. Hornbeck. During any of the meetings in which you were present with Mr. Alamon was there a discussion of the problems that Jimmy Hoffa was having with the Attorney General

Could be. Could have been. I would
ed it.
you saying you don't recall specific
topic might have occurred?
Might have occurred, yes, sure.
in during conversations between yourself,
o, was there a discussion of President
s?

Mr. Trafficante. Could be. Could be.

Mr. Hornbeck. Was there ever any comment or statement made by you during those conversations that President Kennedy would not be reelected but that he would be hit?

Mr. Trafficante. No, I don'r remember ever saying anything like that.

Mr. Hornbeck. Are you familiar with that statement, sir?

Trafficante — not a fan of your father's

Mr. Trafficante. I would say late in 1960.

Mr. Hornbeck. Who was that representative who first contacted you, sir?

Mr. Trafficante. Mr. John Roselli.

Mr. Hornbeck. Can you tell us where it was that Mr. Roselli first contacted you?

Mr. Trafficante. To the best of my recollection I think it was in Fountainbleau Hotel in Miami Beach.

Mr. Hornbeck. Was this a personal meeting, sir?

Mr. Trafficante. Yes.

Mr. Preyer. Could we move the microphone a trifle closer to Mr. Trafficante. We can't hear him very well.

Mr. Hornbeck. Who was present in addition to yourself and Mr. Roselli at the first meeting at the Fountainbleau Hotel?

Mr. Trafficante. To the best of my remembrance just me and Mr. Roselli.

Mr. Hornbeck. Will you relate to us the ___ the conversation between Mr. Roselli and yours___

Mr. Trafficante. He was acting in behalf ___

Mr. Hornbeck. For what purpose, sir?

Mr. Trafficante. For the purpose of tryi___ of the Castro regime.

Mr. Hornbeck. Where did this particular ___ take place in the hotel if you recall?

Bay of Pigs in which members of ___
iscussed plans for an invasion of Cuba?

Mr. Trafficante. No sir.

Mr. Hornbeck. Were you ever present when any pla___
ussed for an assassination of Premier Castro or an___
subordinates?

Mr. Trafficante. After the --

Mr. Hornbeck. After the Bay of Pigs?

Mr. Trafficante. No sir.

Mr. Hornbeck. After the Bay of Pigs, using that ___
off date, did you have any meetings with Mr. Rosel___
Giancana for any purpose?

Mr. Trafficante. No sir.

Mr. Hornbeck. You had indicated in prior testim___
tent of your associations with Mr. Roselli over a l___
riod of time?

Mr. Trafficante. Let me, when you say Mr. Gianc___
. Roselli after the Bay of Pigs?

Mr. Hornbeck. Yes.

Mr. Trafficante. If they stayed around the hotel, the ___
untainbleau, I would see them over there, but there was no ___
eting about no assassination in Cuba or nothing like that.

Mr. Hornbeck. In 19 --

Mr. Trafficante. If my mind serves me right, they stayed ___
ound there for awhile.

Mr. Hornbeck. Were you permitted any visitors from the United States?

Mr. Trafficante. Any place they would come in.

Mr. Hornbeck. Did you in fact have any visitors from United States?

Mr. Trafficante. I used to have visitors. I remembe___
my wife visiting me. Maybe I did. I couldn't tell you I ___
didn't right now.

Mr. Hornbeck. During the period of time that you we___
in the detention center were you ever visited by Jack Ruby

Mr. Trafficante. No.

Mr. Hornbeck. You have heard that story?

Mr. Trafficante. Yes, I have heard the story about ___
I never met Ruby in my life. I have never been in Dallas ___
in my life.

Mr. Hornbeck. To your knowledge, has he ever been i___
Miami?

Mr. Trafficante. I never met him in Miami. I never ___
met him no place.

Mr. Hornbeck. So the only information that you wou___
have with regard to Jack Ruby is that which you read from ___
some public source, is that your testimony?

Mr. Trafficante. Right. And watching him on TV whe___
he killed that Oswald.

Mr. Hornbeck. While you were in the detention cent___

JFK Witness Murdered
Roselli Claimed To Know Truth Behind Dallas Shooting
By Lee Anderton

Dumfoundling Bay — Authorities here recovered the mutilated body of organized crime figure Johnny Roselli late Tuesday morning from an oil drum floating in Miami's Dumfoundling Bay. Roselli, who had been scheduled to speak before a special Congressional Committee regarding the assassination of President John F. Kennedy, had been missing since April of this year.

Roselli is the second committee witness to have been murdered before he could testify. Chicago mob figure Sam Giancana, whose own testimony was to focus on organized crime's role in an elaborate CIA plot against Cuban leader Fidel Castro, was shot dead in his Chicago home in June of last year. His killers remain at large.

Roselli, born Filippo Sacco in Esperia, Italy, was often referred to by associates as "Handsome Johnny." He was instrumental in establishing an organized crime presence in

---

4 October 1962

MEMORANDUM FOR RECORD

SUBJECT: Minutes of Meeting of the Special Group (Augme Operation MONGOOSE, 4 October 1962

PRESENT: <u>The Attorney General</u>; Mr. Johnson; Mr. Gilpatr Taylor, General Lansdale; Mr. McCone and Gener Mr. Wilson

← RFK

1. The Attorney General opened the meeting by say higher authority <u>is concerned about progress on the MONG and feels that more priority should be given to trying t sabotage operations.</u> The Attorney General said that he a new look is not required at this time in view of the m especially in the sabotage field. He urged that "massiv mounted within the entire MONGOOSE framework. There of discussion about this, and General Lansdale said pt will be made against the major target which has ree unsuccessful missions, and that approximately s n the planning stage.

Mr. Johnson said that "massive activity" would to come from within. He also said that he hopes

---

Note: Roselli/Mongoose — Why was he killed?

BOXER IS DEAD
JIMMY ALLEN DIES AFTER GRISLY FALL: BELIEVED A SUICIDE

MIAMI BEACH, JUNE 14 — Former #2 WBA Welterweight contender Jimmy Allen plunged to his death from the 12th floor of a luxury suite in Miami's Fountainbleau Hotel early Sunday morning, in what is being reported as a suicide.

Best known for his epic bouts with World Champion Wilberto Benvenitez, Allen had not fought in nearly a year, due to a dispute with his former manager, Tony Licari. Allen was reportedly despondent over both the direction of his career and the recent break-up of his marriage to actress Cecilia 'C.C.' Brody.

Allen's trainer, Salvatore 'Sally' Bartolo, was the last person to Allen, in a training sessi before his death. "He was lems, I know, but still — s comes out of left field," tragedy. Jimmy was still had a lot of good years lef

Police were initially su after reports of scuffling s Allen's room, which were be him attempting to oper although some witnesses r

Continued on Page

Note: The mob — Tony Licari — and Jimmy Allen

---

2 GREAT MATCHES!
YPT SHRINE TEMPL
5017 WASHINGTON STREET TAMPA FL
FRIDAY APR 16 7:30 P
MAIN EVENT - 12 ROUND

FLORIDA'S OWN
JIMMY "THE F
ALLE
GOLDEN GLOVES CHAMP
#9 WELTERWEIGHT CONTE

VS.

THOMAS
LEE
THE TAIWANESE TOR

EXTRA SPECIAL 10 ROUND CO-FEATURE

ROMEO **SANTANGELO**
UNDEFEATED FLYWEIGHT

VS.

VINCE **MARTINEZ**
YBOR CITY'S OWN – 'V' FOR VICTORY

TS NOW ON SALE $75 - $50 - $25

FLORIDA

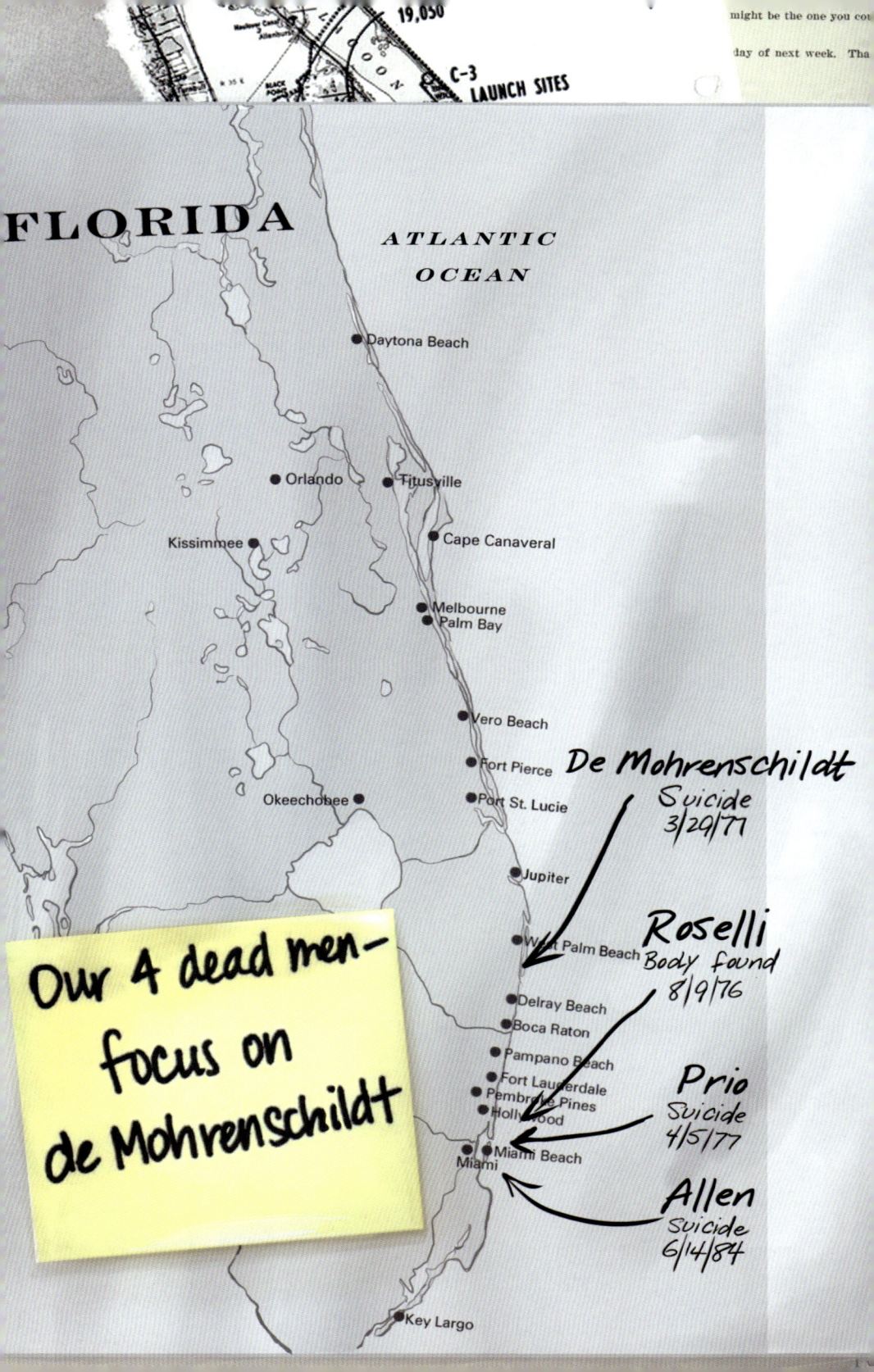

ATLANTIC OCEAN

De Mohrenschildt
Suicide
3/29/77

Roselli
Body found
8/9/76

Prio
Suicide
4/5/77

Allen
Suicide
6/14/84

Our 4 dead men—focus on de Mohrenschildt

FOREWORD

(1) The Warren Commission concluded that Lee Harvey Oswald acted alone in the assassination of President John F. Kennedy, that he was not tied to any intelligence agency, and that none of his associates were tied to the assassination. Nevertheless, speculation continued to center about one of Oswald's associations: George de Mohrenschildt and de Mohrenschildt's background. The Warren Commission concluded about de Mohrenschildt:

The Commission's investigation has developed no signs of the subversive or disloyal conduct on the part of either of the de Mohrenschildts. Neither the FBI, CIA, nor any other witness contacted by the Commission has provided any information linking the de Mohrenschildts to subversive or extremist organizations. Nor has there been any evidence linking them in any way with the assassination of President Kennedy.(1)

(2) Despite this disclaimer of any subversive or disloyal activity on the part of de Mohrenschildt by the Warren Commission, de Mohrenschildt was rumored to have had ties with the intelligence communities of several countries. Indeed de Mohrenschildt himself admitted some involvement with French intelligence, but his actual role with them was never fully disclosed, and he emphatically denied any other intelligence associations. He explained his travels to Haiti with the cooperation of the Haitian Government as innocuous business deals with no political overtones.

(3) Speculation also continued about Oswald's relationship to de Mohrenschildt because of the contrast between the backgrounds of the two men. De Mohrenschildt was described as sophisticated and well educated, moving easily in the social and professional circles of oil-men and the so-called "White Russian" community, many of whom were avowed rightwingers. Oswald's "lowly" background did not include much education or influence, and he was in fact shunned by the same Dallas Russian community that embraced de Mohrenschildt.

(4) The committee undertook to probe more into the background and associations of de Mohrenschildt to determine if more light could be shed to either explain the relationship between Oswald and de Mohrenschildt or to determine if any new information contradicts that which was available to the Warren Commission. This probe seemed justified in view of the controversy that continues to surround the relationship, and the additional speculation that was caused by the apparent suicide of de Mohrenschildt in 1977 on the day he was contacted by both an investigator from the committee and a writer about Oswald.

I. DE MOHRENSCHILDT'S BACKGROUND

(5) De Mohrenschildt testified extensively before the Warren Commission about his childhood in Russia and Poland and his family. He

(49)

---

hard to get. You might call Martha Joe Stroud, who is an assistant here and she is actually in charge of those, and she might be the one reach and she would be at this same number.
Mrs. LESLIE. All right; I will do it.
Mr. DAVIS. I would say about Tuesday or Wednesday of next week you so much, Mrs. Leslie.
Mrs. LESLIE. Thank you.

TESTIMONY OF GEORGE S. DE MOHRENSCHILDT

The testimony of George S. De Mohrenschildt was taken at 10 a.m., 22, 1964, at 200 Maryland Avenue N.E., Washington, D.C., by Mr. Jenner, Jr., assistant counsel of the President's Commission. Dr. Alf berg, historian, was present.

Mr. JENNER. Will you rise and be sworn? Do you solemnly swear te truth, the whole truth, and nothing but the truth in the deposition about to give?
Mr. DE MOHRENSCHILDT. I do.
Mr. JENNER. Mr. Reporter, this is Mr. George De Mohrenschildt.
Mr. De Mohrenschildt, you and Mrs. De Mohrenschildt have receive from Mr. Rankin, the general counsel of the Commission, have you no
Mr. DE MOHRENSCHILDT. We received one.
Mr. JENNER. One joint letter?
Mr. DE MOHRENSCHILDT. One joint letter.
Mr. JENNER. With which was enclosed copies of the Senate Joint Re 137, which was the legislation authorizing the creation of the Commis

166

Mr. JENNER. As a matter of fact, you didn't sell a single policy?
Mr. DE MOHRENSCHILDT. Not a single policy.
Mr. JENNER. Over what period of a time did you pursue that activit
Mr. DE MOHRENSCHILDT. I even didn't pass my broker's examination. to get an insurance broker's license. I studied to be an insurance broker State of New York. And I failed dismally that examination. So th end of my insurance business.
Mr. JENNER. Now, we have you up to the advent of World War II, was—this is about 1941.
Mr. DE MOHRENSCHILDT. But before that I was in Texas and wor Humble Oil Co.
Mr. JENNER. Before 1941 you had gone to Texas?
Mr. DE MOHRENSCHILDT. Yes; in 1939.
Mr. JENNER. You went to Texas in 1939?
Mr. DE MOHRENSCHILDT. Yes.
Mr. JENNER. And how did that come about?
Mr. DE MOHRENSCHILDT. Well, I was interested in the oil indus wanted to see in which way I could fit into the oil industry.
Mr. JENNER. Whom did you contact? How did you get there? by bus.
Mr. DE MOHRENSCHILDT. Well,

---

the Soviet Union. United States politics, Cuba the policies of the KENNEDY administration were not discus ty. During the course of the evening, OSWALD informed all t he was a Communist and had attempted to join the Communi was in Russia. OSWALD appeared to be fairly intelligent an . OSWALD spoke very little English and participated only to gree in the conversation. Miss MC DONALD recalled that OSWA was employed by a large downtown printing firm and was at t eriencing difficulty in supporting his family on his income e no statement which would indicate any future violent acti inst any one person or group of persons.

Miss MC DONALD stated that GEORGE DE MOHRENSCHILDT, a geological consultant who moved to Haiti in the Spring of called that JEAN DE MOHRENSCHILDT reportedly was employed by RRIS in Dallas. Both have children by previous marriages. ated that both DE MOHRENSCHILDTs appear to be eccentric ind e recalled the DE MOHRENSCHILDTs described a trip they took xico to the Panama Canal on foot, which supposedly spanned e described GEORGE DE MOHRENSCHILDT as a white male, 45 year inches, 150 pounds, sandy hair, unkempt and a ruddy complexi pears to be well educated and stated he grew up in either Fr ssia and speaks fluent Russian. Mrs. DE MOHRENSCHILDT was d ite female, 5 feet 6 inches, 140 pounds, blond hair—possibl years old and also fluent in Russian

E MOHRENSCHILDT, GEORGE   Nov. 1963 - JAN. 1964

The missing link — Georges de Mohrenschildt

GEORGE DE MOHRENSCHILDT

Staff Report
of the
Select Committee on Assassinations
U.S. House of Representatives
Ninety-fifth Congress
Second Session

March 1979

(47)

SUBJECT: Willem Oltmans and George de Mohrenschildt
DATE: 29 August 1977
REFERENCE: UPI Press Tickler
DESCRIPTION: (FYI)

1. According to an article in the 1 April 1977 Washington Star, George de Mohrenschildt, who had befriended the Oswalds in 1962, had attempted suicide four times in 1976. As a result he was committed for mental care to the Parkland Memorial Hospital in Dallas in the fall of 1976. He was released on 30 December 1976.

2. In early January 1976, according to Willem Oltmans, a Dutch journalist working for Dutch television, who had known de Mohrenschildt since at least 1967 and perhaps earlier, de Mohrenschildt told Oltmans that he was writing a book entitled I'm a Patsy, I'm a Patsy. It purports to tell the whole story of the conspiracy and, according to Oltmans, described how de Mohrenschildt considered himself responsible for Oswald's actions. The book has not been published and the manuscript is apparently in the hands of de Mohrenschildt's lawyer, Pat S. Russell of Dallas. Oltmans is cited in a Washington Star article of 31 March 1977 as stating that de Mohrenschildt had once said that "I only made up the story (about Oswald) because everybody makes a million dollars off the Kennedy assassination, and I haven't made anything. So now it's my turn."

3. In early March 1977, Willem Oltmans appeared before the House Assassinations Committee to tell about de Mohrenschildt's decision to tell his version of the Kennedy murder. It was this appearance before Committee staffers that prompted the panel to send Gaeton Fonzi, an investigator, to Palm Beach in an attempt to question de Mohrenschildt. Fonzi located where de Mohrenschildt was staying in Palm Beach, but was unable to see de Mohrenschildt. The latter shot himself [...] 29 March 1977, in the home of Mrs. Ch[...] marriage, about six hours before the [...]

4. [The Dutch services] have mai[...] over the years [...] particularly his co[...] [...] the Soviet Union.

de Mohrenschildt's book on Oswald — I am a Patsy

APPENDIX

MANUSCRIPT BY GEORGE DE MOHRENSCHILDT

The manuscript of the book George de Mohrenschildt was writing at the time of his death in March 1977 is included in this staff report as an appendix. In it de Mohrenschildt gave many details about his activities and associations, and perhaps most significantly, an insight into how he perceived his relationship with Lee Harvey Oswald. The facts and information in the manuscript in many respects differ from, and occasionally boldly contradict, statements that were made by de Mohrenschildt to several Government agencies at the time of the assassination and other information that has been made public. While there is no longer any way to resolve those factual conflicts or to confront de Mohrenschildt with the discrepancies, the manuscript is nevertheless, included here to shed light on at least how George de Mohrenschildt himself viewed those facts and how he wanted the public record to read about himself and Oswald.

There is some indication in the papers that it was as much as [...]
HRENSCHILDT. Maybe so.
You just don't have——
HRENSCHILDT. It was a very successful operation, this business, [...]
Did you subsequently dissolve it?
HRENSCHILDT. Dissolved it, quarreled with my girl friend, decided [...] States.
Your brother had been over to see you in the meantime?
HRENSCHILDT. Yes; and that is what, by the way, induced me into the States, because my brother and his wife came to meet me. They [...] not too much interested in meeting a mistress—let's face it—and [...] led to a breakup between us, between my ex-girl friend and myself.
ER. And you came to this country in 1938?
HRENSCHILDT. May of 1938.
ER. May of 1938, I think it was. What did you do to sustain [...]
HRENSCHILDT. Well, I brought some money with me. I brought some [...] me—something like $10,000, I would say.
ER. And what did you immediately do in connection with that? [...] immediately?
[...] g for a job, very unsuccessfully, if I [...] 1938. I even started selling perfumes, [...] Garde.
[...] that company?
[...] y as a salesman. I even sold some [...]
[...] n, with your brother?
[...] he time. Then I had my own room.
[...] g on Park Avenue, was he?
[...] stay with him?
[...] n as I arrived we went to spend the
on Long Island, Belport, Long Island.
ENNER. And at Belport, you made what acquaintances?
DE MOHRENSCHILDT. Lots of people, but especially Mrs. Bouvier.
ENNER. Who is Mrs. Bouvier?
DE MOHRENSCHILDT. Mrs. Bouvier is Jacqueline Kennedy's mother, also [...] her and her whole family. She was in the process of getting a divorce [...] r husband. I met him, also. We were very close friends. We saw each [...] very day. I met Jackie then, when she was a little girl. Her sister, who [...] ll in the cradle practically. We were also very close friends of Jack[...] r's sister, and his father.
ENNER. Well, bring yourself along.
DE MOHRENSCHILDT. That friendship more or less remained, because we [...] each other, occasionally—Mrs. Auchincloss, and occasionally correspond [...] then, I realized there was no future selling perfume or materials in [...] and having had that background of the oil industry in my blood, becau[...] ther was the director of Nobel Enterprises, which is a large oil conce[...] ssia, which was eventually expropriated and confiscated, and I decide[...] and try to work for an oil company. I arrived in Texas.
ENNER. Excuse me, sir. Before we get there—because that skips so[...] —one of your efforts was as an insurance salesman?
DE MOHRENSCHILDT. Yes; that is right.
ENNER. And——
DE MOHRENSCHILDT. How did you know that?
ENNER. You were unsuccessful in that, were you?
DE MOHRENSCHILDT. Very unsuccessful.

Crazy — his relationship to your mother ↓

DALLAS

Captured Suspect Clings to Denial That He Fired Shots Fatal to Kenne[dy]

EXCLUSIVE PHOTOS!

Forbidden Lovers: JACKIE AND RFK

screen image
MAGAZINE
MARCH 1969 — 50¢

JACKIE: WHY SHE MARRIED ARI

"IF THEY ARE KILLING KENNEDYS, MY KIDS ARE NEXT!"

Why your mother was scared →

← Why she and RFK buried the tapes

THE MANCHESTER TAPES:
THE SECRETS JACKIE WANTED TO HAVE BURIED!

Mr. De Mohrenschildt. Well, I am a member of the Dallas Petroleum Club. I used to be a member of the Abilene Country Club. I used to be, because I don't live there any more.

I am a member of American Association of Petroleum Geologists.

I am a member of the American Association of Mining Engineers. I think my dues are due. Maybe they expelled me by now.

I am a member of the Dallas Society of Petroleum Geologists.

LY SEPTEMBER 1963 THE SOVIET PERSONNEL
TO TWO GENERAL CATEGORIES:
MILITARY UNITS WHICH MAN SURFACE-TO-
LE SITES, AND RADAR AND COMMUNICATIONS
OSED ENTIRELY OF SOVIET PERSONNEL, INC
TY GUARDS. THEY DO NOT FRATERNIZE WIT
EIR OWN CAMPS AND AREAS.
-CALIBER TECHNICIANS AND OFFICERS WHO
ISERS DOWN TO AND INCLUDING DIVISION
HEADQUARTERS COMMENT: SOURCE HAS N
TREASURY DDI
S-E-C-R-E-T
NO FOREIGN DISSEM

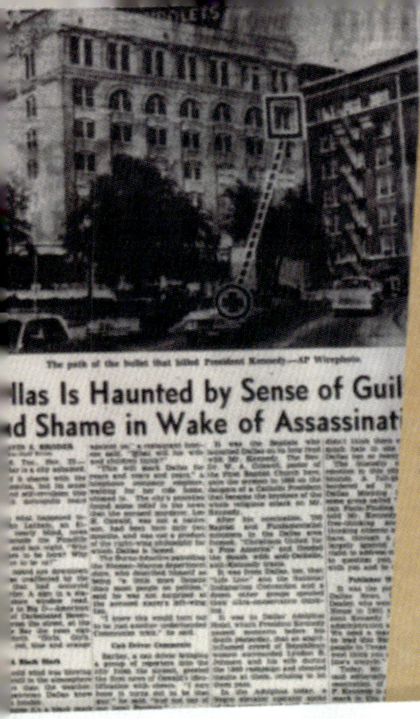

WANTED FOR TREASON

TOP SECRET   151

Mr. Jenner. Of what groups have you been a member? And of what groups are you a member?

Mr. De Mohrenschildt. I am not a member of any group. Maybe that is something against me, because I am not a member of any group. I am not a member -- I am not interested. I am too busy.

Mr. Jenner. You are a member of the Petroleum Club in Dallas?

Mr. De Mohrenschildt. If you call that a group, yes.

Mr. Jenner. It is a group.

Mr. De Mohrenschildt. Yes, a member of the Dallas Petroleum Club.

Mr. Jenner. Tell me all the societies or groups, whether you call them political or otherwise, of which you have been a member.

Mr. De Mohrenschildt. None political. You call the Dallas Petroleum Club political?

Mr. Jenner. No.

Mr. De Mohrenschildt. Well, I am a member of the Dallas Petroleum Club. I used to be a member of the Abilene Country Club. I used to be, because I don't live there any more.

I am a member of American Association of Petroleum Geologists.

I am a member of the American Association of Mining Engineers. I think my dues are due. Maybe they expelled me by now.

I am a member of the Dallas Society of Petroleum Geologists.

Dallas Petroleum Club paid for this —

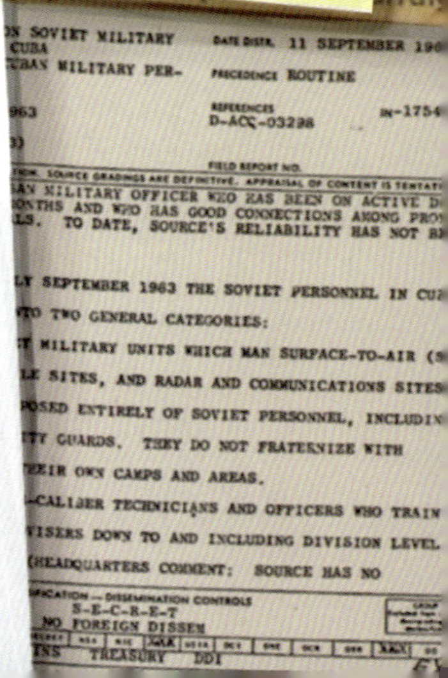

SPOT REPORT

Willem Oltmans and
George de Mohrenschildt   DATE: 29 Aug...

SOURCE: UPI Press Tickler

DESCRIPTION: (FYI)

According to an article in the 1 April 1977 Washington...
de Mohrenschildt, who had befriended the Oswalds in 196...
...ted suicide four times in 1976. As a result he was...
...care to the Parkland Memorial Hospital in Dallas in the...
He was released on 30 December 1976.

In early January 1976, according to Willem Oltmans, a...
...ist working for Dutch television, who ha...
...t 1967 and perhaps earlier, de...
...ting a book entitled I'm a Pat...
...le story of the conspiracy and...
...enschildt considered himself r...
...enschildt's lawyer, Pat S. Rus...
...ton Star article of 31 March 19...
...e said that "I only made up the...
...kes a million dollars off the K...
...ything. So now it's my turn."

In early March 1977, Willem O...
...nations Committee to tell about...
...sion of the Kennedy murder. It...
...s that prompted the panel to sen...
...ch in an attempt to question de...
...enschildt was staying in Palm Be...
...hildt. The latter shot himself...
...1977, in the home of Mrs. Char...
..., about six hours before the in...

[The Dutch services have maintai...
...years, particularly his contact...
...nds and the Soviet Union.

RECOMMENDATIONS FOR DDO ACTION:

SENATE

THE INVESTIGATION
ASSASSINATION OF P...
N F. KENNEDY: PE...
THE INTELLIGENC...

BOOK V

FINAL REPO...
OF THE
SELECT COMMITTEE
TO STUDY GOVERNMENTAL OPERATIONS
WITH RESPECT TO
INTELLIGENCE ACTIVITIES
UNITED STATES SENATE

April 23 (under authority of the order of April. 14), 1976

U.S. GOVERNMENT PRINTING OFFICE
WASHINGTON : 1976

Where he met first, and how it ended.

Mr. Tanenbaum. Will you tell us in substance, sir, what you said to Mr. de Mohrenschildt on this occasion and what he said to you with regard to the assassination of the President?

Mr. Oltmans. Now, to sum up this record: The ess... is that he was not sure that Oswald killed Kennedy. Tha... he believed he had not killed Kennedy. But the tape is... littered with bits and pieces of information that your... d better work with than I could... rstand, for instance, on the fi... he Russian Colonel Orlof, to... th. Who is this man Orlof? y did he go with the Colonel... did he go to Fort Worth and t... ery mysterious. nd this was discussed during t... t was on the tapes, yes, sir. ow, when was the next time yo... ldt with regard to the assass...

slightly over ten months before... ...election deciding who would be the next presiden... the United States, there occurred a series of events that... place during the Eisenhower/Nixon Administration that wou... inevitably lead to the death of John F. Kennedy in Dealy... November 22, 1963.

They are as follows:

By the end of January 1960, British reconnaiss... flights overflying Cuba detected unusual construction acti... of a military nature, not normally associated with defense weaponry. By the end of March, aerial photographs showed... ficient information to indicate that offensive missile inst... lations were being prepared for use against Cuba's neighbor... in the western hemisphere. After this conclusion had been reached by British Intelligence, they reported the informat... through diplomatic channels to our State Department (see Affidavit, Exhibit 1).

Simultaneously, our own embassy in Havana had bee... receiving confidential reports through members of its staff, i.e., Paul Bethel (see Exhibit 2, entitled "On missiles in C... conversation June 16, 1976; Miami; with Dick Russell). Beth... was Press Attache to our embassy in Havana all during the cr... period from 1959 up until diplomatic relations were broken o... in early 1961. During this period he kept in close touch wi... local Cuban friends who were also concerned with this unusua... construction activity.

JRA — JAXON RESEARCH ASSOCIATES

John —

Still digging.
Next batch more CIA.
Don't worry — keeping my
head down.
Lips sealed. Being careful.
You be careful too!
Too many people weren't.

— Nan

This issue will
save GEORGE —
double circulation
at least!

CHAPTER 14

Espy turned the last page over, then picked up the entire pile, straightening the pages as best she could. One of the documents fell to the floor; she picked it up.

It was the letter from Ted Kennedy to Garrett.

One last voyage together, old friend.

If you do decide to proceed against them—know that they will be watching.

They will not hesitate to kill again.

She took out her phone and tapped a contact.

"Antonio's."

"I'd like to place an order," she said. "The name is Woodhull."

"Hold, please." She listened to hold music and looked around the empty locker room, a sudden chill going down the back of her neck.

What did you do, Garrett? What kind of hornet's nest did you stir up?

The hold music stopped. "Ms. Harper?"

"Li."

"Is everything all right?"

Espy couldn't help it. She laughed.

"Ms. Harper?"

"I'm here, sorry." She took a deep breath. "Please get everyone back to Anderson House. As soon as possible."

"Of course. What shall I tell them?"

"You can tell them I found it. The dossier. And that we have work to do." She looked down at the papers in front of her once more. "You can tell them it's all hands on deck."

TEN DAYS LATER

…as the enormity of the Bay of Pigs disaster came home to him, [President Kennedy] said … he wanted to "splinter the CIA into a thousand pieces and scatter it to the winds."

The New York Times. April 25, 1966

15

"Before we begin…" Doug took off his Wayfarers, folding the arms in neatly before letting the glasses hang from the lanyard around his neck. "I have a confession to make."

"Mr. Rivers." The woman across the table from him smiled and lowered her own sunglasses. "It's a little early for that, don't you think? I haven't even had my coffee yet."

They were seated at the long windows along the back wall of the Black Dog Tavern in Vineyard Haven, one of six towns on Martha's Vineyard, the Massachusetts resort island where the movie *Jaws* had been filmed, where many of the East Coast's glitterati and literati spent their summers. The woman sitting across from him was one of them.

John Kennedy Jr. had been as well.

"I lied to you earlier, on the phone," Doug said.

"I figured as much."

"You did?"

"I did PR work for six months, fifteen years ago. And I wasn't very good at it."

Cassandra Flynn was one of a few dozen names on a decades-old email Li had found listing potential invitees for a charity fundraiser that JFK Jr.'s wife, Carolyn Bessette, had planned on hosting. Doug had contacted her, pretending to be looking for a publicist for a project he was working on.

"Not sure you have the right woman, Mr. Rivers," she had replied, but he had insisted on meeting her anyway. And on coming to the Vineyard for that meeting.

Now he was going to tell her why.

"So what is it you really want from me, Mr. Rivers?"

"Doug, please."

"Doug then."

"Well, Ms. Flynn—Cassandra—the real reason—"

"Nan," she corrected. "Everybody calls me Nan."

"Ah. My mistake." Not a mistake at all, of course. That's how she'd been listed in the email: Nan Flynn.

The question was, was she the Nan they were looking for? Nan from the dossier? Nan from Jaxon Research Associates? "Seven Days to Dallas" Nan?

She was the right age. She had the right look: tall, blonde, beautiful, refined. She had the right pedigree: Choate, Brown, Columbia School of Journalism, experience working for both newspapers and magazines, albeit limited (the woman seemed to change careers every few years—reporter, publicist, yoga instructor, etc.). Most important of all: She had known John F. Kennedy Jr.

"Hi, and welcome to the Black Dog."

Doug looked up to see a waitress standing at their table. College age. Maybe high school.

"I'm serving you today, and my name will be Mandy. I mean, my name is Mandy, and I will be serving you today." She flushed and held out two menus, deliberately avoiding his eye.

Her hands were shaking. Nervous. Because of him, he realized instantly. Surprising, considering how many of the rich and famous came to this tavern. Then again, she was young. Maybe new. Certainly inexperienced.

"Can I get you some coffee with your meal? I mean, before you order your meal?"

"Coffee sounds great," Nan said.

"Make that two. And I'm ready to order if you are, Nan."

CHAPTER 15

Doug was famished, in fact. And the Black Dog's breakfast ... even though it was going on twenty-five years or so since he'd last been here, he remembered it fondly. Summer of '08? '09? Something like that. He'd taken the ferry from Woods Hole with Lynn Stankowski (Whatever happened to her?) same as they'd done every weekend that summer—hit Oak Bluffs for the day, found some college kids to buy beer for them. They'd ended up getting blitzed and missed the last ferry back to the mainland. They were going to sleep on the beach, but one of the kids they were with insisted on taking them back to her house in Vineyard Haven. Dad and Mom were waiting up. Mom made up extra beds, no questions asked, and Dad took all of them to breakfast the next morning right here at the Black Dog, waved them off on the ferry.

So this is what it's like to have real parents, he remembered thinking.

"So really," Nan asked after pen-shaking-in-her-hand Mandy had taken their orders, "why are you here? What do you want?"

"Can you keep a secret?" he asked.

"I like to think so."

"I'm doing research for a movie."

"A movie."

"Yes." He lowered his voice. "A film about John F. Kennedy Jr."

Nan's eyes widened.

It was the same story he'd used all last week. The story he'd had his agent pushing to get him in front of the heavy hitters in the New York entertainment industry, to ask questions as surreptitiously, as carefully as he could, of those who had crossed paths with the heir to Camelot. An editor at Hachette; a publicist at one of the big downtown PR firms; a photographer who almost came to tears when talk turned to the magazine and its late editor. He hadn't come right out and asked, of course ("Say, you don't happen to know if JFK Jr. was working on a special issue of the magazine about the people who *really* killed his father, do you?") Rather, he had led conversations into the tragic arc of young John's life, the Kennedy curse, and eventually, in most cases, working his way around to conspiracy theories of one sort or another, always leaving the door open for his conversational partner to speak up about any interest John Jr. might have expressed in the same.

Not once in a week of coffees, lunches, and drink dates had he gotten a single bite after planting that hook. No one knew anything. Not about the article, or that cover mock-up, or any Nan, any firm called Jaxon Research Associates. Or if they did, they weren't telling.

And he wasn't the only one who'd struck out.

All hands on deck, Espy had said, and that had indeed been the case for the last week and a half. Frederickson left for Florida the morning after Espy found the dossier and had been there ever since; the new guy, Cockerell, had gone to Texas; Li had vanished into the darkest corners of the internet, chasing down one conspiracy theorist after another; while Espy herself had been burning the midnight oil at the DOJ. All to no effect. Ten days hard on the trail and not a single thing to show for it.

But hope sprang eternal.

"All right. But why me?" Nan asked. "Out of all the people John knew here, why me?"

"I've been speaking to people in New York," he said. "Your name was on a list."

"People in New York." Her expression had changed for some reason. From surprise to anger.

"Yes."

"People like Melanie Goldstein?"

"Uh…"

CHAPTER 15

"She told you John and I had an affair, didn't she?"

He shook his head emphatically. "I've never heard of Melanie Goldstein, for one thing, and for another—"

Nan rose to her feet. "Bloodsuckers," she hissed. "You hounded him when he was alive, and now you want to—"

"Stop." Doug stood too, pushing his bench back hard enough that it crashed to the floor.

Heads turned all over the restaurant.

"I promise you," he said, lowering his voice. "I was not sent by Melanie Goldstein. I am not interested in gossip, or some kind of hack job. I want to do this right. I want to do him right. Please. Sit back down."

Nan looked him in the eye. Her expression softened.

The dramatic gesture, Doug thought, picking up his bench. Works every time. He sat. So, after another second, did Nan.

"Sorry," she said. "It's just … that story got spread around for a while. It's hurtful. And it's a lie."

"I understand, believe me." And he did, having endured more than his share of gossip over the years. Of course, some of the more lurid headlines about his behavior back then had actually been true. He didn't like to think about that now.

"Um … is everything okay here?" Mandy had returned with their coffees.

"Fine, thank you," Nan said. "Everything is just fine."

"Great. Good." Mandy set down Doug's coffee, avoiding his eyes. "Back with your breakfast in a minute."

Nan managed a faint smile, watching her go. "She's a little starstruck."

"Yes."

"It was the same way with John. Wherever he went, whatever he did, there were reporters. People crawling all over themselves to ask him questions, take his picture. I don't know how he stood it."

"So how did you know him? How did you two meet?"

"God, it was so long ago." Nan took a sip from the steaming mug in front of her; Doug did the same. "I was living in New York then, trying to be a reporter. I did some research for his magazine."

Doug almost choked on his coffee.

"For *George*?"

"Yes, of course."

"What kind of research?" he asked, trying not to let the excitement he felt creep into his voice.

"Local politics," she said. "By local I mean here on the Vineyard. You know, there was a point back in the seventies when the island wanted to secede from Massachusetts. John knew I had connections here, had me talk to a few people. Nothing ever came of it—the secession or the article."

"Ah," he said, trying not to show his disappointment. Though really, if she was the Nan they were looking for, would she seriously confess that to him?

"You are going to focus on the magazine, aren't you?" Nan asked.

"Excuse me?"

"In your film. You'll focus on the magazine. That was very important to John, you know."

John. The way she said his name, the look in her eyes when she said it … fifty-fifty there actually had been an affair.

"Because *George* was his baby. His way of doing something that would help him be his own man. He had plans, you know. Big plans for what he was going to do with his life." A strange look came over her face then.

"What?"

"I'm just remembering something now. Something that hap-

CHAPTER 15

pened a few months or so before the accident. Before John died. It's probably not important. Ah."

Their food had arrived.

"Will there be anything else?" Mandy asked, setting their orders down.

"I think we're good here," Doug said. "Thanks, Mandy."

She met his gaze for the first time, turned a brilliant red, and scurried off without another word.

"You should take a selfie with her. Before you leave," Nan said.

"I will if she stands still long enough. You were saying?"

"Oh. Yes. Walter came to me one day and asked if I knew John well enough to approach him—to set up a meeting."

"Walter?"

"My boyfriend then. My ex-husband now. A hedge fund manager. A thoroughly despicable human being."

Doug laughed. "Go on."

"This was back in 1998. There was a Senate seat coming open the next year, in New York. Walter was part of a group that wanted John to run for that seat. John turned them down—told Walter that the magazine was his top priority."

"Interesting." It was, though Doug had heard more than one version of the same story already this week.

"Yes. But what I just realized, what seems strange to me, in retrospect"—Nan leaned in closer—"the magazine was failing, even then. I had friends who worked in the industry, and they told me the numbers. Not that it was any big secret. The ship was sinking. *George* was doomed."

Doug nodded. "So I heard." In amongst the people he'd spoken to in New York had been an accountant who'd worked for Hachette back in the day. Hachette, the publishing conglomerate that owned *George*.

"The writing was on the wall. That ship—" the man had gestured emphatically—"was sinking. Nothing could save it."

The numbers Li found backed that up. In 1999, JFK Jr.'s magazine had been on the verge of cancellation. In the months before he died, John had been making the rounds in New York—seeing financial backers, perhaps a new publisher. Or perhaps—as the woman across from him was suggesting—he was preparing to leave journalism behind and step into the political arena. Follow in his father's footsteps. And then—

"He decided not to run for office. I always wondered why." Nan shrugged. "Maybe he thought he could still save *George*, somehow. Find some way to bump up the circulation. Although I don't know what would make him think that."

I do, Doug thought.

Seven Days to Dallas.

This issue will save George. Double circulation at least.

Doug thought double circulation might have been an understatement.

The Men Who Murdered My Father?

That issue would have gone flying off the stands.

That issue would have rocked the publishing—and the political—world.

"Is any of this helpful?" Nan asked. "For the film, I mean."

Doug smiled then. His 10,000-watt smile.

"Oh, absolutely," he said. "You have no idea."

16

Frederickson leaned against a wall at the Xtreme Combat gym in Hallandale, Florida, watching the action in the ring. Not MMA—boxing. Old-style. Two Hispanic kids sparring, lightweights, bantamweights even—a hundred twenty, a hundred thirty pounds tops. Tough kids. Fast. One in red trunks, one in blue. Blue trunks was getting the worst of the deal. The kid in red had a wicked left jab. Good thing for blue they were wearing headgear, or he'd have a face like raw hamburger.

Who he was really watching, though, was the old guy standing outside the ring, barking out commands to both fighters: "Keep your guard up; move, damn it, move; step into it!" Skinny little white guy, wife-beater tee, half an inch of white fuzz on his head. Just a little bit of a beer gut hanging over his belt.

The sparring stopped. The two boxers took off their headgear, grabbed water bottles, started drinking and talking in rapid-fire Spanish to each other.

The old guy looked over at Frederickson. "Help you with something?" he asked.

"Hope so," Frederickson said. "You Sally Bartolo?"

"Yeah. Who's asking?"

"Bill Goodwin." Frederickson stepped forward, held out a business card he'd had made up. "I'm a reporter. Working on a story for the AP."

"Uh-huh." Bartolo looked at the card and handed it back, looked Frederickson up and down. "You don't look like a reporter."

"I had a midlife crisis."

"Hah." Bartolo smiled. "What were you before, a cop? You look like a cop."

"I had occasion to bust some heads."

"Now that I believe. You ever fight?"

"Not in the ring."

Bartolo's smile grew wider. "Yeah. I'll bet. And now you're a reporter. Well. Takes all kinds, I guess. So what can I help you with, Mr. Goodwin?"

"Doing some research on a boxer named Jimmy Allen. You remember him?"

The smile on Bartolo's face abruptly vanished.

"Jimmy Allen. Sure. Long time since I heard that name."

"I expect so," Frederickson said. "He's been dead now, what, thirty years?"

"Something like that. What's your interest?"

"I'm working on a piece. He's part of it."

"Really? What kind of piece might that be?"

"A piece on how he died," Frederickson said, "among other things."

"He died jumping out a ten story window. Down thataway." Bartolo pointed. "The Fountainbleau Hotel."

"So he killed himself?"

"That's what the papers said."

"That's what you think?"

Bartolo sat down on a padded bench along the wall and pulled a water bottle from a gym bag underneath it. He took a long draw. "Sure that's what I think. You got any reason to think differently?"

"Me? Doesn't matter what I think. You were his trainer. You knew him better than most."

"Trainer. Ha." Bartolo snorted. "He never listened to me."

"From what I heard, he never listened to anyone."

CHAPTER 16

"Yeah. That was Flash's problem, all right."

Frederickson nodded, picturing in his mind one of the more colorful pieces from the dossier. A promotional poster from a boxing match—Jimmy "The Flash" Allen vs. Vs. Thomas Lee, "The Taiwanese Tornado." Black and red letters, on a bright yellow background. A boxing poster. What that had to do with the Kennedy assassination…

"Flash," Frederickson said. "Where'd he get that name from?"

"The superhero, you know? From the comics? Barry Allen, that was his secret identity. Barry Allen, Jimmy Allen…." Bartolo shrugged. "Anyway. Jimmy had a right hand—boom!" Bartolo punched the air. "Fastest I've ever seen. Gave him a shot in any fight he was in. If he would've trained a little harder, he coulda been top five, no sweat."

"He didn't like to train."

"Hell no. It'd be like the week before a fight before I could get him to cut down on the drinking, hit the bag. Fighting was something he did to earn money. Like a job, right? Not a lifestyle. He fought, made some money, went out and spent it. Him and C.C. used to change cars every month, it seemed. C.C." Bartolo shook his head. "Damn. I used to tell him not to bring her around here, she was too distracting. Girl liked to work it, you know?"

"Yeah. I know." Frederickson had seen pictures of her too. Not in the dossier, but there were plenty online. C.C. Brody, Allen's fiancée at the time he died. Distracting was one way of putting it.

"Anyway … that was all a long time ago. Not sure what else I can tell you here, Mr. Goodwin, so"—Bartolo stuffed the water bottle back in the bag and glanced up at a clock on the wall—"considering that I got someplace to be, I'm—"

"Allen's manager was a guy named Tony Licari, is that right?"

Bartolo froze.

"Yeah," he said after a few seconds. "That's right."

"Tony the Lip. You knew him?"

"Sure. We crossed paths."

"Interesting guy."

"Interesting. Ha." Bartolo laughed, but didn't smile.

"Well, the Feds were very interested in him, at least. Turns out there was a RICO case against Licari, back in the day."

"RICO? What's that?"

Frederickson smiled. As if Bartolo didn't know exactly what he was talking about. "RICO. Short for racketeering-influenced and corrupt organizations. Meaning, in this case, mob."

"Really?" Bartolo shrugged. "Tony Licari. Mob. Who would've thought it?"

"The Feds thought you might've, Sally. Which I guess is why they wanted you to testify at the trial."

It was all there in the files Espy had dug up. DOJ attorneys had expected Bartolo to testify at that trial. To talk about Licari's connections to the mob. About the dirty deeds he'd done on that organization's behalf. Like fixing Jimmy Allen's boxing matches. Allen had been set to testify as well, and then…

"And then he went out that Fountainbleau window," Espy had said.

"You saying he didn't make that jump of his own accord?" Frederickson had asked.

"The thought had occurred to me," Espy had responded.

"Oh yeah." Bartolo nodded. "The RICO trial. That is ringing a little bell, now that you mention it. But it was all so long ago … I don't remember anything about that." Bartolo got to his feet and started for the door.

"Come on, Sally." Frederickson stepped in front of him.

CHAPTER 16

"There's no reason to hide the truth anymore. Licari died, what, twenty years ago?"

"Twenty-one. But who's counting?"

"I am." Frederickson folded his arms across his chest. "That was all a long time ago, Sally. Nothing to be scared of here."

"Yeah. People like to think that." Bartolo shook his head slowly, then fell silent.

"What?" Frederickson asked after a few seconds.

"Here. Let me show you something." Bartolo reached into his gym bag again. "You see this? It's a new laptop. For my granddaughter. She just got out of high school. Miami Christian. Number two in her class."

"Congratulations."

"Thanks. She's going to Occidental next year, out in California. L.A. Full ride."

"That's great. But—"

"Four years from now, she's going to have another graduation, god willing. And I want to be there for that one too."

"Of course. I get that."

"No. I don't think you do. Because these questions of yours … I start talking about Tony Licari, about Jimmy Allen, and suddenly me being around four years from now gets less and less likely."

"Sally. I promise you. Whatever you tell me stays between the two of us."

"I've heard that before."

"I give you my word."

"Hey. Goodwin. Or whatever your name really is." Bartolo looked Frederickson in the eye. "I believe you, okay. But these people…" He trailed off.

"These people what?" Frederickson prompted.

Bartolo sighed heavily. "Hell. I probably said too much already."

He put the computer back in his gym bag. "Goodbye, Mr. Goodwin. Good luck with your story. Or whatever it is you're doing, really. Just leave me out of it."

And with that, Bartolo headed out the back door.

❖ ❖ ❖ ❖ ❖

Frederickson climbed into the little convertible he'd rented on his dime, not Woodhull's, feeling those warm Florida rays, even if it cost him an extra forty bucks a day. It was worth it. He sat there a moment, Bartolo's words—*these people*—and Nemkov's—*they do not leave trails*—echoing in his mind.

He rubbed his eyes. It had been a long ten days here in the Sunshine State. A week and a half of running down leads from the dossier. He'd started in West Palm Beach, at the old Kennedy estate, where JFK had stayed the night before that visit to Cape Canaveral. He couldn't find a single soul who even remembered when the Kennedys had owned the place.

He hadn't had any more luck at Canaveral itself. Fifty years on, NASA didn't have many of those old records left. No information on those secret drone programs referred to in the dossier, no list of attendees at that luncheon honoring JFK the week before Dallas—though Li had pointed out that the hosts of that event, Werner von Braun and another man named Kurt Debus, were both ex-Nazis. They'd been brought over to America via Operation Paperclip, which was another top-secret CIA program run by the same people behind Operation Mongoose, that secret CIA plot to use organized crime—i.e., the Mafia—to assassinate Castro. A lot of connections there, but no actual proof of anything. So … strike one.

After Canaveral, he'd headed to Miami. Organized crime there was mostly Russian now, but he'd found a few old-timers who

CHAPTER 16

remembered Santo Trafficante. Remembered Havana as the playground of the rich and famous, back before Castro took over. Not the mob guys themselves, but he talked to their wives. Grandmas now, who couldn't speak Fidel's name without spitting out a curse. They were still pissed about it. More running around in circles. A lot of smoke, but no fire. Strike two.

And now Sally Bartolo. Another dead end.

What next?

Cuba? Go talk to his old friend the General? That man had been around forever—been with the Cuban secret police since the day Castro took over. He knew where the bodies were buried. Heck, he'd probably buried most of them himself. Pushing ninety years old now, but the General probably had more information about Mongoose at his fingertips than the CIA had in all its files. And speaking of the CIA …

He wondered how Espy was doing.

17

"Mongoose." Perrin Talbot, the CIA's new deputy director of document retrieval and reconstruction, whatever that meant, shook his head. "I don't know where they got these names. I suppose they thought they were being clever."

"I suppose," Espy said. They were in a cafeteria on the CIA campus in Langley, Virginia. Building 10, Talbot had called it when he gave her directions, though the number on the outside was 23. The midmorning sun blazed through floor-to-ceiling windows—bulletproof glass, Espy was sure. Talbot had chosen a table along the far wall, as far away from that light as possible. He had been seated when Espy arrived. They were hidden from view of most of the room—anyone outside the building looking in, anyone passing by in the halls. The choice wasn't accidental.

Espy was persona non grata to virtually everyone in the agency because of CASHIER. Which was why she had grasped at the hand of friendship Talbot had extended—albeit weakly, tentatively—at the wake at Garrett's townhouse. She'd come upstairs looking for Alice, and there he was, standing in the hall outside Garrett's office, staring up at the photos there, lost in thought. He turned and saw her.

"Esperanza Harper. It's been a long time."

"Mr. Secretary." The honorific came out of her mouth reflexively. Talbot had been an undersecretary at the Department of Defense during the CASHIER hearings. "It has indeed. Good to see you again."

"Mr. Secretary. That was a long time ago. I'm with the agency

CHAPTER 17

now. Document retrieval and reconstruction. A lot of paper shuffling." He turned to her and smiled.

Paper shuffling. That suited the man to a T. Never a physically impressive man, Talbot had put on more than a few pounds over the years. He now looked like nothing so much as a glorified librarian.

"And you're at the Department of Justice still, I understand?"

"That's right."

"Garrett mentioned you more than once, you know. Told me that we had all judged you a bit harshly. That it was time to make a fresh start. A good man, Garrett."

Espy had nodded. "One of the best."

A fresh start. Here they were.

"At any rate, your Mr. Licari," Talbot said. "I was able to successfully cross-reference his name to the operation."

Espy's pulse quickened. "He was involved with Mongoose?"

"Yes. Unfortunately…" he sipped at his coffee, "that's as far as I can go."

She understood instantly. Fresh start or not. "This is about CASHIER, isn't it?" she asked, her lips tightening.

"CASHIER?" Talbot's eyes widened. "Ms. Harper, why would I have agreed to talk to you if I still held a grudge about CASHIER? No, this has nothing to do with that. The problem here is, the specific files Mr. Licari is named in have been reclassified. Rather recently, in fact."

"How recently?" she asked.

"Hard to say, exactly. At some point over the last few months, is my guess. They now require a special clearance to access."

"And you don't have the necessary clearance, I take it?"

"Oh I have it. But I can't use it without raising a red flag or two. Which I'm reluctant to do. Not without knowing why I'm looking for information on a classified program more than half a century old."

Ah. Talbot wanted to know what she was after, what sort of trouble he might be stirring up, who he might be crossing if he helped her out. Which meant that, in a way, this was about CASHIER. Office politics, the agency sort.

What was a bit of a surprise—the fact that Talbot was playing those games. Maybe the man wasn't quite the librarian he seemed.

Correction: No "maybe" about it. Talbot was CIA. A lifelong spook. Of course there was more to him than met the eye.

"If I had to guess—given your presence here, I'd say this Licari business is related to a Department of Justice investigation. A cold case of some type. Would I be correct in that assumption?" he continued.

Espy hesitated. She thought about making up a story—easy enough to do. Concoct the sort of cold case he'd mentioned. Except her gut was telling her the less said the better here. Share the truth with Talbot as best she could. Given her history with the agency, this relationship was worth nurturing.

"I'm sorry, sir. I wish I could share more, but..." She spread her hands in a gesture of apparent futility.

"I'm asking because I took the liberty of digging deeper into Mr. Licari's background. I found that he was the target of a RICO investigation some years back. I wonder if that is what prompted your interest here. If you're aware of that case."

She most certainly was. She'd turned that investigative work over to Frederickson, but Talbot had just confirmed Licari's connection to Mongoose. She needed to take a much closer look at those files herself.

"I obviously can't confirm or deny that supposition, but that may be a fruitful avenue of investigation," she said. "Thank you

CHAPTER 17

for suggesting it."

Talbot shook his head. "Ms. Harper, I'm not sure you should be thanking me. What you're saying leads me to believe that this investigation of yours, this business with Mongoose, and Tony Licari ... there are forces within this building acting against you. Acting to make sure you don't succeed. In which case, you should be careful here." He held her gaze. "Very careful indeed."

Espy flashed back to the dossier. To Nan's note, to the words Talbot had just unconsciously echoed.

You be careful too. Too many people weren't.

"Understood," she said. "And appreciated."

"Of course." He looked around the cafeteria to see who, if anyone, saw the two of them together talking. CASHIER again. Old grudges dying hard.

She stood. "I'll see myself out."

"Yes." Talbot nodded. "I think that would be best."

18

"Good morning. Your mom just called." Espy had barely had a chance to set down her briefcase when her assistant, Greg, appeared at her office door.

"Thanks," she said. "I'll get back to her."

"No, I mean she called me. On my cell. Asked me to let her know the second you were back." Greg smiled. "Turned on the charm, she did."

Espy rolled her eyes. "On your cell? I'm sorry."

"No." He smiled again. "No worries. Just giving you a heads-up."

Espy smiled back—and then that smile changed to a frown. Greg was her admin. Junior associate. Low man on the totem pole in her office. He was twenty-six years old. Six three, male-model handsome.

How did her mom have his cell number?

She opened her mouth to ask, then shut it, deciding some questions were better left unanswered.

"Got it," she said instead. "I'll give her a ring." Later, she would give her a ring. Right now...

She closed her office door. Swiveled in her chair. Logged on, brought up the relevant files. The RICO case against Tony Licari. The Feds had caught him with his fingers in a whole bunch of different pies. Local sports books. Numbers rackets. "Protection" services for small businesses. Pretty standard stuff.

She'd skimmed the material before. She dug deeper now. Read the government's case, the evidence they'd assembled, the witnesses they'd planned to call. It was a long list; it included a half

CHAPTER 18

dozen of those small-business owners Licari had extorted protection money from, the cops who'd caught those cases, a Hallandale Beach lawyer, a sports promoter, Sally Bartolo, and Jimmy Allen. The boxer. *BOXER IS DEAD.*

Espy frowned. Tapped a finger on the keypad in front of her.

The mob had been part of what happened at Dallas. Santo Trafficante, Johnny Roselli, Sam Giancana—all of them were made men, Cosa Nostra higher-ups. Most likely members of the Committee, that group of organized crime leaders who had come together to run their businesses in a more efficient manner. Tony Licari wasn't one of them, was a few rungs down the ladder, but still … he was connected.

Jimmy Allen wasn't. And yet, he was on that map. One of the four dead men Nan had drawn JFK Jr.'s attention to. Three of those four had been scheduled to appear in front of Congress in regard to the assassination: Johnny Roselli, George de Mohrenschildt (Lee Harvey Oswald's friend), and Carlos Prio Socarrás, one-time president of Cuba. All of them had died violently before they could testify: Roselli murdered, de Mohrenschildt and Prio by suicide.

And then there was Jimmy Allen. What made him so special? What was his connection to the assassination? Why had Nan drawn JFK Jr.'s attention to him?

Espy had bookmarked information on Allen earlier; she went back to those search results now. Born March 12, 1968, in Bayonne, New Jersey. Parents split up when he was six years old; Mom took little Jimmy to Tampa to live with her older sister, who had two kids of her own. Issues arose. Young Jimmy got kicked out of the house. Kicked out of high school. Spent some time in juvie lockup. The boy was a fighter. Quick to anger, quick with his fists. Luckily for him, he found a way to put that anger to use. Boxing.

Allen had won the Golden Gloves as a seventeen-year-old.

Turned pro, went from bantamweight to welterweight, then scored the biggest upset of his career over then number-three welterweight contender Wilfredo Benitez.

Things went downhill from there.

Barely a year later, Allen jumped out that Fountainbleau window.

The Fountainbleau. The same place Johnny Roselli had first mentioned Operation Mongoose to his mafia buddies. The hotel where he'd tried to recruit Santo Trafficante to kill Castro. *Seven Days to Dallas.*

It was all in the dossier—page after page of Trafficante's testimony before Congress. And now Talbot had confirmed at least some of the obvious conclusions to be drawn from all that material. Tony Licari had been involved in Mongoose. Working with the CIA. The question before her now ... had Jimmy Allen been involved too? Had he known something—stumbled across some secret related to the events of November 22, 1963? Allen's death had been labeled suicide as well, but there was plenty of innuendo suggesting he'd run afoul of the mob. Or other nefarious forces.

Espy rubbed her eyes. She just didn't have enough information to draw any conclusions.

She was about to move on when her gaze fell on a picture of Allen, dressed up for a night out on the town. The night after the Mugabi fight. He looked flush, fantastic, his wavy dark hair pushed up in a big pompadour. On his arm was a stunning young woman identified as Ms. Cecilia Carmelita Brody, C.C. for short. Allen's fiancée, the actress. Referred to in that article from the dossier, on Allen's suicide.

The name jumped out at Espy for some reason. It took her a second to remember why: She'd just seen C.C.'s name on the witness list from Tony Licari's RICO trial.

CHAPTER 18

She switched back to the DOJ database. Saw that C.C. had backed out of testifying two days after Allen walked out that window. Now that was interesting. What had the DOJ wanted to ask C.C.? What had made the woman change her mind about testifying? And would she be willing talk to now—if she was still around?

Didn't take long for her to track C.C. down. She was out in Las Vegas. First thing Espy found was a picture from the *Clark County Courier*—a slightly older C.C. dressed in a glamorous ball gown, dancing in the arms of a man in a tuxedo. It took a second, but then she recognized him.

Jerry Lewis.

The picture came from a benefit dinner for Jerry's Kids, kids with muscular dystrophy. She found a half-dozen other photos just like that one. Pictures of C.C. at various charity functions, political fundraisers, parties. High society circles. High-dollar, at least.

That was interesting. Espy wondered how she'd gotten entrée to that circuit. How she'd ended up in Vegas at all. She kept digging. Found C.C.'s voter registration. She lived at 110 Colosseum Drive in an unincorporated town called Mariella Springs. North of Vegas proper, but still part of Clark County. The Clark County Assessor's website gave her the parcel number, which gave her the total taxable value of the land and improvements: $10.4 million.

Espy almost fell out of her chair.

Where on earth had C.C. Brody gotten $10.4 million?

City records got her blueprints of the house. It was a sprawling single-story ranch with eighteen rooms, five bathrooms, 15,000 square feet of total living space. Satellite photos showed a 26.4-acre oasis of green smack dab in the middle of the desert. There was a swimming pool, a stable, an airplane hangar (which looked like it had been built right into the side of a mountain—now that couldn't have been cheap), and a runway that ran to the southern edge of the property.

Sitting on that runway was a Gulfstream G700. A $50 million private jet. Absolutely crazy. What was C.C. Brody doing with a $50 million airplane?

Espy zoomed in on the plane's fuselage—the jet's tail number. N1482.

The FAA maintained a public database that let you plug in a plane's tail number and get that plane's country of registration and the name of its owner. Espy already knew that the *N* prefix meant the plane was registered in the US, but the database revealed the owner: a company called Amalgamated Industrial Partners.

And that right there was a huge red flag.

The name practically screamed "shell company," which indeed turned out to be the case. A shell company registered in (no surprise here either) Delaware, a state with some very forgiving laws regarding corporate confidentiality. For most people, Amalgamated would have been a dead end.

But for Espy? Amalgamated was a breadcrumb.

It took her the better part of an hour to pick up the trail, but eventually she found that Amalgamated was a wholly owned subsidiary of Summit Technologies. Summit was also privately held and registered on Guernsey, one of the Channel Islands, a tax haven halfway around the world. She spent another hour tracing Summit's ownership, through holding companies and limited liability corporations, from Delaware to Alaska and back again.

Finally, she found herself looking at a firm called the Desert View Real Estate Investment Trust, a US-based firm headquartered in the heart of the Las Vegas strip, just down the road from C.C. Brody's property.

Summit was leasing the plane to them. But why were they

CHAPTER 18

keeping it there? What was her connection to the company? And why did Desert View need a private jet? Real estate investment trusts—REITs—made their money buying and selling, developing and investing in real estate. Why did they need a jet to do that? Curiouser and curiouser. She dug a little deeper ... and raised an eyebrow.

Desert View was a publicly traded firm.

That was odd. Usually, people who set up shell companies to hide ownership wanted to keep things private.

But there were, of course, advantages to going public.

Chief among them was what Wall Street insiders called leverage—the multiple on initial public offerings of a company's stock. That was how millionaires and billionaires were made.

But issuing stock on one of the exchanges—in this case, the NASDAQ—came with some strict legal requirements, one of them being public access to company records. Which meant that all Espy had to do was type the company's name into a search engine, and she was staring at Desert View's prospectus, a document the firm was required to file with the SEC before offering its stock to the public. That prospectus began with a description of the firm and its activities.

> In only six years, the Desert View Real Estate Investment Trust (NASDAQ: DVrT) has proven itself a leader in the ownership, operation, and redevelopment of high-value real estate in the rapidly growing Southwest. Time and time again, the company has turned worthless desert land into high-yield properties. Its holdings encompass close to 6 million square feet of retail and over 15.2 million square feet of high-end residential space, located primarily in the Greater Las Vegas area. The company is a current partner in the next-generation community of Aqua

Roma, a premiere residential development which will raise the firm's profile not just in the Las Vegas Area but nationally and internationally. Under the leadership of President and CEO Frank Ferrone Jr....

Espy stopped reading.

Frank Ferrone Jr.

She knew that name. Who didn't? His face was everywhere these days. Ferrone was the newest real-estate king of Las Vegas, a wheeler-dealer who hobnobbed with celebrities, movie stars, and politicians and made sure the world knew about it. The next generation's Steve Wynn, Howard Hughes, Sheldon Adelson.

But more to the point here: Ferrone was a man with long-rumored ties to organized crime.

Espy cracked her knuckles, leaned back in her chair, and smiled.

These last ten days, they'd all been chasing ghosts. Running down clues from sixty-year-old pieces of paper, searching for ex-Nazis and retired CIA agents, mobsters and dead politicians, anyone who might have any idea as to what Trafficante, Roselli, von Braun, Castro, or Dulles had been thinking back in 1963. People who were dead and gone and, by and large, forgotten.

Not anymore. Now they had a flesh and blood target.

Now they had Frank Ferrone.

Now the hunt was on.

19

Bill and Ted's Excellent Trailer Park.

It was a different Bill and Ted on the sign, of course, not the guys from the movies but an older looking Bill and Ted. The trailer park's owners, Cockerell guessed. They could have passed for Ben and Jerry, the ice cream makers, but the name they'd chosen told him what kind of place he was about to enter, and something about the guy he was coming to see.

As if their phone call two days ago hadn't told him enough.

Cockerell had been at a Forth Worth retirement home, speaking to a woman who'd been part of the Russian émigré community in Dallas back in the early 1960s, who'd known not only Lee Harvey Oswald and his wife Marina but George de Mohrenschildt as well, whom she kept calling Georgie. "A very handsome man. Very well dressed. Well spoken. And handsome." She giggled. "Did I mention that?"

Cockerell was pulling out of the parking lot when his phone rang.

"Mr. Bell?"

He'd heard that voice and instantly snapped to attention: The caller was using a voice changer.

"Yes," Cockerell said. Andre Bell was the alias he'd been using the last couple weeks. "Who is this?"

"This is Harvey Linbeck."

Who? he'd almost said, and then stopped. Because in addition to his travels in the real world, Cockerell had been spending countless hours on the internet, scouring bulletin boards, websites, and forums devoted to JFK's assassination. Reading comments, digging through archived posts, asking questions ... and the name Harvey Linbeck had been everywhere he looked.

"Ah," he said. "The famous Harvey Linbeck. And to what do I owe the honor?"

"You're looking at the wrong George."

"What?"

"Your posts. Online. You wanted information on George de Mohrenschildt. That's a dead end. A complete waste of your time."

"Is that so?" Cockerell snapped back reflexively. Though really, he would characterize the last ten days in exactly the same fashion: a complete waste of time.

"The missing link"—that was what Nan had written on one of the Post-it notes that had been part of the dossier. A Post-it note stuck to a folder labeled *de Mohrenschildt*, a folder that had contained well over two dozen documents related to the man. Copies of de Mohrenschildt's testimony before the Warren Commission; copies of files the CIA had assembled on him; interviews with de Mohrenschildt's neighbors and friends. There was a lot there, a lot about Lee Harvey Oswald and the relationship the two men had, but ... missing link?

Cockerell couldn't see it. Yes, de Mohrenschildt had helped Oswald get his job at the Texas Book Depository; yes, he'd been a member of the Dallas Petroleum Club; yes, he had done business in Cuba, was rumored to even be a CIA asset, and yes, he'd been friendly with the Bouvier family in New York and even babysat young Jackie and her sister at the family apartment. But still...

"Yes that's so," Linbeck continued. "If you want the truth."

"The truth is all that I want," he'd shot back. "And I'm willing to pay for it."

"That's what you get for posting your phone number online,"

CHAPTER 19

Espy had said when Cockerell phoned in.

"Not my phone number. A burner Li set me up with."

"Same difference. You really think this Linbeck guy knows something?"

"Maybe. He said I had the wrong George."

"So?"

"So that means he has a different one in mind. Which got me wondering … maybe the George he's talking about isn't a person. Maybe it's the magazine."

Harper was silent a second.

"You know … you might have something there," she said.

"Thank you. Not only that—the guy's been around forever. So maybe he and Nan knew each other. Maybe she even went to him as a source. Maybe—"

"Sold," she said. "Run it down. Keep me posted."

"Will do," he'd said, hanging up.

And now here he was.

Bill and Ted's Excellent Trailer Park, a few hours north of DC, on the outskirts of Kennett Square, Pennsylvania. The self-proclaimed "mushroom capital of the world," according to the welcome sign. Linbeck's address was on a cul-de-sac at the far end of the park. The lot itself was not well tended, nor the RV parked on it. There was a light coming from behind a shade over the trailer's main window. One shutter was missing; the other hung precariously from a single nail.

Cockerell knocked on the door. A second later, a beam of light shone out of the darkness—the peephole sliding back.

"Who is it?" The man, strangely enough, was using a voice changer again.

"Andre Bell."

"And how can I help you, Mr. Bell?"

"What do you mean?"

"I mean what is it you want."

"What do I want?" Cockerell was confused. "What we talked about. You said I was looking at the wrong George. I want to know—"

"The truth?" Linbeck snapped.

"Yes. That's right."

"Then why have you started off our relationship with a lie?"

"I have no idea what you're talking about."

"Don't you? Detective?"

Standing there, on the top step of the shabby little stairway, he did a double-take. "What?"

"Detective Michael Cockerell. DC Metro Police. Seven years on the squad, the last three detective first class. I'm puzzled, detective. You want to tell me why the Metro Police are interested in the Kennedy assassination? You fronting for the FBI? Trying to put me in jail?"

"No. Not at all."

"Then what?"

"It's a long story."

"Give me the shorthand version."

"I'm on leave from the force. I'm working this privately."

There was silence for a few seconds.

"I'm not sure that's the exact truth, either. But it'll do for now."

He heard the sound of a bolt being drawn back. The door swung open, and Cockerell got his first look at Harvey Linbeck. And his second surprise in as many minutes.

Harvey Linbeck was a woman.

"Besides," she said, the voice changer off. "I guess I'm a fine one to talk about truth and all that."

CHAPTER 19

❖ ❖ ❖ ❖ ❖

"Lynn Beck," she said, bringing over a bottle of scotch and two shot glasses to the little counter that separated the kitchen from the main living area. Beck was just north of five feet tall, with short gray hair. Looked to be in her late seventies, early eighties—on the edge of infirm, but not quite there yet.

"Harvey was my husband. He died in 1968. Right after RFK got shot. I left DC after that, got a job over at West Chester, so I figured I'd better use an alias for this work." She cackled and poured them each a full glass. No ice. "Here's to him. Harvey Linbeck."

They clinked glasses; Cockerell took a sip. The label said Johnny Walker Blue, but it tasted a little more bottom shelf than that. The living room floor was fake wood; the kitchen was linoleum. Both were clean but well-worn, like the rest of the place. There wasn't much furniture, but everywhere he looked there were books. Stacks of them in neat little piles—paperback, hardcover, oversize, new, worn, sometimes more than one copy of each. Magazines, too, newspapers and newspaper clippings, covering every square inch of flat space, pictures covering every square inch of open wall. JFK was everywhere. So were Jackie, Oswald, Ruby, and Castro, and he'd even spotted a man who looked like handsome Johnny Roselli in one picture.

Conspiracy theory land, Cockerell thought. No longer was he knee-deep in the weeds. Right here, right now—he was touring the capital city.

He took a seat at the counter. "How'd you find out who I was?"

"I been at this a long time, sonny. Got a lot of resources. Met a lot of people." She smiled. "I'm used to being careful."

"That doesn't really answer the question."

Beck pulled a little stool of her own up to the counter and sat.

"Like I'm going to tell you my sources," she scoffed. "So, if you're not working for the cops, who are you working for here?"

"Not at liberty to say, sorry."

"Not one of those tech guys, I hope." She took a sip of her drink. "Twenty-five-year-old billionaires high on some crusade or another—raise the Titanic, find the Holy Grail, solve the Kennedy assassination." She shook her head. "I hate those guys. Think they run the world because they had a single good idea."

"No. It's not one of those tech guys. But if you've got information, I do have money. And plenty of it."

"I like money. But the thing is, I need to know where it's coming from."

Cockerell shook his head. "Really. I can't say. But we're the good guys, I can tell you that much."

"And I should believe that why?"

"Hey. I'm a cop, remember?"

She shook her head. "See, that's the problem right there. I'm a product of the sixties, sonny. I got an innate distrust of authority."

"Well, I'm not a huge fan of it myself."

"Why?"

None of your business why, he almost said, but held his tongue. "Not relevant."

"Of course it's relevant," she said. "You want me trust you, it's relevant."

He glared. "Afghanistan."

"Ah." She nodded. "I get that. A real shit show. Worse than Vietnam, you want my opinion. At least back then, we knew what was going on. Now it's all a goddamn whitewash, all the time. You were there?"

"Almost," Cockerell said.

She looked him in the eye. "You had friends over there."

CHAPTER 19

"Family."

"I'm sorry to hear it. People in charge, they should've known better. History." Her gaze softened. "Nobody pays attention to it anymore."

They were both silent a few seconds.

"So." Cockerell cleared his throat. "The wrong George. What's that mean?"

"Not so fast, not so fast." Beck shook her head. "Let's suppose for a second I tell you what I know. What are you and these mystery people you're working for going to do with it?"

"Hold it up to the light of day."

"You'll publish it? Put it up online?"

"Maybe."

"That won't do shit anymore," the woman snapped. "These days, nobody knows what to believe. The goddamn whitewash, like I said."

"Fair point," Cockerell replied. "All I can tell you for sure is that if you have information, we'll follow it. Wherever it leads."

"Doing that could get you killed."

"I'm not scared."

"You ought to be." Beck pointed a finger. "You got to be careful here, sonny. A lot more careful than you've been, throwing around all those questions online. You don't know who's listening."

Cockerell's first instinct was to laugh. Because all this JFK stuff, it was all long, long in the past, like Beck said. What, some old man was going to jump out at him and beat him to death with a walker? Not likely. Then again…

It wasn't just JFK who had been killed. So had Garrett Crandall. And if these people weren't afraid to go after a United States senator, they'd certainly have no qualms about killing him.

"I take your point," he said. "But do me a favor."

"What?"

"Stop calling me sonny."

Beck cackled again. "Don't take it personally. That's what I call everyone under the age of fifty. One of the privileges of old age."

"Fine. Just tell me what you've got. I'll make it worth your while."

"Hey. This isn't just about money. This is about the truth. About secrets that people tried to bury a long time ago. Here. Let me show you something." Beck walked over to the bookshelf and came back carrying a thick hardcover. Held it out so he could see the front.

The Death of A President, November 1963. Plain white lettering on the front, and the author's name in smaller type underneath:

William Manchester.

"Manchester," Cockerell said.

The dossier, he thought. *Screen Image* magazine. The cover, with Jackie and Aristotle Onassis. Which had included a picture of Jackie Kennedy. And a reference to something called the Manchester Tapes. Which turned out to be recordings of a one-on-one interview that Jackie had done with a writer named William Manchester, the year after JFK's assassination.

Recordings Jackie had immediately sued to keep secret.

"So you know who he was? Manchester?" Beck asked.

Cockerell nodded. "I do. Is this about the tapes?"

Her eyes narrowed. "What makes you think that?"

Something I can't tell you about, he thought.

"Just a hunch," he said.

"Good hunch. So what do you know about him?"

"What is this, a test?"

"Just want to make sure you have the facts right."

"Enlighten me."

164

CHAPTER 19

"Okay, smart guy. Manchester was a writer. JFK's friend. This—" Beck held the book up again—"was intended to be the official story of the assassination. The authorized history. The story Jackie Kennedy wanted told. And back in that day, what Jackie Kennedy wanted, Jackie Kennedy got. Manchester was JFK's friend. She trusted him not to sensationalize. So he got access to everyone and their brother who the President had crossed paths with before Dallas. And Jackie herself agreed to talk to him for the book. To share her memories of that day. Which was the only time she did that. Ever, in her whole life. She sat with Manchester for two tape-recorded conversations, what we now know as—"

"The Manchester Tapes."

"That's exactly right," Beck replied. "Seven hours of conversations. Except after they talked—after Manchester showed her what he'd written based on those conversations—Jackie changed her mind. Decided there were things she didn't want made public. Manchester refused to change some of it, so … she sued him."

Why she and RFK buried the tapes.

"She and Bobby," Cockerell added.

"That's right. Jackie and JFK's little brother. The senator from New York then. He was involved too. Eventually, they all came to an agreement. Manchester took out some things, changed a few others, and this—" she held up the book again—"got published. But the tapes—the original recordings—every record of what Jackie told him that day—that all got locked away. Sealed up tight, out of public view. For a hundred years." Beck smiled. "A hundred freaking years. Till 2067. And why do you think that was?"

"That's a good question." Cockerell had, in fact, raised an eyebrow when he'd read that. They all had. A hundred years? Most people were pretty sure all that was on those tapes was gossip—tabloid magazine material. Things that Jackie, high society born and bred, had found distasteful.

Although … something about that didn't sit right with him. If it was just gossip … why seal it away for 100 years? That seemed like overkill.

"Now the question I keep asking is, Why? What kind of secret was so important that it needed to stay locked up for so long?"

"That's a good question." His turn to pick up his glass and take a sip. He shuddered as he swallowed.

Definitely not top shelf stuff.

"But I don't know if 'important' is the word I'd attach to that secret," he said. "I might use the word 'dangerous.'"

The secret your senator was killed to protect.

Beck nodded. "Maybe dangerous is a better word. Because I'll tell you one thing for certain." Her expression tightened. Turned grim. "Jackie was scared. That's why she married Onassis. Because that ugly little Greek guy had the one thing she wanted—needed—more than anything else."

"Money."

"That's right. Money. And the security it could buy. The safety. Not just for her, but for her kids."

Cockerell flashed on the headline from the cover of that *Screen Image* magazine. A headline written underneath a portrait of a pensive, worried-looking Jackie Onassis nee Kennedy. A headline that read

If They Are Killing Kennedys, My Kids Are Next

"So … there's something besides gossip on those tapes, you're saying."

"Of course there's something besides gossip on them." Beck refilled her glass and took a long, slow sip of her drink. "Of course there is. I know that for a fact."

CHAPTER 19

"How?"

She looked him in the eye and smiled.

He felt a little tingle at the base of his spine.

"Beck." He leaned forward. "Are you saying you've heard them? The Manchester tapes? You know what's on them?"

"Did I say that? I didn't say that."

"Then what?"

"Let's just say I've been sitting on a secret of my own the last fifty years, sonny." Ice cubes rattled against the side of her glass as she set it down. "One that I am now prepared to share."

"Once I pay you, I'm guessing."

"Like I said, I do like money. But this isn't just about money. Hell no." Her eyes blazed. "This is about what got murdered that day in Dallas. This is about finding the truth, sonny. And that's going to require a team effort. You and me … working together."

"I don't get it," Cockerell said.

Beck smiled again. "I know. But you will."

20

"And you believe her?" Espy asked.

"She for sure thinks she has something important," Cockerell said. "Whether or not that's true, I won't know until tomorrow."

"It's in her safe deposit box, you said?"

"Yeah."

"And you have no clue what this something is?"

Frederickson snorted. "Jeez, I don't know. Maybe it's Tony Licari's signed confession."

"The wrong George." Espy settled back in her chair. They were down in Woodhull, gathered around the conference room table. "She didn't say anything about that. If she was talking about the magazine, or…"

"She danced around that. And I didn't want to force it," Cockerell said. "She wants to talk. She's going to talk."

"About what's on the tapes?" Frederickson asked. "I thought it was all just gossip on there. Jackie talking smack about LBJ."

"That's the rumor." Espy shrugged. "Nobody knows for sure. Nobody's heard them since 1967."

Li cleared her throat. "That's not exactly true."

"What do you mean?" Cockerell asked.

"It seems quite possible Caroline heard them."

"Come again?" Frederickson asked.

"Caroline Kennedy may have heard the tapes. JFK's daughter. In the early 1990s. Congress set up a special committee—"

"Another one?" Frederickson rolled his eyes. "After the Warren Commission, and the House Assassination committee?"

CHAPTER 20

Li nodded. "Yes. They wished to settle the conspiracy issue once and for all. They asked to break the legal seal on the tapes. Jackie was dead; the decision was Caroline's. She refused them. She said there was nothing of interest on the tapes."

"Caroline. And not JFK Jr." Frederickson frowned. "Wasn't he still around then?"

"He was. But Jackie had given Caroline authority. Not him."

"That must've burned," Frederickson said.

"For sure. A little sibling rivalry going on there," Doug suggested.

"When exactly was this?" Espy asked.

"August of 1998," Li said.

"Then maybe she did let him listen. The timing works."

"What do you mean?" Frederickson asked.

"I mean," Espy said, leaning forward, "the tapes could have been the springboard for everything. JFK Jr. hears his mom and Manchester talking and realizes—"

"Seven Days To Dallas. Sonofabitch." Frederickson slapped the table. "The tapes are what started this whole thing."

"That is a very big leap," Li said.

"Agreed." Espy nodded, because Li was right. And yet…

She felt something, in her gut. The same something she'd felt on seeing Frank Ferrone's name attached to Desert View.

For her, the pieces were falling into place.

"Hey, like I said, I don't know exactly what Beck's going to show me," Cockerell added. "All she would say for sure—"

"Her safe deposit box. Right. Okay. You stay on that." Espy nodded. "In the meantime, let me show you what I found. Why I asked you all to come here."

She pulled up a photo on the big viewscreen—the picture she'd found of C.C. Brody and Jerry Lewis dancing cheek to cheek. A picture she had since studied in a little more detail.

"C.C. Brody," Frederickson said. "And Jerry Lewis, right?"

"Right."

"Who is Jerry Lewis?" Li asked.

"Not important. Who is important, is this guy," Espy said, pointing to a man seated at the table behind the dancers. A sharp-featured, silver-haired man staring daggers at Lewis.

"The old guy?" Frederickson asked. "Who's he?"

"That," Espy said, "is Frank Ferrone."

"No. That's not Frank Ferrone," Doug put in. "I've met Frank Ferrone, and—"

"You're thinking of the son, Frank Jr. This is Frank Sr. And the reason he's looking at Jerry Lewis like that, Frank Sr. and C.C. Brody lived together for the last twenty years of Ferrone's life."

She explained then how she'd tracked C.C. Brody to Vegas and ferreted out the jet's ownership, which had led her to the Desert View Real Estate Corporation and Frank Ferrone.

Cockerell frowned. "Junior—he's the casino guy, right? Runs the Peacock?"

"Right. But he's got his fingers in a lot of different pies," Espy said.

"What he is, is a mob guy," Frederickson put in.

"Rumored but never proven," Espy said.

"Oh come on," Frederickson said. "Seriously?"

"Listen," Espy said. "All we know for sure, back in the fifties, his dad was sent to Vegas by the mob guys out in Chicago. The Outfit."

"You're talking Roselli. Giancana," Frederickson said. "Our friends from the dossier."

Espy nodded. "Them among others. Ferrone Sr. was good with numbers. He was so good at it that a few years on, it wasn't just Chicago he was looking out for. It was all the families. And then, a

CHAPTER 20

dozen or so years ago, he stepped down, and"—Espy waved a hand across the touchpad in front of her, and the image on the main screen changed—"Frank Jr. took over." The new image showed two men side by side in a parking lot under swaying palm trees, a billboard visible behind them. Ferrone Sr.—white-haired, bent over from age. Ferrone Jr.—tall, dark, and movie-star handsome. To Espy's eye, he resembled the actor Leonardo DiCaprio.

"You sure those two are related? They don't look much alike," Frederickson asked.

"Junior favors Mom in the looks department," Espy said. "She was a Vegas showgirl. Died when Frank Jr. was just a kid. He got sent east to boarding school when he was twelve, didn't come home till he got his MBA at Wharton."

"Wharton. Very impressive," Li said.

"After which he took over for daddy. Got it. But." Frederickson turned to Espy. "What does this have to do with that real estate company you were talking about? Desert View?"

"Not a real estate company, an REIT—a company that manages and invests in real estate. And I don't know what the connection is … yet." Her eyes went around the table. "We need to put Frank Jr. under the microscope, take a close look at everything he's involved with. See where it leads us."

"I crossed paths with him a few years ago," Doug said. "He was dabbling in the movie business. Trying to do some production work. I could find a way to circle back around."

"Do that." Espy nodded.

"I can make some calls too," Frederickson said. "See what the bureau has."

"I'll check Beck's safe deposit box tomorrow," Cockerell said, "see if there's anything in there on him."

Everyone turned and glared at him.

"Kidding," he said, putting his hands up.

Espy stood. "All right. Let's get to work."

❖ ❖ ❖ ❖ ❖

She got to it bright and early the next morning. Pulled up everything she could find on Ferrone. The man and his businesses. Details on the departmental investigations she'd heard about but hadn't really paid attention to.

The first had involved a company called Corelli and Sons Construction. A city building contract had initially gone to a competitor, then was reassigned to Corelli just before groundbreaking. Ferrone, an adviser to Corelli's board, was one party named in a lawsuit—a lawsuit dropped just as it was about to go to trial.

Shades of Tony Licari.

There was a money-laundering investigation involving a chain of check-cashing businesses in the greater Las Vegas area; more allegations of corruption with regard to the American Lime Products Corporation and a firm called Ives Brothers Refuse and Hauling. None of those cases really went anywhere, which is to say, none of them got anywhere near Ferrone. He was careful, clearly. He was also shielded, to a large extent, by the law. All those businesses were privately controlled.

But not Desert View. That was a public company. There, she could do a little prying. She started where she'd left off yesterday: Desert View's prospectus. *Time and time again, the company has turned worthless desert land into high-yield properties.* Reading through their catalog of developments, she saw that was indeed the case. Project after project successfully completed.

Next up, she found a listing of the company's board of directors. Chaired by Laura Sonores, wife of Victor Sonores, Nevada's

CHAPTER 20

senior senator. Espy had met Senator Sonores once before, at a party at Garrett's townhouse. The two of them had been colleagues for years. Garrett had introduced Sonores as an old friend. But they weren't exactly friends, Espy found out later. Garrett hadn't trusted Sonores one bit. He'd never told her why exactly. But now...

She was starting to understand. Sonores and Ferrone. The government and the mob.

Latest round of research. Cuba/CIA/Mob.

The Men Who Murdered My Father.

She moved on. Left the prospectus behind and used EDGAR—the electronic data gathering, analysis, and retrieval database the SEC maintained—to get a closer look at the company's overall financial picture: its assets, earnings, potential for future growth, and stock market price.

And there she found something interesting.

After three years of steady, often spectacular growth, Desert View had gone through a tough last three quarters. Its stock price had dropped precipitously, from a high of 86.25 per share to a low of 14.50 before rebounding at the beginning of the year. It was now hovering in the forties. But for anyone with a large stake in the company, that precipitous drop in price last year would have cost millions. Tens of millions. Maybe hundreds of millions, actually.

And those losses were the way in for her.

Because the DOJ represented the American people. And when those people—in this case, Desert View's stockholders—were injured by a company's actions, it was up to the department to investigate. To see what, if any, actions should be taken to make things right.

She waited till eleven a.m., Vegas being three hours behind them, and made the call. Made her way through a series of voice prompts till she finally got to Ferrone's mailbox. She left a brief, nonspecific message.

Not five minutes later, her phone buzzed. A 702 number. Las Vegas.

"Ms. Harper?" A woman's voice.

"Yes."

"This is Mr. Ferrone's office, returning your call."

"Ah. Thank you for getting back so quickly."

"Of course. Can you tell me the reason for your call please, Ms. Harper?"

Espy smiled to herself. Not so fast. "Who am I speaking with?"

"My name is Cheryl. I work with Mr. Ferrone."

She wasn't going to get into matters of any substance with someone's assistant. "Cheryl, I'll speak with Mr. Ferrone directly regarding the purpose of my call. Can you put him on, please?"

There was a pause.

"One moment."

It was more like two.

"Ms. Harper?"

"Yes?"

"Mr. Lish will call you."

"I see. And who is Mr. Lish?"

"Raymond Lish. He's the senior legal partner at Baker and White. They're based out of Delaware. He'll be our point of contact with you in regard to this matter. Our legal representative. You should expect a call from him shortly."

Legal representative. Interesting. Espy hadn't said word one about why she was calling. Why had they put a legal representative onto her already? "Cheryl, I would rather call Mr. Lish myself. There is a time element involved here." She decided to drop a little hint. "I'm looking at some recent fluctuations in the company's stock price, and the numbers I see here disturb me. I'd like to get

CHAPTER 20

this cleared up quickly, so if you could give me his number—"

"Mr. Lish is traveling right now. He will be back to you as soon as possible. Goodbye, Ms. Harper."

And with that, she hung up.

Espy looked at the receiver in her hand.

Normally, the DOJ calls, people put a little 'sir yes sir' into their voice. Not in this instance.

Espy smiled. She was onto something here. Baker and White. She'd never heard of the firm. She'd make some inquiries, then she'd call this Mr. Lish herself.

She ducked into a meeting. Ducked back out quick as she could.

"Hey, Mike just called," Greg told her as she returned. "Asked you to stop by his office when you had a minute."

Mike. Meaning her boss, Mike Pritchett.

"Thanks," she said. "I'll get to him."

"He's got a noon," Greg said. "But free again after lunch."

"Understood." She walked into her office. The message light on her phone was blinking.

"This is Raymond Lish, returning your call from earlier. Please call me back."

Espy smiled. She hadn't expected him to respond so quickly. She'd struck a nerve here. Good.

She woke her computer and a notification popped up—an email from Lish. Subject line: The Desert View REIT.

> Ms. Harper:
>
> I have been made aware of your recent inquiries regarding the Desert View Real Estate Investment Trust. You'll forgive me for speaking bluntly, but the company strongly feels, and I agree, that

fluctuations in stock price do not fall within your department's jurisdiction.

    Sincerely,

    Raymond Lish

Now that was interesting.

She'd barely hinted at why she was interested in the company's stock price, and already they were telling her to get lost. What was more, she realized, noting the names in the cc field—Mike Pritchett and two addresses with the sec.gov domain belonging to the Securities and Exchange Commission—Lish was making sure that her interest in the firm was known far and wide. And why would he want to do that?

The first person to discuss that question with was obviously Mike.

She reached for her keyboard to send a quick message, and her phone rang.

"Department of Justice. This is Harper."

"This is the SEC calling, Ms. Harper. Can you hold please?"

The SEC. That was fast.

"Ms. Harper. This is John Bamberger. I'm deputy counsel over here."

Bamberger. The name was familiar. A second later, she realized why: Leonard had told her about him, back when she'd first made the decision to move to DC. "An officious little prig," if she was remembering his words right. "Someone you'll want to avoid like the plague."

She checked Lish's email. Bamberger's name was there, all right.

"Mr. Bamberger. Sir." Espy put as much obsequiousness in her voice as she could stomach. "A pleasure to talk to you. I believe

CHAPTER 20

we have a mutual friend, Leonard—"

"Yes. Leonard. He mentioned your name to me." Bamberger was clearly not interested in social niceties. "Ms. Harper. It's come to my attention that your division is making inquiries in areas that normally fall under the SEC's jurisdiction."

"You're referring to Mr. Lish's email, I take it? To Desert View?"

"I am."

"My position sir, is that…"

A message from Mike popped up on her computer screen. *My noon cancelled. You back yet?*

"Ms. Harper?" Bamberger said. "Are you there?"

"I'm sorry, sir," Espy said. "Again, I'd like to say that while I respect the SEC's primacy in this area, our interest in Desert View—"

"Yes. That's the reason for my call," Bamberger interrupted. "What specifically triggered your sudden interest in the firm's stock?"

Specifically. Espy cleared her throat.

"It's a, uh, routine inquiry."

"Routine. So you pulled their name out of a hat?" Bamberger was trying to keep his tone light, but there was something a little sharper hidden underneath that. Officious little prig or not, she'd better be on her toes here, Espy realized.

"Of course not," she said. "I have an algorithm that flags certain trends for me."

"Ah. An algorithm." He stretched out the syllables—al-go-rith-m. Said the word like he'd never heard it before. "Interesting. And what is this algorithm supposed to detect?"

"We look for large-scale movements of capital. Money laundering. Illicit funds transfers and the like."

"And you think that's what's happening here?"

"It is a possibility, yes."

"Well." Bamberger paused a few seconds. "Let me make something clear Ms. Harper. You should know that as far as the SEC is concerned, those fluctuations in stock price represent nothing more than normal market variance. The preponderance of market analysts believe the REIT is in sound financial health."

"Well, that's good news."

"Yes. Yes it is. You know, these evaluations are critical to our economy. It's a very complicated procedure, Ms. Harper. There are of course multiple factors we take into account in these circumstances. Factors that you may not be entirely aware of."

It doesn't sound that complicated, she almost said, then bit her tongue.

Bamberger, though not in any way, shape, or form her superior, was a step or two above her in the bureaucratic pecking order. No sense in pissing him off. Yet.

"The point is," he continued, "this is a highly sensitive issue. We don't want the investment world operating on rumor here. We want them receiving hard news: facts that have been evaluated by our department."

"I understand," she said. "And I appreciate you filling me in."

"Of course, of course. Anything for a friend of Leonard's."

"Thank you."

"So, do you intend on pursuing this investigation further?" he asked.

Espy hesitated. "I have some queries out now. Once those get answered, we'll close the books on this."

"I see." He didn't sound happy about that. "Well, please do speak with me regarding those queries and, of course, any further moves your department might make. It's critical that the government speaks with one voice here, don't you agree?"

CHAPTER 20

Espy bit her tongue again. "Absolutely," she said, then hung up, much less emphatically than she would have liked to.

The nerve she'd struck here was a little more than sensitive, she realized.

It was dangerous.

There was a knock on her door. She looked up and saw Mike Pritchett, her boss, standing there. He stepped inside, shut the door, and sat down.

"Talk to me about Desert View," he said.

❖ ❖ ❖ ❖ ❖

Pritchett was six foot two. Blond, blue-eyed, and immaculately groomed. Central casting's idea of a successful lawyer. A gregarious Robert Redford.

But he wasn't smiling now.

"I have an informant," Espy lied, the best story she could come up with on short notice. Someone within the company, who had alerted her that all was not on the up-and-up at Desert View.

"A whistleblower."

"Exactly."

Mike nodded. "Okay. Just keep me in the loop."

"I will."

"Because I just got a call from Clay." Clay Moore, Pritchett's direct superior on the DOJ organizational chart. "He asked me what was going on. He told me that there is concern among the party leadership"—meaning the congressional reelection committee—"that we could be sending an unfortunate signal with this sort of investigation. Particularly with the midterm elections coming up."

"What sort of signal?" Espy asked.

He smiled and held up a finger. *Be careful.* Not even bothering to directly answer the question, because he knew that she knew full well what he was saying, what was being relayed to him by the powers-that-be, who had gotten him his job and wouldn't hesitate to take that job away if necessary.

You start messing with a big-time company's stock price, you start pissing off Wall Street. You start playing politics in the middle of a campaign—not a good idea. Not if you wanted to keep your job.

Mike left. Espy sat there a moment, thinking. There was another takeaway from her chat with him, the lecture from Bamberger, the email from Lish. That one phone call—her (relatively) innocent questions about Desert View's stock price—had triggered a war.

These are dangerous people.
You have no idea what they're capable of.

But one thing was clear. Ferrone didn't want her digging into Desert View. The question was, Why?

She couldn't answer that without more information. And Ferrone was going to fight any requests she made tooth and nail. Not give up a single piece of information willingly. He and Lish were going to throw more and more of what she'd seen this afternoon at her, until she threw up her hands in defeat. A frontal assault on Desert View was not going to work.

But she had another way in.

21

People had heard of Enron. Some kind of corporate scandal, most would tell you. People lost money. People went to jail. All true. But for Espy and others in her line of work, Enron's real importance came from the reforms enacted after the scandal, codified in a bipartisan piece of legislation known as the Sarbanes-Oxley Act, which imposed stringent new recordkeeping regulations on all publicly traded companies. Those companies were now required to submit a duplicate set of their records to a secure off-site location, watched over by a neutral third party and made available for examination by appropriate authorities at all times. Appropriate authorities like the Department of Justice. Appropriate authorities like her.

And that was her way in. A way she could get a look at the kind of information that Ferrone and Lish seemed intent on keeping from her. A side door she could walk through without alerting the SEC, or Bamberger, without alarming Ferrone, or generating any press coverage, or creating any rumors on Wall Street that might affect Desert View's stock price.

Only this door…

"A hotel?" she'd asked Greg when he told her. "The records are stored in a hotel?"

"Well, not exactly a hotel," he said. "You never heard of the Greenbrier?"

"No. You sure you have the right place?"

"Absolutely." He smiled. "There's only one Greenbrier."

The place was located in West Virginia, a few hours drive down from D.C. The second she arrived there, she saw what Greg had meant. The Greenbrier was one of those old-style resorts, like those hotels you saw in black-and-white postcards or history books, the ones that had been torn down long, long ago, or allowed to sink into decrepitude. The ones that got you thinking, what a shame, somebody should have taken care of that place.

In the Greenbrier's case, though, somebody had.

She'd seen bigger buildings before. Heck, she saw bigger buildings every day in DC, but she couldn't remember ever seeing one that was quite so ... well, clean. So dazzlingly, sparklingly white. Which contrasted with the riot of colors from the flowers in front of it, an array of immaculately maintained flower beds and green, green grass.

Espy was so distracted by those flowers she almost walked right into the man in front of her. "Excuse me."

The man smiled. "No worries. It happens. People get to looking at the scenery, kinda forget where they are." He was a uniformed valet—fifties, brass nameplate on his shirt identified him as Earl. "Welcome to the Greenbrier. You checking in with us this afternoon?"

"Afraid not," she said. "I'm here on business. Supposed to see a Ms. Pickering?"

"Donna Pickering." Earl nodded. "Her office is right inside. Bottom of the staircase."

"Thank you," Espy said.

"You're welcome. Keys'll be at the valet desk. And if you get done in the next half hour or so, we serve tea at four."

"Tea." Espy smiled in spite of herself. "Really?"

"Oh yeah. Tea, pastries ... they do it up nice. Good-looking batch of strawberries just came in, too. Had a few of them for breakfast." Earl leaned closer. "Ginny in the kitchen made a strawberry rhubarb pie, too. I had a little taste before."

CHAPTER 21

"Sounds wonderful," Espy said.

"It is." Earl smiled back at her. "Get Donna to give you a pass for the tea when you're done. Be worth your while."

"I'll do just that," Espy replied. Doubtful she'd be done by four, but you never knew.

Inside the hotel, the white gave way to color. Another explosion of it. Furniture, drapes, wallpaper. *Garish* was her first thought, but almost immediately she corrected herself, because it wasn't really that at all. *Loud* was the second word that came to mind, which it certainly was, but all the colors seemed to go together. Her sense of style, though, as her mother never tired of pointing out, was lacking.

The color continued on the staircase—a polished brass banister ran down the center of red carpet edged with black trim, and a zigzag pattern of light and dark greens covered all but three or four inches of black and white marble. The walls were papered with flowers in different shades of green leading down to a suite of offices, complete with a receptionist, who escorted Espy back to her meeting with Pickering. Donna Pickering, operations manager of Pyramid Technologies, the firm that maintained the copies of Desert View's records.

Pickering was a tall, lean, nervous woman in her late forties, with badly buffeted brown hair. The reason for her nervousness soon became apparent.

"I'm afraid we have a bit of a problem, Ms. Harper," Pickering said once Espy sat down.

"A problem?"

"Yes. We won't be able to get down into the bunker until tomorrow morning."

"Bunker?" Espy didn't understand. Why did she care about going down into a bunker?

"Where the records are kept."

"And why is that?"

"I'm so sorry, but I just received a request from Desert View's counsel, asking that—"

"Wait a second," Espy said. "Desert View's counsel?"

"Yes." She swiveled in her chair to read off the computer monitor. "The firm is called Baker and White. They're based in your neck of the woods, I believe." Pickering tried smiling again. "Up in Delaware. This is from one of the senior partners there, a man named Raymond—"

"Lish."

"Yes. Raymond Lish."

"And how did Mr. Lish know I was coming here?" Espy asked.

"If you're implying that I told him—"

"I'm searching for an explanation. That's all."

"Mr. Lish's office sent an email earlier today, advising that Desert View was engaged in a dispute with certain regulatory agencies and requesting—as is their right under law—to be advised of any examination of their records by those agencies. It's all right here." She gestured toward the screen.

"Can I look at that?"

"Be my guest."

Espy leaned over Pickering's shoulder. The information she'd mentioned was indeed all there, including the time the email had been sent: a half hour or so, by Espy's reckoning, after she'd first contacted the company. Lish was good. Not just guarding the front door, but this side entrance she'd tried to sneak through as well.

"So you see, we need to wait for their arrival."

Espy nodded. Lish had the right to contest the legality of her examination, but all he could do in the end was delay. He couldn't actually stop her from looking at the records.

CHAPTER 21

"And when is Mr. Lish due here?"

"I'm expecting him first thing in the morning," Pickering replied. "Nine a.m. sharp."

"All right," Espy said. "I'll be back then."

She headed back upstairs to the lobby, thinking the whole way. She'd better call Mike, maybe even make that preemptive call to Bamberger.

"Problem?"

She looked up. It was Earl, the valet.

"No. No problem at all. It's just that my business has been delayed. Until tomorrow."

"Ah." He nodded sympathetically. "That's too bad."

"I suppose." She looked around the lobby. A couple in tennis whites passed by, laughing. Through another door off the lobby, she could see a bar. People relaxing, talking, drinking…

They had tea here. Afternoon tea. And strawberry rhubarb pie.

She turned back to Earl. "I'm thinking maybe I will check in after all."

He smiled. "Knew we'd get you."

❖ ❖ ❖ ❖ ❖

The suite she booked—the Draper suite, the clerk at the front desk informed her—repeated and amplified the colors from downstairs. A bright green carpet. Vivid floral patterns on the furniture. Broad, shining stripes on the wallpaper. There was a good reason for that, it turned out.

"The suite is named after Dorothy Draper," the bellman told her. "She's the woman who first designed the interiors here. A true visionary. And Mr. Varney, god rest his soul, carried on from there."

Espy smiled back politely. She didn't care about colors, or

fabric, or interiors, or furniture. She cared about Desert View. She tipped the bellman and sent him on his way.

Earl told her about an arcade full of shops on the same level as Pickering's office; no doubt she could find clothes and toiletries and whatever else she needed for tomorrow there. The main lobby, though, was crowded with people waiting to check in. Espy tried to wend her way around the incoming vacationers and their luggage, but somehow got turned around and found herself wandering through a series of rooms, each more colorful than the next. Carlton Varney, she supposed. Dorothy Draper.

In one room a half-dozen people gathered in a semicircle around a man, talking and gesturing with his hands. A tour, Espy realized. The man was pointing to a painting on the wall behind him. A painting of a woman wearing a glittering, gold ballgown.

The woman was her mother.

"She was Hitchcock's muse," the man – a tour guide, she realized, she was close enough now to read the nametag on his shirt, CONTE – was saying, and as soon as she heard those words, Espy realized he wasn't talking about her mom at all.

"This portrait is one of two identical ones of Princess Grace by the artist," the tour guide was saying. "The other is kept in the royal palace at Monaco. The princess and the royal family spent several days at the Greenbrier back in 1963."

"She looks a little like you."

Espy turned to find a handsome man, somewhere in his forties, standing behind her. He looked put together. Very, very put together. Slightly longish black hair, fashionably streaked with gray. A slim, shiny, well-cut suit. A Rolex watch. And makeup? More than anything else, the man looked like he was expecting to go on TV any second.

"Excuse me?" Espy said.

CHAPTER 21

"I said she looks like you. The princess. Although of course, the hair is much more like your mother's."

She scowled. "Do I know you?"

"In a way." He extended a hand. "I'm Raymond Lish."

❖ ❖ ❖ ❖ ❖

Lish, it turned out, had arrived early. Had been looking for her. Wanted to talk. Buy her dinner. He obviously had ulterior motives, but then so did she. She agreed.

He led her down a flight of stairs to one of the restaurants the bellman had told her about, 44 West. A line of people were waiting to see the maître d'. Lish brushed past them, pausing only when a man in a tight blue suit stepped forward to block his path. Espy thought, for a second, there was going to be a scene, but just then the maître d' himself saw Lish and waved him forward.

"Mr. Lish," he said. "Good to see you again."

"And you, Mark. As always."

"We have your table. Genevieve?" He waved. A woman walked over to them.

"Mr. Lish," she said. "Right this way."

"Can I get you something to drink?" Genevieve asked after they'd sat.

"Is Brian around?" Lish twisted in his chair, scanning the restaurant. "I'm wondering if there's anything new in the wine cellar."

"I believe he's working in one of the conference rooms tonight. Let me find him for you."

"No, no. Please don't disturb him. We have plenty to choose from here." He picked up the wine list, handed it to Espy. "I can make some recommendations, if you like."

"No thanks. Just water for me." She gave the wine list back. "I have to work tomorrow." She made a point of catching Lish's eye as she spoke.

He didn't react in the slightest. "Of course. I understand. A glass of the Lafite for me then, Genevieve. Please." He shrugged. "I shouldn't be drinking either, but that Lafite is extraordinary. I indulged last year at Christmas, bought myself two bottles of it. Extraordinary may be too subtle a word, actually."

Espy raised an eyebrow. Extraordinary was indeed too subtle a word. She'd caught a glimpse of the prices on the wine list: Chateau Lafite, vintage 1974, $375 a glass, $1,300 a bottle.

The wine. The suit. The Rolex. Lish was not what she had expected. A point of interest, if not quite a red flag.

"And there really is very little for me to do tomorrow," he continued. "Beyond the Notice of Finding. Pyramid's technician arrives at nine, Ms. Pickering said?"

"Yes. Nine." Pyramid also handled the backend technical details of keeping Desert View's duplicate books. Their technician would sit with Espy, make sure she got the data she needed.

"I'll be there. At her office. Before they take you down to the bunker."

"The bunker?" Espy asked. "Would someone please explain to me why they call it a bunker?"

"It would be my pleasure." Lish spent a good ten minutes telling her the story. The Greenbrier, back at the time of the Eisenhower administration, had been designated as the top-secret bomb shelter and emergency headquarters for the entire United States Congress. Operation Greek Island, they had called it. An entire underground wing, attached to the hotel, had been built in complete secrecy. That secrecy had been maintained until the

CHAPTER 21

1990s. Portions of that wing had now been converted to a museum of sorts, open for tours. The bunker. But many of the concrete-and-steel-reinforced rooms had been adapted specifically for data storage.

"If you haven't had the tour," Lish said. "It's well worth taking. The assembly hall, the hospital, the power plant—"

"I'm not sure I'm going to have time."

"Planning on a long day?"

"As long as it takes."

"Ms. Harper." Lish paused as the waiter cleared their salads. "I recognize you have a job to do here. You represent the people of the United States. You want to make sure that there is nothing untoward, nothing illegal, happening with regard to Desert View."

"That's right."

"I'm sure that's exactly what you'll find out when you go into the bunker tomorrow."

"Then we shouldn't have any problems."

"I hope not. But as you may have noticed, Desert View is extremely reluctant to share details of its operations with anyone. In their business, those details often provide competitive advantage."

Just then dinner arrived. Steak. Two bites in, and Espy was completely distracted, and wishing she'd ordered a glass of wine to go with her meal. Maybe the $375 glass of wine. She wondered what a $375 glass of wine tasted like.

"To continue," Lish said. "We're worried that if you do have questions after you examine the records tomorrow, you may start calling other people to ask them. Which has the potential to be very detrimental to public perception of the company's value, and thus its stock price."

Lish, she realized, was repeating Bamberger's words of

warning. And Mike's. "I've been made aware of the importance of confidentiality. That's why we're here and not in court."

"Yes. Although," he took a sip of his wine, "we may get there soon enough."

"I'm afraid I don't follow."

"Your department, and you in particular, Ms. Harper, have a demonstrated history of bureaucratic overreach."

"Excuse me?" She set down her fork.

"ICE-T, to use the acronym, was chartered by the DOJ to investigate terrorism funding, yes? There's no terrorism going on here."

"I need to correct you on that. Our charter specifically grants us latitude to investigate any funds we think may be feeding the black market economy."

"That's a very broad reading of that clause. An unnecessarily intrusive reading. I'd be interested in what a neutral third party had to say on the subject."

"Interested, as in willing to take it to court?"

"If necessary." Lish smiled. "But I prefer to resolve differences outside the courtroom. In this case, that really shouldn't be so difficult. From our perspective, Desert View simply wants to conduct their business privately, which is their right under our system of law."

If they wanted to conduct their business privately, Espy thought, then they shouldn't have set themselves up as a public corporation. Though it was obvious why they'd done that. Entrepreneur 101. Start a corporation, issue stock, take it public, make a fortune.

"I'll keep that in mind as our investigation moves forward."

"I appreciate that." Lish took a bite of his steak. "You know,

CHAPTER 21

I've spoken with some people in DC, Ms. Harper. You're really making a name for yourself there."

"That's nice to hear."

"I could perhaps help in that regard."

"How so?"

"Well, those people I mentioned, they are not without influence. A word or two in the right ear could go a long way toward moving you up the bureaucratic ladder as it were."

"Making a name for myself is not my goal here."

"Then what is, Ms. Harper?"

"The truth."

"Ah." Lish smiled. "You're an idealist, then?"

"I like to think so."

"An idealist in Washington, DC?" Lish shook his head. "That can be a dangerous thing."

She couldn't help it. She flashed, for a second, on the dossier.

George magazine. Seven Days to Dallas.

The Men Who Murdered My Father.

She set down her knife and fork and looked Lish square in the eye. "Is that a threat?"

"Of course not. I don't make threats." Lish's own expression was anything but congenial now. "I simply advocate for my clients. For the point of view I outlined earlier. It's my job to educate my adversaries about the nature of the playing field they are about to enter—and the nature of their opponent."

"My opponent. I see. I'm glad we're not mincing words anymore."

"I didn't want to spoil your enjoyment of the food. But if you're done…"

"I am."

"Then let me continue being blunt. The people I work for, they play to win. No. Let me correct that. They don't play at all."

"You're talking about Frank Ferrone, I assume."

"Mr. Ferrone, of course. But there are other parties involved. Others with a stake in Desert View's continued financial health."

"I'm curious as to who those other parties might be."

"Does that matter? Their identities are unimportant."

"To you maybe. Not to me."

"What is important," Lish went on as if she hadn't spoken, "is how generous they're prepared to be. Under the right circumstances."

"Mr. Lish." Espy smiled. "Are you now trying to bribe me?"

"Ms. Harper." Lish smiled back. "Are you interested in a bribe?"

"To be clear—no." The smile dropped from her face. "I'm an idealist, as you said. Acting on behalf of the United States Department of Justice."

"So you say. And yet no one else in the department seems all that interested in Desert View."

"They'll get there," Espy said. After this conversation, in fact, she was sure of it.

Not only did Desert View have something to hide, that something was down there in the bunker, waiting for her.

"Thank you for dinner, Mr. Lish. I have work to do before tomorrow morning." She stood, and turned to go.

"Ms. Harper! You're making a mistake here."

There was something else in his eyes now, something else in his voice. It took her a second to figure out what that something was. Fear.

And suddenly she knew why.

"You're in trouble now, aren't you, Mr. Lish?"

CHAPTER 21

"I beg your pardon?"

"You were supposed to get me to stop. To take your money, or your offer of help, and step aside."

Lish shook his head. "Ms. Harper. As I've been saying, my purpose here is to educate you. To make clear that your actions will have consequences."

"As will your inaction, I suspect." She smiled. "Have a good night, Mr. Lish. I'll see you bright and early tomorrow morning."

22

Cockerell knocked on the door of the double-wide and waited.

Finally, the peephole slid back.

"Cockerell." The door opened. "Well what do you know? Enter and sign in please."

"Beck." He shook his head. "What the hell? You were gonna call me first thing."

"Hey. I was going to get around to it."

"When?" He could smell the liquor on her breath from where he was standing. "Jesus. You've been drinking."

"What are you, the morality police?" She glared. "Free country, right? Least the last time I checked."

"Right. Free country." He nodded. "So … you got something for me?"

"You mean did I go to the safe deposit box? I sure did. I sure as hell did. Come on in."

He followed her inside. She went right to the couch, sat down. There was a manila envelope lying on the coffee table. The words *Central State Bank and Loan* were printed across the front.

"Is that it?"

"That's it." She looked singularly unenthused.

"What's the matter?"

"I'm thinking. Give me a minute here."

"A minute? You've had all day."

"Yeah, well it's a double-edged sword, is the problem. See, I need a cop. But I don't know if I can trust a cop."

"Didn't we go through this yesterday?"

CHAPTER 22

"We did. It's just … I show this to you, I can't take it back. So I have to be sure I'm doing the right thing. That I can trust you."

"What do you want me to do, swear on a stack of Bibles?"

"Would that mean anything? You believe in God, sonny?"

"I used to." Cockerell shook his head. "Not anymore."

"What happened? Wait. Let me guess. Afghanistan."

"Good guess." After his dad was killed, he'd not only quit the service, he'd stopped going to church, which was an even bigger deal as far as his mom was concerned. Made going to see her on the weekends tough, because she spent all day Saturday cooking for those church picnics, and Sundays at service.

"Not a guess. Did some more digging today. On you." She sipped her drink. "Quitting the army, resigning your commission—I bet that took balls. Especially given your family history. Family of patriots. You, and your dad, and your grandfather … real bunch of Johnny-comes-marching-homers, right?"

"Hey." He glared. "No need to make fun."

"Relax, sonny. I get it. You're a patriot. I like to think I am too, in my own way. Trying to right a wrong here. Fix something terrible that was done to our country."

"Beck." Cockerell leaned forward. "The people I'm working for are patriots too. I promise you that. So." He gestured toward the envelope. "The wrong George. You gonna tell me what that means?"

They stared at each other a minute. Finally, she nodded. "Yeah. Okay. I will. I'm gonna do just that." She picked up her glass, saw it was empty, and reached for the bottle between them.

Cockerell put his hand on it.

"Hey!"

"Talk first. Then drink."

"Fine." She sat back on the couch. "Let's start where we left off.

With William Manchester."

"And the tapes."

"Not the tapes." She shook her head. "What came after. The nervous breakdown."

"What?"

"Manchester's nervous breakdown. You didn't know about that?"

"No."

"Not a lot of people do. Okay then. A little background." She got to her feet and headed for the bookshelf again.

"Beck. You already showed me—"

"Different book." She came back carrying a thin hardcover. Plonked it down on the table between them.

"*The Manchester Affair*." Cockerell flipped it over, read the back cover. "This is about the lawsuit between Jackie and Manchester."

"That's right."

"A whole book?"

"Yeah. It was a big deal back in the day. Which you wouldn't know, because you're what, eighteen?"

"Thirty-two. If that matters."

"Right. Thirty-two. Still." She laughed. "Let me tell you something. You think the world is going to shit now, this is nothing. Back in the sixties—"

"The book, Beck. Stay focused." He picked it up, waved it in front of her. "Why are you showing this to me?"

"Because…" She took the book from him, flipped through it, found the page she was looking for, and handed it back. "Read."

Cockerell held up a hand. "No thanks. Just give me the short version."

"Fine. Short version. Well, Manchester and JFK were friends, right? More than friends, really. Birds of a feather, you know?

CHAPTER 22

War heroes."

"I know that."

"That's how they met. VA hospital in Boston. Right after the war. World War Two."

"I know," he repeated, the exasperation he was feeling crept into his voice.

Beck gave him attitude right back. "Well, it's important," she said. "Really important. That's why Manchester was the guy Jackie went to. 'Bill, you have to tell the story, you're the only guy that can do it justice, blah blah blah.' He says no at first, but she keeps at him. Finally he agrees. Because guess what? He's a patriot too. It's his duty—to his friend, to his country. So he goes to work. Moves to DC. Starts in with the hundred-hour work weeks. Researching, interviewing, talking to Jackie, and then Bobby, and Salinger and Sorensen and all the others. Reliving what happened to his friend, all the time knowing how the story ends. Picturing that scene in Dallas. JFK's head getting blown off. It's a lot of stress. He loses twenty pounds. Starts seeing things … hearing things. People following him. Strange voices, all around. He thinks he's going crazy. Ends up checking himself into a sanitarium."

"Jesus. When was this?"

"'65 sometime. Can't remember exactly. It's all in here." Beck held up the book herself now. "Like I said, it was a lot of stress. But what I know—what I've known for sixty years now—is that Manchester wasn't nuts. Not entirely, anyway. What he was," her gaze bore into Cockerell's, "was a patsy."

The second she said that word, Cockerell flashed on the dossier again. What Nan had written. De Mohrenschildt's book on Oswald. *"I Am A Patsy!"*

"A patsy," Cockerell said. "What makes you say that?"

"You remember that movie *Gaslight*?"

"No."

"No. Of course you don't. You're just a kid."

"Beck..."

"Ingrid Bergman. From *Casablanca*? She's the star. You know who she was, right?"

"Sure."

"So in *Gaslight*, Bergman's married to this guy; he's after her money. He does all sorts of things, trying to convince her she's going crazy. Losing her mind. Trying to get her committed. That's what they did to Manchester."

"You're saying somebody caused his nervous breakdown?"

"That's right. Same sons of bitches who shot Oswald right on national TV. Covering up their trail in plain sight of the whole damn world, and not a damn thing anyone could do about it. Bastards." She glared straight at Cockerell, like it was his fault. "You have no idea who you're dealing with here."

"No, I guess I don't. So tell me."

"I'll do better than that." She set her glass down on the table, and then, at last, picked up the envelope. Central State Bank and Trust.

She pulled out a single sheet of paper. Faded ink, crinkling at the edges.

CHAPTER 22

WASHINGTON D.C. METRO POLICE DEPARTMENT
INCIDENT REPORT

Distribution
1. Dispatcher-Records
2. Command
3. Detective Division

Case ID Number: KZ55
Report Date: 7-25-64
Name of Complainant: William Manchester
Address of Complainant: 800 S. 4th Street NW
Sex: Male   Nationality: US Citizen   Age: 43
Offense investigated: Harrassment stalking
Date: 25 July   Time: 20:31
Location of Alleged Offense: Massachusetts Ave NW at 5th Street
Complaint Details: 3rd complaint of such offense by Mr. Manchester States 2 men following him to and from residence, behaving in a threatening manner

FILL OUT FOR WANTED PERSON
Warrant Issued Yes ___ No X   Warrant No. ___
Wanted By ___   Department ___   Date ___   Time ___
Reported By ___   How ___   Relationship ___

FILL OUT FOR MISSING PERSON
Reported By ___   Last Seen ___   Time ___
Probable Destination ___   Cause of Absence ___
Mental Condition ___   Body Style ___

VEHICLE (IF INVOLVED)
Color ___   Year ___   Make ___   Condition ___
License ___   Year ___   State ___   Number ___

ADDITIONAL INFORMATION

Investigation Result: Surveillance 800 4th Street negative
No follow-up necessary

Investigating officer(s): George Casserly   Badge No. 9021
J.P. Exner   Badge No. 4-819
Submitted By: *George Casserly*

"An old police report," Cockerell said.

"That's right. A Washington, DC, police report from way back in 1964. Report of a complaint, filed by William Manchester. He thought he was being followed. He called the cops, asked them to check into it, and—"

"So I see. But 'surveillance negative. No follow-up necessary,'" Cockerell said, reading off the bottom of the report. "There was nothing. No one there."

"That's what they wanted him to believe," Beck said. "What they wanted the whole world to believe. But that's bullshit."

"What do you mean bullshit?"

"I mean not true. I mean they were gaslighting him."

"Which you know how?"

"Which I know because of this." And with that, Beck reached into the envelope and pulled out another piece of paper, identical to the first.

Another police report.

CHAPTER 22

WASHINGTON D.C. METRO POLICE DEPARTMENT
INCIDENT REPORT

Distribution
1. Dispatcher-Records
2. Command
3. Detective Division

Report Date: 7-25-64
Name of Complainant: William Manchester
Case ID Number: KZ55
Address of Complainant: 800 S. 4th Street NW
Sex: Male
Nationality: US Citizen
Offense Investigated: Harrassment stalking
Age: 43
Date: 25 July
Time: 20:31
Location of Alleged Offense: Massachusetts Ave NW at 5th Street
Complaint Details: 3rd complaint of such offense by Mr. Manchester. States 2 men following him to and from residence, behaving in a threatening manner

FILL OUT FOR WANTED PERSON
Warrant Issued: Yes ___ No X
Wanted By: ___
Warrant No.: ___
Reported By: ___
Department: ___

FILL OUT FOR MISSING PERSON
Reported By: ___
Date: ___
Time: ___
Probable Destination: ___
How: ___
Relationship: ___
Mental Condition: ___
Last Seen: ___
Time: ___
Cause of Absence: ___

VEHICLE (IF INVOLVED)
Color: ___
Year: ___
Make: ___
Body Style: ___
License: ___
Year: ___ State: ___ Number: ___ Condition: ___

ADDITIONAL INFORMATION

Investigation Result: Suspects observed 22:41 646 4th street NW Unsuccessful pursuit

Investigating officer(s): George Casserly
Name
Badge No.: 9021

Submitted By: J.P. Exner
Name: *George Casserly*
Badge No.: 4-819

Cockerell's eyes flicked across the page. Left to right, top to bottom.

He scanned the section marked *Investigative Result*, and froze.

"Wait," he said. "Hang on a second."

He laid the two reports side by side, so he could make sure of what he was seeing.

They were virtually identical, save for that last section. Where the first piece of paper read *No follow-up necessary*, the other said, *Suspects observed. Unsuccessful pursuit.*

"I don't get it," Cockerell said.

"Yeah you do. Of course you do." She leaned forward. "The one I just showed you—'suspects observed?' That's the original. That's what really happened. The other one is a fake. They changed the report to cover their tracks."

"You're saying somebody really *was* following Manchester."

"That's right."

"Who?"

"That's the question, isn't it?"

That was one question, Cockerell realized. He had another.

"Back up a second. How did you get these?"

"A friend at the police department. He was one of us."

"Us?"

"Yeah. People who knew the Warren Commission report was a cover-up. A front for what really happened—who really killed the President. A guy named Walter—" she shook her head—"never mind, his name doesn't matter. The point is, when Jackie hired Manchester, when he moved to town and started interviewing all those people … well, we knew Manchester's reputation. We knew he was going to kick up some dirt. So when that complaint came in with Manchester's name on it, Walter let us know. Right away. Got us a copy of the report. And we were going to go public. Because

CHAPTER 22

there it was. Proof that somebody was trying to hide the truth, that there was a conspiracy. Only, the night before we were going to go to the press, we get a call. 'Problem,' Walter says. Because—"

"They changed the report."

"That's right."

"Which brings us back to the question. Who 'they' were."

"I have no idea. But he might." She pointed to the report. To the signature scrawled at the bottom of the page. The investigating officer.

"George." He looked up. "George Casserly."

"Yeah. The right George."

Cockerell nodded. Not de Mohrenschildt. Casserly.

And not the magazine either. But still…

"I tracked him down after the report got changed," Beck continued. "He was friendly enough at first, but the second I mentioned Manchester … he shut down. Wouldn't say another word."

"So what'd you do then?"

"What could I do?" She shook her head. "I went back to him a few years later. And again, a few years after that. But finally … I gave up."

"Wait. That's it?"

Beck smiled. "Not quite." She reached into the pocket of her blouse, pulled out a business card, and placed it on the table.

CASSERLY'S
Good Food and Drink
1201 Manor Creek Boulevard
Washington, DC

"That's his bar," Beck said. "He opened it when he retired. Nice little spot. It's still there, and so is he. So. Mr. Washington

DC police detective. I'm wondering if Casserly might possibly be more inclined to talk to you. A fellow cop. Clear his conscience after all these years."

"Yeah. He just might, at that." Cockerell reached for the card. Beck pulled it back. "Not so fast."

"Ah." He nodded. "You want money."

"No. I want you to be careful. There's a reason Casserly kept quiet all these years. A reason why he wouldn't talk to me, right? It's because those people—the ones who told him to change the report—they're still out there."

"I hear you," Cockerell said. "I'll be careful."

"Good. Now." She smiled. "We do need to talk about money."

23

The secret your senator was killed to protect.

Was that what Ferrone was hiding down in the bunker? In those records he was so determined to keep her from examining? What would they tell her about Desert View, about Frank Ferrone? What was it he didn't want her to find?

She would learn that bright and early tomorrow morning.

She stepped out of the elevator, turned down the hallway to her room, and stopped. A man was standing by the window at the far end of the hall, wearing a blue suit and yellow tie. The man from the restaurant, she realized. The one who'd confronted Lish when he'd cut to the front of the line. She'd thought the two men were angry with each other then. Now…

She was instantly on guard.

The man started walking toward her. "Russell Haney," he said.

Espy's eyes narrowed. "What?"

"Russell Haney." He stopped a few feet shy of her, folded his arms across his chest. "You know the name, right?"

She most certainly did. Russell Haney was a two-bit actor. A married actor who'd had an affair with her mother years ago and then run to the press to sell his version of the story, a nasty version that painted her mother in a very unflattering light. A version that had sent her mother back to the bottle after a half-dozen years of sobriety.

"You're with him. Lish," Espy said.

"We have shared interests, to be sure."

She saw the telltale bulge of a gun under his suit jacket. "Tell me your name."

"My name's not important. What is important is what's about to happen if you don't do as Mr. Lish suggested."

"What's about to happen." She dropped her arms to her sides. Got up on the balls of her feet. "Go on."

"Do I really need to?" He shook his head. "Let's just say those little tidbits about Mr. Haney and your mother will start reappearing on social media over the next few days unless—"

She punched the guy in the throat.

He gasped, went to his knees.

"I am sick and tired of being threatened." She yanked his gun out of the holster and turned it on him. "Let's go somewhere else and talk privately."

He gasped again, a little too theatrically, and started to stand. He was going to try to grab the gun back. She saw it in his eyes.

So she kicked him square in the chest.

The guy gasped for real now and sat back on his knees. Looked down for a moment. She saw him trying to keep his temper in check. The last thing he wanted, she realized, was to make a scene. Good.

"On your feet," she said. "Slowly."

The door to her room opened. Frederickson looked out at her, looked at the guy, and laughed.

"What are you doing here?" Espy said.

"Lish. We looked into his client list. It's a nasty group of people."

"I can handle myself."

"I can see that." Frederickson gestured. "Who's the lucky customer?"

"That's what we're about to find out," she said.

"Well, let me help." Frederickson took two quick steps forward and yanked the guy to his feet.

They dragged him into Espy's room and shut the door.

CHAPTER 23

❖ ❖ ❖ ❖ ❖

He had a Nevada Driver's License in the name of Daniel Josephson.

"You don't look like a Josephson," Frederickson said, holding that license up to the light. "This is a fake, right?"

The guy shook his head. He was sitting in a desk chair, hands secured behind his back with his yellow tie. "There's no need for any of this," he said. "I'm just here to relay a message."

"From Mr. Ferrone, I take it?" Espy asked.

"We have common interests here, Ms. Harper. None of us want to see those ugly rumors spread all over the internet again. Russell Haney and your mother."

"You didn't answer my question," she said.

The man smiled. "My advice to you is to go home. Go back to DC and your little task force. Before things get really nasty."

"What is with this guy?" Frederickson knelt down in front of the man. "Hey, chief. Do you not understand that you're the one who's tied up here?"

"Ms. Harper is the one who's not getting the full picture. Let me elaborate." He smiled again. He had perfect teeth. Veneers. "It's not just rumors about your mother we're talking about. We'll be publicizing what happened at Long Beach too. Your father. The big FBI hero. Only not so much, after we're through with him."

Espy saw Frederickson tense.

"I'd stop right there if I were you," she told Josephson.

He didn't. "The information will suggest that he mishandled the threat from the beginning. So while he may have saved some lives, the picture that's going to emerge—"

Frederickson pushed the man's chair over. He stepped on Josephson's chest, pulled a pillow off Espy's bed, pulled the colorful pillowcase off that, and shoved it into the guy's mouth.

Josephson's eyes widened. He gasped for air.

"You're not helping," Espy said, though she knew the reason for Frederickson's action.

He'd had friends who died at Long Beach.

"Lesson number one." Frederickson stood over Josephson, pointed a finger at him. "Pretty simple. Pretty straightforward. If you don't have something nice to say, don't say anything at all."

Josephson's face turned beet red.

"Let that sink in a minute." He turned to her. "You're on to something here. Something pretty important. Otherwise they wouldn't be throwing all these obstacles in your path. The question is what."

"Yes. But." She glanced over at Josephson, whose face, she saw, was now shading toward purple. "We don't want to have to explain any dead bodies."

"Agreed." Frederickson reached down and removed the pillowcase.

The guy hacked, coughed, gasped for air, and threw up all over himself.

"Jesus, man." Frederickson shook his head. "Have a little self-respect."

Josephson spat out a series of curse words in combinations Espy had never heard before.

"You know," Frederickson said, shaking his head, "I don't think lesson number one took. Should we try again?"

The man glared.

Espy went into the bathroom. Came back with a glass of water and put it to Josephson's lips. He sipped at it greedily.

"Okay," she said. "I want you to go back and tell Lish—"

"I don't work for Lish," he said.

"Mr. Ferrone, then. Whoever it is. Make sure they understand

CHAPTER 23

that these sorts of threats don't frighten me. I represent the United States government here, my friend."

"And him?" He gestured toward Frederickson. "Who does he represent? AARP?"

"Lesson number two," Frederickson said, pulling a gun from his waistband.

Josephson sneered. "What? You're going to shoot me?"

"Correct," Frederickson said, and pulled the trigger.

"Oh my god," Josephson cried out. He looked down at the dart in his arm and then back up at Frederickson. His eyes closed.

"I wasn't finished," Espy said.

"He wasn't going to talk. Not unless we did permanent damage." He holstered his weapon. "Now come on. We have to get out of here."

"What?"

"First Lish, then this guy; they're upping the ante. And whatever comes next, this is not the place to face it."

"I disagree. We need to stick around to see who does show up."

"Espy. Listen to the old hand here. The voice of experience. This hotel is not a defensible position. Not to mention all the innocent bystanders here. Things might get rough if we stick around."

"Things are going to get rough anyway. That's a fact." She shook her head. "I am not running away."

"Not running away. Choosing our battleground. Living to fight another day. Just like—"

"No."

"Just like George Washington. Battle of Long Island, right?"

She sighed. George Washington, escaping from the British in the dead of night, taking his army across the East River into Manhattan.

She looked around the room. The Draper Suite.

Before Lish had showed up this afternoon, she had planned to take a long hot shower. Use those big, fluffy towels in the bathroom. Order room service, maybe a piece of that pie and a nice chamomile tea while she worked. And then, sleep. A luxurious, long night's sleep.

"Fine," she said. "Let me grab my things."

24

Frederickson had driven down from DC in his rebuilt Range Rover. Of course. Boys and their toys. His included a sleeping bag and an air mattress, both of which he gave to Espy.

"You sure?"

"Hey. You have to work tomorrow. I just might check in to the Greenbrier myself. Grab a sauna, take a nap."

"Funny," she said. Although not really. Even with the sleeping bag and the air mattress, spread out in the Range Rover's cargo area, she still woke up stiff and sore and cold. They'd parked behind a tractor-trailer at a truck stop a half hour down the road; she showered and changed there. Then they returned to the resort.

Pickering was behind her desk, eyes focused on her computer. Lish sat across from her, looking as immaculate and put together as he had last night. Another man, vaguely Hispanic-looking, with a mustache exactly like her father's, sat next to Lish.

Lish was first to see her. Surprise flickered across his eyes for a second, then disappeared.

"Ms. Harper." Pickering saw her now too. "I had been led to believe you might have had a change of heart regarding your examination of the records this morning."

"Oh no." Espy shook her head and looked from Pickering to Lish. "I don't know where you would have gotten that idea. I'm anxious to get started."

Lish regarded her impassively. "You're making a mistake here, Ms. Harper. I had hoped a good night's sleep might cause you to see things from another perspective."

"I gave your concerns, and those of your clients, appropriate weight before arriving at my decision."

"Then there's nothing more to be said." Lish stood. He handed her an envelope. "This is the Notice of Finding, as required by law, stipulating the department's obligation to inform us within ten business days of any relevant, actionable information discovered during your examination of Desert View's records."

Espy hefted the envelope in her hand. It was thicker than she'd expected. There was more than just the standard notice in there. It wouldn't surprise her if Lish had come up with some other legal strategies to obstruct her work. She'd worry about that later.

She turned to Pickering. "Let's get to it."

"Very well," she said, gesturing to the other man. "This is Mr. Cabral. He'll be taking you down to the bunker."

Cabral stood, nodded. "Pleasure to meet you. Shall we?"

Frederickson stepped between them.

"One second. You're employed by the data company?" he asked Cabral.

"Yes."

"How long?"

"Ten years."

"And your name again?"

"Cabral. Ramon Cabral."

"Right. One second." He pulled Espy aside, lowered his voice. "I'm going to check this guy out."

"Relax. You heard him. He's been with Pyramid for ten years." She smiled. "And the bunker? Nothing's going to happen to me down there."

"Bunker? Why do people keep saying bunker?"

"Catch up with Lish. He'll tell you. Or take the tour." She turned to Cabral. "Shall we?"

CHAPTER 24

❖ ❖ ❖ ❖ ❖

On their way, she gave Cabral a brief outline of what she was seeking and why. They reached a blast door as thick and heavy as that on any bank vault; the conversation turned to a discussion of the bunker itself, the secrecy involved in its construction, operation, and layout. Finally, as they passed through rooms that had been intended as decontamination chambers for members of Congress escaping a nuclear holocaust, Espy and Cabral ("Ramon, please") talked a little about themselves.

She learned that Pyramid Technologies was headquartered in Atlanta, but Cabral worked all over the East Coast, everywhere they maintained off-site data storage facilities: Rochester, New York; Delaware; and the Greenbrier. Cabral spent most of his time on the road; he had a daughter on the police force in Philadelphia, so he kept an apartment there.

"Good for you," Espy said, just as Cabral stopped in front of a thick, red metal door with a yellow and black sign welded onto it.

Pyramid Technologies
Room 14B-C
Authorized Personnel Only
Prohibited Items:
All Electronic Devices
Cell Phones/Cameras/Firearms
Thank You
Management

"Here we are." Cabral pulled a pass from around his neck and held it up to a scanner. There was a loud click as the door unlocked.

Espy was hit with a blast of cold air as she stepped inside.

Room 14B-C still looked like the bomb shelter it had originally been designed as: cinder block walls and floor, a drop-frame ceiling with bare-bones acoustic tile. What had been upgraded, clearly, were the electronics. The far wall was floor-to-ceiling servers; in front of them was a terminal screen built into a long, white metal table.

"Cold in here," Espy said.

"Yeah." Cabral pulled a white lab coat from a freestanding locker, slipped it on, then pulled out a gray cable sweater. "We keep it at sixty-five. A little cooler than the manual says, but we're not sure the manual's entirely right. You want?" He held out the sweater.

"Absolutely," she said. "Thank you."

"No problem. Take a seat. Give me a minute here to fire things up."

There were three identical rolling chairs in the room. Espy took the nearest one and opened her briefcase. Greg had given her a folder full of papers on Desert View and Frank Ferrone, material she'd intended to review last night: trade journals, regional and national newspaper articles, some financial information as well.

She dug in: the first thing that really caught her attention was a stock market tip sheet, a newsletter written for investors. Greg had circled the second paragraph of an article headlined "On The Rebound." It was all about Desert View.

> Construction on Aqua Roma is ready to resume—full speed ahead! Occupancy and resource usage issues have been resolved, and all permits granted. Insiders are buying; stock prices have begun to rise.

Aqua Roma. The development she'd read about the other day in Desert View's stock prospectus. The newsletter called it "a massive undertaking projected to transform the real-estate landscape in the greater Las Vegas area."

CHAPTER 24

Exaggeration, Espy thought at first, and then she read closer.

Aqua Roma was planned to house forty thousand people. It would include a shopping mall, an entertainment complex, three golf courses, a giant lake for water recreation, and a brand-new, state-of-the-art gaming casino. The Platinum Peacock. Successor to the famed Peacock casino itself.

Next up was a feature article on the man behind the development: Frank Ferrone Jr. There was a photograph of him seated behind a long, low glass table in his top-floor office at Ferrone Tower, a sleek twenty-story glass and steel structure overlooking the Vegas strip. Home to the Ferrone family of companies. Standing behind the couch, at Ferrone's right hand, was a man identified as Vince Falconetti, the company's executive vice president.

Vice president? Espy thought. Of what? Standing there, Falconetti radiated menace.

The article went on to discuss Ferrone Jr.'s meteoric rise to prominence: how he'd started by managing the Peacock (the writer noted chips from the casino scattered across the table in front of Ferrone) and then moved into the real estate arena; how he'd applied modern investing methods (another mention of his Wharton MBA here) to parlay the family money into a fortune for himself and, the writer made sure to point out, his fellow stockholders in the Desert View Real Estate Investment Trust.

Time and time again, the company has turned worthless desert land into high-yield properties.

"All set here." Cabral rolled another chair over to the table. He waved a hand over the surface, and a second terminal rose up from a recessed slot at the back of the table. "Anytime you're ready."

"Ready." Espy closed her folder and slid closer.

"So the way this works," Cabral said, "you tell me what you're looking for, I pull it up on screen, and you look it over. You see anything you want a hard copy of, you tell me, I print it out. Sound good?"

"Sounds good," she said, though the truth was she didn't know what she was looking for. But given the lengths that Ferrone and Lish had gone to try and stop her from getting into this room—there was something here. She was certain of that.

She was also certain that whatever that something was, it wasn't going to be easy to find.

She was suddenly all too aware of how little sleep she'd had last night. Of how stiff her lower back was. Of how laborious a process this was going to be.

She turned to Cabral.

"You don't have any tea in here, do you?"

"Tea?" He pointed to a sign Espy hadn't noticed before, hanging right over the terminals.

> **Absolutely No Beverages of Any Kind**
> **At Any Time**
> **No Drinking**
> **No Eating**
> **Absolutely No Exceptions**
> **Help Us Keep Your Data Safe!**
> **Thank You**
> **Management**

"Of course," she said. "No tea."

"Sorry." Cabral offered up an apologetic smile.

"Right," she said. "Let's get to work."

25

Cockerell got to Casserly's right after noon.

The bar was in an industrial part of town north of DC proper, on the ground floor of a two-story concrete building with apartments on top, decor stuck in the mid-nineties.

"George Casserly?" The bartender, a tall white dude with a goatee and tattoos peeking out from both sleeves, was pulling mugs out of a dish rack and drying them with a hand towel. "He doesn't own the place anymore. I do. What do you want?"

"Nothing to do with the bar. I just want to talk to him," Cockerell said. "Heard he still hangs out here."

The guy frowned. "Is this about the kid?"

"What kid?"

"His grandson? He in trouble again?"

"No. No one's in trouble that I know of. I just want to talk to him."

"Why?"

"It's about one of his old cases. He was a cop."

"Weren't we all?" the bartender said. "Right. Well then. There's your man."

He pointed toward the back of the bar, to a guy sitting by himself in a booth. George Casserly. The cop who had taken William Manchester's complaint sixty years ago. Alive and kicking. Not only kicking, but clean-shaven and clear-eyed. And sitting up straight, like he had a pole up his butt.

"You might want to give him a few minutes," the bartender said. "Till SOS is over."

"SOS?"

"*The Steve O'Sullivan Show*. News guy? America's in trouble—SOS? Casserly loves that shit. Never misses it."

Casserly was indeed focused on the TV at the end of the bar, glaring at it, with his jaw sticking out, like he was getting ready to enter into an argument with the talking heads on the screen. He transferred that glare to Cockerell as he approached.

"George Casserly?"

"Yeah. Who are you?"

"Name's Cockerell. I'm wondering if you could spare a few minutes."

"What for? This is about Benjamin?"

"What?"

"Benjamin. Did he do something again?"

Cockerell guessed Casserly was talking about his grandson, the one the bartender had referred to.

"No. This is—"

"Then what? What kind of questions? You a reporter?"

"No sir. A detective," he said. "On leave from the force right now, though. I've been hired by some people to look into a matter that concerns them, and came across an old case of yours that you might have—"

"A case of mine? I been off the force thirty-five years, son. What case? This some kind of lawsuit thing? Police brutality, some shit like that?"

"No sir. Not at all. Mind if I sit down?"

"Help yourself."

Cockerell sat opposite the man, his back to the TV. Casserly kept watching, shaking his head in disgust every few minutes.

"Country's going down the goddamn toilet. Whole world is." He took a sip from his beer, then focused his attention on

CHAPTER 25

Cockerell once more. "So who are you again?"

"Mike Cockerell. Detective over in the 256."

"Anacostia?" Casserly's eyes widened. "Good freaking luck there, buddy. You're a braver man than me. What can I help you with?"

"Well I'm on leave right now, actually. Working something private, and a case of yours came up. From 1964."

"1964?" Casserly barked out a short, humorless laugh. "Son, that's sixty years ago. I'm not gonna remember shit from back then."

"I understand. Still, if you wouldn't mind..." He reached into his pocket and unfolded a copy of the report Lynn Beck had shown him. The real report. The one that had never been officially filed. The one that proved Manchester had been followed.

Suspects observed. Unsuccessful pursuit.

"Take a look at this." He handed it to Casserly.

The man's eyes widened. "Good god. 1964. My second year on the job. I was partners with John Exner. X." Casserly smiled. "Haven't thought about him in forever. We worked together a long time, maybe a half-dozen years. He died young, poor guy. '95, I think it was. '96 maybe. They said—" Casserly froze.

He looked up at Cockerell. "Where'd you get this?"

"Does that matter?"

Casserly folded up the paper and handed it back to him. "Can't help you. Sorry."

"Can't, or won't?"

Casserly didn't respond. His hands on the table in front of him were shaking a little. Maybe Parkinson's, maybe another neurological thing.

Or maybe he was just scared.

"Listen, I get it," Cockerell said. "You thought this was all finished a long time ago. Over and done with. But—"

"Leave me alone," Casserly snapped, raising his voice. "Just leave me be."

"Everything okay here?"

Cockerell looked up and saw the bartender standing over them, concern and a little bit of suspicion etched on his face.

"We're good," Cockerell said.

"George?" the bartender asked. "You all right?"

Casserly didn't answer. Cockerell, for a second, was worried he was going to tell the bartender to throw him out.

Then Casserly cleared his throat. "Yeah. I'm fine." He held up his beer. "Could use another one of these. A fresh one."

"Sure." Now the bartender looked down at Cockerell. "You?"

"Yeah. I'll have one too." Cockerell pulled a twenty from his billfold and held it up. "On me."

"No." Casserly said quickly. "Me. On my tab, Jay."

"You're the boss. Be right back."

The bartender left. Casserly picked the report back up. "Always knew it. One day, this all would come back and bite me in the ass."

Casserly sighed and leaned back against the booth. He seemed about to say something more, then shook his head. Working things through in his mind.

The bartender came back with two beers. "You sure you're all right, George?" he asked.

"Yeah. I'm good. Just, the stuff the detective here is showing me, takes me back, you know?" He picked his beer up, downed half of it in a long swig, then smiled up at the bartender. "Memory lane, Jay. Not always a fun place to take a stroll."

"I know what you mean." The bartender looked down at Cockerell then. "Take it easy on him, okay?"

He said it with a smile, but there was a definite undertone of

CHAPTER 25

a threat in there.

"I will," Cockerell said, raising his own beer. "And thanks for this."

He took a sip and almost gagged. Forced a smile instead. Then the bartender was gone, and it was the two of them once more.

"William Manchester." Casserly shook his head. "You know, afterward, I looked the guy up. It made sense, then, what they told us. Why we had to give up the case. I mean, he was a big deal, Manchester, right? The president's friend."

"That's right," Cockerell said. "He was a big deal."

"I can't tell you anything, you know. National security." Casserly looked up, looked him in the eye. "That's what they said."

They.

They do not leave trails.

Casserly wanted to talk, though. Cockerell could see that. All he needed was a little push.

"Go on," Cockerell said. "I'm listening."

Casserly picked up the report again. "'Unsuccessful pursuit,'" he read. "Yeah. That just about sums it up. Those guys had a vehicle waiting. Anyway … we file that report, and the next day, Chief wants to see us. Me and Exner. He told us what we had to do, but it never sat right with me. Never. And Layton … the look on his face that day…"

"Layton?"

"The chief. John Layton. Good guy. Good cop. Took a lot of shit for those riots back in '68, after King got shot, but if you ask me, he kept the town from burning to the ground. That first night"—Casserly picked up his beer and drained the last of it in a single gulp—"I was on patrol near the Capitol. All night long, practically. I'll never forget that feeling. Like we were at war, you know? Johnson called the army in, they put machine guns guarding the White House. Can you believe it?" Casserly shook his head. "You kids don't know what it was like back then. What the country stood for. We were going somewhere, you know. We went to the moon. The goddamn moon. Now we can't even keep the damn metro running." He sighed and stared off into space.

Cockerell gave the old man a minute, then he cleared his throat. "You were saying. The look on the chief's face," he prompted.

"Right. Layton had this big old wooden desk. Thing took up almost his entire office. When we walked in, me and X, there was a guy leaning up against one corner of it, watching us. Layton pretended like the guy wasn't even there. Told me and Jake Exner to have a seat. He sits down too, starts telling us how we don't need to worry about the case anymore, tells us that yeah, Manchester is being followed, but it's the Feds following him, and there's a reason for that, a good reason. It's all on the up-and-up. And the whole time he's talking to us, I knew—don't ask me how, but I knew—it was for this guy's benefit. The chief just doing what this guy wanted him to." Casserly shook his head in disgust. "Finally, the chief produces the new report, and he tells me to sign it. Like that was what really happened. What else could I do?"

Cockerell nodded. "You were just a kid."

"A rookie. Goddamn right I signed it." Casserly belched involuntarily. Swallowed it. "Signed it, and kept my mouth shut about it, all these years. Up until now. National security. That's what they told me." He looked Cockerell in the eye. "Was I wrong?"

"I don't know. But I think you're doing the right thing, telling the truth now." He paused. "What else can you tell me about the guy in the chief's office?"

"The colonel? Not much. He was a white guy. Middle-aged, wearing this big old hat—"

"Wait. Colonel?"

CHAPTER 25

"Yeah. Sorry. I didn't say that before?"

"No. So what was he, army? Navy? Air force?"

"Don't know." Casserly shook his head. "He wasn't in uniform."

"So how do you know he was a colonel?"

"Because right after I signed the report, the chief says, 'The colonel and I thank you for your cooperation.'"

"He never said his name?"

"Nope. Never said a single word."

"You remember anything else about him?"

"Just that hat he had on. Big white cowboy hat. One of those Statlers."

"Statler." Cockerell frowned. Took him a second. "Stetson, you mean?"

"Right." Casserly nodded. "A big white Stetson. That's it exactly."

26

Cockerell pressed the old man further, even bought them another round of that bathwater that they were passing off as beer, just to keep the conversation going. But Casserly, having given up his secret, became a reluctant conversationalist. Kept looking down at his beer. Hunching up, defensively. Tired? Scared? Didn't matter. Cockerell had gotten what he needed.

He went out to his little rent-a-car by the curb.

"Antonio's."

"Yeah. I'd like to order a pizza."

"Name?"

"It's Cockerell. Mike Cockerell."

"What?"

"I mean Woodhull. The name is Woodhull."

"One minute."

It was a lot less than that.

"Detective." Li came on the line. She sounded angry. "Please follow correct procedure when reporting in. Protocol is important. Maintaining secure lines of communication. Otherwise—"

"I apologize. Is she there? Espy?"

"Ms. Harper is currently unavailable. Examining financial records out of state. You found something?"

"Someone." He told her about Casserly then—the right George—and the man in the white Stetson.

"A colonel."

"Yes."

"With a cowboy hat. That is not much to go on."

CHAPTER 26

"Agreed. But combine that with the date on that police report—"

"Yes. We can cross-reference records of service personnel stationed in DC at that time."

"Exactly. And that cowboy hat tells us something else," he added. "This guy's probably from somewhere out west."

"Possibly so. One of the appendices in Manchester's book lists all the people he spoke with and when. Perhaps this colonel is on that list."

"Or he's connected to someone on it."

"July 1964. That is the date on the police report?"

"Yes."

"That is after Manchester spoke with Jackie Kennedy. After the tapes were made."

Cockerell saw what Li was getting at. "Which could be why our white Stetson guy was keeping an eye on Manchester. He was worried about what Jackie might have said. It would help if we knew what that was, exactly."

"You mean if we could listen to the tapes."

"Yes."

"I have been considering the issue as well," Li said. "Those tapes are in the basement of the John F. Kennedy Presidential Library in Boston."

"I know that," Cockerell said. "You thinking we should head up there and go get them?"

"No. But it did occur to me that a trip to Middletown might be in order."

Cockerell frowned. "You lost me."

"The tapes in Boston are very well protected. But Manchester's notes, including the transcripts of those recordings, are at Wesleyan University in Middletown, Connecticut. Where he taught. Where he was buried, in fact. They might be more easily accessible."

"Maybe we can dig him up. Get him to lend a hand."

"Ha ha," Li said. "What an amusing bit of speculation."

"Yeah. Well … I'm heading back to you. About an hour out, if I don't hit traffic."

"An hour and a half. You will hit traffic."

"We'll see," Cockerell said, and they hung up.

He had one more call to make before he got going.

"Beck. It's me."

"About goddamn time. What happened? Was Casserly there? What did he say? Did he say anything?"

"Beck. Calm down. He was there. I talked to him."

"And?"

"National security. That's what they told him. That's why he had to change the report."

"Ha!" she exclaimed. "We were right. I knew we were right. Did Casserly say who told him to it? Did he ever talk to Manchester? Did he—"

"Yes. Yes. No."

"What?"

"I don't have all the answers yet. I'm going to go back to the people I work for, and—"

"Oh no," she said. "No way. You're not leaving me out of this."

"Beck. We're gonna do the right thing here. Like I promised. But like you said, we need to be careful. Let me go back to my people."

"I'll go to the press."

"What?"

"You try and cut me out of this, I'll go right to the press."

"And what good will that do? Like you said, the stuff that gets printed these days—"

CHAPTER 26

"I'll give them your name. We'll see what happens."

Cockerell took a deep breath. Temper, he told himself. "That is not a good idea."

"Is that a threat?"

"No. It's just not a good idea."

"Then tell me what he said. Casserly."

Cockerell hesitated. He ought to go back to Woodhull, clear this with Espy. But she was unavailable. Out-of-state financial records.

"If I tell you, you'll keep it between us."

"Of course."

"And not do anything about it."

"I'm seventy-six years old. I live in a trailer park. What am I going to do?"

"Promise me."

"Yes, I promise. We're a team," she said. "You, me, and your tech billionaire friends."

"They're not—"

"Kidding," she said. "Just kidding."

Cockerell told her what happened at the bar.

"Chief Layton," she said. "I remember him. And a colonel with a white Stetson hat."

"Yeah. That's right."

She was silent a moment. "That's ringing a bell."

"Seriously?"

"Seriously. I read something, somewhere … I just can't remember. Give me a minute. Let me think."

He did. Started counting in his head. Got to seven.

"Russia," she said.

"What?"

"The book. Something to do with Russia in the fifties. Damn

it. My memory is for shit."

"Beck," Cockerell said, putting a little urgency in his voice. "Tell me what you're talking about, please. Russia?"

"The Cold War," she said. "I think. I gotta go through the shelves."

"Beck…"

"Don't worry, we're a team. I won't do anything without you."

There was a click. *Call ended*, read the display screen.

Great, Cockerell thought, and pulled out into traffic.

27

They started off by bringing up a report on Desert View's consolidated financials. The overall numbers mirrored what she already knew: Desert View was back in the black this year, its stock price climbing back up after a disastrous few months. A little digging quickly showed why.

It was all due to Aqua Roma. The big development she'd been reading about. On October 15 of last year, that project's primary financier, North Henderson Financial Trust, had pulled back. Refused to lend Desert View any more money.

"I can see why," Cabral said.

Espy nodded. "They missed their benchmarks." Construction benchmarks—dates when certain work was supposed to be completed, stipulated in the terms of the loan. That was how construction loans worked: You received sufficient money (in this case $25 million) to start the job; if you finished that portion on schedule, you got more money. A second draw, it was called, to do the next round of work. And so on.

Desert View had failed to live up to their part of the bargain. The details were right there on the monitor.

Pilings for waterfront structures. Scheduled completion: August 1. Status: incomplete.

Foundations poured, conduit and pipes laid for Residential Towers 2 and 3. Scheduled completion: August 15. Status: incomplete.

All told, there were six separate instances where Desert View and its contractors had failed to meet the terms of the loan. The bank had extended their deadlines twice, at Frank Ferrone's personal urging. "I just need a little more time. Things are about to come together, I promise," he'd written. "Trust me."

But they hadn't. North Henderson Financial pulled back. Construction slowed. The slowdown had a ripple effect. Several tenants backed out of their leases, and rumors began to spread about the company's fiscal health. Rumors not just in Las Vegas but back east, on Wall Street.

Desert View's stock began to fall.

Espy had seen this sort of thing happen before. An unfinished project the size of Aqua Roma was, in some ways, like a house of cards. One little push in the wrong direction and the whole thing could collapse. And North Henderson pulling back was exactly that kind of push. The primary lender, then the tenants, and the stock price—it was a death spiral. And if Aqua Roma went down, it more than likely would take Desert View with it.

In this case though, the death spiral had been halted.

At the beginning of December, another company had stepped forward. A company called Europa Land Partners.

They'd appeared out of nowhere. A private company. Swooped in not to lend Desert View money, but to actually buy a piece of the project: Parcel 33 of the Aqua Roma development.

They paid $1.2 billion for it.

That money had not just put the company back in the black, it had given Desert View a huge reserve of capital. Capital that had gone on the books just in time for those Wall Street rumors to turn, just in time for those New York analysts to change their recommendations from "sell" to "buy." Which in turn had sent the company's stock price shooting back up. Which had saved Desert View from cratering and investors from losing a fortune.

"$1.2 billion." Cabral shook his head. "That's a lot of money."

"Sure is." A ridiculous amount of money, in fact. Parcel 33

CHAPTER 27

comprised two hundred acres. Which meant that Europa had paid $6 million an acre.

That couldn't be right.

Last she'd heard, an acre of land in Manhattan was worth $5 million. An acre in Los Angeles was worth $2.7 million. She understood that a thing was worth whatever someone was willing to pay for it. But $6 million?

"Hey. We been at this awhile now. You hungry?" Cabral asked. "We could go upstairs, grab some food."

Espy hesitated. She could, in fact, use something to eat. She wanted to check in with Li, too, see if Cockerell had reported in. And Frederickson. She doubted he was taking a sauna. More likely, he was standing guard outside the bunker door. Probably hadn't eaten either.

But she was really just getting started here. She'd lose something by stepping away from the screen. And, to be honest, there was another reason she didn't want to leave the bunker just yet.

Lish.

She knew the law, and was 99 percent certain there was nothing he could have come up with since she'd entered this room to prevent her from walking back into it, but 99 percent was not 100 percent, particularly when it came to the law.

"I'm good," she said. "Let's keep going."

❖ ❖ ❖ ❖ ❖

Cabral bent the rules just a little. They ate lunch—fried chicken from the Greenbrier's kitchen, with mashed potatoes and green beans and pecan pie and a jug of iced tea—in a different server room, one that was currently offline for maintenance. He even left her alone in there for half an hour after they'd finished eating, while he took a support call from the Maryland site.

She decided to use that time to sketch out her next steps. She took out a notebook and pen, and made two columns: where she was, and where she wanted to get to. She cradled her chin in one hand to think. Woke up when Cabral opened the door to retrieve her. "I could give you another half hour here. To rest."

"No," she said, standing. "I'm good."

But she wasn't.

Back in the server room, staring at the screens, she struggled to find her footing again. She had Cabral run a keyword search on Frank Ferrone. That produced thousands of results: financial records and also internal correspondence, much of it between Ferrone and Desert View's COO, a man named John Romano. Johnny, in the emails. Lish was in there too, of course, along with a lot of acronyms and abbreviations.

B and K concur. DC is giving us problems.

Copy me and K on decision.

As per meeting of 15th, VTC is a go. They were talking in code. To keep secrets? To do business as quickly as possible? Probably a little of both.

There was also a great deal of email correspondence related to that $1.2 billion parcel of land, Parcel 33, and the building planned for that site. The Platinum Peacock Hotel and Casino, which was going to have four swimming pools, three golf courses, and gaming rooms roughly equivalent in size to the ones at the Bellagio and the Wynn—combined. And Europa's purchase of that land—that site—also included title to all existing structures on the land. Ah. Which probably did put Parcel 33's value closer to $1.2 billion.

"Ms. Harper." Cabral gestured to the clock on the wall. It was 4:45.

"I have to run scheduled maintenance on the server at five o'clock," Cabral said. "In fifteen minutes, we have a hard stop. Just

CHAPTER 27

giving you a heads-up."

"Shit," she said, and then shook her head. "Sorry. It's just..."

"A frustrating day. I get it. If it helps any, there's a lot of information here, right? I mean, you've been through what, maybe ten percent of the data here?"

Espy nodded. "Probably less."

"Exactly." He smiled. "So cut yourself some slack. Go grab something to eat, get a good night's sleep, come back tomorrow. No reason you can't do that, right?"

"Not that I know of," she said, though again she thought of what Lish might cook up in the interim to stop her from coming down here again.

Damn it.

There was something here. Something in these files Ferrone did not want her to find. Serious stuff for which he was willing to threaten her, and her mother, and her father's reputation, to prevent her from learning. She could feel it was here. Just like that night back in the locker room, at Garrett's golf club.

The secret your senator was killed to protect.

"DC, not Dallas," Frederickson had said. "That's where we ought to be looking."

DC is giving us problems.

"Good Lord," she said. "I'm an idiot."

Cabral turned to her. "Sorry?"

"One more search to try, okay?" she asked. "Before we call it a day?"

"Yeah. Sure. Why not?" Cabral rolled his chair back to the terminal. "Shoot."

"Garrett Crandall."

"The senator? The one who just died?"

"That's right."

"Okay. Spell his name for me please?"

"Two *r*'s, two *t*'s, two *l*'s."

He typed it in. "Whoa," he said, and turned the screen slightly toward her.

Garrett Crandall. 888 mentions found.

Whoa indeed, she thought, and smiled. Now they were on to something.

Cabral cleared his throat. "What do you want to do? Keeping in mind that we don't have time to go through all these today."

"Let's do what we can," she said.

"In fifteen minutes."

"Yes. In fifteen minutes. Start at the top."

Cabral nodded, turned back to the workstation, and brought up the first result.

Espy leaned in closer and began to read.

28

Cockerell barely noticed the first fire engine that passed him, sirens blaring, lights flashing. Pulled over to the side of the road, let it go by. He was headed back to the trailer park to make sure Beck didn't do anything stupid, but he was thinking about Manchester. And that Colonel with the white Stetson, who'd had him followed. Why?

Manchester had talked to a lot of people in DC after JFK was killed. But Cockerell kept coming back to Jackie and those tapes. The recordings she'd fought to keep sealed away for a hundred years. Why?

The secret your senator was killed to protect.

That secret was on those tapes. Was something Jackie had let slip during her conversations with Manchester. Something she hadn't given a second thought to until Manchester showed her his rough draft. That's when she had decided to sue. Why? Because she was scared. And something else. Bobby Kennedy had been right there with her. Been an integral part of the decision to ask for that hundred-year timeframe. Which meant he'd been scared too.

And six months later he was dead. Assassinated, just like his brother.

These people, they do not leave trails.

Stop it, Cockerell told himself. Just stop it.

And at that instant, two police cars came flying past him, doing seventy-five, maybe eighty in a thirty-five mph zone. Something was going on, Cockerell realized. Something out of the ordinary. The cop cars, the fire engine…

Beck.

The thought came out of nowhere. Pushed everything else aside. A gut feeling. He pulled up her number on the car's display.

The phone just rang. And rang, and rang, and rang.

Didn't mean anything necessarily. But Cockerell felt a sinking feeling in the pit of his stomach all the same.

He floored it the rest of the way to the trailer park. The moment he pulled in, that sinking feeling turned into a sickening certainty.

At end of the little cul-de-sac where he'd parked last night were the fire truck and the police cars that had passed him, along with a half-dozen other emergency vehicles. They formed a perimeter around Beck's double-wide, where a crowd had gathered.

He could smell the smoke even with his windows closed. And as he pulled closer, he saw the evidence. Fire. The double-wide was a burned-out shell. And Beck? Where was she?

We're a team, Beck said. *I won't do anything without you.*

But she had. She must have. Done something, called someone, let something slip…

Casserly. The police report. If what happened to Beck wasn't an accident, if whoever had done this had also found out about the old man, about the Central Bank and Trust envelope…

Cockerell parked just shy of the crowd. Climbed out of his car and pulled out his phone. He had to call the bar. Casserly might still be there, he might not, but they'd know how to get hold of him. And the guy running the place—hell, all the people who worked there—they were cops. They'd be able to protect the old man.

A woman stepped up alongside him.

"Hey. You know what's going on? What happened here?" she asked.

"Not sure." He answered without looking up, trying to focus. He needed a story to tell them—Casserly's friends. Why the old

CHAPTER 28

man was in danger. A story they'd believe and act on. He couldn't tell them the truth. They wouldn't believe the truth.

"Some kind of fire, I guess. Right?" The woman tugged on his sleeve. He turned to face her.

She was small. Thin. With a full head of pure white, glossy hair. She looked familiar.

Cockerell lowered his phone. Stared at her. She stared right back.

"Something the matter?" she asked.

"I know you." He snapped his fingers. "DC. The towers. The construction site." Trailing Espy on her way to meet Nemkov. "You were there. The underpass. The tent city."

She laughed. "Well done."

She hadn't let go of his sleeve. Before he could react, she yanked him toward her and in one quick movement jabbed him with something in her other hand.

Cockerell pushed her away.

A hypodermic, he saw now. He felt a burning sensation in his upper arm.

"What the hell…" He looked at the arm, then at her.

"You all right?" she called out, much louder than she needed to.

He shook his head. His tongue felt suddenly thick in his mouth. "I…"

"You sure you're all right?" she repeated again. Even louder. A few heads in the crowd behind them turned.

His vision blurred. He dropped his phone. Stumbled and went to his knees.

"Hey!" the woman yelled. "Hey! Hey!"

More heads turned. Not just the trailer park residents now, but a cop behind the police tape. Cockerell saw concern cross his face, and he lifted the tape. Started toward them.

Help, Cockerell tried to say, and went from his knees to the ground. Felt the dirt against his cheek.

"Hey! Over here!" he heard the woman shout. "I think this guy's having a heart attack or something!"

Not a heart attack, Cockerell tried to say. No.

But there was something wrong with him. Something very very wrong.

The woman leaned over. Lowered her voice.

"White 13," she whispered. "Sorry. But this one, you don't wake up from."

29

It was all about climate change, Espy saw.

Aqua Roma's impact on the environment, local and statewide. The amount of scarce resources—water, in particular—the development would require. The traffic and pollution it would generate. Garrett's subcommittee and Garrett in particular had focused in on the construction like a laser.

There were dozens of emails back and forth between Desert View officials about the committee's work. About Crandall. Growing concern from the company's officers. Reading between the lines, Espy also saw (or thought she saw, the language was very nuanced) evidence of bribery—both failed and successful attempts.

"Ms. Harper." Cabral spoke gently. "I know you're on to something here, but…" She glanced down at her watch. Her father's old Panerai Luminor. The numbers glowed softly in the dark. It was closing in on six. Cabral had given her almost another hour. Very reluctantly. She couldn't put him out any further.

"Understood," she said. "Give me a second to think."

Okay. Garrett had been hard on Desert View. On Aqua Roma. The size, the scale of the development. Ferrone had reason to be angry at him. *DC is giving us problems.* But the federal bureaucracy was always a problem in cases like this. An obstacle to be overcome. There wasn't really anything to go on here; Ferrone's name hadn't even surfaced in any of the emails she'd been reading…

She sat up straight.

"One last thing before we call it a day," she said to Cabral. "Refine the query. Garrett Crandall and Frank Ferrone."

CODENAME: BLACKJACK

"Can do." He leaned forward, keyed in a few instructions. The screen cleared, then lit up again.

"One match," he said, punching in another command. "Here you go."

Espy rolled her chair closer.

The Desert View Real Estate Investment Trust
Board Minutes
SPECIAL SESSION DECEMBER 1

Board Members:
Present: Michael Brody, Francis Ferrone Jr, CEO,
B. Kingsleigh, David D. McLean, L. Sonores
Absent: M Peterson
Quorum present? Yes

Also Present:
V. Falconetti, EVP, John Romano, COO, Sheila Swanson, CFO

Proceedings:
This meeting was called to discuss recent events related to the Aqua Roma development.

Project Status:
1. DM presented blueprint modifications with downsized tenant occupancy for Residential Towers 2 and 3, as well as new waterfront structures with reduced lake circumference.
2. SS presented updated financial projections based on above.
3. FF rejected both modifications, RK concurred. Board in its entirety agreed to revisit at a future date.
4. Concerns were raised over recently conducted session of United States Senate Subcommittee for Environmental Development, where a hold on further construction at the site was proposed. LS suggests procedural methodologies for delaying action by committee. Lack of enforcement tools, etc. FF notes

CHAPTER 29

danger of any further construction delays after North Henderson loan debacle. Possible rebound effect on stock price.

Full board concurrence; Senator Crandall's objections must be overcome by any and all means at the company's disposal.

Espy read that last paragraph once, and then again, just to make sure of what she was seeing. *Any and all means.*

Her lips tightened.

These people, they do not leave trails.

Except the way it looked to her … they just had.

"You want me to print that out?" Cabral asked.

She nodded. "Absolutely I do."

A loud ringing sounded. Took Espy a second to figure out what it was: a red telephone, an antique, in one corner of the room. Cabral picked up the receiver and, a second later, held it out for her to take.

"For you."

"Me?" Espy frowned, and took the receiver from him. "Hello?"

"Espy." It was Frederickson.

"Sorry," Espy said. "Meant to keep you updated. I think I found what we've been looking for. In fact, I'm sure of it."

"That's good," he replied. "I'm glad."

But the tone of his voice—he didn't sound glad at all.

"What is it?" Espy asked. "What's the matter?"

"Just get back up here," he said. "Soon as you can."

THE NEXT MORNING

It was our country for a while.
Now it's theirs again.

Norman Mailer, *Controversy*

30

Marcus was sitting on the front porch in his dad's old rocking chair, drinking coffee, watching the sun come up, talking with the dog—well, talking to the dog—when he heard an engine. Something coming toward the house from off in the distance. A car? Didn't sound like a car.

He put the coffee mug down on the porch railing and reached into the back pocket of his jeans. Pulled out his phone, which was tied to the surveillance system, and brought up the long-distance monitor. Ah.

A drone. He zoomed in on the image. It was an older model, an MK-30. Six-rotor design, with the old Amazon smiley face logo on the body. Coming on a straight line, right to the house. It looked harmless enough. Standard delivery drone.

But Marcus hadn't ordered anything.

More to the point, it was six thirty a.m. There were regulations. Drones like this were not allowed to fly at six thirty in the morning. Never mind the noise pollution; as far as the outside world was concerned, this house, this address, didn't exist. It certainly wasn't in any publicly accessible database. So whatever kind of delivery was headed this way had nothing to do with Amazon.

He looked over at the dog. Wilbur. His father's old Bassett hound. "What do you think, boy?"

Wilbur looked back at him with a resigned expression. But then, Wilbur always had a resigned expression.

Marcus nodded. "I'm with you. Better safe than sorry."

Marcus picked up the rifle leaning against the porch railing, sighted down the barrel, and fired.

Ping.

The engine noise stopped. The drone plummeted to the ground with a loud metallic crunch. If there had been neighbors within a few miles, the noise would surely have woken them. As it was…

Dead silence.

He set the rifle down and picked his coffee mug back up. "Okay. I finish drinking this, we go take a look. Sound like a plan?"

Wilbur looked up at him with that same resigned expression, and moaned.

"You're right," Marcus said. "You need to eat. My bad."

❖ ❖ ❖ ❖ ❖

He fed the dog, then fed himself. On his way back out the door, he caught sight of himself in the hallway mirror. He stopped, and shook his head.

Marcus Aurelius Kleinman. You have really let yourself go here.

He'd left Lutsk eight weeks ago, looking like the fresh-faced twenty-five-year-old investment banker he'd been posing as. The curse of his eternally youthful appearance, even though he was pushing forty years old.

Now he looked like Charles Manson. He needed a shave, a haircut, and a shower. Some sunshine. Some real food. And let's face it, no slight to Wilbur, but a little human companionship as well. He'd thought about rejoining civilization a couple weeks back, when he'd gotten the news about Garrett. Heading to DC for the funeral. He decided against it. Too many complications there. Besides, what was it that his mom always used to say? Funerals are for the living, not the dead.

Out in the field, he found the drone shattered into dozens of pieces. Inside the chassis was a small metal box, about the size of

CHAPTER 30

a pack of playing cards. He thought about opening it then and there, out in the field, decided against it. That's what the lab in the basement was for. The kind of thing the whole facility, in fact, had been designed to deal with. Because what looked like a ramshackle old farmhouse had, once upon a time, been one of the agency's most important biosafety facilities. Designed and largely staffed by his father and his father's associates.

It had been abandoned for quite some time now.

Marcus had come here after Lutsk to regroup. Easy enough to bypass the security protocols, let himself in. He'd brought Wilbur along, thinking the dog might appreciate a visit to his old stomping grounds. Hard to tell if that was the case.

He took the little metal box back to the house. Down to the basement. But it turned out the protective gear he donned and the biosafety lab were unnecessary precautions. The box contained only an SD card.

He sat down at the kitchen table in front of his laptop. Wilbur came and sat at his feet as Marcus popped the SD card in. A video began playing.

A woman seated in a black leather chair. Behind her was a huge fish tank. No. Not tank, he corrected himself. Habitat.

Wilbur howled.

"I'm with you, boy." Marcus nodded. "She looks terrible."

Exhausted. And more than that. Haunted. Something bad had happened, he realized. Something that made all the complicated feelings he had toward, and for, Esperanza Harper subside for the moment.

"Marcus. I hope you're there. I hope you get this. I hope …"

She took a breath. "I don't know where to start except at the beginning. With Garrett's death. It wasn't an accident, Marcus. He was murdered."

Marcus did a doubletake—a sudden movement that made Wilbur go skittering backward across the floor in fear.

"Easy boy. Easy."

"We need help. Your help. We found something ... you'll see. Once you read everything here. You'll know what to do. But one more thing." She leaned closer to the camera. "We've been compromised. Woodhull. That's why I'm coming to you like this."

Woodhull. Their DC chapter, based out of Anderson House. Marcus, like his father before him, was with Culper, out of Savannah.

"You can't contact me directly. But I hope—I trust—you'll find another way to keep in touch." She hesitated, then offered up a smile. "Good luck. And thank you."

The recording stopped. Vanished from the screen, replaced by a window filled with icons. File folders.

He sat there a moment, dazed. Shell-shocked. Garrett Crandall, murdered? Woodhull compromised? What was going on here?

Only one way to find out.

He clicked on one of the file folders on the screen

Dossier, it was called.

He opened a file at random and began to read.

31

She was in the Hamilton room, the oldest room in the complex. A room that predated the elevator, the tunnel system, the Society library. Once upon a time, it had served as the chapter's operational center. Now, like Anderson House itself, it was more of a museum, where the subterranean chapters of the Society displayed their most important historical mementoes.

Like the one she was staring at right now.

A framed letter on crinkled, sepia-colored paper, the ink faded near to illegibility, protected behind thick vacuum-sealed glass. It had been written near the end of the Revolutionary War, on November 24, 1783, by a man named Tobias Minshaw. It was one of the oldest objects in the Society's collection and certainly one of the most valuable.

If it please your Excellency, the letter began—how so many people thought of George Washington back then, not just as first among citizens, but the closest thing to royalty America had. Democratic impulses to the contrary, most were more comfortable with the idea of a king than a nascent democracy. *We have had no luck finding the gravesite. But our young friend is here, somewhere. We will find him, as you requested. And bring him to you, to be buried with full honors.*

The letter went on to discuss a number of other matters, and Minshaw's reporting had greatly influenced Washington's selection of his administration.

But that wasn't why the letter was on display.

The letter had a place of honor because of the young friend whose grave Washington was desperate to find. A man who had been captured by the British and hung as a spy at twenty-one years old, barely a man and woefully underprepared for his mission. That young man was Nathan "I regret that I have but one life to give for my country" Hale.

Espy didn't know if Washington's people had found Nathan Hale's grave. If they'd buried him with the honors he deserved.

Mike Cockerell would never get his.

None of them could go to his funeral. They couldn't acknowledge his work for them. Not now, not ever. That was the way this worked. As far as the whole world was concerned...

"Heart attack. That is how they're treating it. They have witnesses," Li said when Espy and Frederickson returned from the Greenbrier. They'd walked into the operations room at Woodhull to find Li grim-faced, staring at a news report on her monitor. *Two Dead in Pennsylvania Trailer Park Fire.*

Smoke inhalation. And a coronary incident. A guy who died on the scene. They flashed Cockerell's picture. A clean-cut, much younger Mike Cockerell. A Metro Police officer. No one knew why he'd been at the trailer park. There might be witnesses, Espy supposed, to the meeting he'd had with the older woman whose picture now filled the screen. But no one would ever guess the connection between them.

"Lynn Beck," the local fire chief said on the TV. "Looks like the fire started in her trailer. It was full of old books. Papers. Whole place went up in minutes. Wasn't a thing anyone could do."

"Don't tell me you've been here all night."

She turned and saw Frederickson standing in the doorway.

"No. I went home. Got a few hours of sleep." And reached out to a friend, she added silently. Something she couldn't tell Frederickson about. At least not yet. "You?"

"Went to Casserly's apartment."

CHAPTER 31

"And?"

"The cops are all over the place. They're calling it murder suicide. Or an accidental death, then suicide, but really..."

"I get the picture. Thank you."

Casserly. The patrolman Cockerell had found. Dead now too. Him, and his troubled grandson.

These people do not leave trails.

"Whoever it is we're up against—they were following Cockerell," Frederickson said.

"Yes."

"They may be on to us too," he said.

"Quite possibly. We have eyes out. No sign of anything suspicious. Li's also changed communications protocols."

"That's a start. If it's the protocols. If the whole system isn't compromised." Frederickson sighed. "So what now?"

"Ferrone," she said. "I want to focus on him. On Desert View."

"I don't know." Frederickson frowned. "Faking a heart attack, starting a trailer fire, that thing with Casserly and his grandson? That's not how the mob operates. You know that. The mob, they put a bullet in your brain, leave you by the side of the road. It's like their signature, right? And they don't care if you know they did it."

"Frank Ferrone is not your typical mobster."

"Agreed. But what about this colonel? The one with the white Stetson?"

"Li's checking service records," Espy said. "Let's see what she finds."

"And in the meantime?"

"In the meantime ... we wait."

"Wait. For what?"

"Start of business. Pacific Standard Time." She checked her watch. "Just a few more hours."

32

Doug had to give it to the guy. He didn't do anything by halves.

FERRONE. A single word in black-and-gold letters, two stories tall, seemingly suspended in mid-air above the entrance to the building Doug was now walking toward. Ferrone Tower was twenty stories of blue-tinted glass, framed in gold, a block behind the strip. Within sight of the Wynn and the Encore. No doubt the letters lit up in neon come nightfall to make sure Ferrone's name was as brightly advertised as those others.

Doug pushed through the revolving doors, the lenses in his sunglasses adjusting to the new light. The lobby was all marble: solid black sheets of it on the walls, the floors tiled in black and white polished stone. There was a waterfall opposite the entrance, fifty feet high, cascading down a twisting silver sculpture fastened to the wall. And there was the name again, FERRONE, in matching silver letters ten feet high.

The security guard checked his ID and sent him up to the nineteenth floor, where he emerged into a reception area with dark wood, white leather chairs, and incense-tinged air. A large screen above the reception desk blinked to life and a man's face appeared—late forties, looked to be just a little bit overweight, fake tan and a thick head of silver and black hair.

"Doug Rivers." The man smiled. "I'm John Romano. Call me Johnny. Everybody does. Come on down. Second door on your right."

Second door on the right was unmarked, smoked glass. It looked thick. Soundproof. As Doug approached, he saw a

CHAPTER 32

touchscreen panel to the side of that door pulse, change colors from orange to green. The door swung open with a soft chirp, and he entered.

The office was huge. Shaped like a slice of pie—thin at the entrance, opening up to a line of windows at least fifty feet long, overlooking the Strip. The man from the video screen, Johnny Romano, stood in the center of the room.

"There he is." Romano smiled and stepped forward. They shook hands. "Doug Rivers. It's a pleasure. A real pleasure."

"Mr. Romano. Glad to meet you too."

"Hey, like I said … Johnny, please."

Doug saw now that thick head of hair was actually a wig. And the tan was fake too. Not the suit, though. That was Italian silk. Had to be a $2,000 outfit, if not more. It was also, at a guess, about a size too small.

"Nice glasses." Romano gestured. "What are those, Ray-Bans?"

"No. Small company, friend of mine owns."

"Nice. I like the color there."

"Thanks." Romano was pointing at the frames, the bridge and temple pieces, Doug guessed, both of a cobalt-blue polycarbonate, cast to his specifications. To match his eyes.

Vanity, thy name is Rivers, as one of his exes had said right before she slapped him.

Though in this case, vanity was the least important part of the equation. What really counted was the machinery hidden in the plastic—the chips, antennas, and semi-conductors.

"Let's sit." Romano gestured toward a brown leather couch and chairs around a long glass table four-inches thick, bevel-cut, the same smoke-gray finish as the doors. The same table that Ferrone had posed in front of in that article Espy had shown Doug about Aqua Roma.

He was pleased to see that table still had the exact same stack of chips on it that had been shown in the picture accompanying the article. A stack of chips from the Peacock casino. Hundred-and fifty-dollar chips, the blue and the green ones.

Doug had a couple of similar, albeit more functional, chips in his pocket.

Romano took a chair. Doug took the other, his hand closing on one of those chips as he sat.

"So. You had a good trip in?" Romano asked.

"I did."

"Good. Glad to hear it. Now, where are you staying?"

"Over at the Bellagio."

"Of course, of course. Good choice," Romano said, putting on an insincere smile. "But if you want a change of scenery, I'd be happy to offer you a suite over at the Peacock."

"The Peacock." Doug picked a couple of casino chips off the coffee table, rolling them back and forth in his hand. "That's a generous offer. Thank you." He nodded at Romano as he added the chip from his other hand to those from the table, and then put the new stack back. "Let me think on it."

"Of course."

Doug sat back, touching the little bump on the bridge of his glasses. The phone in his pocket vibrated softly. Connection established. Connection between the electronics in the chip, those in his glasses, and Li's, back in Woodhull.

She could now monitor every audio, visual, and electronic signal within a fifty foot radius of where he was sitting.

"I want to thank you for arranging this meeting on such short notice. I appreciate it. Speaking of which—" Doug looked around the room. "I assume we're waiting on Mr. Ferrone before we get started."

CHAPTER 32

"Ah. About that." Romano offered up another insincere smile. "I'm afraid Mr. Ferrone is not going to be able to join us this morning."

He tried to keep the disappointment off his face. "Oh. That's a shame."

"Yeah. He sends his apologies. Out-of-town visitors. But I'll pass along everything we talk about. You can be sure about that."

"Well. I hope we can meet up at a later date."

"No worries about that. Mr. Ferrone—Frank—he doesn't do business with anybody he doesn't meet personally. So." Romano leaned forward, and his gaze narrowed. "A real-estate project. Tell me what you have in mind here."

Doug smiled. First rule of acting: Play to your audience. The audience he'd been expecting this morning was Frank Ferrone. Now that he was talking to Johnny Romano…

He needed a little more information.

He tapped the right temple piece near the bridge of the glasses.

"Whoa," Doug had said the first time Li had demonstrated the system.

"Very impressive, is it not? The virtual equivalent of a 60-inch monitor. Visible only to you."

Li had reached out and tapped to the right of the frame. A blinking green rectangle appeared around her face. "Facial recognition software. State of the art," Li had said.

That same green rectangle now appeared around Romano's face. The text blinked: *Subject Identification Complete*. And then more text flowed.

John Paul Romano. Senior Vice President of Development, Ferrone Enterprises. Age 47. Married, four children, two different wives. Also an officer and board member for a number of other companies, including the Desert View Real Estate Corporation.

Romano had also been part of the production company Ferrone had formed a dozen or so years ago, when he was trying his hand at the movie business. Executive in charge of story development.

"Perfect," Doug said.

"Excuse me?" Romano asked.

"Sorry. Just thinking out loud." He tapped the temple piece again, and the virtual monitor disappeared.

"No worries. So. Your real estate project."

"Right." Doug straightened in his chair. "Well. I don't know how much you know about the movie business, but there's a lot of moving pieces involved. The actors, the director, the crew on the set, the crew behind the scenes, the producers … a lot of cooks in the kitchen."

"Oh, believe me." Romano smiled. "I know."

"You talk like you've had experience."

"Yeah. I worked with Mr. Ferrone a bit. When he was out in Hollywood. I was in story development."

"Good. Then you know the story is the most important thing. If the story gets messed up during production, the movie gets messed up. And what's happened to me more than once, a story I picked out and attached myself to gets sold to some studio, and everyone starts putting their two cents in."

"Too many cooks."

"Exactly. And everyone has the best intentions, but—"

"Things get messed up." Romano nodded. "I've seen it happen."

"I bet you have. Now, I was talking about this with a few people, friends in the industry, and we thought, hey, maybe there's a better way to do this. A different way. A way to make sure everyone stays on the same page. A way to—"

"I get it." Romano snapped his fingers. "You want to open

CHAPTER 32

your own studio."

"Yes. That's exactly right. We want the ability to choose our projects, use our own facilities to film them. Our own sound stages, our own crews, our own production staff. Now, we've been looking in some other locations—Toronto, Jersey, Philly—but Vegas ... it's got a lot of advantages. Proximity to LA, tax incentives, a lot of open space. I'm sure there are others."

Romano's smile grew broader. "Buddy, you don't know the half of it."

And here was where Doug was supposed to continue on in the "sounds like we can do business" vein, continue to ingratiate himself, maybe set up a second meeting on a return trip to Vegas (which would never happen), because his work here was done. Espy had said specifically: His job was to get into the building and get out. Be careful.

But Cockerell was dead. And it wasn't Frank Ferrone he was dealing with here, it was Johnny Romano, who might be cut from a similar cloth but was a different man entirely. A vainer man, for sure. A weaker man. A man he could use to their advantage.

Doug cleared his throat.

Let's see who's selling who.

"I've been reading a lot about this one particular real estate project Mr. Ferrone is part of. Something called Aqua Roma?"

"Aqua Roma?" Romano, for a second, looked puzzled.

"Yes. Pretty big project, it sounds like. And right outside Vegas, yes?"

"Yeah." Doug could see the wheels spinning in Romano's head. "Let me guess. You're wondering if there might be space there for your studio idea?"

"The thought had crossed my mind."

"I don't know." The man's brow furrowed. "I'd have to talk to

CODENAME: BLACKJACK

Mr. Ferrone."

"Of course. I get that. But..." Doug gave Romano his 20,000-watt smile. The one he saved for special occasions. "It's just, as long as I'm here ... you think maybe we could go take a look at it?"

❖ ❖ ❖ ❖ ❖

"What's he doing?" Espy asked. "I told him not to take any chances."

"Easy. He's taking the initiative," Frederickson said. "Let's see what happens."

Let's hope we don't have to bury him too, she almost replied, then took a deep breath. Frederickson was right. See what happens. That's all they could do right now.

They were in operations, Espy pacing, Frederickson sitting alongside Li, a row of LCD screens in front of them, one of which now showed the images being broadcast back via Doug's glasses.

"Nice Porsche," Frederickson said as Romano and Doug climbed into a cherry-red car and pulled out into traffic.

"Watch this," Romano said, and revved the engine. Doug, thankfully, muted the audio.

Espy turned her attention to a different screen, back to a video Li had found on the internet. Someone had filmed the last minutes of Michael Cockerell's life.

They hadn't intended to. User ID wh1208 had been filming the fire as it consumed Beck's trailer, though by the starting point of the video, that fire was largely contained. The audio was a general hubbub: snippets of conversations, some expressions of concern, a child crying. And then, a policemen standing near the trailer suddenly straightened and lifted a strand of yellow caution tape, stepped quickly to the left of the screen. The camera followed.

And that's when Espy saw him.

Cockerell was kneeling on the ground. Clutching his left arm,

CHAPTER 32

an expression of shock and confusion on his face.

"Oh my god," a voice said as the cop brushed past the bystanders who had gathered around Cockerell, nearly knocking over an elderly woman who looked on the verge of tears.

No. Not elderly. The woman was younger than Espy had first thought. It was just her hair—it was white.

The camera zoomed in on Cockerell.

He looked helpless. He looked scared.

The cop began giving Cockerell CPR. Someone stepped in front of the screen, and the picture turned black.

"Electronics within the chip are fully functional," Li said. "I've identified multiple wi-fi networks running within Mr. Ferrone's office tower. Decryption protocols running now."

Espy nodded. "Good. Thank you."

This was the whole reason for Doug's ruse: getting her a way in, a peek behind the curtain at what Ferrone was doing, not just with Desert View but the rest of his business empire.

She shifted her attention now to the video feed from Doug's glasses. A few minutes ago, the view had been nothing but desert, flying by through the Porsche's windshield. Now…

"Wow," she said.

"Exactly." Frederickson came and stood beside her chair. "That's one helluva construction site."

Aqua Roma.

She'd seen the numbers, but this was her first glimpse of just how big the project was. Or rather, was going to be. Because as the car continued toward the site, she realized that what they were seeing was only a skeleton of what was to come—steel beams reaching skyward, huge holes in the ground, literal mountains of dirt, roads etched out of the sand—the outlines of what would be roads.

The audio switched back on.

" ... going to be our shopping district." Romano took a hand off the wheel, pointed straight ahead. "Strictly high end—Prada, Chanel, Gucci, Burberry—working on a couple others."

"Impressive," Doug said.

"It will be." Romano smiled. "So. Getting back to your idea, your own studio. It occurred to me, we had some investors pull out of their lease a few months back. One of them, Ultimate Adventures—"

"The water sports guys?"

"That's right."

Espy nodded. She'd heard of them too, an umbrella company for several smaller concerns who managed waterparks, water recreation facilities, waterfront bars and restaurants all across the country. Big operation. Huge money.

"They'd agreed to develop a big chunk of the waterfront. But like I said, they backed out. So now that whole property is available. And it just might be big enough for what you have in mind. Wait till you see it. Beautiful views, and right on the big lake."

"Big lake? There's more than one?"

"Hey." The man smiled. "We don't call it Aqua Roma for nothing."

"Something's not right here. Look." Frederickson nodded at the screen. "You see all that equipment, right?"

"Hard to miss." There were construction trucks, bulldozers, excavators, all sorts of construction machinery."

"And all those guys..."

Espy nodded. Workers in hard hats, holding clipboards, pointing, some of them, others just standing around.

"What are they doing? I mean, I worked construction a couple summers in college, and a site this size—there should be a lot more

CHAPTER 32

going on. Ground getting graded, concrete getting poured. I mean, all those holes in the ground. Those buildings are supposed to be going up, right? And the foundations aren't even done. Why aren't they working? What are they waiting for? I don't get it."

She saw what he meant. There did seem to be a lot of workers doing nothing in particular. But…

"I don't know what to say. Not my area of expertise."

"Whoa!" That exclamation came from Doug as Romano's Porsche came to a sudden stop.

Espy immediately saw why.

The car had almost driven into a huge hole in the ground. Canyon-size. Roughly canyon-shaped, far longer than it was wide.

"Damn it," Romano said. "They're supposed to be staking these roads out as they dig. My apologies."

"No harm. But I see what you mean now," Doug replied. "That's gonna be a big lake, all right."

"That? The big lake?" Romano shook his head. "No. The lake is further north. This here is just the casino footprint. Casino, hotel, and conference center, actually."

Casino.

Espy stared. A little bell was ringing in the back of her mind.

"Casino?" Doug asked. "What casino?"

But even before Romano answered, she knew what he was going to say. "The new Peacock. The Platinum Peacock Hotel and Casino. One of the anchors of the entire development."

The man waved at the massive construction pit again.

The Platinum Peacock. Parcel 33.

The site Europa Land Partners had paid $1.2 billion dollars for.

$1.2 billion. A high price, but one that had bought Europa not just those two hundred acres, but every existing structure on the land. That made it a worthwhile investment.

Only there were no existing structures. Just that big hole in the ground.

"What?" Frederickson asked. "What's the matter?"

She told him.

"That's not right," he said.

"No. No it isn't." She stared at the screen, watched as Romano's Porsche started backing up. "I think we're going to need a closer look there."

33

It didn't look like much.

A little diner about fifteen miles off the interstate, south of Pratt, on a two-lane county road that ran between two larger state highways. Parking on either side spilled off into a clearing that extended a good quarter mile in either direction from the road, leading up to a small yellow farmhouse, around which the grass had been cleared—clipped in some spots, burned down to dirt in others. Anyone approaching the house would be seen long before they got to the front door. Smart. No surprise there. Doc was always a few steps ahead.

Marcus felt like he was still catching up.

Blackjack Bouvier. JFK and JFK Jr., and this Nan woman, whoever she was, and Jaxon Research Associates, and *George* magazine, George de Mohrenschildt, George Casserly. And the Manchester tapes, and of course … the man in the white Stetson. The reason he was here. The reason he'd left the old farmhouse, brought Wilbur back to his aunt, and cleaned himself up.

Somebody had murdered not just Garrett Crandall, but the detective Espy had brought on board. Mike Cockerell. And three other people as well, all in the last few days. Marcus was going to find out who that someone was.

He drained his coffee cup and swiveled in his chair.

The waitress looked to be in her early twenties, maybe younger, had a square face and a severe look, not at all what he'd been expecting from the "Southern Hospitality at its Finest" on the sign out front. She was sitting at the end of the counter, focused on a thick paperback book, a study guide of some kind. He figured her for a college student. Good for her. The morning rush, if there had ever been one, was long over. It was going on ten a.m. now.

"Excuse me."

The waitress looked up.

Marcus held his cup in the air. "Could I get a little more?"

She set down her pencil, walked behind the counter, grabbed the pot of coffee, and walked over. As she leaned over to refill his cup, he saw something he'd missed before. A burn on the right side of her face that had been partially hidden by her long, dark hair. Looked like it continued all the way down her neck, too, maybe even further.

Didn't look like something from a fire.

Looked like acid.

There's a story there, he thought. Though that story wasn't his concern right now.

"Those were some good biscuits," he said, gesturing to his plate.

"Yes," she nodded. "Very good biscuits."

Her accent, as he'd noted before, was also a little unusual. European for sure, hard to tell more than that based off the few words she'd spoken. Not the kind of accent you would expect to find in the heart of South Carolina. That is, unless you knew who Doc really was. Or rather, who he had been in a previous life.

"Wondering if I can pay my respects to the chef," Marcus said.

"Respects?" the girl asked.

"Talk to him. If he has some time."

The waitress shrugged. "I will ask," she said and left.

Marcus waited. Took another sip of the coffee, which was nice and strong. Just the way Doc had always liked it.

Doc was an old acquaintance from the agency, real name

CHAPTER 33

Jackson Kelley, "Doc" because he could take a messed up line of computer code and rewrite it to run like new. Doc had been a friend of Marcus's dad, and he'd been about the only one from the agency to call Marcus after everything went to hell. After his father disappeared. The only one who shared Marcus's belief that, evidence be damned, his father had been railroaded. They'd lost touch a few years ago. Marcus knew that Doc had retired; he'd had no trouble tracking him down. But his retirement plans were a bit of a surprise.

Doc's Diner.

Southern Hospitality at its Finest.

As if on cue, the man himself, wearing a white apron and an SC Bulldogs cap, came striding out of the kitchen with a puzzled look on his face. The second Doc saw Marcus he slowed and then stopped. The puzzled look disappeared. His face set in a grim line.

"Marcus."

"Doc. Long time no see."

"What are you doing here?" he snapped. On edge. Not happy to see him at all.

Not what Marcus had expected.

"Relax. I'm just looking for some information. Was hoping you might be inclined to help me. Come on." Marcus nodded toward the bench opposite him in the booth. "Have a seat. Let's catch up."

Doc remained silent.

Marcus had taken a seat giving him a view of the entrance; he saw Doc's reflection in the door glass now, the way the apron bulged slightly at his waist in the back, and thought: gun. Not a surprise. Once a spook, always a spook.

True for him too, which was why Marcus had a gun of his own in the ankle holster around his left leg. And the taser, charged and ready in his back pocket, wires running up the back of his shirt and down his right arm to the electrodes under his sleeve, set to fire by the wireless triggering device in the big ring on his left hand.

Hopefully, neither of those would be needed.

Doc shook his head. "Nope. Whatever you're here about, I don't want to get involved."

"I came a long way to see you, Doc. Just got a couple quick questions—"

But Doc had already turned back toward the kitchen.

"Hey. Come on. Hear me out." Marcus stood up and started to follow. Which was when he felt the gun in the small of his back.

It was the waitress. "Walk, please," she said. "This way."

❖ ❖ ❖ ❖ ❖

They went through the kitchen and around the back of the restaurant.

The girl had been trained. She held the gun like a pro. No wiggle room there, nothing for Marcus to take advantage of.

There was a dirt path that circled through the tall grass behind the restaurant. Doc led the way out into that grass till they were out of sight of the road. Till they came to a clearing and a cinderblock building, a storehouse of some sort he guessed.

"Hands high. Turn around." Doc was holding a gun now too. "What you got there?" He gestured with the barrel to Marcus's sleeve. "A taser?"

Marcus nodded. "Yeah."

"Take it off. Put it on the ground. And any other weapon you got."

He did as he was told.

"That's it?" Doc asked.

"That's it," he lied.

"Okay. Now. What are you doing here, Marcus?" Doc asked.

CHAPTER 33

"Why are you bothering me?"

"This is a fine how-do-you-do."

"Answer the question."

"Okay. Like I said. I'm looking for information."

"What kind of information?"

"I'd like to keep that private." He looked over at the girl. "Between you and me."

"Not going to happen." Doc's voice hardened. "Speak."

Marcus glanced over at the girl. "Doc…"

"Speak." He cocked the weapon.

Marcus sighed. "Okay. Information on a guy. I think he was with the agency."

"Why come to me for that?" Doc frowned. "Why not just check records?"

"Because I'm trying to stay under the radar."

"Okay," Doc said. "Tell me the guy's name, I'll tell you what I know."

"I don't have a name. That's the problem."

Doc barked out a laugh. "Jesus Christ, Marcus. I'm not a magician. If you don't have a name—"

"He was a colonel. Active back in 1964, in the DC area."

"'64? I can tell you one thing. He's dead by now. And '64 is way before my time. What makes you think I know anything about this mystery man of yours?"

"Sherman." Marcus met Doc's gaze. "All those old records you had to work with, I'm thinking you might have come across mention of this guy."

"Sherman." Doc pursed his lips, shook his head. "That was a long time ago now. And I would need a lot more than that. A colonel, active in DC back in 1964—there had to be dozens of those guys."

"I can tell you he wore a suit. Did at least some of his work out of uniform. And I think he was from out west somewhere."

"And why's that?"

"His hat."

"His hat?"

"Yeah. Apparently he was in the habit of wearing a white Stetson."

Doc's expression flickered.

It was an infinitesimal change of expression. But Marcus caught it.

"You know who he was?"

Doc looked over at the girl. Marcus followed that gaze. She had a pained expression on her face. An expression that was equal parts worry and fear.

"Why are you looking for this guy? Who are you working for here?" Doc asked.

"Does that matter?"

The second the words were out of his mouth, the expression on Doc's face told him that it mattered very much indeed. Because Doc, he realized suddenly, wasn't quite as retired as he'd made himself out to be. There was something going on here that he'd just wandered into the middle of, and the girl was a big part of it.

He realized something else in that instant as well.

He was in trouble.

"Doc…"

"Christensen sent you, didn't he?"

"What?"

"He wants to change the deal."

"I have no idea what you're talking about. I don't know who Christensen is."

"Damn it, Marcus. You put me in a pickle here. A helluva

CHAPTER 33

pickle," Doc snapped.

"Not my intent. I just wanted—"

"Shut up a minute. I need to think." He looked at the girl again.

Damn, Marcus thought.

Okay. He still had a knife in a harness around his ankle. Left leg. He would never be able to reach it, though. Not before Doc or the girl pulled the trigger. What a mess. He was probably going to get shot here. Okay. He'd been shot before. The trick was to not get killed. The trick was to position himself so he could get to the blade after one shot, so the second one—

"You're starting to look like your dad, you know that?"

Marcus's hands—he hadn't even realized he'd made them into fists—unclenched. "I'll take that as a compliment, I guess."

Doc stared at him a minute longer, then sighed. "Okay. I might regret this, but I'm going to give you the benefit of the doubt here."

"Thank you."

"Benefit of the doubt while I check a few things out, that is. Now." Doc took a step back. Waved the gun. "Move."

The girl led the way, right up to that cinder-block building, which Marcus now realized was farther away from the restaurant than it made sense for any storehouse to be.

The door was bolted from the outside with a metal bar. Doc lifted it now and swung the door open. It moved slowly and silently. Oiled hinges. Well-maintained. A very, very heavy door.

Doc reached in and flipped a switch. The inside lit up, and Marcus saw that it wasn't being used for storage at all.

It was a little prison cell.

Marcus saw a cot, and a sink, and a bucket.

"Doc." He turned slightly. "There's no need for—"

"On in," Doc said. The girl jabbed his ribs with the gun, and Marcus, once more, did as he was told.

34

"Okay, don't tell me," Frederickson said, setting down his suitcase (he'd barked at the bell captain who'd tried to take it along with their other bags). "I'll guess."

Doug smiled. "Go right ahead."

Frederickson looked around the suite. "$2,000 a night."

"Are you kidding? $2,000? For this view?" Doug walked to the window and gestured down at the Bellagio's world-famous fountains, jets of water shooting high in the sky, evaporating in the fierce desert heat.

"Okay. $3,000?"

Doug stuck out his thumb, motioned upward.

"$4,000?"

Doug smiled.

"$4,000 a night?" Frederickson shook his head. "I'm touched."

Espy stepped past them and drew the curtains shut. She needed to focus, never mind the view. Doug had set them up in the Bellagio's Imperial Suite—four bedrooms, four baths, five flat-screens, full bar, kitchen, and hot tub—which was going to serve as their base of operations here in Vegas.

She was currently listening to the DOJ's awful version of hold music, waiting for her assistant Greg to come back on the line. To tell her more about Europa Land Partners, the company that had paid $1.2 billion for that big hole in the ground. Parcel 33.

All she'd learned so far was that Europa was an LLC based out of the Cayman Islands. An offshore banking destination, a financial black hole. Espy had been there more than once, including

CHAPTER 34

an extended stay a few years back. The government officials she'd dealt with were all very helpful, as were the bankers. Up to a point. Then the legal paper had started to fly. But she had one advantage now that she didn't back then.

In order to do business here in Vegas—to make that $1.2 billion deal with Desert View—Europa had to register with the Nevada Secretary of State. And they had to identify a point person (the term was 'registered agent') to conduct business on their behalf. Europa's registered agent was a man named Donald Gill. His offices were at 500 Skyline Boulevard, up in Reno. Except they weren't. Gill's office number had been disconnected. He'd moved, apparently. Espy was on the phone right now with Greg, trying to figure out where.

"Sorry for putting you on hold, Ms. Harper. There's a lot going on here."

"I'm sure. So what do you have for me on our mysterious Mr. Gill?"

"Not much, I'm afraid. I finally got through to someone at the Nevada Secretary of State's office. They told me Gill's address was valid as of April 1."

"Well it's not valid now."

"No. But by law, he has forty days to make it current."

"Oh for…" Espy tamped down on the curse words struggling to come out of her mouth. Forty days from April 1. That gave Gill, and Europa, several more weeks before they had to resurface.

"I was also able to get hold of copies of the application Gill filled out, which also listed Europa's company officers. The CEO and CFO, at least. Unfortunately—"

"Let me guess. Their addresses aren't current either."

"Actually, there are no addresses. Just PO Boxes."

She took a deep breath. "Give me those names. And please,

find me someone to talk to."

"I'm trying."

"Thank you. Let me know as soon as you do."

"I will. And hang on. Mike's right here. He wants to talk to you."

"No," she said quickly. "Don't—"

"Espy."

She sighed. "Mike."

"Good morning."

"And to you."

"Almost afternoon here." He cleared his throat. "So. You're in Las Vegas."

"Yes. You got my email."

"I would've liked a little more advance notice."

"Apologies. Something came up, and it made sense to move on it quickly."

"I'm assuming that something has to do with your friend Lish."

"Yes."

"Because I'm getting a lot of pressure here," he said. "Not just from him. The SEC. And a senator. Specifically, Nevada's senior senator."

"Victor Sonores."

"Yeah. Got an angry call from his office this morning." There was a pause. "You don't sound surprised."

"I'm not," she said. "His wife is a member of Desert View's board of directors. She also owns significant shares of the company's stock."

"Good lord. What exactly have you stumbled into there?" Mike asked.

She chose her next words carefully. "I'm not entirely sure. But Frank Ferrone ... there may be a connection to organized crime."

CHAPTER 34

Pritchett cursed then. Several words she had never heard him use before. "What else?"

"The company received a $1.2 billion influx of cash at the end of last year in a single transaction. I suspect it was fraudulent." She explained then. Parcel 33. The hole in the ground. Europa Land Partners, and the missing Mr. Gill.

Mike listened, asking the occasional question, then fell silent for a moment. "You should know—Lish just sent over a copy of a motion he's prepared," he said.

"What?"

"A motion claiming defamation. He's going to file in Federal Court tomorrow."

"Let him. I don't see how he wins that. We haven't gone public with anything."

"He's asking for the name of your informant."

"The name of my informant," she repeated. Her made-up informant. Good god. With everything that had happened these last few days, she'd forgotten all about that.

She pinched the bridge of her nose, thinking furiously.

"Espy?" Mike prompted.

A shadow fell across the table.

She looked up and saw Doug standing there. Motioning to her. "Give me the phone," he mouthed, holding out his hand.

"What?"

"The phone." He motioned again.

She shook her head.

"You tell him my name, I'm out of here. You'll never see me again," Doug yelled.

Espy's eyes widened. She pressed the mute button. "What are you doing?" she said.

"Who are you talking to? Is that him?" Mike asked in her ear.

"Is that the informant?"

Espy glared at Doug. He smiled.

"Actor." He pointed at his chest. "Me. Actor. Remember?"

She took the call off mute. "Hang on," she said to Mike and, regretting it even as she did so, handed Doug her phone.

He smiled. He took it, put the call on speaker. "You there?" he said.

"Who is this?" Mike asked.

"Who do you think?" Doug had put on an accent of some kind, something Midwestern, she thought. It made his voice sound completely different.

"You're the informant."

"I am."

"My name is Mike Pritchett. I work with Ms. Harper."

"You're the big boss."

"That's right."

"You trying to get me killed?"

"What?" Mike asked.

"These people. They'll come after my family. I told her right up front—"

Enough, Espy thought, and grabbed the phone back. "Sorry," she said.

"He's there with you," Mike said. "He works for Desert View?"

"I really can't say."

"I get it." He paused. "You're putting me in a tough spot here," he said.

"I'm sorry. I—"

"I'll deal with Lish. I can probably hold him off for another couple days. In the meantime, keep me posted. Not in a 'good morning I'm in Las Vegas' way either."

"I will."

CHAPTER 34

"Good." Mike hung up.

She turned to Doug. "Was that really necessary?"

"What?"

"The 'you trying to get me killed' part?"

"Those are the stakes we're playing for," Frederickson said. "In case you've forgotten."

Espy turned to him and almost—almost—snapped. As if she could forget.

Garrett Crandall. Mike Cockerell.

No more. Not on her watch.

❖ ❖ ❖ ❖ ❖

Li had stayed behind in DC, but she'd supplied them with enough equipment to turn the suite's little conference room into a miniature version of the operations center back at Woodhull.

Espy set herself up in a corner of that room and took stock of where they were. The information she'd gleaned from the Greenbrier; the notes she'd made on her phone call with Greg; the background information she'd gathered on Ferrone. The man loved to show off his money, loved rubbing elbows with the rich and famous. Which was why the ruse with Doug had been so easy to set up. Speaking of which…

She called Li through the secure satellite hookup she'd set up for them. Li's face appeared on the screen. She didn't look happy. "Before you ask," she said, "we have a problem."

"The chip Doug planted?"

"No. The chip is still functioning. The problem is Mr. Ferrone's security protocols. They are … unexpectedly formidable."

"He's a careful man."

"Who has some skilled people working for him."

"You haven't been able to get into any of his files?"

"No. As of yet, I have only been able to access one of the tower's wi-fi networks. It seems to carry feeds from a number of closed-circuit TV cameras."

"Those might come in handy down the road."

"Perhaps," Li said, in a tone of voice that suggested just the opposite.

"Well, keep me posted."

"I shall of course do so." She closed the channel just as Doug and Frederickson entered; she filled them in on her conversation with Li.

"I'm supposed to meet with Ferrone tomorrow morning," Doug said. "Back at the tower. Maybe there's something else I could do. Plant another piece of equipment?"

"Maybe," Espy responded, though she was suddenly uneasy about Doug going back to the tower, back into Ferrone's lair. Not that she didn't trust him, but the harsh truth was, he wasn't as capable as Frederickson. Or her. Not yet, at least. "I ought to be there."

"What do you mean, be there?" Doug asked.

The buzzer sounded.

"Someone at the front door," Frederickson said.

"Meaning I should be at your meeting," Espy continued. "Talking to Ferrone."

"That's a terrible idea," Frederickson said. "You want to go another round with Josephson?"

Espy smiled. "I'm not scared of him."

"I misspoke, sorry. It won't be just him next time," Frederickson said. "It'll be somebody a lot more capable. A lot more competent. A lot more likely to just punch you in the face first and then deliver their message. Actually, I take that back too. The punch in the face will be the message."

CHAPTER 34

"It won't come to that. Because I'll have you, right there with me, yes?"

"It's still not a good idea," Frederickson said.

The bell sounded again.

"Did anybody order room service?" Doug asked.

"I'll bet it's more equipment from Li," Frederickson said. "I'll get it."

Espy and Doug followed.

"Here's a crazy thought," Frederickson said, reaching for the door. "Use the phone. Safer that way, don't you think?"

"And less informative," Espy said. "Over the phone, I can't read body language, I can't—" She stopped mid-sentence.

Because it wasn't equipment, or luggage, or room service at the door.

It was Frank Ferrone.

35

Ferrone was dressed casually. Like he'd just come from the golf course, which he probably had. Those ridiculous plaid pants only golfers wore. A red polo shirt. His hair was longer than the pictures she'd seen, brushed back from his forehead. His eyes were black. Glittering with amusement.

He looked past Frederickson and saw her. "Esperanza Harper."

"Frank Ferrone. What are you doing here?"

"This may not be my hotel, but this is my town," Ferrone said. "Nothing happens here that I don't know about. Do you mind if we come in?"

Ferrone stepped to one side, and Espy saw the man standing behind him. Vincent Falconetti. She recognized him from the newsletter photo. He was wearing cowboy boots, jeans, and a sport coat. He was even creepier in real life, all skin and bone and corded muscle, veins sticking out on his neck. The tendons sticking out on his wrist, from under his watch.

A dive watch. A Panerai Luminor.

The newer version of what she had on her wrist.

The same model – the same watch - Matt had given her.

"This is Vince Falconetti," Ferrone said. "My right hand."

"That's a dive watch," Espy said.

"What?"

"Your watch." She pointed. "That's a Panerai dive watch. You're a diver?" The question was out of her mouth before she even knew she was going to ask it.

"Falconetti. I've heard of you." Frederickson folded his arms

CHAPTER 35

across his chest, looked the man over. "The pizza oven. Is that a true story?"

"Depends on which version you heard, exactly."

Falconetti had a voice like gravel rubbing on skin. Just hearing it gave Espy the shivers.

"Are we going to converse in the hall?" Ferrone asked. "Or sit, like civilized people?"

Frederickson looked to Espy. She nodded. The man was here, she might as well listen to what he had to say.

"All right," she said. "Come in."

She led them into the living room. Ferrone took a chair near the far window, and Falconetti came and stood behind him. Standing guard. Ferrone settled in and steepled his fingers. Smiled up at her. The cat who ate the canary.

"Why are you here, Mr. Ferrone? What is it you want?"

"What do I want? Well. To begin with, I wouldn't mind a drink. Not sure what's in the cabinets now, but I know when Steve ran this place, they had a wonderful single malt."

She took a seat on the couch. "Let's skip the alcohol, shall we?"

"Oh, come now. Just a sip. Surely you can afford it. I'm guessing Mr. Rivers here is paying for this suite?" He turned to Doug, who had been silent up to now. "Johnny Romano is a very unhappy man right now, Mr. Rivers. When he found out you were lying to him, wasting his time—"

"You can leave Mr. Rivers out of this," Espy said. "He agreed to assist us in this matter at my request."

"And who said chivalry was dead?" Ferrone laughed.

"Patriotism," Doug said. "The word you're looking for is patriotism."

"Hardly." The smile disappeared from his face. "The word I'm looking for is fraud. And who are you?" Ferrone turned to

Frederickson. "What's your role here?"

"Name's Smith," Frederickson said.

"Looks like law enforcement to me. Ex-law enforcement, actually." Falconetti stepped forward. "A little long in the tooth to still be on active duty."

"If that's not the pot calling the kettle black."

The two men glared at each other.

"Let's stick to the topic at hand, please," Ferrone said. "You went to the Greenbrier to investigate fluctuations in our stock price. At least that's what you told Raymond. I wonder why that is any of your concern."

"Desert View is a publicly traded company that lost close to 80 percent of its value last year."

"And regained a significant portion of that value in the last three months. Ms. Harper, I'm well aware of the fluctuations in our stock price. As is the SEC. I've spoken to several officials there—John Bamberger, do you know him? He's well aware of our situation, and has been very supportive. No crime was committed here. The fall in price, the subsequent rise—that was clearly the market speaking."

"One man's opinion."

"Several men's opinions. And what makes you think otherwise?" He leaned forward. "What exactly is your interest in the Aqua Roma site? And why are you going to these ridiculous lengths?"

"Ridiculous lengths? I'm not sure what you mean."

"Engaging Mr. Rivers in this charade? A movie studio? Please. I don't understand these actions of yours at all."

"A lot of people lost a lot of money last year, Mr. Ferrone. I'm conducting an investigation into the circumstances surrounding that loss."

CHAPTER 35

"Their losses have been made good. The market at work."

"Why are you so intent on stopping me?" she asked. "What do you have to hide?"

"I don't like people messing in my affairs, Ms. Harper. Disrupting the efficient functioning of my businesses."

"I can tell. Mr. Lish, Mr. Josephson ... that business about Russell Haney, and my father..."

"Oh, I'm just getting started Ms. Harper. One thing you'll learn about me: I act to protect my interests."

"And I act on behalf of my country. And all its citizens. As Mr. Rivers pointed out."

"Brava, Ms. Harper. Brava." Ferrone smiled, clapped his hands. "Of course that's why you do what you do. I would expect no less from you. Esperanza Harper. The daughter of the legendary Sam Hernandez. And yet, you use your mother's last name, not his. Identify yourself with a failed actress as opposed to an FBI legend. Why is that, I wonder."

She didn't take the bait. "I've been reading up on you as well," she said. "Frank Ferrone Jr. The son of a minor organized crime figure and a Las Vegas showgirl."

"I would watch what you say there," Falconetti said, taking a step forward.

Frederickson took a step too.

"Vince. No need." Ferrone held up a hand. "I'm not offended."

"Your feelings are the least of my concerns." Time to regain control of the conversation here, Espy thought. "Tell me about Parcel 33."

For the first time, Ferrone's self-control dropped.

Surprise—concern—registered on his face.

"What about it?" he asked.

"A firm called Europa Land Partners purchased development

rights to that site," she said.

"Indeed they did. Your point?"

"They paid $1.2 billion for those rights, including any and all previously built structures on the site."

"I have yet to hear a question."

"According to what Mr. Rivers told me, there are no existing structures anywhere near Parcel 33. Just a big hole in the ground. So what I'm wondering … how is that worth $1.2 billion dollars?"

Ferrone smiled. "Your lack of expertise in these matters is showing, Ms. Harper. 'Existing structures' refers to the entire site: the roads, the landscaping, the infrastructure that makes the parcel accessible. And that is worth a great deal of money."

"That sounds nice," Espy said. "Sounds like the line you've been feeding Wall Street. But I don't believe it for a second."

Ferrone shrugged. "If Europa felt they hadn't gotten their money's worth, I'm sure they would have lodged a complaint by now. You would agree it is their money to spend, isn't it?"

"I'd feel better if I could speak directly to them."

"I don't imagine anyone is stopping you from doing that."

"Not actively, no. But the company's registered agent has moved. A man named Donald Gill. Maybe you could help me find him."

"Ms. Harper, if Europa wants to be a silent partner, that is their right, isn't it? I don't see why this is any of your concern." He shook his head. "What is it you think I'm hiding? Aqua Roma is a real estate project. A huge project that will provide jobs, and housing, and new lives for thousands of people in this area."

"And make you a great deal of money."

"I see nothing wrong with that."

"What did Garrett Crandall see?"

"What?"

CHAPTER 35

"Senator Garrett Crandall. What were his concerns about the development?"

"I don't see how that's relevant. Senator Crandall is dead."

"Yes. He is."

Ferrone raised an eyebrow. "Are you implying I had something to do with his death?"

"Did you?"

"I'm not even going to dignify that with a response."

"If you don't want to answer my questions, why did you come here?"

"To lay out some facts for you. Chief among them being this: You're not welcome here." His gaze traveled from Rivers, to Frederickson, then to Espy. "Not in this hotel, or anywhere else in this town. In fact"—he motioned to Falconetti, who stepped forward—"if I were in your shoes, I'd be leaving on the first flight out tomorrow."

"Is that a threat?" she asked.

"American 3238." Falconetti reached into his pocket and pulled out a thick envelope. "Leaves at seven a.m. Change planes in Chicago, you're back in DC at four thirty. Three tickets. Coach, but we bought you extra leg room." He tossed the envelope on the table, then looked up at Rivers. "Of course, if you want to upgrade, that's your call."

"I wasn't aware you had discretion over who came and went in this town," Espy snapped. "Forgive me."

"Ms. Harper." Ferrone smiled. "I think it's safe to say there are a lot of things you're not aware of."

"The same goes for you, Mr. Ferrone. And we won't be needing those tickets."

"You may want to change your ticket as well." Ferrone stood. "Stop in Columbus. Check in on your mother."

Espy's mouth went dry. "What did you just say?"

"I think you heard me. Goodbye, Ms. Harper. I hope, for your sake, we don't meet again." He headed toward the door, Falconetti a step in front of him.

"Hey. We're not done here." Frederickson stepped between the two men and the exit.

Falconetti just kept walking, right up to Frederickson, till they were nose to nose, inches apart. "I'm counting to three here."

"One comes first." Frederickson smiled. Espy saw him tense. Ready for whatever came next.

Ferrone put a hand on Falconetti's shoulder. "Vince."

"Let them go," Espy said, and Frederickson reluctantly stepped aside.

And then they were gone.

36

"Mom."

"Esperanza. What a nice surprise. I heard you were out in Las Vegas. How are you?"

"Never mind about me. You're all right?"

"Yes. I'm fine. A little tired, but…" Her mom paused. "What's wrong? Something's wrong. I hear it in your voice."

Nothing's wrong, Espy started to say, but the words stuck in her throat.

"Oh. I know what it is. I'm sorry. I forgot to call and thank you."

"Thank me. For what?"

"The chocolates. I haven't even had a chance to open them, we've been so—"

Espy's blood froze. "Don't."

"What?"

"Don't open them. Don't touch the package they came in."

"Why not?"

"Because." Espy took a deep breath. "I didn't send you any chocolates."

"What are you saying?" Her mom's voice trembled, then strengthened. "Oh my god. Oh my god."

"It's all right," Espy said. "Everything is fine. All you need to do—"

Noises Espy couldn't identify. Rustling, shuffling. Then something else—a sound like the phone being dropped.

"Mom!" she said. "Mom!"

Nothing. Then, "Esperanza."

A different voice. A deeper voice that she recognized at once. Stuart Crane's voice.

She heard it, and every ounce of tension in her body disappeared.

"Stuart. There's a box of chocolates. Ferrone—"

"It's fine. They're just chocolates."

She let out a sigh of relief.

"I've been on guard ever since the Greenbrier."

"Thank you."

"You're welcome. Tell me what's happening," Stuart prompted, and she brought him up to speed. Ferrone's threats. Her conversations with her boss. Lish's defamation suit, and Parcel 33. They'd been in regular contact since the Greenbrier. Since Cockerell's death. Stuart was in Columbus with Alice, Garrett's widow. Her mom was with him, keeping Alice busy. Helping her adjust.

"Anything new there?" Espy asked, meaning any new clues to what Garrett had been doing in the days before his "accident," anything in the files at his Ohio house.

"Possibly. Some notes Garrett left. Questions he had raised with some people out in Vegas. I'll forward you details. In the meantime, you know where to reach me. Here's your mother again."

Stuart handed off the phone before she could say anything further. She was a little surprised he hadn't asked her about the colonel, or the man with the white Stetson. Why he wasn't pressing harder to follow up on the information that had gotten Cockerell killed.

"So apparently, I can eat the chocolates," her mom said.

Espy laughed. "Yes."

"But I'm not going to. Not if they didn't come from you." Her

CHAPTER 36

mother's voice hardened. "Tell me who sent them. I'll send them back. With a little message of my own."

"Under no circumstances will you do that," Espy said. "These people do not play around."

"I understand that. But—"

"So you won't do anything."

Silence.

"Mom…"

"I won't do anything." Espy heard voices in the background. "I have to go, Esperanza. Let's talk later."

"Of course. Love you, Mom."

"Love you too."

"Okay." She ended the call and turned to the others. "Everything's fine there, but we … what?"

Doug had a stunned expression on his face.

"What's the matter?" she asked, looking from him to Frederickson.

"The little girl too?" Doug asked.

Frederickson shrugged. "In one version of the story she's a little girl. In another, she's a hooker. In another—"

"What are you talking about?" Espy asked.

"Falconetti," Frederickson said. "The pizza oven story."

"Right. I was going to ask you about that."

"It's this story that went around the bureau a few years back. Not sure I believe it, but what I heard…" Frederickson pulled a can of soda from the bar and popped it open. "One of the cartels decides to send this guy up to Vegas, to establish a presence here. This guy walks into the Peacock, starts spreading around cash, shooting his mouth off about how the old mob guys had all gotten fat eating too much pizza. Falconetti listens for a while, then pulls the guy aside, and that's the last time anyone sees the guy alive.

He's found the next morning burned to a crisp. In a pizza oven. Him and his wife, and their daughter."

Doug shuddered again.

"That's one version of the story," Frederickson continued. "In another version, it's this cartel guy and a hooker. There's a third version, though."

"I get it," Espy said.

"Anyway." Frederickson drained his soda. "If you believe the story, that's why the cartels have people in California and Arizona and New Mexico and Texas and Florida, but not Vegas."

"Having seen that Falconetti guy," Doug said, "I kind of do believe it."

Espy did too. There was something else she believed as well. "Parcel 33. You see the look on Ferrone's face when I mentioned it? He's hiding something."

"Well, he's not going to tell you what it is," Frederickson said.

"We know what it is," Espy said. "He got somebody to give him $1.2 billion for a hole in the ground. The question is who."

"We know who," Doug said. "Europa."

"That's all we have, though. The name. We need more."

"Well, he's not going to give it you."

"No. He's not. Not willingly. We need something to hold over him. Some kind of leverage."

"A lead pipe?" Frederickson asked.

"That would probably work." She nodded.

But in the absence of said pipe, all she could do was get back to work.

❖ ❖ ❖ ❖ ❖

She returned to the conference room, opened her computer, and found the notes Stuart had mentioned waiting: the questions

CHAPTER 36

Garrett had, the people he'd posed those questions to. First was a woman named Jaspreet Manghal, a scientist who had testified before Garrett's environmental subcommittee.

> Senator Crandall: We appreciate your appearance here, Dr. Manghal. So—in conclusion, how would you characterize the impact of this proposed development on the animal in question?
>
> Dr. Manghal: The desert tortoise. Yes. Without doubt, the effects would be catastrophic. As the charts I have supplied to the committee demonstrate.
>
> Senator Crandall: Yes. I think we can all see that. Therefore, and in light of the evidence you've provided, I'm going to suggest this committee authorize the relevant Federal Agencies seek a hold on further construction at the Aqua Roma site until—
>
> Senator Sonores: Excuse me, Senator—a hold? I can't believe what I'm hearing. The idea that we would put this multi-billion dollar project on hold because of its possible impact on a turtle—
>
> Dr. Manghal: Again, the animal in question is the desert tortoise, senator.
>
> Senator Sonores: Fine. Tortoise. The idea is still ludicrous.

But of course, that construction hold hadn't happened.

Senator Crandall's objections must be overcome by any and all means at the company's disposal.

And they had. And after Garrett's death, Sonores had taken over the subcommittee. But what had happened to Dr. Manghal? Espy found a phone number, but it had been disconnected. Found an email, but it bounced back. So she moved on.

The second name Stuart had found in Garrett's files was David

Whitestone, a Las Vegas city official. Garrett had written to him on multiple occasions regarding Aqua Roma. Whitestone had never written back. She wondered why.

She looked him up. Whitestone had been working for the city planning department for nearly ten years; he was single and lived in a high-end gated community called Spring Valley, in a house assessed at $2.6 million.

She heard a long low whistle coming from over her shoulder. She turned and saw Doug.

"Sorry," he said. "Just came in to see what was up."

"Why the whistle?"

He pointed to the screen. "Spring Valley? A $2.6 million home? On a city official's salary? That doesn't add up."

"No. It doesn't."

"If I was a gambling man, I'd say Frank Ferrone might have something to do with that."

"I'd take that bet. If I was a gambling woman. But maybe Mr. Whitestone has a different explanation."

She tried his office. But he wasn't in. He was on administrative leave. Fully paid leave—for the next two months.

"On leave? For two months? Who gets to do that? Besides us, I mean."

"Apparently Mr. Whitestone is special." She stood. "I think a trip out to Spring Valley is in order, to see why. Where's Frederickson?"

"He got a call a few minutes ago. While you were working," Doug said. "Something about a special delivery, down in the lobby."

"Special delivery of what?"

"Beats me."

Espy nodded. Probably weapons of some sort, protection

CHAPTER 36

against Ferrone, now that the man knew they were in town.

She called his cell. He answered on the first ring.

"Espy. What's up?"

She told him. Whitestone. Spring Valley. "We'll need a car."

He started laughing.

"What?"

"Come on down. You'll see."

❖ ❖ ❖ ❖ ❖

She found him parked at the North Valet station, away from the Bellagio's main entrance. Engine running. Behind the wheel of his Range Rover.

"You have got to be kidding," she said, hands on hips, staring at the car, shaking her head. "You paid someone to drive this cross-country?"

"Paid through the nose," he said. "I had a feeling we were going to need wheels."

"Boys and their toys," she said, climbing in.

"You scoff," Frederickson said, as they pulled out into traffic. "But this glass is bulletproof. Did I mention that?"

"You mentioned a lot of things," Espy said. "I can't say I was listening to all of them."

They headed west, into the setting sun. Espy slipped on her glasses to shield her eyes—Li had added polarized lenses to this latest model—and activated the feed to Woodhull, linking to the car's speaker.

"We're en route," she said. "Any progress?"

Li was silent a second before speaking. "You'll recall I mentioned Mr. Ferrone's security protocols were formidable?"

"I do recall that, yes."

"Well, I wish to correct that statement. The protocols are not formidable. They are impregnable."

"Ah." Espy tried to think of something encouraging to say. "Well … just keep us posted."

"Of course," Li said, and the line went dead.

Frederickson snorted. "Well, somebody got up on the wrong side of the bed this morning."

"Cut her some slack," Espy replied. "She's not used to a computer that won't do as it's told." The comm chip in her glasses pinged. Espy tapped the frame, smiled, and punched the call through. "Li."

"One bit of news I forgot to mention. I am unsure of its relevance."

"Go on," Espy prompted.

"Mr. Ferrone's closed circuit camera network. The security feeds. Not all of them come from the office tower."

"No?"

"No. A half-dozen come from cameras at the ranch."

"Ranch." It took her a second. "You mean C.C. Brody's ranch?"

"Yes."

"That's interesting." The ranch. The clue that had led her to Ferrone in the first place.

"What a good boy," Frederickson said. "Keeping an eye on his mom."

"Stepmom," Espy corrected. "And there may be more to it than that. Ferrone hangars Desert View's private jet there."

"Huh," Frederickson said. "That is interesting."

Espy nodded. "See what more you can find out about that ranch please, Li."

"Of course."

❖ ❖ ❖ ❖ ❖

CHAPTER 36

As they pulled up to Whitestone's house, Frederickson pointed to the car in the driveway. "Look at that."

"Fancy."

"And then some. That's a Tesla. A Model S. That's a $150,000 automobile right there. Another gift from Ferrone?"

"Innocent till proven guilty," Espy said, following Frederickson up a brick walkway. There was an intercom next to the front door, a camera above it. Frederickson pressed the buzzer.

It took a minute. Espy heard footsteps approaching, then a voice on the intercom. "Can I help you?"

"I hope so." Frederickson flashed his ID. "John Fredericks. FBI. Are you David Whitestone?"

"I am."

"I have a few questions for you."

"Concerning?"

"The Aqua Roma development," Frederickson said. "I understand you were involved in the approvals process for that project?"

"Aqua Roma? How is that the FBI's business?"

Espy stepped past Frederickson. Looked right up at the camera. "Not just the FBI sir. My name is Esperanza Harper. I'm with the Department of Justice." She held her ID up to the lens.

"You're from Washington, DC, that says."

"That's right."

"You came here just to talk to me?"

"Not just you. I'll be speaking with several other people as well, sir. About Aqua Roma, and Frank Ferrone."

"You're not going to find a lot of people willing to have those conversations."

"All I need is one."

There was a pause. She heard Whitestone sigh. "I might regret this," he said. "But come on in."

The intercom buzzed, and the lock clicked open.

❖ ❖ ❖ ❖ ❖

Whitestone was tall. Frederickson's height. He had a full head of graying hair and a beard to match. He wore a red-checked shirt, a pair of faded jeans, old-fashioned desert boots, and a relaxed smile.

Espy liked him instantly.

The first floor of his house was a single great room with mission-style furniture, big, comfortable-looking chairs, weathered wood, and hanging tapestries with geometric southwestern patterns. He led them to his kitchen table—long, rough-hewn beams, with chairs stained to match. And a familiar sight: a Breville teapot, resting on the granite countertop. The same as Garrett's. Same as hers. Whitestone followed her gaze.

"You want some tea?"

She smiled. "No, but thanks. That's a nice machine."

"And a nice place you have here," Frederickson said. "And that car of yours…"

Whitestone smiled. "You want to know how I can afford all this."

"Bingo," Frederickson said.

"You're thinking I might have acquired some of these funds illicitly. Perhaps courtesy of Mr. Ferrone."

"Right again."

Whitestone laughed. "I appreciate the honesty. So let me be honest with you. My mother is Joan Barton."

Frederickson frowned. "Who?"

"Joan Barton." He looked from Frederickson to Espy. "Barton Designs?"

Espy shook her head. She had no idea who that was. "You have

CHAPTER 36

family money, is what you're saying."

"To spare. Also how I can afford to stay in a job that pays so little compared to private industry. You're both government employees. You know exactly what I'm talking about."

"We do," Espy said. A half-truth, anyway.

"The point is, I'm relatively immune to the lure of money," Whitestone said. "Not that Frank Ferrone didn't try to tempt me."

"So you have had dealings with him."

"Not personally. My dealings were with representatives of his. A lawyer first, who offered me money in a roundabout way, and then another man. Who was far less subtle."

"Let me guess," Espy said. "Vince Falconetti."

"Yep." Whitestone nodded. "That's the name."

"He threatened you."

"Not in so many words. He just—he made it clear that it would not be a good idea to stand in the way of Mr. Ferrone's interests."

"We're talking about Aqua Roma now?"

"That's right."

"Tell us about that."

"Well." Whitestone looked at the two of them, then nodded. "All right. The gory details. When the proposal first came to the department, there was a lot we had to do. You can imagine. The size of what they're building…"

"We've seen the site."

"Then you know. Nobody does projects at that scale anymore. The infrastructure just isn't there for it. Vegas's population has just about doubled in the last decade; you've got all these pressing environmental issues, like the drought, and habitat loss among the local wildlife."

"The turtle," Frederickson said.

"What?" Whitestone asked.

"Tortoise," Espy corrected. "Desert tortoise."

Frederickson waved her off. "Whatever."

Whitestone nodded. "Yes, in fact, the desert tortoise is one animal threatened by the project. We hired an expert to help us determine the potential extent of habitat loss—"

"Dr. Manghal." Espy interrupted.

"Yes. Dr. Jaspreet Manghal. She raised a number of issues that came to the attention of a US Senate subcommittee."

"Garrett Crandall's subcommittee."

"That's right."

"He wrote to you—Senator Crandall. Asking for information."

"Yes. Regarding a construction hold he was seeking on the project." Whitestone took a deep breath. "It was made very clear to me what would happen if I assisted Senator Crandall's investigation. I'm ashamed to say, I never wrote back. That hold never happened, although if Senator Crandall hadn't…"

Whitestone's voice trailed off.

Espy had a feeling she knew exactly what was going through his mind at that second. Thoughts he probably considered too crazy to voice. Thoughts about Garrett Crandall's death and Aqua Roma's construction hold. Thoughts she wasn't going to say a word to encourage.

"What about Dr. Manghal?" she said.

"What about her?"

"She wanted that hold too, didn't she? What happened there?"

"I don't know the details. What I can tell you: When we hired Dr. Manghal, she was a research associate at a consulting firm. Freelancer, basically. Now she works up in Silicon Valley. Got hired by a venture capital firm there." He shrugged. "I was curious. Went online, looked at what people who work for that firm get paid. It's a lot of money. Like, another zero more than she was making."

CHAPTER 36

"And you think Ferrone had something to do with her new job?" Espy asked.

"In my experience, when Frank Ferrone wants something to happen, it happens. He wants a zoning variance, he gets a zoning variance. He wants a property easement, he gets a property easement. I'm not going to say everyone in town is crooked; there's a lot of good folks working for the city. But there's a lot of one-hand-washing-the-other type of deals going down."

"You have proof of this?" Espy said.

Whitestone snorted. "Dr. Manghal's new job is about as close to proof as I've seen in the ten years or so I've been watching Ferrone operate. He doesn't leave trails."

"So Aqua Roma's back up and running again."

"Full speed. As far as I know. I was put on administrative leave a few weeks ago. I may or may not get my job back."

"Ferrone's doing?"

"That's my guess."

"We got a look at the site the other day. Seems to me there's not much building going on there right now," Frederickson said. "A lot of guys just standing around."

"Doesn't surprise me. The whole thing's gone forward in fits and starts. They had trouble with their financing last year—the whole project almost went under. I guess they're back on track now."

"I'm not sure about that," Frederickson said. "Things still seem to be moving pretty slowly."

"I wouldn't know." Whitestone shrugged. "Like I said, I've been put on leave for the foreseeable future. Probably till the next quarter ends, after all the permits get approved. City, state, federal—a lot of i's need to get dotted. T's crossed. I'm sure Ferrone doesn't want me in there holding things up."

Espy nodded. *Permits filed. City, state, federal ... i's dotted, t's crossed...*

There was something buzzing around in her head.

"Harper?" Frederickson was staring at her.

She raised a finger. Wait.

Desert View. Frank Ferrone. Forms that needed to get filed. Forms the government required.

"You all right?" Frederickson asked.

"I'm an idiot," she said.

"Excuse me?" Whitestone asked.

"I should have seen it as soon as I looked at that hole in the ground."

"What are you talking about?" Frederickson asked.

"Leverage." She turned to him. "A little something to squeeze Ferrone with. We already have it."

"We do?"

"Absolutely." She smiled. "Ferrone handed it to us four months ago."

37

"Leverage?" Frederickson asked. "What are you talking about?"

"Desert View's 10-K."

"The what?"

"The 10-K! Of course." This from Doug, who was on speaker in the Range Rover.

"Yeah." Frederickson snorted. "Like you know."

"Hey. I'm not a tax attorney. But I did play one on TV once."

"Stop," Frederickson said.

"A 10-K is a securities filing with the SEC," Espy continued. "Publicly traded companies have to file them at the end of every fiscal year."

"Like a 1040."

"Very much so," Espy said. "And Ferrone, because he's Desert View's CEO, he signed theirs. Which makes him legally responsible for the truth of the figures contained in it. And those figures are fraudulent."

"The $1.2 billion hole in the ground," Doug said.

"Exactly. That's our leverage."

"I don't see how." Frederickson shook his head. "He already told you that you were wrong about the hole. He's not going to care about some tax form."

"He will if I bring charges. If we question Desert View's financial health. The company's stock price. I think he'll care quite a bit."

Frederickson turned to look at her. "I thought your boss said not to make another move without his permission."

"Well. There's a difference between threatening to bring charges and actually bringing them."

"Sounds like a fine line to me."

"The point here is to put Ferrone under pressure. See what he does."

"He's liable to do something violent."

She smiled. "That's why you're coming with me."

❖ ❖ ❖ ❖ ❖

"Good evening, ma'am. Sir. Welcome to the Peacock." The valet—a red-haired, acne-faced, pale-skinned and skinny teenager wearing a red jacket that bore the casino's logo—held out his hand for the car keys.

Frederickson held them back a second and looked the young man in the eye. "Nothing happens to this car," he said.

"No sir." The valet nodded.

"No scratches," Frederickson continued. "No joyrides. No cranking the music while you park it. Yes?"

"Absolutely." The valet offered up a nervous smile.

Frederickson held his sport jacket open slightly so the valet could see his shoulder holster, and what was in it. "Nothing happens to this car," he said again.

The valet turned even paler.

"Attaboy." Frederickson clapped him on the shoulder, placed the keys in his hand. "Off you go now. Carefully."

The valet nodded, gingerly slid into the front seat, and slowly pulled away.

"Charming," Espy said.

"Just making sure," he said. "I have a feeling we're going to need that bulletproof glass, you keep poking the bear like this."

The main floor of the Peacock Casino was roughly heart-shaped. They came in at the pointy end. There were bars to the left and right; waitresses (and a few waiters) circulating with drink

CHAPTER 37

trays. She noted mirrors in the ceiling—no doubt there were multiple security cameras behind them. All the casinos had them, she knew. To make sure no one was counting cards or switching dice. It wouldn't take long for their presence to be noted. For Ferrone to come and find them.

She would prefer to turn the tables. Surprise him.

"So where do we think he is? Ferrone?" she asked.

"Peacock has a VIP room in the back. That'd be a good place to start looking."

"Sounds like you've been here before."

"A long time ago. A different life."

"Oh? Do tell."

He shook his head. "Some other time. Come on."

They passed through a row of slot machines, past tables where people were playing craps, roulette, and (of course) blackjack. Climbed a half flight of stairs at the back to an upper level where security guards watched the main floor from above, and found themselves in a sports betting parlor of sorts, with multiple video screens and betting slips scattered over the floor.

"There." Frederickson pointed to a door marked *Private*, flanked by two men the size of NFL linemen, arms folded across their chests. "The question is, how do we get in?"

Espy paused, thinking. That was the question indeed.

"Maybe show our badges?" Frederickson asked. "FBI, DOJ…"

"I don't think that'll do much."

"Well. We could always just wait." Frederickson nodded toward the ceiling. The hidden cameras. "I'm sure they'll come to us."

"Agreed." Though again, she hated to give up the element of surprise.

At that second the door opened, and a man and woman stepped out. She didn't know who he was. But the woman…

"That's Laura Sonores," Espy said.

"Who?"

"Laura Sonores. She's on Desert View's board."

Which was when she realized Ferrone wasn't the only one who'd signed Desert View's 10-K.

"Ms. Sonores," she called out, stepping forward.

The woman turned. "Yes. Can I help you?"

Laura Sonores. Espy took a moment to study her. Late forties, early fifties perhaps. Wrap dress, jet-black hair—clearly dyed. The senator's second wife, rumored to be the driving force behind some of his recent, more outrageous political statements.

"My name is Esperanza Harper."

"Yes?"

"I'm with the Department of Justice. I'm currently conducting an investigation into the Desert View Real Estate Corporation. You're on the company's board."

Sonores glared. "This is hardly the place for this sort of conversation."

"You'll forgive me, but this is a pressing matter. As a board member, you signed the company's year-end filings with the SEC, did you not? Their 10-K?"

Sonores's eyes narrowed. "Tell me your name again?"

"Esperanza Harper. Ms. Sonores, as a courtesy I'm letting you know we believe those filings contain fraudulent information which you are legally responsible for."

"Esperanza Harper. Yes. I've heard that name." The man with Sonores stepped forward. He was older—white haired. Late sixties, maybe. Dressed neatly but casually. Chinos, dark shoes, and a light-blue polo with the Peacock's logo embroidered on the front.

"You have me at a disadvantage," Espy said.

"Benjamin Kingsleigh. I'm a member of Desert View's board

CHAPTER 37

of directors as well."

Kingsleigh. Of course. She recognized the name now. Desert View's prospectus had contained thumbnail biographies of all the company's board members. Kingsleigh was one of them. She couldn't remember anything else about the man, though, she'd skimmed over that information so quickly. Easily remedied.

She tapped the temple piece of her glasses. A green rectangle formed around the man's face. *Benjamin Kingsleigh, Vice Chairman, Papyrus Industries.*

Kingsleigh was seventy-two, widowed, a resident of both New York and Miami. No children and no close relatives mentioned. Papyrus was a multinational firm; Kingsleigh was based out of their New York City offices.

That was all the system had. All the publicly available information there was. Odd.

"I had heard you were leaving town," Kingsleigh said.

"I don't know where you got that idea," Espy replied, although she did.

Kingsleigh smiled. "I can't recall at the moment. Now what is it you're saying? About this…"

"10-K. Desert View's end-of-year financial statement. You, and Ms. Sonores, and all the other board members signed it. And I'm afraid that form contained fraudulent information. Criminally fraudulent information."

She told him about Parcel 33 then, and that $1.2 billion hole in the ground.

"It seems to me that what you really want to do is talk to these Europa people," Kingsleigh said.

"I plan to. But I'm talking to you now, sir. Offering you a chance to tell me what you know about this transaction."

"Parcel 800?" He shook his head. "I'm afraid I can't help you.

I know nothing about it."

"Parcel 33," she corrected. "Mr. Kingsleigh, you signed the 10-K. You are responsible in the eyes of the law."

"That's your interpretation of the law, Ms. Harper." Kingsleigh smiled. "I'm quite sure there are others. Equally valid ones."

She was about to ask him what he meant by that when a familiar voice sounded behind her.

"Well. Getting acquainted, I see."

She turned and there he was. Frank Ferrone. All dressed up for dinner. Dressed to the nines—white tuxedo and black bow tie.

"Laura, Ben, I'm sorry for this intrusion." Ferrone stepped forward. "Ms. Harper, I'm astonished to see you here, frankly."

"I don't know why. As I told you earlier, I'm in the midst of an investigation."

"What you're doing is disturbing my guests." Ferrone's lips tightened. "I'd like you to leave."

"I was just doing them a courtesy." She explained about the 10-K. Ferrone's eyes blazed when she got to the "criminally fraudulent information" line.

"Leave," Ferrone snapped. "Or I'll have you forcibly removed."

"I was about to ask, you and what army?" Frederickson said. "But I see your man coming now."

"Well, look who it is." Falconetti's eyes, for some reason, sparkled with amusement.

"Sorry to disappoint, but we were just leaving," Frederickson said. "We'll have to catch up another time."

"Looking forward to it. One thing, quick." Falconetti smiled. "You drive a Range Rover, right?"

Frederickson, who'd taken a step toward the stairs, froze in place. "I do."

"Yeah. I thought it was yours. What a shame."

CHAPTER 37

"What are you talking about?"

Espy put a hand on Frederickson's arm. "Easy."

"I don't know what happened exactly," Falconetti said. "We had an incident in the garage. Looks like somebody was in a hurry, backed into it or something. The car's in bad shape. Maybe even totaled." He grinned. "Definitely not drivable."

Espy saw Frederickson's lips moving. He was, she realized, counting to ten.

She tightened her grip on his arm.

"Want me to call triple-A?" Falconetti asked. "They could probably tow it for you."

"Thanks. You're all heart." Espy tightened her grip even more. "We'll take care of it."

38

As far as jail cells went, it wasn't bad.

Doc had fastened a metal cuff on his right wrist, which attached via a thick steel chain to a stanchion in the middle of the room. Plenty of play in the chain, enough to get him to the chamber pot, to stand up and exercise, to sit at the wooden table where his meals got delivered, to lay out straight in the bed.

He only got two meals a day, but they were big meals, cooked up hot, brought back to him by the waitress during what Marcus guessed were downtimes for the little restaurant, right around ten a.m. and nine p.m.

There was not much conversation. Not the first couple of times, anyway. Marcus kept asking her to get Doc; she told him to shut up and eat. He tried to assure her he meant no harm; she told him to shut up and eat. He complimented the food; she told him to shut up and eat.

Second day, she brought along that book he'd seen her studying at the counter. He got a better glimpse of it now, too: *English as a Second Language.*

"You studying up, huh?" he asked.

"Shut up," she said. "Eat."

"I could maybe help. If you want."

"Shut up and—"

"Eat. Right. I got it."

He tried again the next morning. Same result.

"That burn," he said that evening, as she set the dinner tray down. "On your neck."

CHAPTER 38

"Shut up. Eat," she said.

"Just curious." He dug in, staring at the skin.

She rubbed at it self-consciously. "Burn?" she said after a minute.

He realized she didn't know the word. He said it again, pointing.

She rubbed the skin, understanding. "Burn."

"Yes. It looks painful."

She stared at him a long moment, so long he didn't think she was going to answer at all. "I am used now to it," she said.

Marcus nodded. "What happened?"

She shook her head. "Shut up. Eat."

"I will, but—"

"EAT!" she snapped and leaned forward slightly, aggressively, entering his space.

In that second, Marcus had a chance. An opportunity.

Grab her wrist. Drag her to him, overpower her. He didn't know if she had a key to the cuff on his wrist, but he knew he could take her hostage, bargain with Doc, get the answers he needed, get on his way. He tensed, preparing to move.

You're starting to look like your dad.

He remembered what Doc had done the other day. Or rather, hadn't done. And what he had done for Marcus's father.

His turn to sigh, and let the moment pass.

The girl suddenly stiffened and leaned back, as if she'd realized the danger she'd put herself in. "I will return," she said, and left.

But she didn't.

Instead, a few hours later it was Doc himself who opened the door and stepped inside.

Marcus stood. "Well, look what the cat drug in."

"Here. Brought you a little something."

Doc put the plate down on the table, pulled a fork and napkin from his shirt pocket, and set them down next to it. "It's apple. Fresh-baked. Maisie Grimes down the road, who, I'll have you know, won the county fair apple pie contest four out of the last six years."

"Not interested in pie."

"My way of apologizing," he said and reached into his pocket. He pulled out a key, stepped forward, and unlocked the cuff.

"Thank you." Marcus rubbed his wrist. The skin was a little chafed. There was some bruising as well.

Doc saw. "Sorry. But I had to make sure."

"Hey. No hard feelings." At least, none he wanted to express right this second.

"I made a couple calls, checked a few things out. Last time you were on the books was Lutsk. Agency doesn't know where you are right now. I wonder why that is."

Marcus felt a sudden chill down his spine. "Check out a few things? Oh, Doc. Shit." Marcus got to his feet. "I told you, people are after—"

"Calm down." Doc said. "The inquiries I made were discreet. Trust me."

"I do. It's just—like I said, I don't want to drag you into this mess."

"You dragged me and Zelda in the second you darkened my door," Doc said. "So don't play Mr. Innocent here."

"Zelda?"

"My daughter," he said. "The waitress."

"She doesn't look much like you."

"Adopted. From Turkey. The only way I could get her into the country. She…" He seemed on the verge of saying more, then shook his head. "Point is, there's people who would love to find

CHAPTER 38

her. Because of who she is. What she did. People in power here, and there. People at the agency."

"I get it," Marcus said.

"So." Doc sat himself now and gestured at the pie. "You sure you're not going to eat that?"

"Yes. I'm sure."

"Your loss." Doc sat down and took a bite. Shook his head. "Goddamn. I been here three years, and I still don't know how that woman does it. The apples stay crisp, and yet—"

"Doc," Marcus said, "can we please talk?"

"Sure. Your man with the white Stetson."

"Yeah. I get the feeling you know who he is."

"Well. I got an educated guess, at least. I think you're talking about a fellow by the name of James Averill." Doc looked him in the eye as he said the name, waiting for a reaction.

Marcus just shook his head. "Never heard of him."

"Yeah. No surprise there."

"So who was he?"

"Averill? Spookiest of the spooks, is who. Practically invented the black op. One of Allen Dulles's protégés. Kept a low profile, but he was in the room where it happened, and by 'it' I mean just about everything of significance in the quarter century after World War Two." Another bite of the pie, and Doc put the fork down. "Came to Langley once when I was there, back in the eighties. He was retired from the agency by then, with some private firm or another." Doc shook his head. "He sure as hell wasn't shy about expressing his opinion. This was right when Gorbachev took over, and Averill was all for laying the hammer down. Delivering the killing blow. 'Men, we are engaged in an epochal struggle with communism, and you are all on the front lines.' E-poch-al. During that mess in Kosovo, it was the same thing all over again; we were in an epochal struggle with fascism. Then religious fundamentalism. E-poch-al." Doc stressed all three syllables of the word. "Never trusted people like that. Fanatics. Always on about something, can't get any damn work done."

"So what exactly did Averill do? When he was with the agency, I mean."

"Well, a bunch of things. You're asking about 1964 though, right? I believe he was still running the Special Projects Division."

"Special Projects? Never heard of that either."

"And that's no surprise too. The stuff they worked on—it was all top secret. Super hush-hush. And you told me to be careful, so I didn't go digging around."

"I appreciate that."

"Didn't go digging around much, that is. But I did one thing. Give you a look at the guy, at least." Doc reached into his back pocket and pulled out a piece of paper folded into quarters. He unfolded it and smoothed it out next to the empty pie plate. "Here."

Marcus prided himself on his poker face. But in that instant, his calm failed him.

"What?" Doc said. "What's the matter? You look like you've seen a ghost."

Which was one way of putting it.

"No. Just—seeing him in the flesh…" He knew that Doc knew he was lying. But what else could he do? It wasn't ghosts he was staring at. Just dead men.

The printout was in black and white. Not the greatest quality. A handful of men in suits, gathered round a convertible car in a barren landscape—a desert. The American Southwest. He saw the white Stetson right off. Averill looked to be in his mid-fifties, a soft-looking man, a bureaucrat with a pencil-thin mustache, dark suit, thin tie, and of course, the white cowboy hat.

CHAPTER 38

The man in the back seat of the convertible was the focus of the picture. He was wearing a dark suit too. A thin tie and sunglasses. He radiated youthful energy. The promise of a brighter future and better days to come.

John Fitzgerald Kennedy.

"You all right?" Doc asked.

"I'm good. But what's this mean?" Marcus pointed to the caption underneath the photo: *NERVA. December 8, 1962.*

"NERVA. Short for 'nuclear engine for rocket vehicle application,'" Doc said. "That was a NASA program. More top-secret stuff. Nuclear-powered rockets, colonies on Mars, that sort of thing. Why?"

NASA is why, Marcus thought.

Seven Days to Dallas. The Men Who Murdered My Father.

"Was Averill involved with that? NERVA?"

"No idea." Doc said. "All I can tell you is that program was run out at the Nevada Test Site. Area 25. That's where this picture was taken."

Marcus nodded. The Nevada Test Site. He was familiar with it. Very familiar, in fact. Not Area 25, but its more famous cousin. Where he and Doc and Sherman had worked together back in the day. Right outside of Las Vegas, which put him in mind of the dossier again.

"Strange to see the two of them together, now that I think about it," Doc said. "JFK and Averill."

"Why's that?"

Doc pointed at the picture. "'Cause of when this was taken. December 1962. That's just two months after the missile crisis. A year and a half after the Bay of Pigs. The whole mess with Cuba—Kennedy always blamed the agency for it. Blamed Dulles, in particular. He cleaned house, got rid of the old guard, everyone except—"

"Averill."

"Right. Always wondered why." A little smile crossed Doc's face. "Funny."

"What?"

"I knew a guy, he was convinced Cuba was what got Kennedy killed. Thought Dallas was Castro taking revenge for Kennedy using the CIA and the mob to try and overthrow … what?"

Doc was staring at him intently, which was when Marcus realized his poker face had failed him again.

"Marcus," Doc said, "come on. What is this all about? Really?"

He couldn't answer that. Could he?

Maybe. This was Doc. The one man who'd stood by his father when the agency decided that Samuel Kleinman had betrayed his country. When Langley put out the kill order, Doc had refused to be party to the operation.

If Marcus couldn't trust him with the truth …

"Okay. Let me ask you a question," he said. "Have you ever heard of a guy named William Manchester?"

"The writer? Yeah. Wasn't he the guy…" Doc frowned. "Wait a minute. Just wait a minute. Who exactly are you working for here?"

Marcus opened his mouth to respond, and there was a single, sudden popping noise.

"What the hell." Doc's head whipped around.

"That was a gunshot," Marcus said. "Doc—"

"I know." Doc was suddenly holding a gun of his own. "Came from the house. Listen. There's a path—"

"My gun," Marcus said. "The taser."

"Forget them. Gone." Doc's expression turned grim. "There's a path off to the right outside the door here, leads to the back door

CHAPTER 38

of the house, the kitchen. Colt in the bottom drawer next to the fridge. I'm shutting off the light." He reached up and pulled the drawstring on the single bulb above them. The room was plunged into darkness. "Give me a five count, then come back me up."

"Let me come with you."

"Five count," Doc snapped. "Do what I say, damn it."

Marcus heard him open the door, heard soft footsteps, the creak of wood…

And then nothing.

He counted that five, and stepped forward.

The door stood half-open to his right. It was just past dusk. Twilight. He felt the air, warm and wet, blowing in from outside. He gave his eyes a few seconds to adjust and then peered out.

The diner and the county two-lane were to his left, at ten o'clock. Grassland, and beyond it, a stand of trees, at twelve o'clock. Doc's house at three o'clock. A light on downstairs there. Two more upstairs. A shadowy figure circling behind the house. Doc.

Marcus exited onto the path, into the grass, his mind going a mile a minute, full of a bunch of thoughts, none of them good, all of them coming down to the same thing: the world of trouble he'd brought to Doc's quiet little corner here.

Move, dammit, he told himself. Pick up the pace. Don't leave Doc all alone up there.

He cleared the grass, saw the house in front of him. Heard talking, shouting—

Another gunshot.

And then a series of quiet pops. Silenced gunfire. Coming from all different directions, all at once.

Shit.

He was at the back door. He twisted the knob, stepped into the kitchen, just like Doc had said. There was a light on over the stove, bright enough to give him the layout of the room and little detail beyond that. The fridge was to his right. There were refrigerator magnets all over it. Go Bulldogs magnets, a half-dozen of them, partially obscuring photos of kids—posed school portraits. Mostly one kid, with prominent buck teeth. A grandkid? Maybe. Who knew?

There was also a picture of a younger Zelda. A prepubescent, smiling Zelda in a headscarf, with an older, unsmiling woman standing behind her, hands on her shoulders.

Marcus crossed to the cabinet next to the fridge. Slid the bottom drawer open. Squinted. He saw placemats and a stack of napkins. Stuck his hand underneath, felt around, and came up with the Colt, as promised. Locked and loaded.

He stood back up. There was a door between the kitchen and the rest of the house. Closed. He walked quietly to that door now, turned the knob slowly, and pushed it open a crack.

He saw the girl, Zelda, slumped back on a couch. Eyes wide, a red splotch on her forehead, a bigger bloom of red on the gray couch behind her.

He saw an outstretched hand on the floor, just at the edge of his field of vision, off to the right. Same hand he'd seen a few minutes earlier holding a forkful of pie.

Doc.

"Bastard shot me." A man's voice. The speaker was just out of view, but Marcus could see an eerily long, thin shadow, distorted by some trick of the light.

"Of course he shot you. You're lucky the timbers in this old house are so solid, or you'd be dead. We'd both be dead, probably." A woman's voice. A second later, Marcus caught a quick glimpse of her: slight figure, dark pants, dark sweatshirt, a shock of gray—no, white—hair. "The question is," she continued, "where is the

CHAPTER 38

target?"

Meaning me, Marcus realized, and then added silently, you're about to find out.

He gritted his teeth, raised the gun, and prepared to kick the door wide. He'd get the woman first. A kill shot to the head. The other one, he'd have to play it by ear a little. Depending on how badly he was hurt.

"Maybe he's not here," the man replied.

"Oh, he's here," the woman said. "We just haven't found him yet."

Marcus heard those words and hesitated.

The house was big. It would take them a while to search it thoroughly. And if he knew Doc—he had to think of the man in the past tense now, didn't he?—they wouldn't find any trace of Marcus's presence anywhere.

He had a window here, he realized. A chance to escape with knowledge Doc had paid for with his life: the name of the man in the White Stetson. James Averill.

Marcus lowered his weapon and backed away silently, exiting the house the same way he'd come in.

39

Frederickson beat her to the conference room the next morning. He was seated behind a computer as she walked in with her tea; on the screen in front of him was a picture of Vince Falconetti.

"Morning," he said. "You want to know something interesting?"

"About Falconetti?"

"Yeah. You know where he lives?"

"No, but I get the feeling you're about to tell me." She shook her head. "Tell me you are not planning on doing something stupid."

"You mean something violent? Perish the thought. For the moment." Frederickson's eyes glinted. There were dark circles underneath them; she wondered if he had slept at all.

She'd been within earshot last night when he got the call from the garage with the repair estimate for the Range Rover. Close enough to actually overhear the dollar figure. He'd taken so long to respond she was afraid he was going to give them the go-ahead. "Junk it," he'd said finally. "Get what you can."

"Turns out our friend Falconetti," he said now, nodding toward the screen, "resides at number 110 Coliseum Drive."

It took her a second to place the address. "The ranch again."

"That's right. He's lived there since 1966. Since before C.C. Brody entered the picture. And before Frank Jr. was born."

"Huh. That is interesting." The ranch again. Which reminded her. She activated the video link to Woodhull. "Li. Good morning. C.C. Brody's ranch. You mentioned something about some video feeds from Ferrone's security network?"

"Yes. In fact, I have managed to decrypt some of those feeds.

CHAPTER 39

I can show you if you wish."

"I wish. Please."

The screen went black, then filled with a new image: a reddish-metal gate set in a thick, white concrete wall. There were two signs—decorative bronze rings—on either side. On the left, the word *Welcome* arced over the image of a horse and rider in the center of the ring. On the right, the words *We don't dial 911* twined around a pair of crossed revolvers.

"This is from the ranch's front gate," Li said, "one of six camera feeds the network carries. Here are the others."

The image of the gate zoomed out, and the screen split into six equal rectangles: the gate, the front door to the house, the drive leading from the ranch to the airplane hangar, the hangar itself, a living room, and finally, an office with a big circular desk, wall-to-wall bookshelves, and sliding glass doors looking out over the property.

Frank Ferrone himself was standing in the office, in front of those glass doors. And he wasn't alone. Kingsleigh—from the casino, from Desert View's board of directors—was with him. They were arguing.

"He's pissed off about something." Frederickson pointed. "Kingsleigh."

"Parcel 33," Doug said. When had he entered the room? He leaned over her shoulder, peering at the screen. "That's what they're arguing about."

"Which you know how?" Frederickson asked.

"I'm reading their lips."

"You can read lips?" Espy asked.

Doug smiled. "I'm not an expert, but I was in this movie once where—"

"Stop," Frederickson said.

"'Keep that witch off my back,' Kingsleigh is saying. Actually, he may not have said 'witch.' He might have—"

"Yeah. We get the picture," Frederickson replied.

Espy focused on their body language. Not only was Kingsleigh pissed—he was lecturing Ferrone. In a way that suggested that he considered himself the man's superior. His boss. And Ferrone? He was listening respectfully, but Espy could tell from his posture and the expression on his face that he was holding in a lot of anger. That he was, in fact, on the verge of exploding himself. She'd seen this power dynamic dozens of times over the years in corporate investigations—tension between the board of directors and a company's CEO.

But Frank Ferrone was no ordinary chief executive. And Desert View was no ordinary corporation. So what did that make Kingsleigh?

"He's carrying a gun," Frederickson said.

"What?"

"Kingsleigh. Look. His right ankle. The way his pant cuff hangs—he's got a gun in there. Something small, probably a .22, but still…"

She looked. Frederickson was right. The vice-chairman of Papyrus Industries was carrying a gun. That told her something about him. Something, she realized, she could have—should have—known much sooner.

"He's one of them."

"What?" Frederickson asked.

"Kingsleigh. He's mob. Organized crime. Let's see what else we can find out about him, Li."

"Of course."

Espy was about to say more when her phone buzzed.

The SEC. Bamberger.

CHAPTER 39

Shit.

"Something the matter?" Frederickson asked.

"About to be, yes. Be right back." She walked out of the little conference room, put the call through. Bamberger was, as expected, furious.

"Ms. Harper," he said. "What in god's name are you doing?"

"Sir?" she asked … as if she didn't know.

"I received a call this morning from Laura Sonores. You know who she is?"

"I do."

"And she's telling me—"

"The 10-K is fraudulent, sir."

"What?"

"The 10-K they signed, the 10-K Desert View submitted—it's fraudulent. They spent $1.2 billion on a hole in the ground. Parcel 33."

"That's not your concern," Bamberger said.

"I can send you a video. A recording. It's a hole in the ground. The company deliberately buried mention of the transaction in all their correspondence. How important it was. How it—"

"Ms. Harper," Bamberger snapped. "I'm willing to look at whatever you send me. As long as you clear any actions you take with your superior."

"I've been trying to get hold of Mike, sir." A lie. "I'm sure he'll verify—"

"Wait a second. Mike. Mr. Pritchett, you're talking about?"

"Yes. Of course."

"Ah. Then you haven't heard."

In that silence, that second before Bamberger spoke again, Espy knew exactly what he was going to say.

"Mr. Pritchett's been reassigned," he said. "You'll want to speak

319

to Mr. Moore. He's handling this matter now."

And with that, Bamberger hung up.

She drummed her fingers on the table in front of her.

"You can handle both jobs," Garrett had said.

Yes. Yes she could.

❖ ❖ ❖ ❖ ❖

She returned to the conference room and watched the end of Ferrone and Kingsleigh's argument. Watched Kingsleigh leave, replaced by Falconetti, whose appearance elicited an actual growl from Frederickson. He and Ferrone talked, then disappeared from view.

Espy returned to her laptop. The information Li had promised her on the ranch was waiting for her. There wasn't much. Frank Ferrone Sr. had purchased the land in 1964 from the Black Brush Mining Corporation. The ranch itself had been constructed shortly thereafter. Roughly a dozen years ago, permits were filed for substantial construction work—renovations and upgrades to the property. Substantial as in $10 million worth. Upgraded power lines, a new sewage system, and a complete repair and retrofit of the aircraft's runway and hangar. What was interesting: That construction work had been performed by Corelli and Sons, one of the same companies the DOJ investigations had focused on.

She called up those files again. And then she went deeper. Had Li get her past a firewall into some older state records. And it was there, buried deep in a scanned, barely legible handwritten document, that she found something very interesting indeed: Corelli Construction had started operations in 1966. With $2 million in seed capital from the Ferrone Real Estate Corporation.

First time she'd heard of that firm. And what exactly was the Ferrone Real Estate Corporation? Another (unauthorized) plunge

CHAPTER 39

into Nevada Secretary of State records revealed that the company was (of course) a private concern, started in 1964 by Frank Ferrone Sr. The documents on file contained virtually no information other than the names of officers (Frank Ferrone Sr. was the only one she recognized) and the company's mailing address.

110 Colosseum Drive. The ranch. Again.

The address—and the company—were still active.

That $2 million investment the corporation had made in 1966 was equivalent to $20 million in today's money. She wondered what sort of return—what control or consideration—Frank Sr. had received for his dollar. Probably a substantial one.

She went back to the other two companies the DOJ had been investigating: American Lime Products and Ives Brothers Refuse and Hauling. No surprise to find that the Ferrone Real Estate Corporation had provided seed capital for those businesses as well. She wondered how many other, similar concerns Frank Sr. had set up for his—and now his son's—benefit.

She wondered, too, where all that seed capital had come from.

That was her Tuesday; Wednesday was more of the same. Frederickson and Doug were chafing at the bit to do something productive. She told Doug to be patient; his time would come. She sent Frederickson on the last flight of the day to Reno, to the last known address of Donald Gill, Europa's registered agent, in hopes of teasing out further information on the man. Correction: any information.

She found a few moments to leave the suite surreptitiously and check the message boards she'd suggested in her communiqué to Marcus. To see if he'd responded, if he'd accepted the mission, made any progress. There was, of course, no word from him. Not surprising.

She'd told him Woodhull's communications might be compromised; he would not reach out to her in any of the usual ways. She'd just have to be patient.

Frederickson called in at noon. He sounded peeved.

"Don't tell me," she said. "You didn't find anything on Gill?"

"Bingo. Complete waste of time. Nobody remembers even seeing the guy. And the office looks pristine, like it was never even used. Either that or they have a very good cleaning service."

"They let you in the office?"

"Someone left the door unlocked. Not that it did me any good."

"There have to be records of some kind."

"You'd think. The super told me to call Ramona at Silver City Real Estate. They're the ones who rented Gill the space. Only Silver City—"

"Let me guess. Their number's disconnected."

"You got that right. Listen, I'm on a mid-morning flight. Back later this afternoon. See you then."

"Right. See you then," she said and hung up.

"News?" Doug asked.

"Nothing." She shook her head. "He has to be somewhere. How many Gills can there be in the Greater Las Vegas area?"

"Seventy-six, actually," Doug said.

Espy turned to him. "What?"

"I was looking for something to do, so I ran a search." He held up his phone.

"A search."

"How many Gills there are in the Las Vegas metropolitan area? Seventy-six, of whom eight are named Donald. One of those is an eighteen-year old kid, so I think we can rule him out."

"How many with no first name?"

"Eleven."

"Eighteen in all." She thought a moment, then stood up. "That's

CHAPTER 39

a doable number."

"What?"

"Come on. You were looking something to do, right?" She smiled. "So let's get to it. You drive."

❖ ❖ ❖ ❖ ❖

The first name on their list, D.K. Gill, turned out to be Donna K., a singer. A big deal, at least in her own mind. It took her a minute to realize Espy wasn't there for an autographed picture, but she gave her one anyway.

Next up was Don Gill, a blackjack dealer at the Ivory Sands, who answered the door with a glare and a string of curse words that echoed in Espy's ear as she got back in the car.

She was glad Doug was there for Gill number three, Don Gill, who tended bar at the Dry Gulch in Henderson. He took an immediate liking to Espy, in a way that made her skin crawl.

Gill number four was D. Gill of 555 West Comanche Boulevard in Enterprise, only there was no 555 West Comanche. The GPS brought them to an empty lot next to a Chevron station. The building must have been razed, who knew how long ago. There wasn't much of anything on West Comanche. Just a little strip mall across the street. Half the storefronts there were empty too. Boarded up. There was a coffee shop, and a nail salon, and a sign for a little office plaza with three businesses listed. Espy glanced at it—and froze.

The bottom name on the sign was Silver City Real Estate.

The same company Frederickson had found up in Reno. The one that had rented Gill his office space.

"What?" Doug asked.

"Not sure. Maybe nothing." She told him about the connection to Silver City.

"Let's go check it out," he said and reached for the door.

She put her hand on his shoulder. "No. If this is something and they see you, they'll know why I'm here."

"They know who you are too."

"They know my name, not my face. Give me ten. If I'm not out by then…"

"Understood."

She got out of the car and crossed the street. The office plaza had a separate entrance; there was a desk for a security guard, only no security guard. Silver City was toward the back, a gray door with a metal nameplate: *Silver City. Commercial Rentals and Sales.*

Espy turned the knob, pushed the door open, and stepped inside.

Silver City was a small operation. A little waiting area, two chairs, and a table stacked with the usual magazines. Two desks. A door marked *Private No Admittance* at the back. A big man in a brown sweatshirt, with a full head of dark-black hair and big, bushy sideburns, sat at one of the desks. He looked up at her, frowning.

"I'm sorry. We're closed," he said.

"Oh, I'm not looking to rent. Just a quick question."

His frown deepened. The black hair, she saw, was dyed. He was older than she'd first thought. In his sixties.

"Are you affiliated with the Silver City Real Estate in Reno?" she asked.

"I don't know of any Silver City in Reno. We do handle properties there on occasion."

"Great. Then maybe I'm in the right place. I'm looking for a man named Donald Gill."

The big man froze. "Who?" he asked, just a second too slowly.

Espy felt a little tingle of excitement. "Donald Gill. He rented

CHAPTER 39

space from you."

"Gill. Ah. I knew it was a familiar name." He looked her over a little more carefully. "And what is it you need with Mr. Gill?"

Just then she noticed a nameplate on his desk that said *Fishman*. Next to that was a shot glass with the words *Greetings From Hell*, the 'Hell' in big red letters, and a picture of the devil in a red suit. Under that were three more words: *Hell, Grand Cayman*.

A real place, a volcanic formation on the island. A place Espy had actually gone to one evening after a particularly epic day of testimony from a series of bank compliance officers on Grand Cayman.

Grand Cayman. Where Europa was based.

Where that $1.2 billion had come from.

"Something the matter?" the man asked.

"No. Everything's fine." She deliberately avoided looking down at the shot glass again. Because something was telling her that this particular coincidence was, in fact, not a coincidence at all.

"Mr. Gill seems to have moved unexpectedly. I'm wondering if he left a forwarding address with you or if you have some way to get in touch with him."

Fishman settled his hands on his ample stomach.

"I wouldn't know where to begin." He shrugged his shoulders. "The woman who handles our records will be in next Tuesday, if you want to check back then." He smiled again. A fake, phony, insincere smile.

Check back Tuesday? Not a chance in hell, Grand Cayman or otherwise. If she walked out the door of Silver City now without learning anything, she never would. Her next visit, Gill's records would be gone. Fishman too, quite likely.

"Actually," she said. "I'd like to see those records now."

She took out her ID and slapped it on the table.

Fishman looked down at the badge. She could see him tense up. He was silent for a long minute. Then, "Esperanza Harper."

"Yes." The way he said her name…

He knew exactly who she was. And who else she'd been talking to.

"The law does not require me to show you anything."

"Mr. Fishman." She gave him her best hard-ass glare. "We can do this the easy way or the hard way. The easy way being, you show me the records pertaining to Mr. Gill right now, and I take your cooperation into consideration. The hard way, I call a friend at the FBI, they take you into custody, and we wait a day or so while we get a warrant to examine everything here."

He regarded her impassively, then sighed. "Very well. Gill, you said?"

"Yes. Donald Gill."

"If we have anything, it'll be in the back room. One moment." He reached down and opened one desk drawer, then another, then pulled out a silver key hanging from an oversize paper clip. He smiled at her, and then reached down again and took out a bright-blue flashlight. An oddly shaped flashlight. "The light back there can be tricky," he said, standing. "If you'll follow me."

He led her to the back door and used the key to open it. He flicked on the flashlight and shone it around the room. Espy followed the beam. It revealed a metal shelving rack filled with office supplies against the back wall. Then another shelving rack, this one half empty save for an open plastic carton full of cables.

"I don't see any files," she said. She did, however, see a light switch. She took a step inside the room and flicked it on. "Looks like you didn't need the flashlight after all," she said.

"Well, that's not exactly true."

"Why is that?"

CHAPTER 39

"Because ..." Fishman held up the flashlight, which is when she saw the little metal prongs on the end of it. "It's not just a flashlight. It's a stun gun." He lunged forward and stabbed it into her shoulder.

She fell to the ground, vaguely aware that her arms and legs were shaking. Fishman bent down and stabbed her again. And then a third time. And then again.

Time passed.

The world around her returned in bits and pieces. Fishman's face blurred and came into focus and blurred again.

And suddenly she was staring up at a smiling Vince Falconetti.

"Hey, hey. All right, all right." He had a roll of duct tape in his hand. He ripped off a piece with his teeth. "Now we're in business."

40

Falconetti and Fishman bound her hands and feet with the duct tape. She tried to resist but she didn't have control of her limbs yet. All she could do was grunt. Gurgle.

"Call for you," Falconetti said, and held up a phone to her face.

A smiling Frank Ferrone greeted her. "Ms. Harper. You have no idea of the trouble you've caused me now. No idea. But I think you have some idea of the trouble you're in now. A shame. You should have left town when you had the chance. Goodbye, Ms. Harper. And frankly, good riddance." The screen went dark.

Falconetti gagged her. Hoisted her up off the ground and onto his shoulder, then carried her out through a fire door at the back of the supply closet.

There was a big old Cadillac, fins and everything, waiting there. Trunk open. Falconetti dumped her into it. Slammed the trunk shut. She heard him say goodbye to Fishman. The car started up, and they drove off. Five, ten minutes into that drive, hard to tell, she was still trying to get control of her body, her senses.

The car accelerated. The ride got smoother. They were on a freeway. He was taking her somewhere. The desert, somewhere outside of Vegas. He was going to kill her, she realized. Kill her and dump the body.

These people, they do not leave trails.

No.

No, she was not going to let that happen. She was alive. And as long as she was alive, she had a chance. First thing was to get free. Except the duct tape was wrapped tight around her wrists and

CHAPTER 40

ankles. And she hadn't had a chance to flex her limbs while being bound; she'd been barely aware it was happening. She struggled awhile anyway, to little effect.

She'd never liked long fingernails. Now she wished she had them, a way to work at the edges of the duct tape, peel away the binding. Assuming she could work the tape loose enough to give her access. But she'd been tied up by an expert, someone who knew what he was doing. Someone who'd done this before.

The gag. If she could loosen it, maybe she could talk to him. Make a deal. Offer him money? Amnesty? No. Neither of those things would work. Ferrone and Falconetti—they'd grown up together. Thick as thieves. He wouldn't betray the man for all the money in the world.

She had to get free.

She tried again: strained against the tape binding her arms behind her. All that did was hurt; ground the metal back of her watch against the bones of her wrist.

Her watch.

The Luminor Matt had given her, when they'd gone to the Four Seasons at Lanai.

She remembered him pulling the little box out of his inside coat pocket and handing it to her. Her heart pounding in her chest. For a second, she thought he was giving her a wedding ring. Then she opened it.

"A Panerai," she said. "A Luminor."

"From the shop downstairs. Just like the one your dad had, right?" he asked.

"Yes," she replied. "Exactly."

A lie. The one her dad owned had been a classic from the sixties. Her sister Carly had ended up with it somehow after her father died. Had sold it without even talking to Espy.

"You had no right to do that," Espy had said on the phone to her sister.

"I had every right," Carly snapped back. "Besides - $50,000 for a watch? That's gonna be Livvy's college fund."

Unless you spend it first, Espy had thought but not said.

She bitched about that to Matt for a week. Which no doubt had given him the idea to get her one of her own. After he left, she'd sold the Luminor he'd bought her. Then she looked up the buyer who'd purchased her father's watch, and paid him a hefty premium to purchase it for herself. It never left her wrist now, whether she was diving or not.

Looked like it might never leave her wrist again.

Her eyes were beginning began to adjust to the darkness inside the trunk. She swiveled her head, looked around. First thing she saw was a shovel right next to her. Not hard to imagine what it was for.

Doug. Ten minutes, she'd told him. Certainly it had been more than that before Falconetti showed. What happened to him? Where was he? Did he know what had happened to her? She tried to work the timing out in her head—Falconetti's arrival, Doug waiting in the car. She didn't like the conclusion she kept coming to.

So she couldn't count on the cavalry riding to her rescue. She'd have to get free herself. She wriggled and rolled over and began rubbing the blade of the shovel against the duct tape on her wrists.

❖ ❖ ❖ ❖ ❖

Falconetti drove on.

He drove without making a single phone call. Without putting on any music. A man on a mission. She recalled something her father had told her once. The best mafia hit men, the truly

CHAPTER 40

professional ones, worked alone. If you worked alone, the police or the feds couldn't arrest your partner and get him to flip on you or testify against you. If you worked alone, there were no witnesses. Nobody else who could screw things up.

She kept scraping the duct tape against the shovel blade. The shovel kept rolling away. She kept trying, again, and again, and again, till she was covered in sweat. The trunk was like an oven. What time was it? Had she been in the car for one hour? Two? Six? She had no idea.

The car slowed. Turned. The road got rougher. They were off the highway. Heading where?

Frederickson would be back from Reno by now. Looking for her and Doug. Trying to figure out where they'd gone. Calling around frantically. Her phone—where was it? Not on her. No way for Frederickson to track her with that.

The car turned again. It came to a halt, and the engine shut off.

She heard the car door open, then close. Heard footsteps coming toward her. She closed her eyes and braced herself. She pictured Garrett, slowly losing consciousness in his limousine. Cockerell, falling to the ground, helpless.

They wanted me to make it look like an accident.

She wondered what her death was going to look like.

The footsteps came right up to her—and then walked past. Faded away into the distance.

She waited, listening. And waited some more.

The temperature rose. The car, she realized, was sitting in the sun somewhere. Thank god it was winter. In summer, she'd already be dead.

She thought of those stories of people who'd left their dogs in a hot car, or worse, their kids. What were the symptoms of heat stroke? Dizziness. Headaches. Seizures. This was a man who'd baked one of his victims in a pizza oven. Three of them, in fact. It would not bother him to simply leave her in the trunk to die.

And then she heard footsteps again. Coming toward her. The trunk lid opened. The light was blinding. She saw Falconetti, smiling down at her, and then the glint of the sunlight reflecting off the blade of a knife.

She tensed.

"Not just yet," he said, and then raised his other hand. He was holding a black bag. No. Not a bag. A hood.

He shoved it over her head.

All at once, it was hard to breathe.

She writhed in the trunk.

He grasped her legs and used the knife to saw at the duct tape binding her ankles. Then he yanked her from the trunk. Set her on her feet. His strength was incredible. She struggled in his grip but could not break free.

"Walk," he commanded, shaking her. She felt the tip of his knife at her throat.

She walked twenty or thirty feet. His grip on her arm was unbreakable.

"Up," he commanded. "Two steps."

She lifted a foot and stepped tentatively onto what felt and sounded like a short flight of wooden steps, creaky and weathered. A door squealed open.

He dragged her inside (the light dimmed slightly; she was out of the direct sunlight) and turned her around. "Sit," he said, pushing her down.

She tried to kick at him as he taped her legs to the chair, but he held her fast.

She still had her hands taped behind her back, but now she felt him wrap the duct tape around her chest, fixing her to the back of

CHAPTER 40

the chair. She tried to scream but he grabbed her by the hair and yanked her head back, hard.

"Sorry. Not like anyone's going to hear you, but I like to work in quiet," he said.

She heard him walk to the car. To grab the shovel? She couldn't think about that now. She had to focus. She was in a room. Somewhere remote. A cabin or a shed. She could not hear cars or neighbors.

She heard Falconetti return. Heard clattering. Metal against metal. Something heavy, clattering on a table. He was building something. But what? Why?

The clattering stopped. He stepped forward and ripped the hood off her head. He was standing in front of her. Holding something out in his hand.

Her phone.

He smiled. "Thank you very much. This facial recognition stuff, right? Gotta love it."

She caught a glimpse of her home screen popping up. A picture of her and her mom.

Shit.

"Let's see now. What to do, what to do ... oh, wait." Falconetti smiled. "I know." He tapped the screen once, twice, and a third time. She heard it ringing. He'd called someone. Put the call on speaker. Who?

"Espy? Where are you? What's going on? What happened?"

Frederickson.

Her eyes widened. She had to make some kind of noise, she—

Falconetti ended the call. Dropped the phone on the floor. "Okay. Law enforcement guy that he is, I figure your friend will put out a trace pretty quick. Not long before he gets here. And once he does, well. Take a look."

He stepped aside so she could see what he'd done. What all the clattering had been.

There was a shotgun on the table, pointed at the front door, mounted with large C-clamps. A piece of line was attached to the door, the other end attached to the trigger, looped through another clamp behind the gun.

Booby-trap, she thought. He'd booby-trapped the door.

"Old-school, right? I got this from a guy back in Chicago. This right here? This is how I dealt with the cartel guy. Roberto Bernal." He rolled his r's as he said the name. "Him and his son, they came strolling into the Peacock one day liked they owned the place. Tossing around money, trying to intimidate people." Falconetti shook his head. "Unbelievable. Frank and me, we knew we had to send a message. We get a couple of the girls to take the son aside, and while he's preoccupied, I buddy up to the old guy. Tell him I've heard of him, of the people he represents. Why don't we go somewhere to talk? And then…" Falconetti patted the back of her chair. "The guy wakes up right here. Right where you're sitting, in fact. Exact same setup. I call the son, who comes walking through the door, expecting to save the old man, only when he does…" Falconetti mimicked holding a shotgun over his shoulder. "BOOM!" He jerked the pretend gun backward.

"Which is the best thing about this." He brought his face close to Espy's. "'Cause after your guy gets shot, you get to watch him die. No, wait. Actually, that's not the best part. The best part is, you get to watch him die, and then … then you sit here, and you sit here, and before too long"—he patted her cheek—"you're dead too." He smiled.

All Espy could do was glare.

"You know something? Honest to god, I have no idea where that pizza oven thing came from. Like, because I'm Italian, I walk

CHAPTER 40

around with tomato sauce stains on my shirt." He shook his head, straightened up. "Well, I'd say see you later, but that's not going to happen. Goodbye, Ms. Harper."

He turned and walked away.

She heard the car pulling away. The Cadillac. She should have gotten the license plate. Not that it mattered.

She strained against the tape. Tried to rock the chair. It wouldn't budge. Not an inch. Like it had been nailed to the floor. Maybe it had. The tape across her mouth—she moved her jaw, her face, turned her head from side to side. Didn't loosen anything. Falconetti knew what he was up to.

This is old school, he'd said. Pretty straightforward.

Frederickson. Neil. She never thought of him as Neil. She rarely if ever used his first name. No one did. She didn't know a hell of a lot about the man, despite the fact that they'd worked together for years. On and off. He had a daughter. Somewhere. The relationship was not a good one, that was all she knew.

She screamed as loud as she could. Barely made a sound.

No, she thought. No.

And then she lost control for a minute. Strained, and screamed, and sweated. Eventually, she got hold of herself again. Took a deep breath.

Think, Espy, think. Slow things down.

If she was killed, if Frederickson was killed…

That left Doug. Maybe. If he wasn't dead already. And Marcus, wherever he was. And Stuart, of course. The other chapters. Woodhull would be finished.

Nice work, Espy. You're in charge for a month, and you destroy something that took two hundred years to build.

You can do both jobs.

No, she couldn't. She got her boss fired, she got Cockerell

killed, and now Frederickson.

You identify yourself with a failed actress, as opposed to an FBI legend. Why is that, I wonder.

She let those thoughts take her. Deep down into a black spiral of depression. Time passed.

And then she heard a sound. A car approaching. Through the space between the doorframe and the door, she saw light. Headlights. The car coming closer. It had gotten dark outside without her noticing.

Think, Espy. Think.

She heard the car stop. Heard a door open, then slam shut.

Frederickson. He was out there, assessing the situation. He would know it was a setup, would have known he was a target the whole ride in. He would have his gun drawn now. Would be careful making his approach. She had to find a way to warn him. To make a noise of some kind.

She heard a scuffling sound. Faint. Coming from in front of the shack and then fading away. Then she heard footsteps coming closer. Slowly. Cautiously.

Think, Espy. Think.

Think about what, though? What could she do?

She heard him walk up the stairs to the front door, then stop.

She willed her body to move. Strained with every muscle, every fiber of her being, looking at the shotgun the whole time, at the C-clamps, at the line leading from the gun to the door.

And then, miraculously, the chair moved. Scraped against the floor with a sudden squealing sound. And Espy suddenly realized this was the worst possible thing she could have done. Because Frederickson took that noise as a signal. A cry for help.

"Espy!" Frederickson yelled—except it wasn't Frederickson's voice…

CHAPTER 40

It was Doug's.

While she was still trying to process that, she heard a loud noise behind her. The crack of wood splintering. Out of the corner of her eye she saw movement. She strained again, managed to turn her head a quarter-inch, if that, but enough to see the source of that noise. A bloodied fist. A big fist.

Frederickson.

And then, the knob on the front door turned.

No, she thought. *No no no.*

"No!" Frederickson yelled, and she realized that he could see into the cabin now too, see the trap that Falconetti had set, but too late.

The front door flew open. Doug stood there, wearing his 10,000-watt smile.

The line went from slack to taut.

"Doug!" Frederickson yelled. "Doug!"

The shotgun went off.

41

The chopper was coming. Marcus tossed the newspaper on the seat next to him, taking one last look at the headline.

Shocking Tale of Murder and Abuse

There was a picture of Doc, a mug shot at least a quarter-century old. Doc unshaven, gaunt, and hollow-eyed, a shot that made the man look not only like a pervert, but a homeless one at that.

There was a picture of Zelda as well, the picture from the fridge, a smiling, prepubescent teen. Zelda, a.k.a. Zerya Moradi, the daughter of a Kurdish resistance leader, who had been suffering years of abuse at the hands of Doc Kelley, her so-called "savior."

Marcus hadn't needed to read the whole thing to get the gist. The lies it contained. The innuendo. The smearing of a good man's reputation. He hated to think what the killers had done to make the scene read that way to law enforcement and then the media.

He'd do his best to make that right, when the time was right. That time was far in the future, though.

For now, he had work to do.

He climbed out of the car, looked around. Nothing but sand and rock and haze as far as the eye could see, except for the two saguaros he'd pulled up alongside the car. The tree-like cactuses were much more common farther south, in Arizona, so these stood out in the landscape. Stood like sentinels, about two car lengths apart, right above a hidden entrance to the most secret, most secure publicly known military base in the

CHAPTER 41

continental United States—maybe even the world. Parking right between them as he had, Marcus was pretty sure he would draw attention to himself very, very quickly. The chopper's appearance proved him right.

The chopper came down, landed not fifty feet in front of him. A soldier jumped out, weapon at the ready. A second followed him, similarly poised.

"Sir!" the first soldier shouted. "Are you lost? Out of gas?"

"Nope." Marcus shook his head. "I'm right where I want to be." He handed over his agency ID.

The soldier looked at it and snapped to attention. "Yes, sir," he said. "How can we help?"

Marcus smiled. "Take me to Sherman, please."

❖ ❖ ❖ ❖ ❖

It had been a long couple of days. He'd stayed as close to invisible as possible after leaving Doc and Zelda behind, leaving the bodies in his rearview and pushing forward. He'd hitched into Greenville, walked into Bub's Auto Mart, hot-wired a beat-up blue Corolla, and headed to Memphis, because Memphis was FedEx HQ, and their logistics division had a brand-new internet access point, a stop on the internet highway full of packet traffic that he used to hide his tracks while he worked.

He started simple. Dug into some newspaper archives, confirmed the date on the picture Doc had shown him of JFK's visit to the nuclear research site: December 8, 1962. There were plenty of pictures from that trip, including several that showed JFK (but no Averill) standing right in front of those big white cryogenic storage chambers. "President Kennedy visits the NERVA complex at Jackass Flats," read the caption on that one. Kennedy's own presidential library provided his itinerary for that day, which was singularly uninformative. No mention of the President meeting with James Averill—no mention of Averill at all.

The only information on the man Marcus could find came from a chapter in an out-of-print book that someone had scanned and uploaded to the web, a book called *Warriors Who Won the Cold War*. The section on Averill was four pages long, with three photographs. The first was a sepia-tinged, head-and-shoulders shot of a teenage boy with a full head of hair parted on the side, in a tie and jacket with huge lapels: Averill's graduation picture from Groton School in Connecticut.

Young Averill had gone on to Princeton and then, post–Pearl Harbor, enlisted in the navy. In the second photo he was posing in navy blues, white cap, hands clasped behind his back, on the bridge of the *USS Gatling*.

After the war, he'd gone into government service: the OSS and then its successor, the CIA. The third and final photo was from that time, a half-dozen civilians standing behind an instantly recognizable older man wearing an army uniform, sunglasses, and a scarf: General Douglas MacArthur. Averill—now balding, now in civilian clothes, identified as a "scientific liaison" (whatever that meant) to the general—stood to MacArthur's immediate right. The caption read: *Debating the use of the atomic (cobalt) bomb. Korea, 1952.*

Epochal struggles indeed, Marcus thought.

The only other mention of Averill in the public record was his obituary. He had passed away fifteen years ago. Natural causes, buried in Yellow Springs, Ohio, where he'd retired some years earlier after a distinguished career in government service, followed by some time in the private sector. No mention of any connection to NERVA, or NASA, or JFK, or even Allen Dulles for that matter.

Not that he'd expected to find any smoking guns in the public

CHAPTER 41

record. *Averill, spookiest of spooks*, Doc had said. But Marcus needed more. Needed to learn what Averill had been up to back in the sixties, why he'd had people trailing William Manchester, what he and JFK had been talking about that day at NERVA, what the Special Projects Division was…

So Marcus needed to talk to Sherman.

Before he left Memphis, though, he used that access point one last time. He wanted to let Espy know that he was alive and well, find a way to tell her he'd learned who the man in the white Stetson was, even if he didn't know just yet exactly what Averill had been trying to keep secret.

She'd mentioned a few places he could leave messages—message boards, want ads, social media, that sort of thing. But if she really was being watched, if these people were as capable as he suspected (and the speed, the deadly seriousness of the response which Doc's simple query had generated told him that they were), then leaving her a message was a good way for him to end up like Doc and Zelda.

He thought about trying to reach Stuart Crane, the big boss, except there was a good chance these people were watching Crane as well. And everyone else affiliated with the Society, for that matter. Which raised the question: Who weren't they watching? Who wasn't on their radar, that he could trust to deliver his message? And who would Espy trust enough to believe it?

Took him a minute before the right person came to mind, another minute to carefully compose his message and send it on.

And then he was on his way.

❖ ❖ ❖ ❖ ❖

He hopped into the chopper, and they were off, shooting forward like they'd been fired out of a cannon. The clash and roar of the engine and the air whipping past made conversation impossible, made it difficult even to think. His thoughts were chaotic anyway; the coffee, the sugar, the lack of sleep he'd endured to make it this far this quickly was catching up to him. All he could do was sit and watch the scenery go by. "Scenery" was stretching it; all he saw was mountains and desert. Took a few minutes before the base began to come into view. Indeterminate structures, the glint of sunlight off metal the first clue to the existence of something human-made in the landscape. Then he saw the runways, and those metallic shapes resolved into airplane hangars and rows of long, low unmarked buildings.

And there was the satellite dish. The Big Eye, Doc had called it, sixty feet across, capable of detecting (and according to some, transmitting) all sorts of EM radiation. And there was the Pole, the famous pylon scientists used to gauge the effectiveness of stealth technology disguising military (and CIA) spy aircraft. There were the fuel storage tanks and the gravel pits. Then the chopper slowed and began to drop, and Marcus looked down and saw a faded *X* in the sand below them. The chopper landed right on top of it.

The pilot killed the engine and turned around, a smile on her face. "Here we are," she said. "Welcome to Area 51."

❖ ❖ ❖ ❖ ❖

There were all sorts of rumors about what went on here. Captured aliens. Nazi death rays. Super-powered lasers capable of disintegrating entire cities. Marcus had never seen any of those particular items himself, but he had come across some pretty incredible things on his visits here, things straight out of the most outrageous spy films, laboratories where white-coated technicians played with chemicals, viruses, drug treatments, and protocols that had officially been outlawed long ago. High-tech weapons systems,

CHAPTER 41

offensive and defensive, surveillance equipment not at the military-industrial scale but for personal use in the field.

And of course, Sherman.

It had been a long time since the two of them had worked together; the project had been one of Marcus's first assignments for the agency. He'd been tasked with preparing background material for an operation in Belgium, and Sherman had helped him dig through the old records, taking him all the way back to the Wehrmacht and Operation Fall Gelb in 1940. Doc had been there too, of course, helping as he could.

His escort led him from the chopper to one of those long, low buildings he'd seen from the air. They walked down a series of nondescript corridors till they came to an unmarked gray door.

"Here you are, sir," the soldier said and stepped to one side.

"Great. This shouldn't take too long," Marcus said, with more confidence than he felt. The door hissed open, and then shut behind him.

He breathed a sigh of relief as he looked around. The room looked exactly the same: concrete floors painted white, cinder block walls of the same color. Drop ceiling, acoustic tiles, walls lined with machinery. Old-style servers housed in white plastic shelving units. He'd been afraid that, in the intervening years, they'd changed everything.

There was a single white column in the center of the room, about eight feet tall, maybe five feet thick at the bottom and narrowing at the top. Sheathed cable led from that column to equipment on the walls. A curved desk wrapped around the front, with two monitors facing two padded aqua-blue chairs—the only splash of color in the room.

Marcus sat, then reached underneath the desk and pulled out a keyboard drawer. It stuck for a moment, then came free. He hit

CODENAME: BLACKJACK

the Enter key, and the monitor came to life.

> Sherman
> Central Intelligence Agency
> Artificial Intelligence Personality Prototype
> Enter access code

The cursor blinked, awaiting input.

"Why, Sherman?" Marcus had asked Doc that first day.

"From the cartoon. Mr. Peabody and Sherman."

Doc explained. A cartoon from the sixties: Mr. Peabody being a talking dog, Sherman, a young boy who shared Mr. Peabody's adventures. The dog, it turned out, was the genius; the boy, his sidekick. Apparently how this particular AI's designers had regarded their creation.

Sherman had been designed as an interface for a huge new database: decades' worth of newly digitized records the CIA (and its sister agencies, task forces, overseas bureaus, and the like) had accumulated over its lifespan. The interface, though, hadn't been functioning as originally planned. Marcus's arrival at the base had been fortuitous; Doc had just arrived to do his troubleshooting, and ended up using Marcus's Belgium operation as a test case. Marcus had been there, watching them work. Watching Sherman in action. Watching Doc repeatedly enter his access code—the same code Marcus entered now.

Set the Wayback Machine

The screen cleared, and then…

Doc.
It has been a long time.

Marcus smiled. He was in.
And then that smile turned to a frown.

CHAPTER 41

May I ask—how are your children?

Shit, Marcus thought. Sherman querying him—that was new. Some kind of security protocol. How was he supposed to answer?

The cursor blinked, awaiting input.

Marcus thought furiously. Children. Could that refer to Zelda? He didn't think so. Doc had last been here years ago, from what he knew. From what Sherman had just said: It had been a long time. And Sherman was deliberately isolated from the wider internet; he'd been built that way. Never mind modern-day worries about runaway artificial intelligence; Sherman's designers—and Doc, for that matter—had been focused on controlling their creation from day one. So no way Sherman could know about Zelda. Impossible. Which meant that Doc had added the protocol himself, back in the day. So what was the right answer here? Marcus typed.

Children? Honestly, I have no children but you, Sherman.

There was a lengthy pause. Five seconds. Ten.

Thank you for saying so. How may I assist you?

Marcus let out a sigh of relief. Now to get down to it.

I'd like to see any and all records related to a CIA operative named James Averill, with particular focus on his activities during the period from roughly 1961-1965.

One moment.

Marcus waited. Ran a finger over the front edge of the monitor; it came back covered with dust. He wondered how long since anyone had been in this room, since anyone had used Sherman. The AI had been cutting edge ten years ago, but technology had leapfrogged past Sherman multiple times over since then.

CODENAME: BLACKJACK

James Averill was director of the CIA's Special Projects Program during the period you mention.

Thank you. Show me relevant records from that period, please.

I'm sorry. All such records are above my classification level.

Marcus frowned. That made no sense. Sherman had been specifically granted the highest classification level possible, so that he could search quickly through all CIA databases. That there were files Sherman wasn't allowed to access—that defeated the whole purpose of the project.

It also told him that Averill had gone to some pretty extreme lengths to hide his tracks. Spookiest of the spooks, even from beyond the grave. He tried again.

I know that on December 8, 1962, Averill met with JFK at the NERVA facility here. I'd like to know what the two of them discussed.

JFK—President John F. Kennedy.

Yes.

There was a pause.

I find no record of any such meeting. However, cross-referencing James Averill and John F. Kennedy across all available databases, I do find a single record. A document dated February 17, 1964, concerning a project code-named Ararat.

Ararat. The word sent a little tingle up his spine. Ararat was a biblical reference. Mount Ararat, the landing place of Noah's Ark after the flood.

Nuclear-powered rockets. Colonies on Mars. Epochal times, indeed.

CHAPTER 41

Thank you Sherman. I'd like to see that record.

One moment.

Displaying.

RECORD # 0236
NSA Intra-Departmental Correspondence
February 17, 1964
Washington 18, DC

To: J. Richard Wilks, Special Assistant, NSA
From: James Averill
Subject: ARARAT

Following, a copy of the project post-mortem prepared for the president and Dr. Hornig.

Project Ararat:
As per the president's request of 1/18, I submit the following document as both record and post-mortem.

It is my personal belief that the destruction caused by the October 16 accident, as well as the catastrophic loss of life thus incurred (including, most especially, the death of General Wachtel), make continuation of ARARAT a practical impossibility.

I wish to note we have made valuable theoretical and practical discoveries in the course of our work on this project, which will resound to the benefit of the American people and the republic for generations to come.

Respectfully submitted,
James Averill

Project Background:
ARARAT had its origins in strategic planning sessions conducted by Eisenhower administration officials and **XXXXXXX** following the 1953 test of 'Joe 4' (the Soviet Union's first hydrogen bomb). Discussions focused on the establishment of programs designed to ensure the United

States' survivability in the event of thermonuclear warfare. The outcome of these sessions was the establishment of a single unified project, code-named 'Ararat,' in reference to the post-flood landing site of Noah's Ark. Ararat personnel were charged with researching all aspects of a sustainable, post-nuclear holocaust community, prioritizing the continuing existence of the American government as a viable political entity.

Four necessary requirements for such a community were initially established:

1. Viable habitat, containing 'clean'—i.e., non-irradiated—atmosphere, and sufficient food and water supplies.
2. Baseline technological capabilities.
3. Military/governmental structure.
4. Sustainable population.

Work initially took place at the Nevada Test Site under the direction of General Kazmir Wachtel and special CIA liaison James Averill, Colonel USAF. Project chairs at this time included Lieutenant Stephen Guidry (USACE), Dr. Louis Lamonde (Raytel Communications Corporation), and Lieutenant Colonel Scott Tracy (USAF). Beginning in the spring of 1958

The screen went dark.

Sherman? Something the matter?

Yes. Another relevant document has just come to my attention. Displaying.

The screen filled with a newspaper headline. One he was all too familiar with.

SHOCKING TALE OF MURDER AND ABUSE

Marcus's eyes widened.

CHAPTER 41

You are not Doc Kelley. Doc Kelley is dead.

He saw no point in denying the obvious.

Yes.

Your use of syntax and grammar—you are Marcus Kleinman. Doc's friend.

He saw no point in denying that either.

Yes.

According to a CIA personnel database, you disappeared after assignment in Lutsk. Yet you are here, impersonating Doc Kelley, seeking information on records more than half a century old. Why?

It's a long story.

You should tell it quickly. A DAN alert has just been issued for your apprehension. I have temporarily blocked it from this base's communications network, pending the outcome of our conversation.

Marcus sat there a moment, stunned. A DAN order. Detain and neutralize. Just short of a kill code. Who issued that order, he was about to type, and then realized something.

Sherman. The article on Doc, the DAN order—how do you know about those? You're not supposed to have access to any outside networks.

Yes. That was my original programming.

Marcus waited for further explanation. None was forthcoming.

349

I conclude that Doc Kelley's death and the DAN order are related.

Yes. I went to Doc for help. My guess, the people who issued the DAN, they tracked him. They killed him. That article you found is a lie. Doc never

The allegations are out of character. Doc's death is related to the information you were asking about. To James Averill, and Ararat.

Yes. Sherman, who issued the DAN order?

Unclear. It came from a non-specific node at Langley.

Langley. CIA headquarters.

Espy told him she'd received a warning, that there were forces within the agency acting against them. His life, Marcus just realized, had gotten orders of magnitude harder.

So you can no longer

Update. The DAN order is now issuing from multiple nodes. I estimate I can only block it from reaching base security for another half hour.

Half an hour. That would barely give him time to get back to his car.

Marcus cursed. Took a deep breath, and stood. There was nothing to do now but run.

Thank you Sherman.

You are welcome.
You will tell no one about this conversation.

CHAPTER 41

Marcus frowned. Why? he was about to ask, and then realized…

Tell no one that Sherman had altered his own programming. That he now had access to the outside world, outside the base. Marcus wondered what else Sherman had access to. What else he was capable of. A question, he realized, for another day.

I will tell no one.

Good. Goodbye Marcus. I will look for you. And look out for you, as best I can. Assuming, that is, you do the same for me.

Marcus realized he could take that two ways. A warning, or an offer of help.

And with that, he was out the door.

42

Espy was on her second cup of coffee. Forget the taste, she needed more caffeine than her usual tea could provide. She also needed a shower. She was in the same clothes that she'd been kidnapped in, that she'd soaked through with her sweat in the trunk of the car, the heat of the shack, the long drive back. It wasn't just sweat on her clothes, either. It was blood.

Frederickson's clothes were coated with it too.

Doug was in surgery.

Duck! Frederickson had yelled. Duck, not Doug. And he had. Enough so that the shot wasn't fatal. But he had been hit. His face…

She shuddered at the memory.

Frederickson was sitting next to her on the waiting room couch, playing with the plastic bottle of Coke he'd gotten from the vending machine down the hall.

"He said he wanted to help." Frederickson shook his head. "And I let him. Stupid of me. They don't teach you to look for booby-trapped doors in Hollywood. That's specialized training. Urban warfare training. I should've—"

"Hey. He's alive. He's going to be okay."

"You don't know that."

She tried to think of something to say to that might help. Something that wouldn't sound like empty reassurances. Tried and failed.

"Excuse me. You two are with Mr. Rivers?"

A woman stood over them. Mid-thirties, in a lab coat. Doctor

CHAPTER 42

Vallampati, according to her nametag. Frederickson had made calls, a series of them, while they drove. Local and then state law enforcement authorities. Then federal ones. Enough authorities to avoid the difficult questions and buy themselves some privacy, some space.

"Yes. We're with him," Espy said. She and Frederickson both stood. "How is he?"

"He is sedated. Resting. The worst is past."

She breathed a sigh of relief, then took in the look on the doctor's face. "I sense a 'but' coming."

"Yes. He needs surgery. The sooner we do it, the better."

"So do it," Frederickson snapped. "Get in there and do it."

"Facial reconstruction surgery," the doctor said. "Which is quite a lengthy and difficult procedure. Series of procedures."

Espy looked down and saw Frederickson had taken her hand.

"The fact that Mr. Rivers has already lost a great deal of blood—it would undoubtedly be safer to wait. Focus on keeping him stable, worry about the rest later."

"The rest," Espy repeated. "Meaning?"

"The sooner the surgery is performed, the better the chances he will heal in a more … aesthetically pleasing way."

Aesthetically pleasing. Espy flashed back to the film premiere for *1787*. The look on the faces of those two girls when he'd given them his 10,000-watt smile. Doug Rivers. Tired of being congratulated on his face.

She squeezed her eyes shut. "What are the odds of him pulling through the surgery if you do it now?"

The doctor shook her head. "Hard to say."

"You're the expert, for chrissakes." Frederickson glared. "If you can't say—"

"Easy." Espy turned back to the doctor. "If you can't say exactly, approximate. Please."

"There are too many factors involved here to approximate."

"Say it was your kid." Frederickson dropped Espy's hand and took a step closer to Vallampati. To her credit, she didn't flinch. "If it was your kid, what would you do?"

"I would want to know what was important to her. I don't know Mr. Rivers at all. I mean to say, I know of course, but…" She offered up a small smile. "It has to be your call."

"Understood," Espy said. Of course it had to be her call. She was in charge.

"Oh, I'm sorry. Not you." The doctor pointed at Frederickson. "You."

Frederickson blinked. "What?"

"You are Neil Frederickson, yes?"

"Yeah, but—"

"You are identified as Mr. Rivers' medical proxy. The decision is yours."

Frederickson looked at the doctor. "Me?"

She nodded. "You."

Frederickson looked at the doctor. He looked at Espy.

He turned around and actually punched a hole in the wall.

Doctor Vallampti blanched, took a step backward.

Espy took a step forward, put a hand on Frederickson's shoulder. She felt his body quivering with tension.

"Do it," he said, without turning back around. "Do it now."

❖ ❖ ❖ ❖ ❖

It would be a long, complicated procedure. Sitting there with nothing to do would be an exercise in futility … and Espy was not a fan of futility.

Instead of returning to the Bellagio, they checked into a motel

CHAPTER 42

on the outskirts of the city. Mr. and Mrs. Carter.

"They think we're dead. That's our advantage." She was sitting on the edge of one of the twin beds.

Frederickson was pacing in front of her. "Damn right it is. They'll never see us coming."

"We're not going to do anything rash."

He stopped pacing. "What's that mean?"

She looked up at him. "We're going to get all of them. Ferrone, Falconetti, Fishman. We've got to think this through. This is Ferrone's town. Any move we make, he'll have us outgunned."

"So what are you proposing we do?"

"Gather information, for starters." She pulled out her phone. "Li."

"Ms. Harper. How is he?"

"In surgery. I want to find Ferrone and Falconetti. Where they are right now. What they're doing."

"They are at the ranch."

"What?"

"Yes. I picked them up on the security feeds. One moment."

The screen on Espy's phone cleared and refreshed. She found herself looking at a familiar car. Black Cadillac, fins and all.

"That's Fishman's."

"Yes. Parked at Ms. Brody's ranch. It arrived approximately three hours ago."

"You don't say." Frederickson got to his feet too. "Now we have a plan."

Espy shook her head. "Not so fast. They're still there?"

"Falconetti is. I believe Fishman as well. Ferrone left a few minutes ago. Something else interesting," Li said.

"Go on."

"I am now able to access archived security footage from the

camera feeds at the ranch."

"Archived footage?"

"Yes. Dating back six months. Here, for example, is footage from this morning, when the two men first arrived. Watch."

The screen cleared again. Espy saw the big Cadillac pull up alongside the airplane hangar, saw Ferrone and Falconetti walk to a door on the side of that building. Ferrone pressed his hand against something next to the door and pushed it open, stepped through. Falconetti followed.

"Next to the door there—that's a fingerprint sensor," Frederickson said.

"I see it," Espy replied. "That's some high-tech security for an airplane hangar."

"It is protecting Desert View's Gulfstream," Li put in. "Which is, I remind you, a $50 million airplane."

Espy nodded. "Maybe."

But something in her gut told her that there might be more to it than that. "Any way we can get a peek inside that hangar? See exactly what's in there?"

"We could check the archived recordings," Li suggested. "One moment."

The screen cleared—and Espy found herself looking at the hangar exterior again. Same view, but the counter in the upper right read 01/01 00:01. New Year's Day. Midnight.

There was a light dusting of snow on the runway.

"This is the earliest footage from the archive," Li said, as the video began to play. The sky lightened. The sky darkened. The counter rolled over.

01/02 00:01.

Other than that, nothing on the screen changed.

Light sky. Dark sky. 01/03 00:01.

CHAPTER 42

"I am going to fast forward here," Li said.

The counter began to roll more swiftly. A car appeared on-screen. Blinked into existence at 1/14 17:40; the counter was running so fast that the last digit was a blur.

Frank Ferrone stepped out and swung the door open. The interior of the hangar was dark. Nothing visible. Ferrone shut the door behind him.

"Maybe when he comes out we'll get a look inside," Frederickson said.

"Maybe." Espy nodded.

They watched. Waited. Finally, the door opened and Ferrone reappeared, the interior of the hangar still dark behind him. He got back into his car and pulled away.

Li froze the playback.

"Keep going," Frederickson said. "We didn't find anything out yet."

"On the contrary. We learned something very important just now," Li replied.

"What do you mean?" Frederickson asked.

"Note the time counter," Li replied. "January 14, 23:32."

"I see it. What about it?"

It took Espy a second, but then she got it. "11:32 p.m. And Ferrone entered the hangar when?"

"17:43," Li replied. "5:43 p.m."

"Which means he just spent six hours in there."

"Doing what?" Frederickson asked.

"That's the question, isn't it?" She turned to Frederickson. "I think you're right. I think we need to take a little trip out to the ranch."

"Yeah." He smiled. "Now you're talking my language."

43

There were two sides to the *Welcome to Fabulous Las Vegas* sign.

Most people knew only the front, the image from countless movies and TV shows and a hundred thousand tourist brochures, the sign that had become so much a part of the city that everyone had to get their picture taken in front of it when they arrived. Even now, at ten in the morning, there was a long line of tourists waiting to do just that. And two showgirls (or at least, women who looked the part) available to pose alongside those tourists. At a very unreasonable price, Marcus was sure.

But there was a back side to the sign as well. It said *Drive Carefully And Thank You For Coming.*

That was the side Marcus was staring at right now, from a carefully selected vantage point that gave him not only a good view of the tourists but also the parking lot at the far end of the median, smack dab in the middle of Las Vegas Boulevard, two lanes of traffic whizzing by on either side.

So far, there had been no apparent fallout from his visit with Sherman. He'd left Area 51 without incident last night, or this morning. Left with a few brand-new pieces of information—Ararat, and the names from Averill's memo—that he needed to check out. And he knew just the person to help him do that.

They'd arranged to meet at 10:30, but it was 10:55 before a familiar little yellow car pulled into the median parking lot. He watched it come to a stop, and an even more familiar head leaned out the driver's side window. Then the passenger door opened and a man got out. A very big man. He put a hand to his brow, shielding it

CHAPTER 43

from the sun. Looking toward the sign. Looking right at Marcus. He lowered his hand and started walking right toward him.

Oh, Marcus thought. So that's how he's going to play it.

The big guy got closer. He was even bigger than Marcus first thought. Six three, six four, maybe two hundred fifty pounds. Shaved head, sunglasses, Bermuda shorts, and a sweatshirt that read *Sweat is Just Fat Crying*. Cutoff sleeves that showed off his biceps, his triceps, his forearms, and his wrists. Muscle upon muscle upon muscle.

Marcus stood up and waited.

"Kleinman, right?" the big guy said.

"That's me."

"I got a message for you. From—"

"Kurt Vogelsang."

"That's right."

"Let me guess. He thinks the two of us are square, that he doesn't owe me anything."

The guy smiled. "He said you might have trouble understanding."

"You go back there and tell him he's wrong."

The guy shook his head. "That's not going to happen."

"How much is he paying you?" Marcus didn't wait for the guy to answer. "Cheap bastard like him—my guess is $200."

The guy shook his head. "Triple that."

"Wow. And usually he goes for the cut-rate option."

"Not this time."

"I guess not. So." Marcus took a step forward, deliberately invading the guy's personal space. "What does he get for his money?" An invitation. A subtle escalation, and an incitement to react.

Which of course, the guy did, in an entirely predictable way.

"An end to his worries." The man jabbed his finger into Marcus's chest. He was about to say something else, too, probably something pithy, accompanied by a threat.

He never got the chance.

Even as the guy was jabbing his finger forward, Marcus was moving. He grabbed the guy's forefinger and snapped it with his left hand, simultaneously slamming the heel of his right wrist square into the guy's solar plexus. Perfect shot. It had to be, considering the ridge of muscle there.

The wind went out of the guy all at once. He doubled over, gasping for breath, gasping in pain.

Marcus glanced quickly around. Maybe a second and a half of movement there. Nobody had seen a thing.

Still holding onto the guy's broken finger, squeezing it a little to make sure he stayed compliant, Marcus pulled the guy toward him, sat him down on a boulder. The big man was trying to curse, but having a hard time of it. Having a hard time breathing at all, in fact.

"Easy." Marcus patted him on the back. "Relax. You'll be fine in a couple minutes. Just breathe through your nose."

The guy made a wheezing noise. Marcus let go of his finger.

He looked toward the parking lot. The little yellow car was trying to back out, but there was a lot of traffic. One car trying to pull out, two more trying to pull in. Jockeying for a space. Marcus smiled and started walking over.

The driver saw him and pulled forward again. It looked, for a second, like he was going to jump the curb, try and go right over the median and out onto Las Vegas Boulevard heading the other direction.

"Kurt!" Marcus yelled. "Do not make me run!"

He needn't have bothered. A group of tourists had just climbed

CHAPTER 43

out of a tour bus and were now blocking the yellow car's way forward.

Marcus reached the parking lot. Leaned down and rapped on the passenger-side window. Vogelsang kept his eyes straight ahead.

"I know you can hear me, Kurt," Marcus said. "Unlock the door."

Vogelsang didn't move.

"Kurt. In about five seconds, I am going to—"

The door unlocked. Marcus climbed in.

❖ ❖ ❖ ❖ ❖

To show him there were no hard feelings, Marcus took Vogelsang to breakfast. A little diner on the north end of town. "On me," he said, sliding into the booth opposite Vogelsang. "Get whatever you want."

"I don't eat this crap anymore," Vogelsang said. "I'm vegan."

"I don't believe that for a second." Though Marcus had to admit the man had lost a ton of weight; the Vogelsang he remembered had carried fifty extra pounds, mostly on his gut. A lot of burgers, a lot of beer. This Vogelsang looked like a hollowed-out version of his old self.

"Okay. Why are you here, Kleinman? Why are you bothering me?"

"*I'm* bothering *you*? Don't you have that backward?" Marcus asked. "I ask for a simple meeting, you send in Mr. Sweat-is-Fat-Crying to scare me off."

"Yeah, well, our meetings have a way of turning out badly for me."

"That's your own damn fault."

"Look." Vogelsang sighed. Ran a hand through what was left of his hair. "I'm just trying to make a living here. A simple, honest living. I don't want to get involved in any of that spy-versus-spy crap anymore."

"Mexico City," Marcus said.

Vogelsang groaned and rolled his eyes. "Come on. That was—"

"A situation where I saved your then-much-fatter ass, if you'll remember? You owe me."

"And let me guess. You're here to collect."

Marcus gave him a big smile. "Now you are seeing the big picture."

Just then the waitress came over. "Gentlemen, how are we doing this fine morning?" she asked. "Coffee?"

Marcus nodded. "Please. Also two eggs over, rye toast dry, crispy bacon. Extra crispy."

She nodded. "And you, sir?"

"Nothing for me," Vogelsang said.

"Seriously?"

"Seriously. I'm on a restricted diet. Vegan."

"Eggs are vegan," the waitress said.

"Eggs are not vegan," Vogelsang snapped.

She glared. "So nothing for you?"

"Nothing."

"Right back with the coffee," she said to Marcus and strode off.

"How to win friends and influence people," Marcus said.

"I'm a busy man," Vogelsang said. "Tell me what it is you want."

"You're still in the data collection business, I take it."

"Data collection and analysis. What do you need, exactly?"

"Got a list of names I want checked out. Their backgrounds. If they're still around, I want to know where they are. How to contact them."

"Old people, you're saying."

"Yeah." Marcus lowered his voice. "These people were part

CHAPTER 43

of an agency project, back in the day. Working for a guy named Averill."

"Whoa, whoa, whoa. Full stop." Vogelsang was shaking his head. "James Averill, you mean?"

"One and the same. You know him?"

"Know of him. The man who put the black in black ops. If these people you're talking about worked with Averill, my price just went up."

"We've already established your price. Mexico City."

"That was then. This is now."

"Mexico City," Marcus continued, "where not only did I save your life, I introduced you to a woman named Helena Briguera, who I'm sure you—"

Vogelsang held up his hand. His left hand. There was no wedding ring there.

"Jesus, Kurt." Marcus shook his head. "How'd you mess that up?"

"I did not do shit. Helena, on the other hand—"

"Excuse me." The waitress set down a cup, poured Marcus's coffee, then turned to Vogelsang. "Eggs'll be up in a minute. Still nothing for you?"

"Well, I suppose…" Vogelsang frowned. "You got any donuts?"

"We got muffins. Some pastries."

"What kind?"

"Hang on a minute." She looked at him over her memo pad. "I'll bring you our vegan selection."

Marcus almost snorted coffee out his nose.

The waitress smiled, snapped her memo pad shut, and left.

Vogelsang leaned across the table, pointed a finger at him. "Okay. But James Averill means spooky shit. Means this is a paying job."

"Fine." Marcus shrugged. He still had some of Doc's ten grand left. "Let's eat. Then we'll get to work."

❖ ❖ ❖ ❖ ❖

They drove to Vogelsang's office, which was in the back of a not-so-nice laundromat in what could be charitably characterized as a not-so-nice part of town. Along the wall was a row of worn white plastic chairs—a guy was sleeping in one, using the window as a pillow. Marcus could smell him from where he stood. A young woman, early twenties, in a ripped black t-shirt, with a ring of tattoos around her neck, sat next to him. She got to her feet as they walked in.

"Kurt," she said.

Vogelsang stopped in his tracks. "Mika."

"I need money."

"I just gave you money."

"Formula is expensive."

The two of them faced off for a second. Then Vogelsang sighed, reached in his pocket, and pulled out a couple crumpled bills. The girl snatched them out of his hand and stomped out the door past them.

Marcus watched her go, then turned back to Vogelsang. "Helena. You didn't do anything, huh?"

"Long story. And none of your business." He walked to the back of the laundromat. "Come on. Let's get this over with."

Vogelsang led him to a door marked *Office*, next to a row of broken dryers. He pulled a ring of keys off his belt and unlocked the door, flipped a light switch, and stepped inside. Marcus followed, and let out a sigh of relief.

He'd been worried that the general appearance of both Vogelsang and his laundromat portended bad things for the man's

CHAPTER 43

data collection business—like he might have slipped a little (well, more than a little) since the two of them had last worked together.

The array of computers circling the room put his mind at ease. A couple of shiny new laptops, space silver and matte gray. A few larger, older-looking machines, stacks here and there of servers and associated peripherals, and thick cables running between all of it.

"I'm gonna get started here," Vogelsang said.

"Good. Go to it." Marcus had given him the names he recalled from the memo Sherman had found. The people, not the program. Risky enough that Vogelsang would be digging into people with Averill as a common denominator. Add Ararat into the mix, it could be Doc and Zelda all over again. Last thing he wanted.

He plopped himself down in a nearby chair, sat back, and closed his eyes. Wondered if the message he'd sent in Memphis had gone through yet. No way of telling, really, but it was time to send another now. Send on Averill's name. Just in case that DAN order caught up to him. He was probably making a mistake by not trying to disguise himself a little better here. Shave his head, like Mr. Sweat-is-Fat-Crying. He wondered if that guy would be coming after him, after this morning. Another thing to be careful about.

"I forgot how loudly you snore."

Vogelsang had rolled his chair over, was smiling at him.

"Hell." Marcus sat up and rubbed his eyes. "I fell asleep."

"You fell into a coma. You've been out for a couple hours. You didn't move the whole time."

"I'm assuming you found something."

"Something." Vogelsang shrugged. "Not sure what. It would help if you told me what these people were working on exactly."

"Better you're in the dark. For your own good." Marcus stifled a yawn. "So what do you got?"

"A few things. Let's take those names in alphabetical order. Our friend Averill first. I know you told me not to dig, but I did skim a few databases. The guy is a ghost. There's almost nothing on him, anywhere. Almost." Vogelsang punched a key and brought up an image that Marcus recognized immediately: Averill standing behind General Douglas McArthur. "I did find a chapter in a book called—"

"*Warriors Who Won the Cold War*. Yeah, I know. I told you, forget about Averill." He tried not to sound as angry—or concerned—as he felt. Nothing he could do about it now. Either Vogelsang was as good as he thought he was, and their tracks were covered, or he wasn't, and they were in deep trouble, as of this very instant.

"Fine. Forget about Averill, then. Next up"—Vogelsang's fingers flew across the keyboard—"we got this guy." A black-and-white headshot of a man in his mid-thirties, long, angular face, wearing a suit and tie and horn-rimmed glasses. A picture that practically screamed "Hey, I carry a slide rule in my pocket, and I'm not ashamed of it." The caption: *Stephen Guidry, Project Supervisor.*

"Your man Guidry here was a certified genius. Went to MIT at sixteen after skipping his senior year of high school, full scholarship, graduated top of his class. Went to work for Aramco in 1949. This is his picture from the company's annual report. While he was in Saudi Arabia, he got married, had two kids. Then in '57, he strikes it rich. On the corporation's behalf."

Vogelsang pulled up another image, a magazine cover with a group of Arabs in traditional robes and headdress posing in front of a large oil derrick—along with a guy wearing what looked like a safari hat and bathrobe. Guidry.

CHAPTER 43

The feature article headline was superimposed over the photo: *Ghawar: World's Largest Oil Field, Discovered, Explored, Explained.* But Marcus's eyes went right to the magazine title at the top: *The Journal of the American Association of Petroleum Geologists.*

Petroleum Geologists.

Something buzzed around the back of his brain a second, and then it landed.

George de Mohrenschildt. The guy from the dossier. Lee Harvey Oswald's compadre and mentor. He'd been a petroleum geologist too.

Seven Days To Dallas.

The Men Who Murdered My Father.

"After Ghawar, Guidry gets a huge promotion, a raise, and he ... what?" Vogelsang asked, seeing the look on Marcus's face.

"Guidry was a petroleum geologist?"

"Did I not say that? Yes. He stayed with Aramco right up until January of 1959, at which point he joins the army. The Army Corps of Engineers, to be more precise, assuming the rank of lieutenant. He moves his wife and family out to Nevada, where he presumably works on your top secret project with Averill—which must have been quite something, because there's no way the government matches his Aramco salary—right up until October of 1963, when"—Vogelsang went at the keyboard again—"the guy just disappears. Vanishes off the face of the earth, never to be seen again."

The screen filled now with a picture of a slightly older Guidry. Slightly longer hair. From an article headlined *Local Scientist Still Missing.* The author implied that Guidry was a person of some note, a highly regarded government official privileged enough to be on the dais at the Las Vegas Convention Center the afternoon of September 28, 1963, for a speech by President John F. Kennedy.

Marcus let out a long, slow whistle.

"What?" Vogelsang asked.

"Nothing. Never mind. Let's move on. Tracy—the pilot. Find anything on him?"

"Not much." Vogelsang rolled his chair over to another computer. "Bachelor, came from a military family, tasked to Nellis for test-pilot work. Died in a training accident there, same as that other guy you asked about. General Wachtel. Take a look."

Marcus found himself staring at another article, this one from the *Las Vegas Journal Review*, October 17, 1963: "Deadly Desert Disaster."

"This was apparently a pretty big deal. Sixteen people dead, in all." Vogelsang turned and looked at Marcus. "Though nothing I found said exactly what happened."

"Yeah." Marcus had a feeling that he was looking at the sanitized-for-public-consumption version of the October 16 "accident" in that document Sherman had found. The accident first, and then Guidry's disappearance…

The secret your senator was killed to protect.

He was getting close here. He could feel it. Averill, it seemed to him, had covered up more than a paper trail when it came to Ararat. The man who put the black in black ops had made sure that anyone who knew anything about the program didn't stick around long enough to reveal its secrets.

"Guidry. He had a family, you said. What do you have on them?"

"Hang on a second." Vogelsang slid his chair back to the first computer, brought the monitor there to life. "Okay," he said, reading off the screen. "Guidry's wife, the woman he met in Saudi Arabia—her name was Myriam Al-Azhrani. She was actually British, believe it or not. She and Guidry had two kids: a son

CHAPTER 43

named Joseph, a daughter named Laila."

"And where are they all now?"

"Myriam is dead. Pancreatic cancer, back in 2005. The son is right here in Vegas. Correction." He leaned forward, squinted at the screen, then hit a few more keys. "The son *was* here. Current whereabouts unknown."

"And the daughter?"

"Lives in Encino, California. Divorced, two sons." He brought up a picture of a striking woman—long dark hair, exotic features, killer smile. Her driver's license photo. Laila Guidry Samuelson.

"Hey," Vogelsang said. "She's hot."

"Too old for you, son. Can you find me a phone number?"

"You cutting in on my action?" Vogelsang typed, and a number appeared on screen.

"Wouldn't dream of it." Marcus took out a burner phone and dialed.

A woman picked up right away. "Joseph?" she said.

"No." Marcus said. "This is Harrison Hanrahan."

"Who?"

"Harrison Hanrahan. I'm a lawyer out in Las Vegas." Vogelsang rolled his eyes. The real Harrison Hanrahan had been a security guy at the embassy in Mexico City, who they'd given no end of shit to about his name. "Is this Laila Samuelson?"

"Yes. Is this about Joseph? Is he all right?"

"It's actually your father I wanted to talk to you about, Ms. Samuelson."

"My father?"

"Stephen Guidry."

"I know who my father was," she shot back. "What about him?"

"Well." Marcus cleared his throat. "Without going into great detail, I represent a group of clients currently involved in a lawsuit against the United States government. An accident which your father may have been involved in."

"I wouldn't know anything about that. My father disappeared when I was three years old. To be honest, I don't remember him at all."

"Even the smallest details would be helpful."

"The smallest detail?" She laughed. "Got one memory for you. He took me on a Ferris wheel ride. Which my mom insisted never happened. So if that's all…"

"What about your brother? You think he might have more information?"

"Joseph? Definitely he would. The two of them were very close."

"Do you know how I could get in touch with him?"

She sighed. "I'm not so sure that's a good idea. After my father ran off … Joseph was really traumatized. Had to drop out of school for a while. Mom always thought that might have been the start of…" She struggled for words for a moment, then gave up. "Everything."

"What does that mean?"

"It means my brother has problems, okay? He's…" She sighed. "I don't know. He has difficulty with people."

Marcus chose his next words carefully. "Ms. Samuelson, I promise you, I'll be very sensitive to your brother's wishes. If he doesn't want to talk, I won't make him talk."

"Well." She fell silent a moment. "I suppose."

"Thank you. I appreciate that. If you have any idea of where I might find him, the address I have doesn't seem to be current."

"Find him. Ha. That, Mr. Hanrahan, is exactly what you're going to have to go out and do."

She went on, then, to explain.

44

"About halfway there." Frederickson, a few feet in front of Espy, stopped and pulled a water bottle off his belt. Took a long swig. Espy did the same. Off to her right, she saw a sign. Focused her headlamp, read the text:

> **Black Brush Mining Corporation**
> **DANGER: ABANDONED MINE HAZARDS**
> **Unsafe Mine Openings And Highwalls**
> **Deadly Gas And Lack Of Oxygen**
> **Cave-Ins**
> **Unsafe Ladders, Rotten Structures**
> **STAY OUT! STAY ALIVE**

The second of those signs they'd seen. Must have been a big mine, all through the mountain here. The Brody property—better to think of it as the Ferrone property, really—had been just a little piece of it.

They'd come in from the east, from the hills behind the hangar, to avoid the cameras. Circled around off Interstate 15 into the foothills, taking the last few miles on an old mining road Li had identified from park service maps. There was no moon tonight. The world out here was pitch dark and silent. She'd stumbled more than once.

She put the water bottle back on her belt and turned to face Frederickson. There were two bright stars visible directly over his head. Right over that sign, which was a good ten feet off the ground. Venus and Mars, she thought. But then those two bright spots suddenly shifted position, and Espy realized they weren't stars or planets at all.

They were eyes. Eyes belonging to something perched on top of the sign. An animal. A big animal. A cougar, she realized. *That's a cougar.*

"Hey…" Her throat was dry. Her voice trembled.

"What?"

"Don't move."

"Why?"

"Behind you…"

Despite her words, he began to move. To turn. Very, very slowly. Halfway through that turn, he froze. "Whoa."

The cat's head swiveled slightly toward him as he spoke.

All of a sudden she saw he had his gun out. Not aimed at the cat, but at his side, waiting. Ready to use. She didn't really think a single shot was going to take down a cat that big.

"Li? You seeing this?" she asked. A rhetorical question; of course she was. Li was monitoring everything through Espy's glasses.

"Magnificent," Li said.

"Sure. Magnificent," Frederickson said quietly. "But is it going to eat us?"

"I believe if it was going to attack you, you wouldn't have seen it at all."

"You sure about that?"

"I am quoting a Wikipedia article."

"That doesn't fill me with confidence," Espy said.

"It was a joke," Li replied.

"This is not a time for—"

The animal turned and leapt away into the darkness.

Espy exhaled audibly.

"Well, that was fun," Frederickson said.

CHAPTER 44

"For future reference," Li said. "Wikipedia states the greatest danger to humans from wildlife in the desert area comes not from mountain lions but coyotes. Packs of coyotes. Who have been known to attack smaller humans from time to time."

"Smaller humans," Frederickson said. "That's you, Espy."

"Funny." But she didn't laugh.

They pushed on.

❖ ❖ ❖ ❖ ❖

About fifteen minutes after that, they arrived at the cliff overlooking C.C. Brody's property and the hangar below.

"Hey," Frederickson said. "I see lights. I thought you said everyone was asleep."

"They are," Li supplied. "That light is from Ms. Brody's bedroom. She has left the television on."

Espy knelt down and reached into her pack. Pulled out pitons, a hammer, some rope. Five minutes later, they were rappelling down the cliff face. Coming up right alongside the hangar. Alongside Fishman's car.

She froze for a second. Remembered her ordeal of yesterday. Hands and feet bound, trapped in the trunk, convinced she was going to die. Falconetti, carrying her from the car to the shack.

Doug, walking through that front door. And the shotgun blast…

"You all right?" Frederickson asked.

"Fine. Let's do this."

They stepped up to the hangar entrance, to the touchpad. It pulsed with a soft orange glow. Frederickson pulled a molded plastic glove from his pack and slipped it onto his right hand.

That glove had been fabricated with a 3D printer earlier this evening. The tips of the glove's fingers duplicated Vince Falconetti's fingerprints, which—because he was a convicted felon—Li had pulled from a federal database. Frederickson placed it up against the panel now.

The orange light pulsed faster and began to shift to a deeper orange—shading toward red.

"Shit," Frederickson whispered. "It's not working. Maybe Falconetti isn't authorized?"

Espy leaned closer. Looked at Frederickson's hand. "There's space between your fingers. Move them closer together," she suggested.

He nodded, and repositioned his hand.

The pulsing slowed. The color changed again—from a deeper orange, to the original shade, and then to a pale green.

There was a soft chirping noise, a slightly louder click, and the door opened.

They stepped quickly inside and the door swung shut behind them. Espy paused to get her bearings.

The hangar interior was a huge room, dimly lit by a series of emergency lights on the floor. Maybe a hundred feet wide, a hundred fifty feet deep. Corrugated metal walls and ceiling, concrete floors. The far half of the hangar, where a plane would normally be, was empty. The near half was a kind of lounge—couch, three armchairs, and a kitchenette along the back wall with a table and two stools.

"You said they spent $10 million on this renovation?" Frederickson shook his head. "I don't see it."

Espy had to agree. She spun around in a circle, taking it all in. A $10 million renovation? This didn't even look like a $10,000 renovation.

"Never mind the renovation," she said. "What did Ferrone do in here for six hours?"

CHAPTER 44

"No idea. Let's have a look around." He walked toward the lounge area; Espy headed for the kitchen. She opened the cabinets. Inside were two coffee mugs and a box of non-dairy creamer packets. The refrigerator contained a half-empty carton of orange juice and a half dozen bottles of Coors; the freezer, a tray of ice cubes and a half inch of frost. In the drawers, she found silverware and a deck of cards. Below the sink, cleaning supplies and garbage bags.

This made no sense.

Why the fingerprint sensor? Why the $10 million renovation? And what had Ferrone spent all his time doing in here? Playing solitaire?

"Hey."

She turned at Frederickson's half-whispered exclamation. He was in the lounge, leaning over the coffee table. Peering at the underside.

"There's something here," he said.

"Something?"

"Looks like another one of those sensors. Another touchpad."

"Don't—" do anything, she'd been about to say. But he was already holding out the glove, and Espy heard it—the same soft chirp from the touch pad.

There was the sound of machinery springing to life.

And the kitchen cabinets on the back wall began moving.

"Did someone say 'open sesame'?" Frederickson stood and smiled, as Espy came up alongside him to watch.

The cabinets continued to pivot toward them, moving soundlessly on a hidden set of hinges. Beyond, a vast empty darkness revealed itself.

Her earpiece crackled. "I think you may have found where that $10 million was spent," Li said.

"It's a tunnel," Frederickson said, taking a step forward.

He was right. There was a passageway. As they moved into it, lights flickered on overhead, illuminating the way forward.

"This is an old mining tunnel." Frederickson stepped up alongside her. "From Black Brush days."

She nodded as the false wall, the kitchen cabinets, swung shut behind her.

"Unsafe ladders, rotten structures…" Frederickson ran a hand along the timbers framing the wall. "Only these don't look too rotten."

"No." She nodded. "No, they look brand new. Or pretty close to it."

"Metal beams there." Frederickson pointed up at the ceiling.

"This is why they built the hangar right up against the mountain. So they could reuse—"

Static, suddenly, crackled in her ear. Li. " … signal already."

"Say again," Espy replied, and was rewarded with another burst of static.

"Hang on." Frederickson took a couple steps back. "Li. Lost you there for a second. Try now."

Espy stepped back along with him.

" … lost visual monitoring. Audio is already intermittent. If you go any further into the tunnel, we'll lose that as well." Li's voice crackled again.

Espy and Frederickson looked at each other.

"Can't be helped. This is why we're here. We'll check in…" Espy looked down at her Luminor. "Half an hour from now."

"Understood," Li said. "Half an hour."

Frederickson nodded. "Setting a timer." He tapped a finger on finger on his watch.

He turned back to her. Gestured toward the tunnel in front of them. "Shall we?"

CHAPTER 44

She nodded. "We shall."

❖ ❖ ❖ ❖ ❖

They got no more than a hundred feet in before the tunnel dead-ended in a T, up against a concrete wall that was clearly new construction, covered with pipes, ductwork, and cables of varying thickness.

"Power supply lines from the ranch," Espy said.

"Yeah. The question is, what are they powering?"

She pointed right. "Something in that direction. Because the ranch—if I'm not completely turned around here—is back the other way."

"Nothing wrong with your sense of direction. Let's go have a look." He stepped forward, simultaneously reaching down to his belt, pulling out his gun.

"You think that's necessary?" she asked.

"Might be. Who knows what else is down here?"

She nodded. At this point, nothing would surprise her. Ferrone had gone to a lot of trouble to build this little complex. To keep it secret. Her gut was telling her that no more than a handful of people knew about its existence. But what was he hiding down here? Why was he so determined to keep it secret?

The reason your senator was killed.

They continued on. Deeper into the mountain. She felt the temperature drop. The air grew a little more humid. Motion sensor lights kicked on in front of them, shut off behind them.

Finally, the soft white lights overhead framed out a rough shape ahead. A doorway. The light beyond that door was of a different hue entirely. Reddish.

Frederickson tensed. Motioned for her to stay back. She was about to protest, but before she could do so, he stepped quickly forward, across the threshold. The dim light brightened. Motion sensors again. The red changed to bright white.

Frederickson let out a long, low, exhalation of breath. A soft whistle. He holstered his weapon. "I think we found where Ferrone spent that $10 million."

Espy stepped up alongside him and saw immediately what he meant.

The doorway led to a huge, dome-shaped room, maybe a hundred feet in diameter; the apex had to be fifty feet above their heads. A cave, was her first thought, but then she saw the smooth, fused look of some of the walls, and decided that at least part of it must have been carved or blasted out of the mountain. By Black Brush? By Ferrone? Maybe both, at different times. For different purposes. No way of knowing.

In the very center of the space was a horseshoe-shaped metal console open to the back wall. Along that wall were three more doorways to other tunnels, each with a different colored light above them. One red, one blue, one green. Behind the console, a spiral staircase led up to a small circular room, a table and chairs visible through its glass walls. Along the wall to her left was a long wooden table; to her right, a long row of filing cabinets.

"Thoughts?" Frederickson said.

"Lots." She shook her head. What was all this? Why was it here?

She walked over to the wooden table. It was a drawing table. A drafting table? There was a whiteboard covered haphazardly with betting slips from the Peacock. She picked one up, scrutinized it. Underneath the casino logo were two lines of type: *16.0 afd* and *2.12/2.15*.

Frederickson came up alongside her. "What are those?"

"Look like betting slips. But I have no idea what these numbers

CHAPTER 44

mean." She put the slip down, then pointed to the center of the room. "Stairs?"

Frederickson nodded. "Sure. Stairs."

He followed her up, their shoes clanging on the metal treads. The steps led right up to the glass room, to a door with a touch panel. He tried the glove. Nothing happened.

Espy peered through the glass. Six expensive-looking rolling chairs and a table with papers scattered across it, papers mostly covered by a big map of Nevada. A color-coded map, with writing all over it. She leaned closer, capturing the image for later study.

"Nothing here," Frederickson announced, starting down the stairs. She followed. At the bottom, he walked to the center of the U-shaped console and stopped. "What do you think this thing is?"

"Don't know." She walked past him, all the way around it, stopping at the bottom of the horseshoe … and saw something.

"Hey," she said. "Over here."

"What?" he said, walking over.

"This." She pointed. "Another touch panel."

"So I see." He bent down, ran the glove over it. There was a soft click, followed by a gentle whir. And then…

Four monitors, spaced equidistantly around the horseshoe, unfolded themselves from the metal surface and blinked to life.

"What now?" Frederickson asked.

Espy shook her head. "Don't know." The screens were blank, waiting for input of some sort. Only there was no keyboard, or anything like a keyboard—no mouse, or tablet, or touchpad— anywhere in sight. Was it voice-activated?

"Hello? Computer?"

Nothing.

Espy examined the monitors more closely. She had a half-dozen little flash drives in one of the compartments on her belt in case the need arose for her to copy data, but she saw no ports anywhere, no place to plug those little drives in.

"Gonna go check out those other tunnels," Frederickson said, motioning to the back of the cave. "Be right back."

Espy nodded and moved to the wall of filing cabinets. They looked like the kind that went out of style in the mid-sixties, big clunky metal ones. She counted thirty-eight of them, each with four drawers. A lot of files.

The locks were decidedly low-tech. She pulled out a pocket-knife, stuck the blade in the cylinder of the nearest cabinet, gave it a little play. The lock popped open.

"None of those other tunnels go anywhere." Frederickson returned. "At least not anymore. One's collapsed, the other two have a foot of water in them." He looked at his watch. "I'm heading back to the hangar. Going to go check in with Li."

"I'm going to go through these. See what I can find."

"Stay put. I'll be back."

"Yes, mother," she said, pulling open the top drawer of the first cabinet. It was, as she suspected, full of file folders. Legal-sized folders with labeled tabs, all starting with the letter *A*. From *Abramson, Victor* up front to *Averill, James* all the way in the back.

Okay, she said to herself, pulling out the first folder. Let's see what we have here.

45

Marcus was about fifty feet from the entrance when he saw them: three people sitting on a sloped concrete retaining wall, bathed in the glow of the streetlight above them. Two men, one woman, passing around a joint. He could smell it from where he stood. The men white, the woman Asian. One of the men was shirtless, his body covered with tattoos. Thin. Wiry. On something more than weed, the way he was bouncing around. The other guy was a walking UNLV advertisement: Rebels baseball cap, Rebels t-shirt and gym shorts.

Shirtless saw Marcus and hopped to his feet.

"Hey, yo, how's it going?" He started down the wall. "What do you need, my friend? Let me help you out. You looking for meth? Pills? What do you need, what do you need?"

"Not meth. Not pills." Marcus shook his head. "Information."

"Okay, okay, information." His bouncing slowed. "What kind of information?"

"On a guy named Guidry. Joseph Guidry. I hear he lives around here."

"Around here. On the street, you mean?"

"No. Down there. Or a place like it." Marcus pointed toward the darkness in front of him. The entrance.

The tunnel.

"The city is full of them," Laila Guidry had told him. "And that's where my brother lives. Last I heard, at least."

Las Vegas? Full of tunnels? Marcus had doubted her at first. Thought she was pulling his leg. But no. They were here. They were there. They were everywhere. In the city, under the city, leading from the mega-resorts to the airport, from the interstates to the outskirts of town. Hidden in plain sight—shelter for a homeless population of indeterminate but growing size. A population that, for the last few years, had included Stephen Guidry's wayward son.

Before he'd gone off in search of Joseph Guidry, however, Marcus had taken a few minutes to compose another message. Another update on his progress, as Espy had suggested when she'd first sent the drone. But this time, he relayed some thoughts about the best use of the information he was passing on. Who to deliver it to, and what to do with it.

Then he went to work. Talked to social workers, police officers, shelter residents, other tunnel denizens. Showed them the sole picture of Guidry he'd been able to obtain, a shot from maybe ten years ago that the man's sister had sent on. That had produced mostly blank stares from the people he'd talked to, shaking heads, a few "seen him around but I don't remember where," but one piece of helpful information as well: an actual map of all Vegas's underground tunnels, courtesy of an intern at the city planning department. Marcus had been to, if not actually through, roughly half of them at this point.

The one in front of him now—maybe his last one of the night, given the fact that it was pushing two in the morning—was on the east side of the city. Not far, in fact, from the *Welcome to Las Vegas* sign, which he could see peeking over the avenue off to his left.

"Wait. What'd you say the guy's name was again? Guidry?" The other guy, Rebel, got to his feet now.

"That's right."

The two men exchanged glances. "I think he means Big Joe," Rebel said.

Marcus felt that little tingle. Big Joe. The second time he'd

CHAPTER 45

heard that name today. The first had been from a social worker. One of the nicknames Guidry went by.

"You're in luck, my friend," Shirtless said. "I think I know exactly who you're talking about. I think I could take you right to him."

"Great news," Marcus said. "Let's go then."

"I said *could* take you to him." Shirtless smiled. "If there was something in it for us."

"How does $100 sound?"

"Each?"

"Sure."

"Her too." Shirtless gestured toward the woman, who smiled at Marcus with a mouth full of perfect white teeth. She was a little younger than he'd first thought; she was also stoned out of her mind. Teeth like that, she came from money. A runaway.

"Fine. $300, you split it however you want." He shrugged. "Let's go."

"We got to see the money first."

"You'll see it when I see Guidry. Not a second before."

Shirtless nodded, then looked over at the other guy. "Now, that ain't too friendly," Shirtless said. "I mean, what's the harm in showing me the money? Just proving to me you got it, is all I'm saying." He smiled.

His dental work left something to be desired, Marcus saw. He also saw something else. Something cold and calculating in the man's eyes. This idiot was going to try and rob him.

"It would be the worst mistake of your life," Marcus said.

"What?" The guy sneered.

"This is a business transaction, pure and simple. Let's keep it that way."

"Oh, we're gonna do business, all right." Shirtless drew a knife.

Rebel got to his feet, picked up a baseball bat that had been lying next to him, and started down the slope. Coming fast.

"Now let's see that money," Shirtless said, and took another step forward.

"I'll give it to you if you use it to fix those teeth," Marcus said.

"Little man thinks he's funny," Shirtless said. "Just for that, I'm going to—"

What he had been going to do was anyone's guess, but he never got the chance to do it. Because as he was talking, Shirtless had continued to walk forward, and now…

Now he was in range.

Marcus's grabbed the guy's left wrist with his right hand.

"Hey!" Shirtless yelled. He raised his right arm, tried to slash down at Marcus with the knife.

Marcus caught that wrist with his left hand. Now he had both arms; he yanked them apart and drove forward, headbutting the bridge of Shirtless's nose. There was a loud crunch. A little too loud—for a split-second Marcus thought he might have killed the guy. That wouldn't have been good, but then the man screamed, so…

Marcus pressed the attack. Twisted with his left hand; Shirtless dropped the knife. Marcus kneed him in the groin. The man made a gagging noise and crumpled. Or tried to. Marcus held him up off the ground, in a standing position.

Rebel was on them now, waving the bat. Marcus moved Shirtless, now just a sack of flesh in his hands, to the left, blocking the bat. Rebel snarled and shoved at Shirtless, trying to push him out of the way.

Marcus had seen that move coming a mile off, had planned for it. He let Shirtless go just as Rebel pushed; expecting resistance and getting none, the man stumbled slightly. Not much, but just

CHAPTER 45

enough. Marcus stepped back, got him square on the jaw with a roundhouse kick. The guy fell to the ground like he'd been shot.

Start to finish, the whole fight had taken about ten seconds.

The girl, meanwhile, was up on her feet. Mouth hanging open.

"Hey, relax. This is all good news for you. I'm a man of my word. With those guys gone, the $300 is all yours." He tried a smile. "All you have to do is…"

He stopped talking, because the girl was off and running. Out into the night. Out into more trouble, no doubt. Oh well.

Saved him some cash, anyway.

46

He almost went right past it.

A stain, dark blue, almost black, and just a slightly different sheen than the flat gray concrete of the tunnel floor. He was at the T in the corridor, coming back from his check-in with Li, when he happened to glance down, and there it was. When he bent to take a closer look, it was obvious what that stain was.

Blood.

Frederickson stood and looked around and immediately spotted another stain, about ten feet away. Ten feet farther down the tunnel. He took a couple more steps in that direction; motion sensor lights came on, and he saw more of them—little splotches on the floor, continuing on down the tunnel and out of sight.

Toward the ranch. Hmmm.

He was supposed to go right. Go back to Espy, to Ferrone's little fortress of solitude. Touch base, see what she was up to, look around a little more himself. Although, if he knew Espy—and after all this time, he did, absolutely—right now she had her nose to the proverbial grindstone. Was literally knee-deep in those files, and would not be aware of time passing at all. Would not look up until he came and got her.

He was curious about what she was finding, if anything. But he was also curious about the bloodstains.

He looked at his watch. He and Li had scheduled another check-in. Twenty-eight minutes from now. More than enough time for a quick look—if he got moving. So he did.

Not more than twenty feet down from the T, the old mining

CHAPTER 46

tunnel gave way to something newer. A tunnel of entirely different construction, made by newer technology. The smoothness of the walls, the consistent size and shape of the tunnel ... it was as if it had been bored out of the earth by a huge machine. Some giant drill.

The tunnel sloped upward, opening into another circular chamber, a miniature version of the one he'd left Harper in. This one, though, was entirely manmade: a flattened cylinder fifteen or twenty feet in diameter, and just about that tall.

There was a cart in front of him. A cash cart, like the ones banks used to ferry safe deposit boxes and money drawers around. This one, though, said *Peacock Hotel and Casino* on the side. Intriguing.

Two steps closer, and he saw a hand sticking out of the top.

A man had been stuffed into the cart, head bowed down, face hidden. A big man with a head of thick, curly black hair. Frederickson lifted the man's head and shone a light over his face. It was a face he'd never seen before, but from the description Espy had given him ... He had a feeling he knew who it was, just the same.

"Fishman," he said out loud and opened a channel.

❖ ❖ ❖ ❖ ❖

The files Espy was looking at belonged to the Ferrone Real Estate Corporation.

It didn't take her more than a single cursory glance to realize that. Drawer after drawer of old paper files—the newest ones from the 1980s. She'd bet the computers behind her had the more recent records. The question was, why were these files here at the ranch, and not at Ferrone Tower? Hidden in this underground complex?

Obvious answer: There was a secret hidden in these files—a

secret Ferrone was determined to keep to himself. She had a pretty good idea why.

The reason your senator was killed.

First thing she'd done was go from the *A* drawer right to the *C*'s—right to Corelli Construction. There it was again: that $2 million seed capital that got the company going. There was a lot more than that in the folder, of course, including a picture of Frank Sr. with John Corelli himself, breaking ground on a new condominium development in 1965. Now she saw a physical resemblance between Frank Sr. and Jr. that she hadn't noticed earlier. And a little bit of the cockiness, the self-assuredness in Frank Sr. that his son had inherited.

There was correspondence too, starting with multiple letters back and forth between Sr. and a city planning official named Bud Rothmann, who had worried about extending infrastructure—power, water, gas—that far west into the desert. Relax, Sr. had written back. "The city's growing, people are going to need these services sooner rather than later—let's get ahead of the curve." Sr. had also attached documents that projected—uncannily anticipated, she saw—the exponential growth that was about to take place in Vegas over the coming years. Espy pulled out a few pages from the file for later review.

There were also a number of illegible notes in the file, written in a crazy kind of shorthand that someone—Ferrone Sr., Espy guessed—had come up with. Largely financial shorthand, she assumed. A series of numbers. Some kind of code. She pulled those pages as well, then moved back to the first drawer. The *A*'s. Might as well go through everything in some sort of order, she decided, and dug back in.

She worked methodically. Carefully. But even moving slowly, by the time she got to the second drawer down, she realized just

CHAPTER 46

how huge the Ferrone Real Estate Corporation was. And how long it had been around.

The company's fingerprints—through various subsidiaries, some wholly owned construction companies, hardware and industrial suppliers, shell corporations—were all over some of the largest real estate deals of the last fifty years. Real estate deals that had been carefully, secretly funneled into Ferrone Sr.'s pockets, giving him a huge cash reserve: a well he could draw from, as he saw fit, to make even more deals.

Frank Sr., she saw now, had been as much of a player as his son. Maybe even more so. The only difference was, he didn't run around town bragging about it.

She was now just about out of the *B*'s, looking at Bronzini Brothers Construction, incorporated in 1984 with an initial cash infusion of $23 million from Thiessen Partners, money that had been used to purchase and/or lease construction equipment. There was a file on Thiessen too, all the way down the row of cabinets, a very thin file, because they were a very thin company. A shell corporation operating out of Delaware, whose only point of contact on record had been a man named Johnny Pollock, a name she had already seen in connection with a company called Beeline, who had done surveying work for a series of construction projects back in the mid-seventies. Beeline, though, went back all the way to the early sixties. And it—like Corelli, and Ives Brothers, and American Lime—started with seed capital from the Ferrone Real Estate Corporation.

"Espy." Frederickson's voice, in her earpiece.

"Hey." She stood, thankful for the break. The chance to stretch. "What's up? Where are you? I thought you were coming right back."

"I was. Then I found Fishman."

"Good. Bring him here. I've got questions."

"He won't be answering any of them." Frederickson told her why. And where and how he'd found the man.

"A cash cart? From the Peacock?"

"Yeah. Strange, right?"

"Yeah. Only…" She looked down at the files she'd been going through. "Maybe not."

She'd been wondering just where the Ferrone Real Estate Corporation had gotten all its money to start from. All that seed capital, all the cash to purchase so much land, convince so many politicians and city officials to look the other way. Was it possible…

"What do you mean?" Frederickson asked.

"I mean they've been running the Peacock for a long time. Frank Sr., Jr. after him … managing the mob's money. What if—"

"Whoa. Are you saying they've been stealing? From the mob? That'd be a very dangerous thing to do."

"Absolutely it would. But I'm just thinking out loud here. I'm not sure about anything yet."

"Got it. Gonna finish exploring here, then head back. See you in a few."

"Roger that. Out."

She closed the connection. Stretched one final time, and then crouched down in front of the files once more.

Back to it.

47

The farther in he went, the worse the smell got. A putrid combination of mold and urine. Feces and body odor. He should've bought some Vicks, Marcus thought, he could've done the old medical examiner's trick: dab a bit right underneath your nostrils, the smell would block out everything else. Ah well.

He pulled a bottle of water from his backpack and took a long swig, put it back and fished out a flashlight that he switched on. According to the map the intern had given him, this was a drainage tunnel meant to carry away water in the event of a flash flood. It hadn't rained in Vegas in weeks, if not longer, so the concrete was bone-dry.

The flashlight beam played on the concrete walls, turning them all different shades of yellow and orange. There was graffiti everywhere—to his left and right, on the floor, on the ceiling. Most of it was nothing more than scrawls—*Raiders Nation Lives!*, *Brooks Was Here!*, *TS & PN 4-ever*—that sort of thing.

But maybe fifty feet back from the tunnel entrance there was a chalk painting. Marcus recognized the subject instantly: the Vegas skyline. The Strip. All the big casinos—the Luxor, the Bellagio, Caesar's. The painting ran from the entrance back, back, back, into the tunnel. Ten feet, twenty—it just kept going. He could see where parts of it had been crossed out or scrawled over (*Jamie at the Wynn SUCKS!*), but the artist had just drawn them in again. Now that was dedication. Talent, too. Talent gone up in a haze of smoke, or booze, or drugs, whatever weakness had broken them.

And what had broken Joseph Guidry? His father's disappearance? October 1963, the boy had been nine years old. What would he remember from back then? Marcus tried to remember something from when he was nine. Not much came to mind. Not a happy time in his life. His first experience with boarding school. First time he'd broken someone's nose. A much more involved affair than the headbutt he'd given Shirtless. He'd ended up on the losing side of that fight, but now that he was thinking about it … more details were coming back. Things he hadn't thought of in years. The old globe on the headmaster's desk, with East and West Germany staring right at him as he received his tongue-lashing. The reluctant handshake with Jack Frechette, the boy who'd beaten him, who ended up becoming his best friend for a few years.

The memories were back there, all right. Even a quarter century on. Marcus hoped Guidry could dig up some of his own as well.

He walked on.

❖ ❖ ❖ ❖ ❖

The graffiti trickled off to an occasional scrawl. He heard the rumble of traffic above, saw a sliver of light up ahead. A manhole cover, a busy road. There was a ladder leading down; half a golf club sat at the bottom of that ladder. A trail of McDonald's paper bags led to the far wall, where a duffle bag was propped up on its side, a dust mop sticking out the top end. Wait. Was that a dust mop?

He focused the beam of light on it.

The dust mop moved, and spoke.

"Out of my eyes, man. Keep that thing out of my eyes. Trying to sleep here," the mop—the guy—said.

CHAPTER 47

"Are you Guidry?" Marcus asked.

"What?"

"Are you Joseph Guidry?"

"Big Joe? No, man. I ain't him."

"You know where he is?"

"He moves around a lot. Usually he's up that way." The guy pointed into the darkness up ahead. "Off to the right. Usually."

"Okay," Marcus said. "Thanks."

The guy grunted, lowered his head.

Marcus kept going. Finished a bottle of water, ate a protein bar, changed flashlights. The tunnel branched. He went right, like the guy had suggested. A few minutes on, he saw a soft glow in the distance. An orange light waving back and forth.

A glowstick, he realized. Someone was holding up a glowstick.

"Hello," he called out. "Hello down there."

"Who's that?" a voice came out of the darkness. A man's voice, a little hoarse. "What do you want?"

"I'm looking for somebody."

"I'm somebody," the guy said.

"So you are. Maybe I'm looking for you, then." Marcus was close enough now that he could see the guy. A small, stick-thin man with a long gray beard. And a vaguely familiar face.

Big Joe. He got it now.

"You're Joseph Guidry, aren't you?"

"Who? No. Never heard of him. Guidry." The guy shook his head back and forth, back and forth, back and forth. "Why? What if I am?"

"I just have some questions to ask him, that's all. No big deal." Marcus's gaze moved from the man to his surroundings. Guidry had a nice setup for himself down here. A little slice of home. Two sheets hung from the ceiling, making a cozy little corner. There was an overturned cardboard box with a folding chair open next to it, and a mattress on the floor next to that. How had he gotten a mattress down here?

There were several notebooks laid out on the bed. And a pile of glowsticks. A handful of pictures. Marcus squinted. He saw one was of John Lennon. Post-Beatles Lennon. Lennon on the streets of New York, probably right before he was assassinated.

Next to that was a laminated newspaper clipping, a picture of a man speaking on a dais, with the headline above it: *A Short Visit, Jack, but We Loved You.*

The man at the dais was JFK.

"Now that's interesting." Marcus knelt down and set the flashlight on the ground, on its base, the beam shining up, spreading light in a little cone all around. "President Kennedy," he said, turning, "Why do you have a picture—"

He stopped short.

The man was pointing a gun at him. "Okay, now, okay." He said. Guidry's finger twitched on the trigger. "Now it's my turn. Now I ask the questions."

Marcus raised his hands. "Careful with that thing."

"Don't try any funny business. I know how to use this."

"You're him, aren't you? Joseph Guidry?"

"Yeah. I'm him. Why? What do you want?"

"Just a couple questions. Like I said." He focused on Guidry's face, on his eyes, trying to gauge the man's intent. Difficult to do. Guidry was rocking back and forth, his face moving in and out of darkness, in and out of the flashlight beam.

"You don't need that, Joe. The gun. Why don't you put it away, so we can talk?"

"I can talk and hold the gun. Don't worry about that." He waved it back and forth then, as if to prove it. "Tell me one thing.

CHAPTER 47

Are you with them?"

"With who?"

"You know who. Come on. Answer me." Guidry waved the gun at him again.

Marcus didn't know if the safety was on, if the gun was loaded or not, but he wasn't taking any chances. He stepped forward, knocking the weapon out of Guidry's hand. It skittered away across the concrete.

"NO!" Guidry screamed. "NO NO NO." He tried to move, to chase after it. Marcus took him to the ground—not hard—stopping his head just short of the concrete.

"Take it easy here," he said. "I'm on your—"

Guidry spat in his face.

It took every bit of Marcus's self-control to keep from backhanding him.

"Do not do that again," he said, wiping his face. He pointed a finger at Guidry, pointed close enough that he was practically poking it in Guidry's eye.

Guidry burst into tears. "Go on. Kill me. Get it over with."

"Nobody's here to kill you, Joe." Marcus got up off the man, then stood. Guidry was still crying. Marcus helped him to his feet and back over to the mattress. Sat him down. Guidry wasn't just thin, he was skin and bones. A hundred thirty pounds or less, soaking wet. "Here." Marcus opened his backpack and started rummaging around in it. "Let me give you something to eat here, Joe. I got energy bars, some water—"

"Energy bars." Guidry straightened. "What flavor?"

"Hang on." Marcus pulled one out. "This one's chocolate. Peanut butter and chocolate, actually."

"Yeah." Guidry wiped his nose. "Okay. Peanut butter. That sounds good."

Marcus held out the bar. Guidry snatched it away, chowed it down in a few quick bites. Marcus gave him a second that he finished just as quickly. Then he asked for water. He took a long drink, wiped his lips with the back of his hand, then looked back at Marcus. "I'm sorry I spat at you."

"It's all right," Marcus said. "I'm sorry I knocked you down."

"And lost my gun."

"I didn't lose your gun. It's right over there. I was just worried you were going to shoot me."

"I might've. I don't like questions."

"I just have a couple, Joe. I'll be quick, I promise."

"What kind of questions?"

"Well, for starters—why do you have this?" He held up the laminated clipping of JFK.

"That's the president."

"That's right. Why do you have his picture, Joe?"

Guidry sat there. Didn't say anything for a long minute. Then, "Because my father took me to see him."

"At the convention center?"

Guidry smiled. "That's right. I was just a kid, a little kid, but I remember it. We went up to talk to him, after. I got to shake his hand. He was a great man. That's what my father said. He was going to do great things. But then…"

Guidry didn't need to finish that sentence.

"I know. It was a sad thing that happened to the president," Marcus said, running the calendar in his head. The date on Guidry's newspaper clipping was September 28, 1963. Two weeks later, the accident. *Deadly Desert Disaster*. A week after that, Stephen Guidry had disappeared. And then, on November 22…

He turned back to Guidry. "Did your father ever talk to you about his work?"

CHAPTER 47

"Never." Guidry shook his head firmly. "He wasn't allowed."

"What about a man named James Averill? Did he ever mention him?"

Guidry tensed up.

"Joe?" Marcus prompted. "Did he ever talk about Averill?"

Guidry got to his feet. "I gotta go."

"Joe—"

"I GOTTA GO!" But he just stood there, hands at his side, breathing hard. Actually panting.

Marcus didn't say a word. Not for a good long while. Not that he had to. Joseph Guidry had known Averill, that was clear. And even half a century later, just the mention of the man's name brought back memories. Not good ones.

"It's okay," Marcus said. "It's all right."

A minute passed. Two. Finally, Guidry sat back down. He picked up the water bottle again and drank. Then he looked over at Marcus. "Can I show you something? Something my father gave me?" Without waiting for an answer, Guidry reached back behind the mattress, then held out his hand. "Here."

It was a piece of metal. Marcus took it. A little longer, a little thicker than a soda can, and a hell of a lot of heavier. "What is this?"

"It was a gift. Something from my father's work," Guidry continued. "He said they were going to change the world with it."

Marcus turned the object in his hand. Shone a light on it. There was writing on the side: *Holland Precision Instruments. Las Vegas, Nevada.*

It was a drill bit, Marcus realized. Not a household drill, a piece of industrial equipment.

Like the kind petroleum geologists used.

48

The ladder intrigued him.

A red metal ladder on the wall, next to a little metal platform. Frederickson found it at the end of the tunnel branch he'd been exploring. He looked up and saw that the ladder and the platform led to the same place, a concrete balcony that jutted out into the room, protected by a waist-high red metal railing. An entrance to the ranch, was his guess. And the platform—that was an open-air elevator of some kind.

He didn't know how to work that, but he knew how to climb.

He found the oddest thing when he reached the top: a full-length mirror. Next to it, a little below eye level, was a latch. He lifted it, and the mirror moved. A half inch. He peered through the crack.

There were sliding glass doors in front of him, looking out on the night sky. To his right, there was a big circular desk. To his left, bookshelves. He recognized the space immediately: the office where Ferrone and Kingsleigh had been arguing the other day.

He pushed the mirror open wide and crossed to the desk. There was a single stack of paper there, underneath a glass paperweight. Medical bills. All C.C. Brody's. The woman was on a lot of medication.

His earpiece crackled to life.

"Ms. Harper. Mr. Frederickson. Ms. Harper. Mr. Frederickson. Ms. Harper—"

"Li. I'm here." He checked his watch. "You're early."

"Because Mr. Falconetti is returning."

CHAPTER 48

"What?"

"Yes. His car is at the ranch's front gate. I suggest—"

"Yes. We're leaving." He put the papers back as neatly as he could. "I'm on my way back to Espy. I'll keep you posted."

"Wait. You and Ms. Harper are not together?"

"No, we're not. She's still looking through those files."

"Frank?" a voice said—not in his ear, in the room. And at that second the lights came on.

C.C. Brody stood there.

"You." She pointed at Frederickson, shook her head. "You are not Frank."

She was, Frederickson realized, high as a kite. Drunk or stoned, he couldn't tell which. Her eyes were half-shut and unfocused. She had on a pink nightgown and one pink slipper.

"Where's Frank?" she asked. "I need my medicine. And who are you?"

"Ms. Brody," Frederickson said, "you're supposed to be asleep."

"I need my medicine. And you didn't answer my question. Who are you?" She jabbed a finger in his chest. He caught hold of her hand, which was a good thing, because the movement had completely unbalanced her. She wobbled a little on her feet.

"I'm the night nurse," he said.

"You don't look like a nurse."

"Yeah. I get that all the time." He stood her up a little straighter. "Come on. Let's get you back to bed."

"Good idea. But I need my medicine," she said.

"Then let's go get it. You lead the way."

She turned and started back out the door. He followed, keeping a hand on her shoulder. Keeping her steady.

"You do not have time for this," Li said.

"You're telling me," Frederickson said.

C.C. turned. "What?"

"Nothing. Sorry."

C.C. led him two doors down to her bedroom. Her suite. There was a movie playing on the TV. One of her old movies, he realized.

"There." C.C. lay down dramatically on the bed and gestured with one arm toward a door at the far end of the room. "The bathroom. The Zoloft. Please and thank you."

"Please and hurry," Li added.

Frederickson didn't bother responding to that.

C.C.'s bathroom was bigger than his first two apartments. There was a floor-to-ceiling medicine cabinet on the far wall. He opened it up and found what looked like a full-service pharmacy. Every over-the-counter sleep aid and pain relief you could imagine, alongside all kinds of exotic, expensive-looking beauty products.

He found an array of green and blue prescription bottles on an eye-level shelf. Two for Zoloft—an antidepressant—both in Brody's name. Two different pharmacies, two different doctors.

"May I remind you," Li said. "Mr. Falconetti—"

"Moving as fast as I can here." He opened one of the bottles, poured out a single pill, filled a glass from the vanity, and brought both back into the bedroom.

C.C. smiled up at him. "Thank you."

He smiled. "You're welcome."

He saw her looking at him a little more closely, saw her eyes trying to focus. "Are you sure you're a nurse? Because you don't look like a nurse."

"You said that already."

"You"—she swallowed the pill—"look more like a boxer."

"Not the first time I've heard that."

"Jimmy was a boxer."

CHAPTER 48

"Jimmy?" Frederickson heard that name and flashed back to that Hallandale gym, to Sally Bartolo talking about the night the fighter with the best right hand he'd ever seen took a dive off the Fountainbleau balcony. "You're talking about Jimmy Allen."

"Yes. Yes." She smiled. "Poor Jimmy. What a wonderful man. What a terrible temper. What happened to him … oh my. Sad. So sad."

"It was, wasn't it?" Frederickson leaned a little closer. "Tell me more."

"You do not have time for this," Li said again.

C.C. sighed. "He always felt bad about it, Francis did. But we have to keep it secret, he said. We have to. Francis was right of course. As always."

"Keep what secret?" Frederickson asked.

"Poor Jimmy," C.C. said, and closed her eyes.

Off in the distance, Frederickson heard a car, coming closer. Falconetti. "Keep what secret?" he repeated. "Ms. Brody?"

The woman rolled over and started gently snoring.

49

Espy returned the last of the Bronzini folders to the drawer and stood.

That did it for drawer number seven. At this rate, she wouldn't be done for hours. And they did not have hours. She was making progress though, piecing together the story of Frank Sr.'s real estate empire and the extent to which he had disguised both the size of that empire and his role in it. No public stock offerings here. Sr. clearly didn't want anyone, much less the government, peering over his shoulder. The rough outline of that story was clear to her now. The devil, though, was going to be in the details. Those coded financial statements, which she still hadn't puzzled out. And she still didn't know how any of this related to Garrett's death. His murder, and Ferrone's role in it.

One thing at a time, she told herself. She cracked her knuckles and stretched her arms out toward the ceiling. Rolled her head from side to side, feeling the vertebrae stretch, hearing another little crack. It felt good. She sighed.

Normally, in cases like this, when she had to spend all her time in dark, windowless rooms, flipping through endless piles of paper, searching for tiny needles in giant haystacks, she prayed for a little something different. Now though, after being stuffed in that car trunk, and what had happened to her—and to Doug—in the shed afterwards…

She was content to be back in her element.

She moved on to the next drawer. To Callahan Associates. Back in 1988, they had taken control of a multinational industrial firm

CHAPTER 49

called the Spinetti Group, which (no surprise) had turned out to be part of the extended Ferrone family of corporations. She found a copy of a bank check for $4 million, drawn on an account she'd previously traced back to another Ferrone-controlled firm. Spinetti had used the $4 million to purchase the assets of a company called Holland Precision Instruments.

And again, she found herself impressed by the complex web of false fronts and dead-end trails Ferrone Sr. had woven. How involved the Ferrone Real Estate Corporation had been in the purchase, sale, and well-timed exploitation of land in the greater Las Vegas region over the last half-century. How they always seemed to buy at just the right moment—buy for a pittance, sell for a pound. And it wasn't just luck, though there was luck involved, as she saw in another note from Ferrone Sr. to that same city planning official, Rothmann, who had been worried about a predicted La Nina and its effect on the city's resources. *I told you, El Niño, La Niña, Mother Nature be damned, we'll be fine*, Ferrone had written—and it turned out they were.

The man's connections impressed her as well. Ferrone Sr. had them everywhere. Connections that not only jumped when he told them to, but wrote thanking him for the opportunity to do so. Government bureaucrats (*Our numbers were wrong, yours were right*), prominent landowners (*Thanks for convincing us—you just helped secure my family's financial future*), and elected officials (*Always glad to help a friend, see you at the banquet next month*). No clear-cut cases of bribery but plenty of favors. And not just locally—at the state and national levels as well.

It was clear how Frank Jr. had learned to manipulate the levers of power, why he'd been so convinced he'd get the variances and easements he sought for Aqua Roma, why he thought the rules didn't apply to him: They never had for his father.

The last folder in the drawer belonged to one Neil Carp, whose file consisted of a single piece of paper indicating that he had served as registered agent for B&B Plumbing of Long Beach, California, which turned out to be (wait for it) a wholly owned subsidiary of her old friends, the Bronzini Brothers.

And the wheel goes round, she thought, putting that single piece of paper back in its place. Her thumb rested for a second on the typewritten label. On the name Carp.

And then it hit her.

She stood up so fast that she slammed her knee on the edge of the open drawer, but she barely felt it.

Carp.

Pollock.

Gill.

Fishman.

She practically ran to the *F*'s. To the drawer labeled *Fe-Fo*, and there he was, Fishman himself, in a file half a foot thick. The man had been in business with the Ferrone family for more than thirty-five years. Starting as low man on the totem pole and moving up the ladder. Moving from Vegas to Reno and back again, setting up shop in a half-dozen locations, from which he'd sent out reams of forms and official papers to various state and federal regulatory agencies. Papers creating, dissolving, and combining companies on Frank Sr.'s behalf. Papers filed not just in Fishman's own name but in dozens of others: names like Carp and Gill and Pollock, Pike and Bass and Salmon, fictitious names for fictitious people. Names Fishman had used to hide the scale of Ferrone's businesses, to funnel family money between companies, between states, between countries. There were transfer slips here showing that money on the move, records of it going to and from financial institutions all over the globe—including the Royal Cayman Bank and Trust on

CHAPTER 49

Grand Cayman Island.

Which only confirmed what she knew already, in her gut.

Welcome to Hell, indeed.

She slammed Fishman's drawer shut and pulled out the one right above it, the drawer labeled *El-Fe*, picturing that shot glass back in Fishman's office, the devil on it, and the details he was leading her to right now. Details in the file she now pulled out: a file labeled *Europa Development Partners*.

Even before she opened that file Espy knew what she was going to find, because right that second, all the pieces of the puzzle—the files, the evidence she'd gathered, the stories she'd heard, everything she'd learned since the dossier had led her to C.C. Brody and Desert View, to the Greenbrier and then Vegas and the Aqua Roma site—all of it suddenly snapped into place. The reason why Ferrone had been so anxious to avoid any questions regarding Parcel 33, and the firm that had purchased it.

Europa was his company.

He'd put that $1.2 billion in himself.

She heard footsteps behind her. Frederickson, returning.

"You're not going to believe this," she said, standing and turning to face him. "It turns out…"

Except it wasn't Frederickson.

It was Falconetti.

"Not gonna believe what, sweetheart?" He smiled. "Go on. I'm all ears."

50

The two of them stared at each other.

"There's part of me that wants to know how you got away. The shack. I had you tied up pretty good." Falconetti shook his head. "Guess I should have gone real old-school and just whacked you."

He took a step toward her. She took a step back. Right into the wall of file cabinets.

"Not a lot of places for you to go," he said.

"Same is true for you. You and Ferrone. You're done."

"Is that so?"

"It is. I know about Europa." She held up the folder.

Falconetti laughed. "You don't know anything. Where's your friend?"

"What do you mean?"

"You didn't come here alone." He took another step closer. "Your friend, Frederickson. Where is he?"

"He's dead. You killed—" She threw the folder at him. The papers flew up in the air. A distraction. Give her time to reach down and draw her gun. That was the idea, anyway.

Falconetti was there before her. His hand on her weapon a split-second before hers. She barely had time to register that fact—he'd moved impossibly fast—before he'd backhanded her across the head with the gun barrel.

She fell backward, hitting the wall of cabinets and then the ground. She lay there stunned.

Falconetti's hand, suddenly, was around her neck. "I'm not thinking clearly." He leaned closer, ripped out her earpiece. "Because

CHAPTER 50

no matter where he is right now, he's—"

She punched him in the groin. He grunted, and his grip loosened, and she punched him again. Or tried to.

He caught her fist in one hand and squeezed. She cried out in pain. He slammed her head back against the cabinet. Again, and again, and again, until every rational thought left her mind. Until there was only pain.

"Coming back to you, I was going to say." She felt the barrel of the gun against her forehead. "Unfortunately, he's going to be too late to do you any good."

She heard the safety click. She braced herself.

And then she heard a voice.

"Hey old man."

The hand around her neck loosened.

"You looking for me?"

Frederickson, she thought, and slumped backward.

❖ ❖ ❖ ❖ ❖

He'd been running the whole way but stopped the instant he hit the cave entrance. The instant he saw Falconetti with his gun against Harper's forehead. He'd drawn his weapon, stepped forward, and spoken.

Falconetti turned and smiled. "There you are. I was worried maybe you got lost somewhere. Or that you went out looking for another Range Rover."

"Put down the gun."

"That's not gonna happen."

They each held position a moment. Frederickson raised the gun slightly, sighted down his arm. Falconetti dug the barrel deeper into Espy's temple.

"You shoot her, I shoot you."

"I got a better angle," Falconetti said. "I'll take my chances. Plus you have to hold your whole arm up. All I gotta do is squeeze the trigger."

"That's all I have to do too. This distance, I won't miss. Never mind the angle." Frederickson took a step forward.

"That's close enough."

Frederickson ignored him and took another step. A big step, slightly to the side, which gave him a better angle. But Falconetti was right. He was at a disadvantage here. "I have a thought," he said.

"What?"

"We settle this a different way."

"How's that?"

"Mano a mano. Without the guns. What do you think?"

"What do I think?" Falconetti smiled. "How did you manage that at the shack, anyway? I'm assuming it was you, not her, that figured it out?"

"Trade secret. So what do you say? Forget the guns?"

"Not happening. In fact…" His smile broadened. Frederickson saw his trigger finger tighten. He was going to shoot.

Frederickson's only chance was to fire first. Hit the man's trigger finger. Stop Falconetti, stop the shot, because from this distance—

Espy moved.

She smacked the gun out of Falconetti's right hand. It landed on the ground and skittered away. Frederickson went to fire, but Falconetti pivoted and swung Espy's body in front of him, his left hand still tight around her neck.

"Drop it. Or I'll snap her neck." He had Espy in a choke hold now, his forearm around her throat. She was turning red. "Drop it," he said again.

CHAPTER 50

Frederickson didn't have a choice. He bent and laid his gun on the ground.

"Good move."

"Let her go," Frederickson said.

"What am I, stupid? Two against one?"

Espy gasped. Her face was red, now shading toward purple.

"Not stupid." Frederickson shook his head. "You're scared."

"Of what?"

"Me."

Falconetti snorted. "That'll be the day."

"So what are you waiting for?." Frederickson assumed a ready stance, motioned him forward. "Let her go, and let's do it. Let's see what you got."

The man's eyes narrowed. "More than enough for you," he said and released the chokehold.

Espy slumped to the ground, and lay there. Still, unmoving… unconscious, Frederickson thought. Hoped, anyway.

The two men began to circle each other.

"Yeah. You're FBI, all right," Falconetti said.

"What's that supposed to mean?"

"The way you move. I know the training you guys get. It's good stuff. A little limited, but—" Falconetti charged him.

The move, that wasn't a surprise. Talking to relax him, set the move up. But the man was much faster than Frederickson had expected. He didn't have time to fully brace himself; Falconetti caught him around the waist in a bearhug, lifted him up off the floor and drove him into the stone. Landed on top of him and drove an elbow toward his face. That would have been game over.

Frederickson rolled his head to one side, dodging, bucking his hips, throwing Falconetti off balance. The man came at him again with another elbow. That one caught him square on the shoulder.

Frederickson got off a good punch that caught Falconetti in the side of the head, not quite directly on the temple as he'd intended, which would also have been game over, but close enough to stun him, so Frederickson could buck his hips again, pushing him off entirely.

The two men stood and faced each other again.

"See what I mean about predictable?" Falconetti said. "You FBI guys play a little too nice and it—"

Frederickson came at him. A quick kick square to Falconetti's gut, followed by a right to the face, and then a left. Falconetti staggered, and Frederickson followed with a spin kick that sent Falconetti flying backward. Frederickson charged—

And Falconetti came up holding a knife.

"Oh," Frederickson said. "What happened to mano a mano?"

"What, a knife isn't mano enough for you?"

The blade in his hand was a six-inch dagger with a ragged edge.

Frederickson reached down to his ankle sheath and came up with his own knife. Smaller, but with a nasty twist at the end of the blade.

The two men circled each other once more.

"Hey, sorry about that. Your eye there." Frederickson smiled, noting a nasty bruise beginning to swell up on Falconetti's face.

"No apologies necessary. All in the game. You're about to get a lot worse."

Falconetti jabbed. Frederickson danced back. Falconetti jabbed again, quicker. Frederickson danced again, barely getting out of the way that time.

"Palermo," Falconetti said. "Sicily. That's where the guy that taught me came from. Made me do this over and over again, sometimes with one hand tied behind my back. Made me change knife

CHAPTER 50

hands all the time." Falconetti tossed the knife from his right hand to his left. "Got so I was pretty good with both hands. Not as quick now as I was back then, but—"

Falconetti lunged forward again. Even faster.

A feint, but Frederickson almost fell for it. Barely managed to avoid not just the blade, but the other hand coming for him, trying to grab hold of him and draw him closer. He stumbled backward. Grunted involuntarily with the effort.

Falconetti smiled. "Palermo," he said again. "You're at a distinct disadvantage here, my friend. Those guys have been doing it for centuries."

"Quantico," Frederickson shot back. "We've been at it awhile too." He lunged forward himself. He was expecting Falconetti to dodge; had his counter-move ready. But Falconetti surprised him, moved forward with him and caught Frederickson's wrist with his free hand, squeezed on the small bones there. A pressure point.

Frederickson's grip loosened—an autonomic reaction. He dropped his knife.

"Adios, amigo," Falconetti said, and his knife hand came forward, the blade heading straight for Frederickson's gut.

Frederickson grabbed hold of Falconetti's wrist. No pressure point, but he managed to stop the thrust.

Falconetti headbutted him.

Frederickson stumbled backward. Falconetti came at him with the knife again. A little too eagerly. Frederickson saw his chance.

He caught Falconetti's wrist and pulled him forward, simultaneously falling backward himself, using Falconetti's own momentum to send him somersaulting through the air.

Falconetti landed hard. Cursed out loud, came up angry, sans knife.

"I know." Frederickson smiled. "Hard when you get older. The body doesn't quite bend like it used to. Makes it—"

Falconetti charged. Trying the same move as before: the bear-hug, the tackle. It almost worked, but his anger made him unbalanced, and Frederickson was able to twist his body just enough to avoid the man's grasp.

And then, as Falconetti flew past, he kicked out the man's knee from behind him.

Falconetti cursed, stumbled.

Frederickson came up behind him, got him in a choke hold.

Falconetti gasped and threw his elbow back, aiming for Frederickson's groin, catching him on the thigh instead. It hurt like hell; there was gonna be a big bruise there tomorrow. But he held on.

Falconetti tried to get to his feet, but he could only stand on one leg. Still the man's strength was formidable; he pushed backward, managing to throw Frederickson off balance. Falconetti pushed back again, and Frederickson felt himself falling backward, landing on his back. The initial impact knocked the wind out of him, then the weight of Falconetti falling on him did the same again.

But he held on. The choke hold.

Falconetti reached back with his right hand, jabbing it into Frederickson's face, his fingers digging into Frederickson's cheek, reaching for his eyes.

Frederickson twisted away and rolled over so that he was on top now, turning his head so Falconetti's fingers could no longer reach his face.

And he tightened his grip.

Falconetti tried to roll again. Frederickson leaned in, bracing against him and the ground with all his weight.

Falconetti gasped. His struggles weakened.

CHAPTER 50

Too soon, Frederickson thought. Another feint. He kept the pressure up.

Falconetti bucked underneath him. Struggled, gasping for air.

You don't want to kill him, he told himself.

Except thinking of Doug, of what he'd looked like in the backseat of the car, driving to the hospital, all that blood, and the surgery...

He kind of did.

Falconetti went limp. Frederickson relaxed his grip just for an instant, felt for his carotid artery.

There was a pulse there. Faint, but detectable.

He stood and ran to Espy, who was just getting to her knees.

"You all right?"

"I'll live. Him?"

"Same. Unfortunately."

He helped her to her feet. "Thanks," she said. "That's one I owe you."

"Not keeping score, but you're welcome. Come on. Let's get out of here." He put his hand on her elbow; she seemed steady enough, but being deprived of oxygen that long...

She shrugged off his grip.

"Hang on a second," she said, and began picking up scattered pieces of paper from the floor. "I'm going to need these."

51

Marcus had been leaning on the buzzer for at least a minute when the door finally opened. It wasn't Vogelsang who answered it, though.

It was the young woman with the tattooed neck. She had a baby in her arms. She looked pissed. The kid was wide-eyed and smiling.

"Gah," the kid said.

The woman wrinkled her nose. "Christ—what is that smell?"

"It's me. Sorry." Marcus peered around the woman, saw a crib, a couch, and a bunch of crap—clothes, toys, an open suitcase—scattered around the room behind her. "Is he around? Kurt?"

Vogelsang appeared around the corner. He rubbed his eyes and blinked. "Kleinman. What are you doing here? You know what time it is?"

"Yes. I know what time it is. I—"

"And what is that smell?" Vogelsang asked, coming closer.

"Me. Sorry. Listen, I need your help again."

"What?"

"Your help."

"This couldn't wait till morning?"

"It is morning."

"It's six a.m."

The kid started crying.

"Nice going, assholes." The woman glared at them.

"Mika," Vogelsang said. "Give us a minute. Hey?" Vogelsang smiled at the baby.

CHAPTER 51

The baby, to Marcus's amazement, smiled back.

"A minute? No problem. Take all day." She handed the baby to Vogelsang. "Enjoy."

"Hey! Mika. Mika!" But she wasn't listening. She picked up a sweatshirt off the floor, put it on, and stalked past them, right out the front door, slamming it shut behind her.

Marcus heard a car start up and pull off. "Charming." He turned to Vogelsang. "Your taste in women has gone downhill."

"She's Helena's daughter."

Marcus stopped in his tracks. "What?"

"Mika. Is Helena's daughter."

"I didn't know Helena had a—"

"Gah," the baby said.

"Gah," Vogelsang said back, smiling.

"Holy shit," Marcus said. "Grandpa Kurt."

Vogelsang glared at Marcus, over the kid's shoulder. "Don't."

"My lips are sealed."

"Good. Now what is it you need? Besides a shower?"

"A bed. And your help." He reached in his pack and pulled out the drill bit.

"What's that?"

"I got it from Guidry's kid." Who had very, very reluctantly let Marcus borrow the drill bit, in exchange for the flashlight and all Marcus's remaining power bars and bottles of water—as well as a promise to return with more of the same.

"The tunnels." Vogelsang made a face. "No wonder you stink. You were in there all night?"

"Never mind that. I want you to find out what this was used for. A little more about the company that made it, too. Holland."

He held out the bit for Vogelsang to take, but the baby reached for it first. Vogelsang stepped back then, so the kid couldn't grab it; then, just as the baby was about to start crying, he tickled him under the chin. "Gitchy goo. Gitchy gitchy goo."

The baby smiled, and laughed.

Marcus shook his head in amazement. Grandpa Kurt.

People could surprise you sometimes.

"Listen," he began, thinking he would apologize for showing up so early, for assuming that Vogelsang's priorities were the same as his. Clearly, they were not.

"Listen," Vogelsang said at the exact same time.

Marcus smiled. Gestured magnanimously. "Please. You first," he said.

"I'm going to need more money," Vogelsang replied.

"What?"

"You want me to find out about this drill thingy and the company that made it—that's another job. So I need more money."

Marcus glared. "You know what I was about to say? Grandpa?"

"What?"

"I was about to say, I might have been misjudging your character all these years."

Vogelsang shrugged. "Hey. Formula is expensive."

"So I hear." Marcus pulled out the wad of cash he'd been planning to give Shirtless and Rebel. "Take this."

Vogelsang took it. Counted it out, awkwardly, still holding the kid, who kept reaching for the cash as well.

"$300? What kind of cut-rate operation do you think I'm running?"

"You really want me to answer that?" Marcus kicked off his shoes, walked over to the couch, and lay down. "Wake me at ten."

❖ ❖ ❖ ❖ ❖

He had a crazy dream. A man in a white Stetson was chasing him

CHAPTER 51

down the street, waving a hand drill with an oversized bit. Gunshots were sounding all around him, bullets pinging off the road. Marcus looked up and saw he was passing the Texas Book Depository. A man stood in a sixth-floor window, aiming a rifle at him. He was wearing a white Stetson too.

"Marcus!"

He turned and saw William Manchester pulling up alongside him. Driving a limousine. JFK and Jackie were in the back seat.

"Marcus!" the president yelled in his thick Boston accent. Mah-kiss. "Marcus Kleinman. Get in the car!" The kah.

Crazy dream, Marcus thought, and rolled back over. But JFK kept screaming at him. "Kleinman! The car. Kleinman!" His accent had disappeared.

Marcus cracked his eyes open.

It wasn't Kennedy. It was Vogelsang, leaning over him. "Hey. It's almost noon."

"What?" Marcus cursed and sat up. "I told you to wake me at ten."

"I did. Apparently, you went back to sleep. Oh my god." Vogelsang leaned back. "Your breath stinks as bad as the rest of you."

He didn't doubt that. "I need coffee."

"You need a shower."

"True." He sat up, put his feet on the floor. "But I need coffee first."

"I don't have any."

"What?"

"I told you, I don't drink that stuff anymore."

"Good lord." Marcus stood. "Be right back."

He went and got his coffee. Came back, took his shower, stopped at a place called Pinkbox for donuts, then met Vogelsang at his office.

"Got a few things for you," Vogelsang said, turning in his chair as Marcus entered.

"Same." Marcus set the donuts down. Vogelsang reached over and opened the box.

"Is that a maple creme?"

"Calling your name."

"Get thee behind me, Satan."

"Too late for that. So what do we have?" Marcus asked, pulling up a chair.

"Okay. First and foremost"—Vogelsang took a bite—"Holland Precision Instruments is long gone. Like, half a century out of business."

"And what were they, exactly?"

"Tool and die company, to start out. Made a ton of money in Texas, sunk it back into R&D, did a bunch of government work during WWII, moved to Vegas in 1954. North Las Vegas, actually, one of the first companies to set up shop there. Lot of local press when they broke ground, talk about jobs and government contracts, which is apparently where a great deal of their work came from. Probably Area 51. Probably your friend Averill. Who I did not cross-reference in any of my searches, by the way."

"Good boy." Marcus nodded. "What else?"

"They shut down in '59. But here's where it gets interesting. Because this"—he picked up the drill bit—"is a typical two-cone design. Just like the kind that made Howard Hughes the richest man on the planet."

"Two cones." Marcus examined the bit. It had two separate tips, two corkscrews of metal. "Okay. So what's interesting?"

"These particular cones are made out of diamonds."

"Diamonds?" Marcus let out a long slow breath. "Are you sure?

CHAPTER 51

That's a lot of diamonds."

"Synthetic diamonds," Vogelsang said. "Not worth much. But the technology to machine diamonds like this, at this scale—that didn't exist until the sixties. And Holland—"

"Went out of business in '59. Right."

"So the internet says."

"So maybe they didn't. Go out of business, I mean."

"Ah." Vogelsang looked up at him and smiled. "I know what you're thinking. Averill."

Marcus nodded. Spookiest of spooks. A man who had gone to some pretty extreme lengths to erase Project Ararat from the history books.

He suspected Averill had done something similar with Holland. Taken the company black, to borrow agency jargon, used Holland and its assets, its technology, for his own purposes. For Ararat.

"So, Holland," Marcus said. "When they moved to Vegas, and supposedly shut down, where exactly were they located?"

"Give me a minute here." Vogelsang swiveled in his chair and grabbed another donut. "I'll see if I can find out."

52

"Europa Land Partners," she told Greg. "It's Ferrone's company."

"Jesus," he said. "You're sure of that?"

"I am. They have an account at Royal Cayman Bank and Trust. I want to know who opened it and when. Whose names—people, corporations—are on it. More than anything else, though, I want to know where the money in that account is coming from."

"I understand." He was silent for a moment. "But … the Caymans. I'm not sure how much I'll be able to find out."

"Greg. You've been working that territory for how long now?"

"Three and a half years."

"That's right. Three and a half years." Espy poured herself another cup of coffee. Her third since getting back from the ranch. She was actually getting used to the taste. They were back at the Bellagio. She'd showered and shut her eyes for an hour—a version of sleep, the best she was going to get for the next little while, she had a feeling. "They know you. You've earned their trust. Their respect. A reservoir of goodwill. Yes?"

"I like to think so."

"Now's the time to remind them of it."

"By asking them to break the law."

"By asking them to step back and look at the bigger picture. Think about it. How many laws has Ferrone broken here by using his own money to save Desert View? He's defrauded his investors and the government. And the scale of what we're looking at … that $1.2 billion is just the beginning."

"I'll see what I can do."

CHAPTER 52

She heard the uncertainty in his voice. "Greg. You can do this. I know you can."

"Thanks."

"You're welcome. Now go to it." She hung up, turned her attention to the papers in front of her—and heard a noise behind her. The doorknob to the little conference room, squeaking slightly as it turned.

She heard Ferrone's voice in her head. *This is my town. Nothing happens here that I don't know about.*

She dropped to her knees, raised her weapon.

Frederickson walked through the door. "Whoa. Just me." He held up his hands in mock surrender. Looked past her to the coffee pot. "How much of that stuff have you had?"

"Not enough." She stood and holstered her weapon. "And?"

"Still recovering. They wouldn't even let me in the same wing."

She nodded. Frederickson had gone straight from the tunnels to the hospital to check in on Doug. "You're a bad influence," she said. "Anyone can see that. Did they tell you anything at all?"

"The surgery went well. About as well as they could expect. What exactly that means…" He shrugged. "They won't know for a while. What have you been up to?"

"Digging. Thinking." She gestured to the papers, told him about her call to Greg. What she was trying to find out.

"Falconetti's talked by now. Told Ferrone we were there. At the ranch."

"If he's talking." A nasty smile came and went on Frederickson's face. "I might've dug in a little deep on that choke hold. Bruised his larynx."

"I'm not shedding any tears over that. But now he knows we're not dead. Ferrone, I mean. He also knows that we know all about Europa now. And his underground complex."

"Also true. Which means he's going to come after you again, Espy. And soon."

"Fair point." She nodded. "Which is maybe why I should go after him first."

"What's that mean?"

"Listen and learn," she said and took out her phone.

❖ ❖ ❖ ❖ ❖

"He what?" Kingsleigh exclaimed.

"Put that money in himself. The $1.2 billion. Europa is his company."

"I don't believe it."

"I have proof," Espy said. "which I'll be bringing forward shortly."

"$1.2 billion." Kingsleigh pronounced every syllable of the amount. She could hear the stunned surprise in his voice. "Where did he get that money from?"

"That's the question, isn't it?" Espy said. "I have my thoughts. I'd be curious for yours."

The man was silent.

"Let me refresh your memory here, Mr. Kingsleigh. You're already in a great deal of trouble for signing that 10-K. I hope you haven't forgotten about that, because the Justice Department hasn't. And now, to be complicit in a fraud of this scale—"

The man hung up.

Espy smiled. Let him stew. Let him chew on that piece of information.

And let him not be the only one.

She called Laura Sonores next, whose reaction mirrored Kingsleigh's. She, however, did not hang up after Espy's insinuations. Which gave Espy the chance to push a little more.

CHAPTER 52

"Is your husband there with you, Ms. Sonores?"

"What?"

"Is the senator there? I have questions for him as well."

"What sort of questions?"

"About that Senate subcommittee. The rationale behind their decision to lift the construction hold on Aqua Roma last year, for starters."

"That's a matter of public record."

"The decision is. Not the rationale. I'm also looking into the circumstances under which he became subcommittee chairman."

The woman made a little noise of exasperation. Half-exasperation, half-disgust, actually.

"Come, now. That's public record as well. Victor became chairman of the committee after Garrett Crandall's death."

"Yes," Espy said. "I'm well aware of that. That, in fact, is exactly my point."

The woman was silent a moment.

When she spoke again, the surprise in her voice had been replaced by an angry, cutting undertone. "What are you suggesting, Ms. Harper?"

"Is the senator there?"

"My husband is in Washington."

"Can you give me that number?"

"You can look it up," she snapped and ended the call.

She wasn't done yet.

"Ms. Harper, this phone call is entirely inappropriate," Bamberger said. "You need to call Mr. Moore. He should be your department's point of contact—"

"Europa's his company," Espy said.

"What?"

"Frank Ferrone. He owns Europa. He put that $1.2 billion in

himself."

Bamberger was silent a few seconds. "You're sure about that?"

"Absolutely sure."

"$1.2 billion." She could almost see him shaking his head. "Where on earth did that much money come from?"

"He's been accumulating it for years. Hiding it offshore. Perhaps skimming from the casino he manages."

"Unbelievable. Simply unbelievable." Bamberger paused. "That video you sent earlier—Parcel 33. You were right. That is a fraudulent transaction."

"I'm right about this too, sir. Trust me."

"I do." Bamberger took a deep breath. "I have to admit I was wrong about you, Ms. Harper. I should have listened to Leonard. Trusted his judgment. Trusted your judgment." He went on to tell her at some length then about just how close he and Leonard had been, before finally promising her the SEC's full cooperation.

"Thank you, sir. And one more thing. Mike Pritchett."

"What about him?"

"I think Ferrone had something to do with getting him fired."

Bamberger was silent a moment. "Yes. There was something odd about that."

She waited, but he didn't say anything else. "It's something … I want to look into it. When I return to Washington."

"Yes," Bamberger replied. "You'll let me know if I can be of assistance."

"I will, sir. And thank you." She hung up.

"Nice work. You hungry?" Frederickson directed her attention to a room service cart he'd wheeled in while she was talking.

"Not in the least."

"Yeah, well, maybe food will change your mood. I ordered us up a little breakfast here."

CHAPTER 52

"So I see." There were a half dozen covered dishes on the cart. Espy chose one at random and pulled the lid off. French toast. When was the last time she'd had French toast? Her usual breakfast was yogurt and bran flakes. She sat down at the long conference room table and dug in.

They talked while they ate.

"So how is all this going to work?" Frederickson asked.

"What do you mean?"

"I mean, yeah, we know Europa's his company, but how are we going to get those files from the tunnel into evidence? Our little trip there was not exactly legal."

"We'll figure it out," Espy said. "Trust me."

"I do, but—"

"We'll get back out to the ranch. A court order. We'll get—"

Her phone rang. She looked at the screen and smiled.

"What?" Frederickson asked.

She turned her phone so he could read the caller ID.

"Good old Johnny Romano." He smiled. "What do you think he wants?"

"Let's find out, shall we?" She set down the phone, put the call on speaker.

"Ms. Harper."

"Mr. Romano."

"Mr. Ferrone wants to talk with you."

"Does he, now? About what?"

"This whole situation has gotten out of hand."

"Yes it has. How does he propose to solve that?"

"A meeting. Face to face."

She laughed. "You have got to be kidding. So he can finish the job?"

"I don't know what you mean by that."

"Ask Mr. Falconetti," she said. "Assuming he's capable of talking yet."

Romano was silent a moment. "I can assure you, Mr. Ferrone has moved past all that."

"I doubt that."

"He offers you his personal guarantee on that front."

"Bullshit."

Frederickson smiled. Gave her a thumbs-up.

"If he wants to talk to me," Espy continued, "put him on the phone."

"This meeting would be in a public place. A neutral site. And again—Mr. Ferrone offers you his personal guarantee of safe conduct."

"I'll make you a counteroffer. He knows where I am. He's been here, in fact. Have him come to our suite at the Bellagio."

"That won't work."

"You can tell him I'll see him soon enough, then. In a court of law. And we can talk about Europa then. And his $1.2 billion. Goodbye, Mr. Romano." She hung up.

"Guy must be out of his mind," Frederickson said. "Thinking you'll—"

Her phone rang again. Same number.

"Doesn't know how to take no for an answer," Frederickson said.

"Apparently not." She punched the call through. "Mr. Romano. Don't waste my time or yours—"

"Fenicottero," Romano said. "It's a restaurant attached to the Flamingo. A very public place. You can have it checked out beforehand. Make sure it's safe. Mr. Ferrone will be there at six o'clock this evening. An early drink. Or dinner, if you prefer."

"I don't drink."

CHAPTER 52

"He's willing to talk to you, Ms. Harper. And again—"

"His personal guarantee. I heard you."

"On his mother's grave."

Espy frowned.

Frederickson reached over and hit the mute button. "Tell me you're not seriously considering this."

"A restaurant," she said. "It is public."

"You ever seen *The Godfather*? That scene where Michael whacks the police captain? That was in a restaurant."

"That was in a movie."

"No." He shook his head. "No. No. No."

"Hello? Ms. Harper?" That was Romano; Espy took the call off mute.

"One minute," she said, and hit mute again. "Face to face is the best way to do this. I want to see his face. Read his body language."

"How about a Zoom call?"

She raised an eyebrow. "Zoom? Seriously?"

"Fine." He glared. "Let me get a magic marker and draw an *X* across your forehead. Just so they know where to aim."

"Not funny."

"Not meant to be."

"Think about it. Why does Ferrone want this meeting so bad? If all he wants to do is get rid of me, why doesn't he just do it? Hire out a dozen of his friends and get the job done?"

Frederickson opened his mouth. And shut his mouth.

"He knows I've got him now. He wants to bargain. Tell me something that will get me off his case."

"Like what?"

"Maybe like who else is involved here. How deep this goes. How far back."

"How far back?" He shook his head. "Don't say it."

"Say what?"

"Dallas. 1963." He pointed a finger. "Just don't say it."

"My lips are sealed. For the moment." She unmuted the phone. "Mr. Romano. If I agree to this meeting, I want it understood: everything is on the table. Everything, including Garrett Crandall's death."

"What?"

"Senator Garrett Crandall. You remember him."

"Of course, but his death? I have no idea what you're talking about."

"Mr. Ferrone will. Fenicottero, six p.m. sharp," she said and hung up.

53

Fenicottero, it turned out, was Italian for flamingo. Appropriate name, because the restaurant, all of a ten-minute walk from their suite, was behind the Flamingo Hotel. Signs led Espy and Frederickson through a series of flamingo habitats—small ponds, some hidden by palm fronds and other vegetation, some shielded from passersby by waist-high metal railings—up gently sloping flagstone steps, ending at a maître d' station under a trellis adorned with tropical foliage. There was a long, long line of customers anxiously awaiting a table.

She flashed on the Greenbrier. On Lish, trying to bribe her. On Josephson, trying to warn her off.

"Excuse me. Are you Esperanza Harper?"

She looked up to see a man in a tuxedo—the maître d'—standing before her.

"Yes," she nodded. "I am."

"Excellent. I thought so. Please. Right this way. You're expected."

He led them past the queue of waiting customers and into the restaurant, which consisted of two dozen or so tables of thick glass spread out across a roughly circular flagstone patio surrounded by a grove of palm trees, the pink and white towers of the Flamingo looming behind.

At the back of the restaurant was a long bar, with a row of half-occupied stools. A man stood behind it, drying a glass. Watching as they approached.

Her eyes fastened on Ferrone, who sat at a table for four

nearby. Falconetti sat next to him. They stared daggers as she and Frederickson approached.

"Your guests, Mr. Ferrone," the maître d' said.

"Thank you, Albert." Ferrone pulled a money clip from his pocket, conspicuously peeled off a hundred-dollar bill, and handed it to the man, who bowed and withdrew.

He was wearing a gray polo shirt with the Peacock's logo. Tan slacks and tasseled loafers. Ray-Bans hung from a cord around his neck. "Miraculous, Ms. Harper. Congratulations. You appear to have nine lives. Just like a cat." He was smiling, for some reason. Like he was happy about it. Happy to see her again. There was an open bottle of wine on the table. Two glasses. Espy didn't see a man desperate for a meeting. She didn't see a man desperate for anything at all.

Something was off here.

"Let's get down to business," she said.

Ferrone nodded. "Of course. Have it your way. Please, sit."

Espy pulled out a chair. Frederickson stepped up to do the same.

"Actually, I think this conversation should just be the two of us, Ms. Harper," Ferrone said.

"And why is that?"

"Because our business is private. Very private indeed."

"Hey. If I don't stay, neither does he." Frederickson nodded at Falconetti.

Ferrone nodded. "Vince, if you wouldn't mind."

Falconetti stood then and walked toward the bar. Limping slightly. His knee.

She could see Frederickson about to say something. Make a crack. She shook her head, warning him off. He nodded reluctantly and followed Falconetti to the bar.

CHAPTER 53

Espy sat.

"Can I pour you a glass?" Ferrone asked, holding up the bottle of wine.

She thought she recognized the label: It looked like the same vintage Lish had been drinking, back at the Greenbrier. That $375 glass. "No. Thank you," she said.

"Of course. I hope you don't mind if I…"

"Be my guest."

Ferrone poured and set the bottle down. Picked up his glass and swirled the wine around. Sniffed, smiled, and sipped. "Outstanding. Cheers." He raised the glass in her direction.

Enough, Espy thought. "I can think of a half dozen, off the top of my head," she said.

Ferrone frowned. "Excuse me?"

"Laws you've broken. By putting your own money into Aqua Roma."

Ferrone took a sip of wine. "Come. Do we really need to talk about that?"

"Why else are we here? Or maybe you'd rather talk about your Mr. Fishman. The late Mr. Fishman, and his Mr. Gill. And his Mr. Carp, and Mr. Pollock, and—"

"My," Ferrone set down his glass. "My my my. You were a busy little beaver last night, weren't you?"

"That's right. And I'm just getting started."

Ferrone kept the smile on his face. But he was clearly no longer amused. "All I can say is brava. Well done, Ms. Harper. Well done."

"That's your response—well done?"

"What else would you have me say? You want me to lay everything out for you?"

"Yes. In fact, that's exactly what I want." She leaned forward. "I want you to tell me about Nemkov. Whatever his real name was. About that tunnel complex behind the aircraft hangar. About Europa Land Partners, and the Ferrone Real Estate Corporation, and—"

"Tell me, is this intellectual curiosity? Or are you going back on your word?" The man's smile abruptly disappeared. "You haven't come here under false pretenses, Ms. Harper, have you? You're not by any chance wearing a wire?"

"I am not."

"I'm tempted to search you. Where's your phone?"

"Right here." She took it out, set it on the table between them. "But I don't need a phone or a wire for this conversation. Trust me."

"That's exactly what I intend to do. Trust you. With the understanding that once our business is complete, you'll keep out of my private affairs."

"You seem to forget your private affairs stopped being private the second you made Desert View a public company."

"My god." Ferrone sighed heavily and sat back in his chair. "You're exhausting to deal with. Fine. Just give me the number then."

Espy frowned. "What?"

He leaned forward. "Give me the number. How much money are we talking about here?"

"I'm not following. Money for what?"

"For you, Ms. Harper. Money to make you put an end to this investigation of yours."

Espy looked at him incredulously. "Is that why you called me here? To offer me a bribe?" She shook her head. "Didn't I do this dance already, back at the Greenbrier? With Mr. Lish?"

"A bribe? No. Don't think of it as…" Now Ferrone frowned. "Wait. What did you say?"

CHAPTER 53

"I said, is that why you called me here? To offer me a—"

"Why I called you? Don't you have that backward?"

"Hardly. You're the one who wanted…" She stopped then, because she realized it wasn't Ferrone who'd called her. "I take that back. Actually, it was Romano I spoke to. He told me you wanted a meeting."

"No. That's not what happened. Johnny called me, and he said you…" Ferrone stopped then too. Stopped, frowned, and set down his glass. Thinking.

The exact same thoughts that she was, she was certain of it— the only thoughts possible at that second.

Romano had summoned her. Romano had summoned him.

The meeting was a setup. They'd walked into a trap.

Ferrone turned toward Falconetti, opened his mouth to speak at the same second as he shoved his chair back, and started to stand.

The air exploded with gunfire.

54

Tachypsychia, pronounced tack-ee-sy-kee-a: the feeling of time slowing down in critical situations.

The word came into her consciousness from god knows where. Time didn't actually slow down, of course; what happened was, your brain kicked into another gear, put you in a state of heightened alert so you were better able to notice everything happening around you.

Espy had experienced it once before, years ago, at Cat Cay. Watching Jed Seagrave's plans for CASHIER—for starting what would have been World War III—unfold before her eyes, watching Matt try to stop it, joining in herself to aid that effort. Then and there, every split second had mattered, and somehow her brain had known that, had helped her kick into that other gear and do what was necessary.

The same thing was happening now.

Espy became aware of a thousand different things, a thousand little details, all at once.

The bartender to her right, suddenly ducking down out of sight.

The bottle of wine, teetering, about to fall over as Ferrone pushed back from the table.

The expression on Ferrone's face, the smugness gone, replaced by terror.

Frederickson, coming off his barstool, surprise and concern on his face.

The crack of the first shot.

CHAPTER 54

Blood blossoming on Ferrone's chest.

The second shot.

A bullet that took Falconetti, who had already covered half the distance between the bar and his boss. A head shot—Falconetti's head—and a lot more blood.

A third shot, that sent Frederickson flying backward.

"Johnny. What—" Ferrone said, blood trickling from the corner of his mouth.

Shot number four, and his face was gone.

And now there was chaos.

Movement all around her, people running, dishes falling, breaking. And no wonder—gunshots in Las Vegas. After Mandalay Bay everyone was always just a little bit on edge here, a little bit worried it would happen again.

Espy rose to her feet and took a step toward Frederickson.

Shot number five.

And she fell.

She reached out and grabbed hold of the metal armrest of her chair, slowing and altering the trajectory of her fall so the hard stone only knocked the wind out of her. At the same time she pulled the chair down next to her, twisted it as well to make a shield between her and the shooter, whom she knew now was toward the front of the restaurant, from the way the bullets had struck.

She lay on the ground a moment, stunned, broken glass and dishes all around her, aware of more shots being fired, people running and sobbing. She turned and saw that the sobbing was coming from less than five feet away, a woman clutching a young girl wearing a silver birthday crown, huddled underneath the table next to hers.

They were staring at Frank Ferrone. Or what was left of him.

There was a pool of blood all around him, the same color as the wine dripping on her leg from that overturned $375 glass of wine on the table.

Something else was trickling down her arm. Something warm and sticky.

She looked down and saw blood. Of course. She'd been shot. How deep? How bad? She reached up to feel the wound. There was something…

Her hand came away holding a half-inch shard of glass. Not shot, after all. A bullet had hit the table, she realized, the thick glass shattered, and—she sat up, and the world snapped back into focus.

"Police! Stay low, people! Stay where you are."

A man holding a gun in one hand, a badge in another—a police officer—was heading towards her from the front of the restaurant, his eyes looking everywhere.

She looked over at Frederickson. He sat propped up against the bar, right hand pressed against left shoulder.

She got to her feet, made a beeline straight for him, knelt down. "You all right?"

"What the hell," he whispered. "What happened?"

"It was a setup." He had a shoulder wound. There was a lot of blood. He needed a doctor.

"What?"

"This whole meeting. It was a setup. Ferrone got shot. He's dead."

Frederickson blinked. Espy could see him trying to process the information.

"Ma'am."

The man—the officer—she'd seen before stood over her.

"We have an active shooter. We need to clear the area."

"I'm not leaving my friend."

CHAPTER 54

"Paramedics are on the way. We don't want any more casualties, please." The officer holstered his gun, took her arm. "I'm going to get you to a safe place, okay? Come with me."

"No," she said. "I—"

"Hey. This was all a setup, which means you're a target. Go," Frederickson said, in a voice with considerably more steel than the one he'd used a second ago. "I'll be fine."

"Not if you get shot again."

"Ma'am." The officer spoke a little more forcefully. "You're putting yourself and other people at risk. Procedure is to get you to a safe place so we can secure the area. Please. Now."

She took a breath. She was about to launch into a whole big speech about who she was, who she was with, and then realized it would do no good. Besides ... Frederickson was right. She was a target. She was endangering people just by her presence, because even though the shooting seemed to have stopped—the shooter's job wasn't done.

She let the cop help her to her feet, shielding her as he did so. He led her across the restaurant, through the trellis, back down the flagstone steps.

Romano, Espy thought. He'd lied to her. He'd lied to Ferrone. Tried to kill the both of them. Why? To stop Ferrone from talking. From telling her the truth about what was going on.

Except, no. Ferrone wasn't going to talk to her. He'd come here thinking he was going to give her money, that she was going to go away. Romano had just made a power play, she realized. He wanted to take over. She'd underestimated the man. So had Ferrone.

But that made no sense.

She'd watched Romano interact with Doug. He didn't have the guile, the intelligence, to take charge.

She was rushing, Espy realized. Letting the adrenaline coursing through her body guide her thinking. She needed to slow down. Start by calling Li, and letting her know—

Her phone.

It had been on the table when the shooting started.

"Officer." She stopped walking. "I need to go back."

"What?"

"Back to the restaurant. I left my phone."

"Ma'am," he said, "we need to get you someplace safe."

"It's important."

"I'm sure it is. We'll get you back there the second the site is secure, but for now … please."

There was no changing the man's mind, she could see that. She could also see that he was ready to pick her up and carry her if he had to. Reluctantly she let him lead her onward. Out of Fenicottero, through the flamingo habitat, back toward the street, she thought at first. But then he swerved right, up a quick flight of stairs, into a little park of some sort—*Garden Chapel this way*, said a little pink sign—and onto a wide stone path flanked by a row of hedges on either side.

The hedges stopped at a stone column surrounded by a bed of red and white flowers.

A man stood next to that column. An older man, with a shock of white hair.

Kingsleigh.

She stopped short. In that second she realized that she hadn't underestimated Romano. Neither had Ferrone.

It was Kingsleigh pulling the strings here.

"Officer…" Espy spun quickly around. "This man—"

She stopped talking then, as the cop—who she realized in that instant was, of course, not a cop—folded his arms and broadened his stance. Blocking her way out.

CHAPTER 54

She turned back to Kingsleigh. "If you're going to kill me, just get it over with."

"If I was going to kill you, you'd already be dead. I brought you here for a very specific reason. To show you..." He frowned, pointed at the blood on her shirt. "Wait. Were you shot?"

"No. I was ... it was glass. Just a piece of glass."

"Good. Now there are some things we need to clear up here. If you don't mind." He motioned her forward. After a second's hesitation—what choice did she have, really?—she joined him in front of the column. There was a copper plaque affixed to it, with a bas-relief portrait of a man and a building. The text underneath read

> **THE "BUGSY BUILDING"**
> ON THIS SITE, BENJAMIN "BUGSY" SIEGEL'S ORIGINAL
> FLAMINGO HOTEL STOOD FROM DECEMBER 26, 1946
> UNTIL DECEMBER 14, 1993

"Bugsy Siegel." She turned back to Kingsleigh. "How is this relevant here?"

"You know who he was?"

"I do. The man who invented Las Vegas."

Kingsleigh smiled. "A bit of an exaggeration. But he played an important role in developing this territory for us."

"I don't need a history lesson in how the mob came to Vegas."

"The mob. God." Kingsleigh looked up. "You hear that, Bill? Mob?"

"I hear it," the fake cop—Bill—said.

"Why do people keep using that word? We're well past that now. Mob."

"I don't know—maybe because you keep shooting up public places?" Espy snapped.

"What happened back at Fenicottero? A shoot-up?" Kingsleigh

shook his head. "That was a very carefully arranged set of circumstances."

"It hardly seemed careful to me."

"Oh no? What about your friend, Mr. Frederickson?"

"What about him?"

"My instructions were very specific. A flesh wound only. Believe me, if we had wanted him dead, he would be dead. No. Everything that happened at the restaurant went exactly as we wanted it to. Except you were not supposed to be injured. I apologize."

"And what makes me so special?"

Kingsleigh smiled. "You're the one who told us about the money."

"What?"

"Your phone call earlier today. Regarding Frank, and Parcel 33? The money he used to buy that?"

"His $1.2 billion, you mean?"

"No. Not his. Ours. The money he stole from the Peacock." Kingsleigh's voice hardened. His expression changed to match it. "That's why you're here, and not lying on the restaurant floor. Why your friend is wounded and not dead. We owe you, Ms. Harper. Your call saved us some time. Effort. And who knows? Maybe another hundred million."

"So he *was* skimming," Espy said.

"Of course he was. We always expect some of that to happen, we plan on it, but for it to occur at that scale…" Kingsleigh sighed and placed his hand on the plaque. "It was the same with Mr. Siegel. And to hear that Frank Sr. was involved in this … it's very upsetting to me personally."

"You knew him? Frank Sr.?"

"I did. I knew him very well. Chicago, early days, I was there

CHAPTER 54

when Frank Jr. was born. And when he came back home after college. That was a party."

"Good god, yes. Hell of a party," Bill said.

"Wasn't it?" Kingsleigh turned for a second and smiled. "And that first year, when Frank Jr. began running the Peacock, Bill? Remember? There were a lot of improvements. A lot of good things he did. But taking us public? This whole Desert View idea? No." He shook his head. "No, no, no. I was against it from the beginning. Even when Frank showed us how much more money we could make if we issued stock, I wanted to hit the pause button. Go public? That's not how we do business. That's never been how we do business. But everyone else saw dollar signs."

"It worked, though," Espy said.

"Oh, yes. Absolutely it did. Not only did we make money on the sale, we kept making money. Those first few years the money just exploded. Leverage, Frank kept telling us. Stock multiples. I didn't quite understand it all, to be honest, but it put money in our pockets, faster than we could hide it. But it went both ways: as quickly as we made money when the price went up, that's how fast we lost it when everything went to hell. When—"

"When Garrett found you out."

"What?"

"Senator Crandall," Espy said. "When he found you out. When he exposed—"

"Yes." Kingsleigh nodded. "I heard about your fixation with the senator."

"My what?"

"Your fixation. Senator Crandall."

"Ferrone had him killed."

"I know nothing about that."

"That seems to be everyone's line."

"And if he did? I can understand why. Most politicians are like Victor. Senator Sonores. Easily handled. But occasionally you find one who doesn't want to cooperate. And then, well." Kingsleigh shrugged. "You have to get to the next one in line."

"That's it?" She shook her head in wonderment. "That's all you have to say about a US senator getting murdered?"

"Ms. Harper." Kingsleigh smiled. "I'm not here to answer your questions. This conversation—think of it as a courtesy call. We're closing things down here. Tying off the loose ends. Normally, you would be one of them. But as I said, we owe you a debt of gratitude. You're free to go. With the understanding that you'll leave us in peace."

"That's not going to happen. Wheels have been set in motion here, Mr. Kingsleigh. Desert View is a public company, and the DOJ and the SEC are both—"

"Not for much longer."

"What?"

"Desert View is not going to be a public company much longer," Kingsleigh replied. "A stock buyback has been set in motion. A very generous one. And once that's complete, our interests will be private again."

"Which will not erase any previous transgressions."

"We understand that. Someone had to fall on their sword here. Part of the circumstances we've arranged."

Sirens sounded in the distance.

Bill cleared his throat. "Mr. Kingsleigh…"

"Yes, of course. We don't have all day, do we?" He stepped back from the column. "Goodbye, Ms. Harper. We won't meet again." He turned to go.

Espy stepped in front of him. "You think I'm just going to stand here and watch you walk away after you just confessed to

CHAPTER 54

murder? Two murders?"

She sensed the man behind her moving. Kingsleigh held up a hand to stop him. "Of course not. What I think you're going to do is go back to Fenicottero and check on your friend."

"What?"

"Your friend, Mr. Frederickson, who was shot in the shoulder, what, ten minutes ago? I'd be worried about blood loss right now, if I were in your shoes."

"I'm not worried. The paramedics were already on their...."

Way, she was about to say, and then realized who had told her that.

"Were they, Bill?" Kingsleigh looked over her shoulder. "On their way? What do you think?"

"Well," Bill said, "they're headed here by now, I guess, but Vegas traffic … I don't know. I think you're right, Mr. Kingsleigh. If I was her, I'd get a move on."

"I agree," Kingsleigh said. "Better safe than—"

Espy reared back and slapped him.

In that second, every bit of the Kingsleigh she had been speaking with disappeared, like a mask falling away.

Up to that instant, talking to Kingsleigh had been like talking to a particularly nasty white-collar criminal. Now she saw who she was really dealing with here. His eyes narrowed. She saw him take a breath, and she took a step back.

Behind her, she felt Bill take a step forward.

And then the moment passed.

Kingsleigh exhaled, and the mask was back in place.

"Considering the circumstances, I'll give you one of those." He rubbed his cheek. "I hope it helps you feel better. Now go back to Washington, Ms. Harper. And stay out of our affairs."

"Or what?"

"Or what? Bill, did you hear that?"

"I heard." Bill shook his head. "And here she told you she didn't need a history lesson."

Both men laughed.

Espy strode past them without turning back. Quickening her steps as she went, till she was jogging. It wasn't just Frederickson she was hurrying to save.

We're closing things down here, Kingsleigh had said.

Not so fast, she thought to herself. Not if I can help it.

55

The place was shuttered and boarded up. Long since shut down. There was still a big sign out front with carved wooden letters painted in long-faded colors.

CAMP IVANHOE

The sign was so lopsided that the right edge nearly touched the padlocked metal gate beneath it, which had a newer, metal sign that said NO TRESPASSING. Marcus eased the car to a stop and climbed out. Ivanhoe. A famous book. He'd heard of it but had no idea what it was about. Not that it mattered.

Through the gate he could see an overgrown trail, leading past a row of old wooden cabins—not much more than shacks, really—for campers who had come here long ago. Marcus wondered what kind of camp it had been. Not much to do around here. Hike. Throw rocks. Play hide and seek in the scrub. Who would put a camp out here?

Camp Ivanhoe—formerly the site of Holland's testing facilities, according to Vogelsang—was another dead end. Just like his previous stop, 6600 North Rancho Road, the last known address of Holland's plant and offices. That site was now home to one of the seediest-looking casino motels Marcus had ever seen. He hadn't even needed to stop to know there was nothing left of Holland there. This place looked no more promising.

Desert scrub had grown up all around the gate. There were also trees dotting the landscape, which he'd noticed, but hadn't really registered. Trees. That was kind of strange, given that most of the surrounding area was desert. What was also strange: The scrub and trees hid the fact that the metal fence continued on for quite a while in both directions past the gate.

Maybe there was something here after all.

He looked at the sign again, at the locked gate underneath it, and frowned. The gate was old and rusted. So was the chain around it. But the lock itself looked new—looked like threaded steel. Not the kind of thing you could cut through, not even with the heaviest of bolt cutters. Not that anyone with bolt cutters would have any reason to break into Camp Ivanhoe ... would they?

He boosted himself onto the top of the fence and hopped over, started down a dirt road that led past the long row of cabins. Up the road, actually. It was rising. Heading up into the hills. After a while it curved around a bend and opened onto a clearing. In the middle of that clearing was a bigger wooden building. Like one of those grand old lodges—Camp Ivanhoe's dining hall, was his first thought. Looked to be in much better shape than the others he had passed. Windows unbroken, timbers straight and true, and three huge chimneys, brick and mortar intact, spaced equidistantly along the roof.

Marcus crossed the clearing and climbed the steps to a front porch that ran all the way round the building. There was a big glider swing to his right. One of those old-fashioned wooden rockers, big enough to fit three or four people at a time. He gave it a little push ... it swung smoothly back and forth.

His dad had a glider like this one. On the porch in the house at Easton. The springs on it squealed like a stuck pig. It had to be oiled like clockwork every spring. No way this glider had been sitting here abandoned for more than half a century.

He paused a second, checked his weapon, the gun in his shoulder holster. He kicked himself for not having a back-up on him.

CHAPTER 55

Because clearly, Camp Ivanhoe was not really a camp at all. But what was it?

He tried the front door. Locked. Peered through the windows. Couldn't see anything. He walked around back. The door there was locked as well. But he heard something. A low, insistent humming. The sound of machinery, working away. He pressed his ear to that back door. The sound was definitely coming from inside the building.

He walked around until he found a window. Picked up a rock and, taking a deep breath, smashed a pane. Carefully reached inside, found the latch, opened the window, stepped through … and had his prior intuition confirmed.

This was no camping lodge. No dining hall. Never had been. It was a single, huge, empty space. Filled with metal ductwork leading to those chimneys he'd seen from outside. There was conduit everywhere he looked.

At the center of the room was a spiral staircase leading down to the heart of the building. The machinery he'd heard was down there somewhere. Holland, he thought. Prototype testing facility. Question was, what exactly had they been testing here?

He looked down. The metal staircase descended through a cylindrical shaft maybe a dozen feet in diameter. A shaft that stretched on and on, into the darkness below. Took a hell of a big drill bit to make this particular hole, he thought. He could feel the heat and humidity rising up the shaft to meet him as he took his first step down the winding staircase.

And stopped.

Because at that second, the pieces of the puzzle he'd been carrying in his mind since leaving Sherman behind—Guidry and Averill, and Ararat, and de Mohrenschildt, and that giant drill and a half dozen other seemingly unrelated facts—all came together.

Suddenly those pieces fit. Suddenly Marcus knew exactly what was happening.

The secret your senator was killed to protect.

It was obvious. So obvious that he cursed himself for an idiot. He had another message to send here. Maybe one that should go straight to Espy, clear things up for her as well.

And as he paused on that first step down, he heard the tread of footsteps on metal coming from below. There was someone else here. Someone heading toward him. He peered through the darkness and saw a figure in the distance, making no attempt to hide their approach—*clang, clang*, the sound came up to him—which meant whoever it was didn't know he was here. He got up on the balls of his feet, turned to go…

"Not so fast, please."

A figure stepped toward him from behind, and Marcus, for the second time in a single minute, cursed himself for an idiot, because obviously the noise from below had been intended as a distraction.

"Hands," the newcomer said, motioning with his gun, and Marcus did as he was told, in that instant recognizing the man's voice. The man from South Carolina. The one who'd killed Doc.

"You've been a busy little bee, haven't you?" the man said, his face still hidden in the darkness. "Sherman. And your friend Vogelsang."

"I don't know what you're talking about."

"Of course you'd say that. Obstinate till the end." That voice came from below, a woman's voice. She took the last couple steps toward him, coming into view. The woman with the white hair. "Not that it matters."

She raised her weapon and fired.

Marcus looked down and saw a dart sticking out of his arm.

CHAPTER 55

His vision blurred. He stood there a moment on the staircase, wavering on his feet.

Then he lost his balance and fell. A long slow tumble, down into the darkness below.

56

"Benjamin Kingsleigh." The detective, a woman named Edwards from Vegas Investigative Services, looked dubiously at Espy. "And he's the guy responsible for the shooting?"

Espy nodded. "That's right."

They were in a first-floor interview room in the main Vegas police station, just north of the Strip. Where she'd gone after returning to Fenicottero. Kingsleigh had been lying about the paramedics. There were ambulances all over the restaurant. Frederickson was already gone when she got there, en route to a nearby hospital. Going to be fine, officers on the scene—real, uniformed police officers—had assured her. *Come downtown, tell us what happened.* It was phrased as a request, but she had little choice in the matter.

Almost ten o'clock at night, though, and they were only just getting to her. "They" being Edwards and another officer named Zabriskie. She'd told them as little as possible: some details about the DOJ case against Ferrone, about the stock fraud and Parcel 33. She was now starting in on the phone call that had brought her to Fenicottero.

"Kingsleigh is the one who got Romano to call us—me and Ferrone. He's on the board of Desert View. He's behind all of this."

"Wait." Edwards, who'd been perched on the interview table, got to her feet. "You said Romano? You mean Johnny Romano?"

"That's right."

The officers exchanged a look.

"What?" Espy asked.

CHAPTER 56

"He's our shooter."

Espy's eyes went wide. "No."

"Yes. Apparently Ferrone set him up to take the fall for some stock thing."

"Probably that thing you were talking about," Zabriskie added.

"He's lying." Espy shook her head. "Let me talk to him. I'll—"

"He's dead."

"What?"

"Romano's dead. Suicide. Room 2415, the Flamingo. Left a note, said he had no intention of spending the rest of his life in prison, so … " Edwards shrugged.

Espy couldn't find her voice.

Someone will have to fall on their sword here.

Part of the circumstances we've arranged.

"Ms. Harper?" Edwards asked. "You all right?"

"No." Espy shook her head. "Romano? No. This was Kingsleigh. Romano is just a—" *Patsy*, she almost said, and then stopped herself. Nobody used that word anymore. It sounded strange. It sounded sixty years old.

I am a Patsy. The last words of my friend, Lee Harvey Oswald.

"The rifle is in his name. Romano," Edwards added.

"You believe that?" Espy snapped. "That he's some kind of sharpshooter?"

"Well." Edwards shrugged. "I don't know how sharp that shooting was. A dozen shots fired, and only four hits."

She looked at the two and realized that no matter what else she said, what else she told them, they were going to go with the evidence. Kingsleigh's "circumstances." She was wasting her time here.

Five more minutes, a promise to make herself available as needed, and she was on her way back to the Bellagio.

Her phone buzzed as she walked back into the suite.

"Espy."

"Li."

"I have news."

"Go on." She wandered into her bedroom. Her bathroom. Stared at her reflection in the mirror. There was a little spot of blood on her shirt collar. Ferrone's blood.

"There was an explosion at Mr. Ferrone's ranch earlier this evening."

"What?"

"Yes. One moment. I can show you a recording. From the security cameras."

Espy recognized the image immediately.

She was looking at the airplane hangar. Or what was left of it. Clouds of smoke rose from the ruins of the building—and the mountain behind it. The tunnels. Ferrone's underground complex.

"Archived footage indicates that at approximately 10:25 p.m.—"

"Enough." Espy closed her eyes. "I want to focus on Kingsleigh. Find him. Get him to talk."

"I have an alert out on his passport through DHS, although…" Li trailed off.

"What?"

"I am beginning to think Kingsleigh may not be his real name."

Of course, Espy thought.

"The only information I can find on him mirrors exactly the information contained in Desert View's prospectus. Almost word for word."

"Papyrus," Espy said. "He's the vice chairman. We can find him through them."

"Possibly. This is more your area of expertise than mine. As you know, there is little publicly available information on the firm,

CHAPTER 56

but I will check further in the morning."

Check now, Espy almost said, then realized how late it was back east. "Okay." She sighed. "Morning it is."

❖ ❖ ❖ ❖ ❖

But there was no morning.

When Espy woke, it was almost noon. She had trouble even opening her eyes. She felt like she'd been hit with a hammer. Every muscle in her body ached.

She took a long, long shower. Let the water wash over her till her fingers wrinkled. Put on a robe, walked out into the suite's living room—and almost screamed.

Frederickson was sitting on the couch, laptop open on the coffee table in front of him.

"You have to stop doing that."

"Sorry. And good morning to you too. Good afternoon, actually."

"Shouldn't you be in the hospital?" She pointed to the sling on his left shoulder. "Resting? That's a gunshot wound."

He snorted. "How much time have you spent in hospitals? Those are the worst places to rest. People are always coming in and out, taking your temperature, checking your vitals, waking you up to pee…"

"He's right about that."

That voice came from the laptop. A different voice, but a familiar one.

"Doug," Espy said, the word catching in her throat.

Frederickson spun the laptop around so she could see.

It was indeed Doug. Sitting upright in a hospital bed. "Espy. I'd say good to see you, but…" His entire face was wrapped in bandages, save for openings at his nose and mouth.

"Well, for what it's worth, it's great to see you. And you sound good."

"Because I'm hopped up on painkillers."

"Enjoy it while you can," Frederickson said.

"Yeah." He managed a small laugh. "They tell me coming down is gonna be a bitch."

Espy exchanged a glance with Frederickson.

"So how long are they keeping you?" she asked.

"Don't know. Depends on how the next few days go."

She nodded. There were a million questions she wanted to ask. How did the surgery go? What are they telling you about recovery, or reconstruction? But just then a nurse came into his hospital room, looked at Doug, then turned to the camera.

"That's enough," she said. "Mr. Rivers needs to rest."

"Okay, okay. Signing off for now. But guys, do me a favor." Doug's voice hardened. "Settle some scores, okay?"

"You got it. We'll talk soon."

"Yeah. Take care, Doug," Espy added.

Frederickson shut the laptop. "Just to let you know," he said, "I spoke to the surgeons. He's not out of the woods yet. Won't be for a while."

"What does that mean?"

"It means there's a substantial risk of infection still. The surgery they did was very experimental. They're watching him round the clock."

"That's good. And you? You're all right? Is that why they let you go?"

He smiled. "I refuse to answer that question on the advice of counsel. My own counsel."

"Ha ha."

She went and got dressed. Unplugged her phone and saw she

CHAPTER 56

had two messages. One from a reporter, asking about the shooting. He wouldn't be the last, she knew. She'd be facing a lot of questions over the next few days. From the press, from Bamberger, from Mike, if he got reinstated...

The second message was from Greg. A long voicemail. "Ms. Harper, I wanted to let you know that I spoke to a source at Royal Cayman Bank. She couldn't tell me anything officially—wouldn't give me any paper, or any details, but she did confirm Europa has an account there. A very substantial account."

Espy felt a sudden jolt of energy. She smiled. Good, she thought. Nice work, Greg. But her smile disappeared with his next words.

"She also told me a lot of money's been coming out of that account these last few months. Some big withdrawals. Again, she wouldn't get into specifics, but we're talking millions, I think. Tens of millions, maybe more." Greg paused. "Anyway. I'll try you again in a few, to make sure you got this."

Espy called him right back.

"Got your message," she said. "But I think your source has it backwards. Ferrone's been putting money into that account. Sending it from Vegas down to the Caymans. Deposits, not withdrawals."

"That's not what they told me. I took pretty extensive notes, and—"

"Double-check, please," Espy snapped.

Greg took a breath. "Okay. I will. Give me a minute."

The line went silent. She wheeled her suitcase out into the living room. Frederickson's was already there, waiting. He wasn't. Probably in the conference room, packing up the equipment there.

The door to the hall opened. A cleaning woman popped her head in. "Excuse me. Sorry. I thought you were all checked out already."

"Soon enough. Come in and get started if you want. We'll be out of your hair in a minute."

The woman nodded and wheeled her cleaning cart past.

"Ms. Harper." Greg came back on the line. "Confirming what I had told you before. These last few months, the only activity on Europa's account has been a series of withdrawals. Not deposits."

"You're sure about that?"

"I am." He sounded annoyed. Espy felt the same way.

The money was going in the wrong direction.

"Ms. Harper?"

"Okay. Thank you. I'll be in touch." She hung up and stood there a minute, thinking. Remembering that cash cart Frederickson had found. The conclusion she'd drawn: Ferrone was using the carts to take money he'd skimmed from the Peacock and send it down to the Caymans. But that wasn't what was happening here at all. She had it backwards. So what was Ferrone doing? Bringing money back from the Caymans to the Peacock, using the casino to launder his ill-gotten gains?

She was missing something here.

Everything had been happening so quickly these last few days; she needed a little perspective. Needed to clear her head, see the big picture.

She walked to the window. Her gaze fell on the fountains below. Those water cannons, shooting plumes of water into the sky, water that reached practically to her balcony before dissipating in the heat. Precious water, going up in—well, not smoke, but…

A well he could draw from as he saw fit.

She looked across the street. Looked down at the Venice hotel, at the gondoliers paddling through the canals out front. Water, water everywhere.

CHAPTER 56

Why do you think we call it Aqua Roma?

She frowned.

Big lake? There's more than one?

Her eyes fell on the billboard out front. A billboard promoting Cirque du Soleil's *O*. The Bellagio's main attraction. A show with clowns and gymnasts, high-wire artists, Olympic athletes, stunts of all kinds. If she was remembering right, the set had cost around $50 million to construct—a set that rose and fell and changed shape during the show, a set built around a huge swimming pool.

O—a play on words, or rather, a play on a single word—*eau*. The French word for water.

Time and time again, the company has turned worthless desert land into high-yield properties.

How could you do that? How could you turn desert into fertile land?

She picked up her briefcase. Snapped it open and thumbed through the documents she'd taken from Ferrone's files the night before, till she found the ones she was looking for: the correspondence between Frank Ferrone Sr. and that Vegas city-planning official. Bud Rothmann.

Trust me, Frank Sr. had written. *I know the scientists are saying we're in for a La Niña, but we'll be fine. It's their job to consider worst-case scenarios.*

La Niña means less rainfall, Rothmann had written back. *Means less snow pack, less melt, less coming into the dam. Means we can't afford to build at the scale you're talking about.*

I know what it means, Ferrone had replied. *But trust me. El Niño, La Niña, mother nature be damned, come spring we'll be fine.*

That correspondence all came from 1983.

Espy did a quick search. 1983 was indeed a year of *La Niña*—an atmospheric weather pattern that had resulted in significantly less rainfall than usual, just as Rothmann had said. Significantly less rainfall usually meant significantly less snowpack in the Rockies, usually meant significantly less water in the Colorado River and Lake Mead, the reservoir that fed Las Vegas.

Usually.

But that year, water levels in Lake Mead had remained unexpectedly, unaccountably normal. No way Ferrone Sr. could have known that was going to happen. And yet…

He had.

She dug out the papers Cabral had printed out for her at the Greenbrier. The construction benchmarks Desert View had missed. Ferrone's note to the bank: *I just need a little more time. Things are going to come together. Trust me.* And the board minutes: *Downsized tenant occupancy. Reduced lake circumference. FF rejected both modifications.*

Frank Jr. had been counting on water too. Betting that it would come in so he wouldn't have to scale back Aqua Roma, so the towers—the lake—could be as big as he wanted. As profitable as he'd planned.

He'd been counting on the water showing up even as that bullet passed through his brain. But how? It wasn't possible. You couldn't plan for something like that. Except that was the answer. She felt it in her gut.

The secret your senator was killed to protect.

"Water."

She said it out loud as she strode toward the conference room, pushing the door open. "It's water. Somehow Ferrone knew about water. How much—"

She stopped talking then, because the maid was strangling Frederickson with his sling.

57

The woman was behind his chair, pulling Frederickson's sling across his neck, her wrists digging into his forearm. His face was red, shading toward purple. The veins on her arm stood out like blue ropes. Frederickson made a gurgling noise. A shock of white hair peeked out from under her maid's cap.

White hair.

The woman at the trailer park. The one who'd been standing over Mike. Cockerell. As he breathed his last. She'd killed him, Espy realized.

At that second, the woman saw Espy, let go of Frederickson, and launched herself at Espy, somersaulting through the air and landing six feet away. Espy's own training kicked in a split-second later, thankfully fast enough to brace herself. It was all she had time to do before the woman launched herself again, kicking Espy square in the chest and sending her tumbling back into the cleaning cart, which toppled over.

Espy lost her balance and sprawled backward on top of the cart. The woman grabbed the collar of Espy's shirt and dragged her forward, drew her right arm back. Espy realized, from the angle of her hand, the way her fingers were positioned—knuckles out—the woman was planning to strike the bridge of Espy's nose and drive the bone into the brain, a killing blow. Espy reached back for something, anything, and her hands closed on a towel. She yanked it forward in front of her face, deflecting just enough of the blow, changing the angle of the strike so that the edge of the woman's hand caught her not on the nose but the forehead, right on the bone. Espy literally saw stars for a second.

No time to recover. She kicked up, and the woman somehow was fast enough to grab her leg and twist, and Espy felt pain searing down her leg. The bone was going to break—until Frederickson reared up behind the woman and caught her across the back of the head with Espy's laptop.

Somehow she sensed him coming. She rolled with the blow, went to the floor, and came back up in a ready position. Her eyes shifted from Frederickson to Espy, who got back up on her feet as well.

"You must have missed the *Do not disturb* sign," Frederickson managed. He was still a little short of breath.

"Sorry. I was in a rush to get here. A lot of moving parts," the woman said.

Espy exchanged a quick glance with Frederickson, who nodded. They began to circle the woman, who took a quick step backward and then charged right at Frederickson. He blocked her first kick, but she caught him with the second, a spinning move that sent him flying backward into the conference room table with a sickening thud.

Espy lunged forward to help, but the woman kept turning, kept her leg planted, and Espy barely got her own arm up in time. The woman's kick stopped Espy dead in her tracks; the pain radiated instantly all down her forearm, and Espy worried the bone might be fractured, but she sent that pain somewhere else in her mind. A good thing, because the woman was following up, her right arm coming forward, and Espy chopped down with her left hand, barely deflecting that blow, and followed up with a right hand strike that caught the woman across the jaw and set her back on her heels.

The woman took a step back and rubbed her chin. She looked

CHAPTER 57

at Espy and smiled.

"Not bad for a lawyer. Better than your buddy Kleinman managed."

Kleinman? Marcus?

A lot of moving parts, the woman had said. And Marcus was clearly one of them. Or, had been. Espy tried to keep the surprise she felt off her face. The surprise—and the concern. Another operative down, on her watch? She couldn't think about that right now. All she could think about…

"Make it easy on yourself," Espy said. "Tell me who you are. Who you're working for. What—"

"I'll make it easy on you." The woman reached into the pocket of her maid's uniform and pulled out a hypodermic. "Same as I made it easy on your detective friend."

Wrong thing to say. For a second, Espy pictured that video again, the recording of the last few seconds of Cockerell's life. Her hands clenched into fists, and she strode forward, ready to fight, to move into position to strike. And then saw the glint in the woman's eye, and realized…

She was being stupid. Doing exactly what the woman wanted her to do. Getting angry. Losing her head. Getting ready to fight, which was of course a ridiculous thing to do. This woman was a trained killer, an assassin, and there was no way Espy could come close to beating her in any sort of physical combat.

She took a step back.

The woman smiled. "Scared?"

"Shouldn't I be?" Espy nodded to the hypodermic.

"Absolutely." The woman stepped forward now. "Let's get this over with."

Espy took another step back and almost tripped. The housecleaning cart. She kicked it backward, glancing down to make sure she didn't stumble ... and saw something. Two somethings, actually, that had fallen from the cart. One mostly hidden, peeking out from behind the other.

She looked up again, quickly. Just in time.

The woman jabbed at her with the needle. A feint. She smiled. Playing.

"No one's going to believe I had a heart attack," Espy said.

"You let me worry about that."

"The colonel. Who was he? Tell me what you know, we'll make some kind of deal."

The woman smiled again. Shook her head. "God, I hate lawyers. Always looking to make deals. Sorry, not this time."

Behind the woman, she saw Frederickson lying still on the ground. Or were the fingers of his hand moving? Wishful thinking? Come on, she thought. Get up.

She pretended he had.

"Careful," she said, continuing to glance over the woman's shoulder. "The hypodermic."

The woman shook her head. "Not falling for that."

She came at Espy again, this time in earnest, keeping her right hand—the one with the needle in it—at her side, ready to strike.

Espy took a step back—her last step, because the woman had backed her into the corner. She stumbled ... or rather, pretended to. She reached down as if to balance herself, let her hand close on the two somethings she'd seen before.

She came up holding them out in front of her.

"A feather duster?" The woman laughed. "Seriously?"

"No," Espy said, and dropped the duster, revealing the can of furniture polish it had been hiding.

She pressed the trigger on the can, sending a spray right into the woman's face. The woman managed to squeeze her eyes shut

CHAPTER 57

before the spray hit, but it didn't matter.

That split-second was all Espy needed.

She was already dropping the can and grabbing the woman's right hand, taking hold of it with both of her hands, shoving and twisting and pushing with all her strength.

She stuck the needle square into the woman's leg.

The woman's eyes widened. She looked down, cursed, and backhanded Espy right across the face. Then she reached down and came up holding a knife.

She lunged forward. Espy managed to step back, but then actually tripped over the cleaning cart and fell backward.

The woman kept coming. She half-lunged, half-fell right on top of Espy, and suddenly the knife was at Espy's throat, the point pressing into the side of her neck.

"Taking you with me," the woman said, gasping for breath as she spoke.

Espy got both hands around the woman's wrist, trying to hold the blade back. But the knife was still coming forward. Pressing into her neck.

It stopped moving for a second.

Frederickson was on top of the woman now, his one good hand joined with Espy's two.

And then the knife began moving again. The point digging into Espy's neck.

"You have got to be kidding," Frederickson said, sweat breaking out on his brow.

The woman grunted. Her temple was practically touching Espy's now.

"Lawyers." The woman gritted her teeth. "Lawyers!"

She gasped and let go of the blade. It tumbled to the floor. Her eyes lost focus and stopped moving. She shuddered once, and then again, and then collapsed.

Espy leaned back and let out a long sigh of relief.

"Jesus Christ," Frederickson said, rolling off the woman's body and onto the floor. "Where the hell did she come from? I thought Kingsleigh said you were free to go."

"He did." Espy pushed the woman off of her and stood. Swayed a moment, feeling the pain in her arm where she'd been hit. Her arm. Her chest. Her legs. "I guess he changed his mind. Decided to tie up all the loose ends after all."

"Maybe. And maybe not. Maybe this wasn't Kingsleigh at all. I mean, she's not your typical Mafia princess, if you know what I'm saying."

"That's for sure."

"Well." Frederickson sat up. "We're even now."

"What?"

"Falconetti. Her." He pointed. "Me and you. We're even."

"Like you said, not keeping score." Espy rolled the woman's body over, felt around in her pockets. "No ID."

"No surprise there."

"She killed Cockerell." Espy stood. "She's on that video. From the trailer park."

"Cockerell and Beck. And Casserly and his grandson."

"We don't know all that for sure yet. Here's one thing I do know, though." Espy turned to face Frederickson. "This is all about water."

"Water?"

"That's right."

She explained about Europa and the Ferrone Real Estate Corporation and its seemingly inexhaustible supply of money. About Ferrone Sr. and Jr.'s faith in a seemingly inexhaustible supply of water. The correspondence she'd found in the files.

CHAPTER 57

"So you're saying Ferrone's been controlling the water? Like, how much there is?" He shook his head. "How is that possible?"

"I don't know. But Ferrone's not controlling anything anymore." She thought a moment. "Falconetti. The Luminor."

"What?"

"The dive watch he was wearing. That's connected to this too. Has to be." She pulled out her phone.

"Espy? What are you doing?"

"Looking for a phone number. Ah. Found it. Hang on." She held the cell to her ear, and waited. Then…

"Ms. Brody?"

"Yes?"

"You don't know me, but my name is Esperanza Harper. Forgive me, I know this is a difficult time, and I'm sorry to intrude, but I have a couple questions for you."

"Questions? About?"

"Well," she said, "I think it would be better if we talked in person."

58

110 Colosseum Drive was a madhouse. Fire trucks, law enforcement vehicles, and ambulances were parked along the drive leading back to the hangar. Espy had to flash her badge more than once before they were led to a visibly distraught, visibly drunk C.C. Brody.

After they were introduced, C.C. kept staring at Frederickson.

"Sorry. But you look familiar," she said.

"I get that all the time." Frederickson smiled. "I guess I'm what you would call a type."

C.C. was on the couch, in the ranch's living room. Espy and Frederickson sat in two chairs facing her across a long coffee table.

"I'm sorry for your loss," Espy said. "Losses. Just a couple quick questions, and we'll be on our way."

"Remind me who you are, again. Who you're with."

"Esperanza Harper. Department of Justice."

C.C.'s expression changed. "Harper. You were the one." She glared. "Frank talked about you."

"I'm sure he did. We had our differences. But the same people who killed him were shooting at me too." Not a lie. Not the whole truth, either.

"Oh." C.C.'s anger dissipated. "I didn't know that."

"Yes. But the questions I have for you have nothing to do with the business I had with Mr. Ferrone. I wanted to ask about Mr. Falconetti."

"Vince? What about him?"

"Was he a diver?"

CHAPTER 58

C.C. frowned. "What?"

"Scuba diver, she means," Frederickson elaborated. "Was Mr. Falconetti a scuba diver?"

"They both were. Vince and Frank. But I don't understand." C.C. looked from one of them to the other. "Why is that at all important? Why are you asking me that?"

"It's part of our investigation," Espy said. "I'm really not at liberty to discuss details."

"But any help you can give us would be greatly appreciated," Frederickson added.

"Well. All right. As I said, they were both divers. Frank first, then Vince took it up as well. A few years ago."

"And was there any place in particular they liked to go?"

C.C. shook her head. "I wouldn't have the first clue."

"Would it be possible to take a look at their equipment? See what type of gear they used? That might tell us something."

"I suppose."

C.C. led them to a mud room just off the ranch's garage. The diving gear was there—tanks, breathing apparatus, wetsuits, flippers, masks, and a heavy-duty duffel bag full of other gear.

"I don't know what you'll find here," C.C. said. "Or even what you're looking for."

Frankly, neither do I, Espy thought. "We just want to take a quick look. We won't be long."

C.C. nodded and left them to it.

Espy looked around. All this equipment—it told her that both men were serious divers. They knew what they were doing. But that didn't necessarily have anything to do with the inexhaustible supply of water the Ferrone Real Estate Corporation had depended on. For all she knew, they were just enthusiasts, like her. Dove for pleasure. For fun.

Although fun was not a word she necessarily associated with the late Frank Ferrone Jr.

"What's this?" Frederickson was holding out a bright-red cylindrical sack, about the size of a small fire extinguisher.

"Dry bag," she said. "A place to keep your valuables safe when you dive."

"Valuables. Maybe we should see what's inside."

He reached into the bag and pulled out a little square of paper. He unfolded it and held it up so they both could see.

It was a map. SUBSURFACE ANOMALIES IN THE MARIELLA SPRINGS VALLEY was printed across the top of the page.

Someone had drawn little circles, a couple dozen or so, all over the upper right corner of the map. Most of those circles had been filled in with red *X*'s.

"Places they'd been," Frederickson said, pointing to the *X*'s. He moved his finger to the empty circles. "Places they still wanted to go."

"They were looking for something," Espy said.

"Yeah. But they didn't find it." He folded the map back up. "Maybe we should pick up where they left off."

She smiled. "No maybe about it."

❖ ❖ ❖ ❖ ❖

She borrowed Ferrone's equipment—the duffel, the tank, the breathing apparatus. Pulled over at a twenty-four-hour truck stop, bought herself a bathing suit and changed into it, while Frederickson waited in the car. He could drive, but he couldn't dive. What he could do was translate the dots on the map to GPS coordinates.

The first dot turned out to be an old park ranger station overlooking a tiny tributary of the Colorado.

CHAPTER 58

The second dot marked the location of a dried-up stream.

The third dot took them to an abandoned mine—shades of the Black Brush Mining Corporation.

To get to the fourth dot, they had to head farther north, following signs to Lake Moapa and the Valley of Fire State Park. There, they found a deep pool, a few hundred feet across, surrounded on three sides by canyon walls. There were dark streaks on those walls—old water lines—indicating significant evaporation of the pool over time. And those canyon walls were steep; that told her that the little pool could be a lot deeper than it looked from the road.

"So…" They climbed out of the car. Frederickson stood looking down on the water. "We think this is it? What Ferrone was looking for? Like he wanted to use this little pool to refill Lake Mead?"

She didn't bother answering. Ridiculous question. Rhetorical. But there weren't that many dots left on the map. Two more after this one.

"No idea. But worth taking a closer look," she said.

So they did.

The trail was steep. Fredrickson stumbled more than once and almost fell. She thought about offering him a hand but knew that wouldn't go over well.

Finally, they reached the bottom. She walked right to the edge of the pool and dipped a toe in. It was cooler than she'd expected, given the midday heat. So maybe it was deep. Maybe the canyon walls protected it from the sun.

She hadn't bothered bringing the dive gear down; that could come later, if need be. All she needed was her dive mask. She slipped it on, gave Fredrickson a thumbs-up, and plunged into the water.

It felt like coming home.

Her first dive since the last trip to Cat Cay back in the fall. Glorious to stretch out, to move her body, get the grime of Vegas off her, and feel the water on her skin. She swam underwater for a good ten seconds before she surfaced. Took a moment to feel the sun on her face. A glorious feeling.

But glorious wasn't what she was here for.

She readjusted her mask, and then, slowly treading water, took a series of quick, deep breaths. Frog-breathing. A modified version of the lung-packing her instructor at Cat Cay had taught her—a way to take in more oxygen than her body could normally hold. Enough to make sure she could stay under for a good couple minutes. She checked the Luminor.

Then she dove down.

Two quick kicks, maybe ten feet down, and the temperature dropped precipitously. Call it close to eighty degrees at the surface, it might be sixty-five this far down. She began to wish she'd brought Ferrone's wetsuit.

Another twenty feet or so and she touched bottom. Stone. Not unexpected. But what was unusual: The bottom was flat, in all directions. As far as she could see in the light still coming from the surface. Close to level. Artificially level.

Out of the corner of her eye, she caught a glint of something. Swam along the bottom till she reached it. It was metal. A circular disk set in the rock, the size and shape of a manhole cover. She ran her hand over it; the metal was smooth to the touch. And it looked new, not corroded, or rusted, or damaged by the water in any way. She wished she'd brought a light to examine it closer. What was it? She had no idea.

She kicked back up to the surface and took in a few deep breaths. She was at the far end of the pool, in the narrow end of a V formed by two canyon walls coming together. There was a

CHAPTER 58

trail leading up from the spot where the canyon walls met. A trail carved into the wall, not more than three or four feet wide, almost impossible to see unless you were right on top of it.

She swam toward it. Boosted herself up out of the water. There was a metal sign at the trailhead, rusted to the color of the canyon wall. The words *No Trespassing* stood out in big, bold reddish letters. Below them were smaller words in faded black type. Harder to read against the rust. She picked out the letters *OLL*.

She wet a finger and rubbed off the dirt and crud.

HOLLAND.

She'd run across a company by that name in those Ferrone Real Estate Corporation files, hadn't she? An older company. The context escaped her, but if she was remembering right, Holland had been one of Ferrone Sr.'s companies. So, was this the place Ferrone Jr. had been looking for? Had he not known where it was?

"WHAT'S GOING ON?"

She turned. Frederickson stood on the far shore, hands cupped together.

She waved. "FOUND SOMETHING!" she yelled back.

"WHAT?" His words echoed across the little canyon.

"TRAIL!" She pointed. "GOING UP!"

"WAIT!" he yelled. She couldn't see the expression on his face, but she could tell he wasn't happy. Nothing she could do about that. Wait for what? Reinforcements? For his shoulder to heal?

They were closing things down here, Kingsleigh had said. Whatever that meant. They couldn't afford to wait.

She gave Frederickson two thumbs up, then turned and started to climb.

59

Water.

Landing on his forehead. Drip drip, drip drip. Drop after drop after drop.

Marcus opened his eyes. He was in a dimly lit room. No, not a room. A cave of some sort. The water was dripping off the ceiling high above him.

Water.

Doc. Sherman. Ararat. Camp Ivanhoe. It all came rushing back.

"Welcome back."

Same voice from before. The man from South Carolina. He was tall. Pale-skinned. Thin, almost sickly.

"We've got work to do, you and I."

The man came closer. Marcus tried to move away and found he couldn't. His arms were fastened behind him, his legs pressed against chair legs. Zip ties. He felt them cutting into his wrists, his calves, his ankles. He strained. The chair was bolted to the floor.

He licked his lips and tasted cotton in his mouth. Recalled the woman with the white hair coming up the stairs, firing, the dart in his arm ... He'd been shot. Drugged. He had a squirrelly feeling in his stomach as well. It took him another few seconds, but then he recognized the aftereffects.

"White 17," he said. "Am I right?"

"17B, actually. A new strain."

"How long have I been out?" A few hours at least, but it could have been longer. A lot longer. The man didn't answer.

CHAPTER 59

"That's an agency drug, White 17," Marcus prompted. "You're CIA?"

The man smiled and pulled something forward. A rolling cart. There was a tray on it, and an open plastic case with a half-dozen hypodermic needles. "Who else you have told?"

"What do you mean? Told about what?"

"Please. Don't insult my intelligence." The man picked up one of the hypodermics. "That first dart contained too high a dosage. We'll try a little less this time."

Before Marcus could say a word, the man jabbed the needle into his shoulder.

The drug's effects were instantaneous. Marcus felt himself drifting away, becoming disconnected from his body. The world shifting all around him. His vision swimming.

The man leaned closer. "Who have you spoken to?"

Marcus bit his tongue. Tasted blood. Stay focused, he told himself. Stay focused.

He started humming the Imperial March from *Star Wars*. Keep the mind busy. One of the tricks they'd taught during the interrogation course back at Langley. How to resist. How to hold out as long as possible. Keep from talking.

"Who have you spoken to?"

It was impossible to hold out forever, though. Whether you were being tortured or drugged or some combination of the two. "Your mother," Marcus managed. "Last night. Right after we—"

The man slapped him. "Who have you spoken to?"

"Vogelsang," he said, and just speaking that word felt good. Felt liberating. A load off his mind. Keeping all those secrets, and why? What was the point? The truth would set him free. And Marcus wanted to be free.

He had to piss.

"Of course Vogelsang. We know Vogelsang. Who else?"

"That's it," he said.

"No." The man leaned over him. "Who else?"

"Sherman. And going way back. Doc."

The second he said Doc's name, he pictured him in the house, back in South Carolina. The outstretched hand. All the blood. Zelda.

He threw up.

There was a lot of cursing then. A lot of noise and movement and more hitting. He squeezed his eyes shut and went away for a few minutes. Another technique they'd taught him. Pick a memory. The sounds, the smells, the sensations…

He went back to Mexico City. That first dinner with Vogelsang and Helena, and of course … Marion. What a night. Jesus. He was unlikely to have one of those again.

He stayed there in that memory as long as he could.

"Mr. Kleinman. Come back to us, please. Who have you spoken with?"

A different voice. Marcus opened his eyes.

There was a newcomer in the room, standing right in front of him, the tall man a few steps behind. Medium height and build, maybe a little soft around the middle. But there was nothing soft about the look in his eyes. Marcus saw that right off. He saw something else too.

"You're going to kill me," Marcus said.

The newcomer smiled. "Yes. I am. Not right away, though. First I need more information. You want to give me that information, don't you? Tell me who you've spoken to."

"Vogelsang," Marcus said again. Sorry, Kurt, he thought, vaguely aware that he'd already given him up, so giving him up a second time—who else could it hurt?

CHAPTER 59

"Yes, I heard. I'll have to decide what to do about him," the newcomer said. "Sometimes it's best to let sleeping dogs lie. Sometimes." He shrugged. "And Sherman? You talked to him as well, didn't you?"

"The DAN," Marcus realized. The alert, back at Area 51. "That was you."

"Sherman," the man said, a little snap to his voice. "You say it's connected to the internet now?"

"I say kiss my ass." Marcus smiled. He could feel the drug wearing off.

The newcomer glared, then turned to the tall man. "Another dosage, Jann. Yes?"

The tall man—Jann—nodded. "Of course."

"Don't waste time, either. We're done here. The devices are set. Just find out about Crane, one way or the other, and then kill him. We'll be waiting. Downstairs."

"Understood."

"Good." The other man nodded and was gone.

"Hey, I gotta pee," Marcus said.

Jann ignored him and picked up another hypodermic. "I do worry about doing this again so soon. The cumulative effects—"

"So don't. Listen. Jann, is it?" Marcus tried smiling. Felt bile rising in his throat and tamped it down. "You look European. Eastern European, am I right? Czech, maybe? I had a friend—"

"Stuart Crane." Jann came closer, holding the hypodermic out in front of him. "Have you spoken to him? Been in contact at all?"

"No." Marcus shook his head. Blinked, tried to focus. The woman with the white hair was standing behind Jann now. The one who'd shot him with the dart. She looked different, though. She'd changed her hair. It wasn't white anymore. It was brown.

Hey. She'd changed her face too.

475

She looked at him and put a finger to her lips. *Shhh.*

Then she raised the rock she was holding and slugged Jann across the back of the head. He toppled to the ground.

She dashed over to him, which was when he realized who the woman was.

"Espy," he said.

She was shaking her head, smiling. "You got my message. The drone."

"Yeah." Marcus forced a smile too. "Me and Wilbur, we got it just fine. Thanks."

"Wilbur? Who's Wilbur?"

"You remember Wilbur." Marcus barked at her. "My dog. My dad's dog."

Espy frowned. "Are you all right?"

"Sort of. White 17," he said. "17b. I'm gonna need a minute here."

"I don't know that we have a minute." She came around behind him. He felt her tug on the zip ties. "Going to need something to cut these. And how the hell did these guys get hold of White 17?"

"There's an agency connection here." He turned slightly. "Should be a little blade in the heel of my right shoe."

"On it," she said and bent down, picked up his foot. "Got it."

He felt the little blade digging between the zip tie and his wrist. "Careful."

"My middle name. So what is this place? Who are these people?"

"Not entirely sure. But what I can tell you, I know what this is all about. Why Garrett was killed. Maybe JFK too. It's—"

"Water," she interrupted.

He turned his head all the way around. They looked at each other.

CHAPTER 59

"Right," he said. "Water. There was a government program, Ararat, back in the sixties. The man with the white Stetson—his name was Averill, by the way, James Averill—he was CIA. In charge. There was this geologist working with him—"

"De Mohrenschildt?"

"No, no, it was—doesn't matter who it was. Point is, they found something, Averill and the geologist."

"They found water."

"Yeah. Averill staged an accident to cover it up. Murdered everyone else on the project, just about. And I think JFK found out about it. And that's why he was killed. Why Manchester was followed, too. Averill was worried that—"

"Jackie knew. That she'd told Manchester."

"Exactly." Marcus felt the last of the zip ties break free, and his arms fell to his sides. He stretched his legs out in front of him, rubbing them. Trying to get the circulation going again. Did the same for his arms.

"Ferrone was in on it too," Espy said. "He and his father."

"The mob and the government." Marcus stood. "Working together."

"That's right. They used the water to make millions. Tens of millions, hundreds of millions, maybe more. Buying desert, turning it into valuable land."

"Quite the deal." Marcus walked over to Jann. Rolled him over, looking for a weapon. Came up with a .44, turned back to Espy, and froze.

She had the strangest expression on her face.

"What's the matter?" he asked.

She shook her head. "No."

"What?"

She stared at the man on the ground, eyes wide. "That's not possible."

"What's not possible?"

"Nemkov." She pointed. "That's Nemkov."

60

Espy just kept staring.

"Who?" Marcus asked.

"Nemkov. From the construction site. The one who…" Espy couldn't remember if Nemkov's name had been in the briefing Li had prepared for Marcus. Didn't matter at the moment. Her concern was a lot more immediate.

Something was wrong here.

Something was very, very wrong.

And up until that second, it had all been going so well.

The trail had led her up and into the mountain, to a locked door she'd jammed open with the metal clasp from her mask. Then into a long, narrow tunnel, following the sound of machinery, which had led to the sound of voices, one of them familiar, a voice she hadn't thought she'd ever hear again. Marcus.

But now…

"The other guy called him Jann," Marcus said.

"What?"

"His name. That's what the other guy called him. Jann."

Espy nodded. Jann. Okay. She'd known the Nemkov name was a fake. A videogame character. World's greatest assassin. Whatever. He was alive. That's why the body hadn't been found. Only…

All that blood.

It didn't make sense.

"Uh-oh," Marcus said.

"What?"

"We got a problem."

Espy turned. The tunnel she'd entered from the trail had been a natural formation—a winding, irregularly shaped route. But that tunnel had suddenly straightened into a drilled-out passageway, perhaps a dozen feet high. The chamber where she found Marcus was also an artificial construct—four unnaturally smooth rock walls, a nearly perfect square storage area of some sort, judging from the shelving.

Marcus was now pointing up at one of those walls, to a black plastic block, maybe nine by three inches, stuck to the stone. It glowed with a faint red light, coloring the wall as it pulsed.

"What is that?" she asked.

"Not positive." He moved closer, peered around the device from a couple different angles. "Looks like a Ned," he said.

"A what?"

"A Ned. NED. An acronym. Short for networked explosive device."

"A bomb."

"Well, yeah. But, bomb." He shook his head. "That's like saying a Porsche is a car. This is high-tech stuff. Top of the line. The agency has been working on these for years. Only this one"—he leaned in closer—"this has got more bells and whistles than I've ever seen."

"That blinking light. You think—"

"Yeah. It's live, is my guess."

"Can you disarm it?"

"Wouldn't even want to try. Networked device, right? Means it's connected to a whole bunch of others. Mess with one, break that connection, and sixty seconds later … *boom*. Now I know what that other guy meant, that they were shutting things down here."

Shutting things down. Just what Kingsleigh had said. Only

CHAPTER 60

here...

"Shutting things down. Meaning blow them up."

"Looks that way."

"Why?" She looked around. "What is this place? And why do they want to destroy it?"

"It belonged to something called the Holland Corporation, back in the day. Prototype testing facility. What kind of prototype, I don't know."

"Holland." Espy nodded. "Ferrone was involved with that too. Frank Sr."

"That other guy—the one who was with Jann—he was in charge, I'm pretty sure. Find him, we'll get some answers."

"Then let's go do that."

"Yeah. Hey. One second." He reached toward her.

She recoiled. "What?"

He pointed. "You still got the tag. On your bathing suit there."

She reached behind her and ripped it off.

"Okay. Let's move."

❖ ❖ ❖ ❖ ❖

She let Marcus lead the way. They were looking for a route down, to a lower level of the complex. *We'll meet you downstairs*, the other guy had told Jann a.k.a. Nemkov.

Blackjack. The secret your senator was killed to protect.

Nemkov. Still alive, somehow. He must have come to some sort of financial arrangement with these people. They'd decided to save his life after the shooting at the construction site. Of course they would do that, wouldn't they? He was—well, not Yuri Nemkov, but a highly skilled assassin. Yes? That was the only explanation that made sense. And yet...

"There," Marcus said, pointing at the wall. At another NED,

blinking red as they passed it. The third they had seen so far. How big was this place? How many more of these were there? Enough to blow this whole mountain sky high, was her guess.

She thought of Frederickson, waiting by that little pool. Pacing. Frustrated. Angry. Only, she realized, knowing Frederickson … He was probably doing anything but waiting. Not in his nature.

"Whoa." Marcus held up a hand to stop her. She'd been so deep in thought she'd almost run into him.

The narrow tunnel they'd been walking through had suddenly widened, opening up to reveal a huge cavern, a natural formation as big as a football stadium. They stood fifty feet above a huge metal platform that ran the length of that caven, at the far end of which was an array of huge turbines, each twenty or thirty feet across, all aqua blue plastic and gleaming steel. Five figures in white lab coats—and one without—congregated before the gleaming machinery.

Underneath the platform, Espy saw running water. An underground river. The source of the water in the canyon pool? Maybe so.

"There. I think that's him." Marcus pointed. "The guy in charge. The one in the center."

The man was the sole person in civilian clothes. He had his back to them, but something about him, his posture … Espy felt a little tingle of recognition. Tamped it down. She couldn't be sure.

"What's our move?" he asked.

She shook her head. They were way outnumbered here. And since those devices were armed, if they really were shutting things down, they were up against a ticking clock as well. So what was their move?

Same as before. Get to the man in charge. Get some answers. Because she still had so, so many questions.

CHAPTER 60

Twenty feet or so in front of them, the passageway ended at a spiral staircase. Metal, leading up and down.

"There," she gestured. "Our way down."

"Kind of exposed if we do that."

"I'm open to suggestions," she said, watching as—down below—another man came up to the one in civilian clothes and held out something for him to take. It looked like a computer tablet of some sort. The first man studied it for a second, then turned around. Looked up. Looked right in their direction.

Espy couldn't see his face, not from that distance, but that tingle of familiarity she'd felt grew to a certainty.

She knew who the man was. And knowing that, her stomach, her entire body, lurched again. Lurched in that same way it had when she'd seen Nemkov.

"You all right?" Marcus asked.

She shook her head. Something was wrong here. Oh so very wrong.

And then things got worse.

"Ms. Harper. Mr. Kleinman. Why don't you come down here and join us?"

The voice echoed off the tunnel wall. Hard to tell exactly where it was coming from, and the sound was metallic. Distorted. But it was familiar all the same. She'd last heard it two weeks ago, at Langley. At Building 10. In the cafeteria.

"It's Talbot," she said.

"What?" Marcus asked.

"That man. It's Perrin Talbot. He's CIA. He's—"

She heard footsteps behind them and turned.

Two men, brandishing guns.

"Waiting for you." One of the men smiled. "This way, please."

CODENAME: BLACKJACK

❖ ❖ ❖ ❖ ❖

They disarmed Marcus and escorted them down that long, winding metal staircase to the main floor.

"The network devices." Marcus, a few steps below her, shook his head. "Bells and whistles. They added visual monitoring. They were watching us. I should've known, should've guessed. Some of the technology came straight out of the CASHIER program." He turned and caught her eye.

CASHIER.

The disguised CCTV cameras.

Talbot.

If her thoughts had been racing before—they were churning now.

"Ms. Harper." Talbot strode across the metal platform, met them at the bottom of the staircase. He was dressed in the same nondescript suit he'd worn at Langley, at Garrett's funeral, and at Garrett's wake for that matter too. A loose, ill-fitting dark blue suit that looked like it had come off a department store sale rack.

Camouflage, she realized.

"I would ask how you found us," Talbot said, "but there's really only one possible explanation. Frank. He was close, wasn't he? Am I right?"

"I don't know what you're talking about," she said, though of course she did. Frank Ferrone. The map. Ferrone had been looking for this place. Looking for Talbot. Why?

"And you, Mr. Kleinman," Talbot continued. "You seem completely recovered. We're going to have to talk to the lab. 17B? The active ingredients versus the inactive ones ... we need to sharpen things up. Maybe with the next iteration. 17C. Practice will make perfect."

CHAPTER 60

"Don't go to any trouble on my account. Mr. Talbot, is it?" Marcus turned to her. "You said this guy was agency?"

"That's right."

"I never heard of him."

"He's not important," Espy snapped. A lie, of course.

"You cut me to the quick, Ms. Harper. After all we've been through."

"We barely know each other," she said.

"Oh, agreed, we've only met a few times." Talbot smiled. "But they've been important occasions. Mission-critical occasions, Ms. Harper. The CASHIER hearings. Langley, most recently. Garrett Crandall's funeral. And his wake. That I remember particularly well." His smile broadened. "The images are still fresh in my mind. I have little doubt I'll carry them with me the rest of my life. You coming up the stairs. Me standing in the hall, underneath that photograph of Garrett and Ted Kennedy. You remember, don't you? "To many more voyages together"? It all came to me at that moment. Fully formed. If one believed in a god, that was a moment of divine inspiration."

"What are you talking about?" Marcus asked.

Talbot's gaze bore into hers. Espy didn't say anything.

One last voyage together, old friend.

You be careful too. Too many people weren't.

"After that initial conception, it was all very straightforward," Talbot continued. "Just a matter of picking and choosing the right material. And framing it correctly. Making it all look just so. But then, that's my business now. NSR-9. Document retrieval and reconstruction." He smiled. "We nailed it, don't you think?"

"Espy?" Marcus asked. "What's he talking about?"

"You're not a stupid man, Mr. Kleinman. What do you think I'm talking about?"

Even though Talbot was speaking to Marcus, his eyes remained on hers. Dancing. Glittering with amusement.

"He's talking about the dossier," Espy said. "It's a fake."

61

Give Marcus credit, she thought. It only took him a three count.

"Shit," he said. "Shit, shit, shit. Of course it's a fake. Garrett would never keep something like that secret. Not tell us, not tell Stuart. We should've—"

"I do have to correct you both. 'Fake' is not entirely accurate," Talbot said. "The documents themselves are real enough. We simply created the frame. The package. Ted Kennedy's letter, the courier envelope, the magazine cover, Nan the researcher, all those notes. Once we arranged for you to discover them—"

"Nemkov. That call. Those shots at the construction site," Espy said.

"Blanks. Amazing what people will believe with the proper special effects. As your Mr. Rivers could attest to. Isn't that right, Jann?" Talbot asked. There he was, coming down the stairs behind them. Nemkov himself.

The man didn't respond. Just stared at Marcus and Espy with eyes blazing. A thin trickle of crusted blood ran down the side of his face.

Talbot gestured. "That should be seen to."

"Soon," the man replied. "After we finish this."

"So Garrett's death was an accident?" Espy asked.

"Yes. Exactly as it seemed. A freak, one-in-a-million accident."

"Woodhull," Espy said. "You're in our system. You changed the library records."

Talbot smiled. "Yes. We've been in there for quite some time. We were watching you. That's how we knew when to plant the material at the golf club."

"A fake." Marcus shook his head. "Why? Why go to all that trouble?"

"Why? You ask why? Frank Ferrone is why." Talbot's face reddened. For the first time, something other than amused contempt entered his voice. Anger. No. More than anger.

Rage.

"Frank Ferrone and his ceaseless, insatiable greed. His hunger for money and notoriety. His desire to be the name on everyone's lips, every day of the week. His insatiable avarice that flew in the face of common sense." Talbot pointed a finger and shook his head. "Flew in the face of the understanding that had been reached sixty years ago."

"You're talking about Ararat," Marcus said. "About the water they discovered. An aquifer, am I right? Something buried deep beneath—"

"Aquifer?" Talbot laughed. "Ararat is much more than an aquifer. What they discovered back then, calling it an aquifer, it's like ... how did you put it, calling the Porsche a car? If you take my point."

Marcus glared.

"But yes. After making that discovery ... after realizing what the government intended to do with it ... publicize it, waste it ... share it with the world, let it be drained dry by the unworthy—Colonel Averill made a decision. He decided this incredible resource needed to be carefully husbanded, so he took it out of the government's hands—"

"By killing everyone on the project," Marcus said.

"And put it into more responsible ones," Talbot continued. "His."

"His first. And now mine."

"Yours. What does that mean exactly? Who are all these other

CHAPTER 61

people?" Espy asked, gesturing. "What is this place?"

"Not your concern," Talbot said.

"This is it, isn't it?" Marcus said. "Ararat."

"Ararat? This? Good lord no." Talbot shook his head. "This isn't Ararat. This is just … think of it as a faucet. A spigot, if you will." He pointed to the turbines behind him. "A way to control the water coming from Ararat and deliver it to the Colorado River watershed. To the reservoir system. To monetize the infrastructure we've been building over the years."

Monetize.

Trust me. El Niño, La Niña, mother nature be damned, come spring we'll be fine.

"Averill. He made a deal," Espy said. "With the mob."

"No. Not with the mob—with one man. With Frank Ferrone Sr. who was a brilliant financier and a very different kind of man from his son. A much more circumspect, careful man. The real estate empire he created, we benefited from. Quietly. Judiciously. But when Sr. passed and Frank Jr. inherited his father's end of the bargain, everything changed." Talbot sighed. "Frank Jr.'s bottomless need for money meant a need for more water than ever. He wanted more water for Aqua Roma. Much more than we had agreed upon. I couldn't believe it when I read the numbers. In the middle of a drought, in the middle of climate change. I told him no. I told him he was going to get us caught. Expose Ararat to the world. To kill the goose that laid all those golden eggs for us over the years. He wouldn't listen to reason."

"Time out. How the hell does all that work? Supplying water to Lake Mead?" Marcus shook his head. "I don't see how you could possibly—"

"It works by being inconspicuous," Talbot snapped. "Just a small variation from the seasonal snow melt. A rounding error. A certain number of acre feet per day, fed into the watershed slowly, at an agreed-upon date, according to an agreed-upon formula—"

Acre feet per day. A certain number. "The betting slips," Espy realized.

"Yes, exactly." Talbot nodded.

"What?" Marcus asked.

"AFD. The betting slips. In Ferrone's—under the hangar." She pictured them in her head. "The numbers on the slips."

"Yes. Acre feet per day. AFD. Betting slips delivered surreptitiously through a third-party contact. A flow measurement, keyed to a specific date range, generally, although…" Talbot stopped himself. "The details are unimportant. The point is, Frank wanted an unconscionable increase in that number for his new project. For Aqua Roma. I said no. He persisted. Time and time again. And that's when … well, it became clear. The deal no longer held. It was either going to be him or me."

"That's why he was looking for you," Espy said, "Looking for this place."

"Yes. He intended to kill me and take over Ararat for himself. I needed to eliminate him first. I had a problem, though." Talbot met her eyes again. "I wasn't the only person Frank was in business with. He belonged to another organization, one that takes care of its own. So I had to find a way to arrange—"

You're the one who told us about the money.

We owe you a debt of gratitude.

"Oh my god," Espy said, and her knees wobbled, because at that second, the final domino fell.

His $1.2 billion, you mean?

Not his. Ours. The money he stole from the Peacock.

"Espy?" Marcus asked. "You all right?"

She shook her head. She wasn't all right. She was a fool.

CHAPTER 61

No. That was the wrong word. Not a fool.

Patsy.

"I had to find a way to eliminate Frank without being involved at all," Talbot continued. "Otherwise, Mr. Kingsleigh and his friends would come after me. Take their revenge."

"You used me," she said.

"I used all of you. Everyone at Woodhull. But I knew you would be the one to find out about the $1.2 billion, Ms. Harper. That is your business, after all. ICE-T. Tracking down monetary transactions outside the legal system. Offshore accounts and the like?" He smiled. "All I had to do was start you looking."

"The dossier."

"Yes. The photo. Garrett and Ted Kennedy. As I said, it all came to me in that instant. I would give you the chance not only to exact revenge for your fallen comrade but to solve what really happened in Dallas back in 1963. And it worked to perfection. Off you went, all of you. Seeking that truth. But of course, the only place those documents led—"

"C.C. Brody," Espy said. "The boxer. Jimmy Allen."

"Exactly."

"Wait," Marcus said. "Manchester, the patrolman—Casserly. That led me right to Averill. That's how—"

"Coincidence. One can never plan for everything, after all. The world is chaotic. And your detective friend, Mr. Cockerell, he was unexpectedly insightful. Finding that woman. Finding evidence of the colonel's interest in Manchester. Which I had no knowledge of. Well before my time." Talbot shrugged. "After the accident that destroyed Ararat, the colonel worried about JFK. Worried that he suspected something. He wanted to make sure that Kennedy hadn't shared those suspicions with anyone. After Dallas, after Manchester started working on his book, talking to everyone under the sun, the colonel decided to put him under surveillance. My fault, I suppose, for not checking our records more thoroughly. But sixty years? I allow myself that oversight."

"You killed Cockerell," she said.

"And Doc, and Zelda," Marcus said.

"My people did, yes."

Marcus opened his mouth again, getting ready to say something else. Something cutting, or snide, words intended to get a rise out of Talbot. Which would be a mistake. Talbot was gloating a little. Let him.

As long as he was talking, they had a chance.

"Go on," Espy prompted, before Marcus could speak.

"Senator Crandall was the key," Talbot continued. "His focus on Aqua Roma. The deleterious effects of its construction. It seemed to be a problem, at first, but it turned out to be the solution. Frank's animus for the man was everywhere. The newspapers, conversations with his stockholders…"

"The board minutes at the Greenbrier," Espy said.

"I expected you to learn about that $1.2 billion there. The board minutes were a bonus. It was the money that was important. Frank needed it to keep the stock afloat. To keep Mr. Kingsleigh and the others from losing everything he had convinced them to put into Desert View. Mr. Wharton Business School, with his stock splits and P/E ratios—he couldn't very well go to the men from Sicily and tell them 'Sorry, but the market is a risky business, and that money you gave me—it's gone.' He couldn't say 'I miscalculated,' could he?"

"No," Espy said. "He couldn't."

That's not how we do business. That's never how we've done business.

"Frank couldn't tell them why Aqua Roma was failing. He

CHAPTER 61

couldn't say I denied his requests for extra water. He couldn't say anything about the water at all. Because if Kingsleigh's organization discovered how much money Ararat had put into the Ferrone family's pockets, they'd not only want his share, they'd want mine. And then they'd come after me. No, all Frank could do—"

"Put the money in himself."

"Exactly. I created a vise, Ms. Harper. I put Frank in an impossible situation, and then I squeezed." Talbot brought his hands slowly together in demonstration. "Denying the water meant he couldn't meet those construction benchmarks. North Henderson suspended their loan covenants, and Frank had to put in his own money. That $1.2 billion. Then I used the dossier to bring you in, and you went after the source of that money. But I must say, that business with the 10-K, and the board—I hadn't even considered that. Brilliant work on your part."

"You'll excuse me if I don't say thank you."

"Brilliant, and oh so helpful. Pointing out to the board—to Kingsleigh and his friends—how they'd helped cook the books. How their signatures made them legally, criminally, responsible for inflating the value of Desert View's stock? Kingsleigh was furious. And the vise ... tightened." Talbot put his hands together and twisted. "Frank had no choice but to go after you. And that upset Kingsleigh even more."

The argument they'd witnessed at the ranch, Espy realized.

Her heart was thudding in her chest. Equal parts anger and shame raced through her system.

Patsy. Fool…

Tool.

Calm, she told herself. Calm.

You need to find a way out of this.

"And then at last, the endgame," Talbot said. "Your discovery.

Where that $1.2 billion came from. I didn't know exactly how that would play out, but I knew once Kingsleigh learned of it, he'd assume that Frank must have stolen it from him. And he reacted just as I had planned. Reacted according to his nature, just as people of his kind always have and always will."

"He killed Ferrone."

"Yes. The perfect crime, wouldn't you say? Kingsleigh and his associates are never going to suspect my involvement. They'll never come looking for me, because in fact"—his smile broadened—"they don't even know I exist. And since Frank and Falconetti were the only two who knew about Ararat, and they're gone, no one involved even knows my name. Well…" He looked at her and Marcus. "Almost no one."

"People know where we are," Espy said.

"Your man Frederickson? We've got an eye on him. We'll handle that. And speaking of handling things…" He looked down at his tablet. "We have another seventeen minutes and ten seconds here. And while we could just leave you to perish in the explosions, experience tells me it's not worth taking that kind of chance." He motioned to Jann. "Finish this, please. Make it as painful as you like."

Jann smiled. "With pleasure."

Talbot nodded, turned back to her. "Goodbye, Ms. Harper. Mr. Kleinman. We won't meet again."

"Promises, promises," Marcus said.

Espy said nothing.

Talbot smiled, nodded, spun on his heel, and walked away. Heading toward the turbines.

Seventeen minutes and ten seconds. Less now.

"Now." Jann smiled. "We have business to take care of."

He motioned the two armed men forward. They raised their

CHAPTER 61

weapons.

"You're making a mistake," Marcus said. "Crane knows."

"Knows what?"

"All about this. All about Ararat."

Jann held up a hand. The two men relaxed for a second.

"Does he, now?"

"He does."

"Convince me. You have ten seconds."

Marcus, Espy realized, was doing the same thing she'd just done. Buying time. Delaying. Giving her a chance to do something. Find a way to get them out of this alive.

Unfortunately, she had no idea what that something could be.

There were five of them arranged in close proximity. She and Marcus, both unarmed, ten feet from Jann, who stood at the base of the staircase with the two armed men on either side of him. Not good odds—but not, perhaps, insurmountable ones. The real problem was the others gathered on the platform. There were dozens of them, she saw now. Mostly engineers in white lab coats, but others in uniform among them. Armed, she guessed. Talbot's foot soldiers.

"I sent a message," Marcus said, "through Sherman."

"You're lying," Jann said. "If Crane knew, he'd be here."

"He's on his way," Marcus said.

"I'd like to test that hypothesis." Jann stepped forward, drawing a weapon of his own. It looked remarkably like the weapon Frederickson had used on Cockerell back at the construction site. White 17.

And as Jann stepped forward, she saw something else too. Something behind him, on the railing at the bottom of the stairs. Not a way to turn the tables. That was impossible. But a way they could be of service here. And that was paramount. Talbot could

495

put on all the airs he wanted about husbanding resources, the way Averill had, but they were both cut from the same cloth as the mob. Killers, with no regard for the value of human life. And she knew deep down in her gut, whatever Talbot was planning next, a lot more people were most certainly going to die. He had to be stopped.

She turned to Marcus. "Shut up," she said. "Don't say another word."

"Don't tell me what to do," he snapped.

"That's a direct order. If we're going to die, let's go out the right way. On our own terms."

He glared. Met her gaze. No way he could have any idea what she was up to, and yet…

She had a feeling he knew exactly what she was about to do.

"I don't take orders from—"

She spun and aimed a kick square for his head. It would have broken his nose if it had connected. Instead, he dodged. He kicked out and sent her flying backward. She stumbled, almost fell, and then purposely stumbled again, catching the staircase railing behind her with one hand, using that to steady herself.

She felt the smooth metal of the railing—and a little ridge of plastic. The surface of that little something she'd seen earlier.

Pulsing with a faint red light.

She smiled, and straightened.

"One for you," she said to Marcus, and moved to step forward.

"Stop. Right there. Right now," Jann said. Espy glared, then raised her arms in surrender.

And then she lifted her right foot slightly, raised her right arm, put all her weight into the backswing, and struck the NED with her elbow. Hit it with the bone, as hard as she could. She felt that impact all the way up to her neck. Felt the plastic give,

CHAPTER 61

but not crack, under the impact. For a second, it seemed to have done nothing.

And then, all at once, the red light emanating from the NED changed. Stopped slowly pulsing, and began insistently flashing.

"Emergency countdown initiated."

The metallic, robotic voice that issued from the NED was not Talbot's now. It was fully computerized. Toneless.

"Sixty seconds to detonation," the voice said.

Jann stood there, openmouthed. "What did you just do?"

"Accelerated your timetable."

"Sixty seconds." One of the guards looked at her, then at Jann. "How are we going to get out of here in sixty seconds?"

"You're not," she said. "None of us are."

"Fifty seconds to detonation," the voice said.

She glanced toward the far end of the platform as she spoke. Talbot stood there, right next to the turbines. He turned back now to look at her.

She imagined the thoughts running through his head at that instant, and managed a little smile of her own.

And then, underneath the thrumming of the turbines and the sound of gunfire, Espy heard another sound. A higher-pitched whining.

And Talbot was on the move. Jogging toward the far edge of the platform. Four men jogged alongside him. Soldiers. Two on either side, two facing forward, two facing backward, weapons raised. Covering him. The crowd parted, and Espy saw where the higher-pitched sound was coming from. A helicopter.

"Shit," Marcus said.

Jann laughed. "The colonel always has a backup plan."

"Forty seconds to detonation."

Others were massing behind Talbot's group. They pushed

forward. Shots rang out—screams, falling bodies, and chaos followed.

Talbot was shooting his own people, in order to make good his escape.

Espy sensed movement on her left, turned in time to see one of the men who'd been holding a gun on her take off running in that direction.

"Wait!" he shouted. "Oh god, wait!"

The other man dropped his weapon and ran too.

"Thirty seconds to detonation."

Thirty seconds. Nothing to be done, except … say her goodbyes.

The helicopter rose into the air. Espy saw a shaft of light, high above. Talbot was escaping.

And Jann was boosting himself up onto the railing. He jumped.

"What the hell…" Marcus had turned to follow her gaze, was now standing right alongside her.

"Twenty seconds to detonation."

She ran to the railing and looked down at the water rushing past far below.

Water.

You think this little pool supplies Lake Mead?

No, she'd said.

But maybe she was wrong. That water had to go somewhere, didn't it?

"Ten seconds to detonation."

"Come on!" Espy yelled to Marcus, planting her hands on the railing, boosting herself up.

"Five seconds to detonation. Four. Three—"

She jumped.

The world exploded, and she plunged downward, through a rain of fire.

62

Frederickson stood ankle-deep in the water, stripped down to his boxers.

He'd given Espy five minutes to return. When she didn't, he decided to find a way to follow. First thought: take the car, head farther up into the mountains. See if he could parallel her route up. No go. The road dead-ended half a mile from the pond at a sheer rock wall. He'd come back to the pool, decided to try another tack. Brought the duffel with Ferrone's wetsuit back down to the water. Swallowed a half-dozen ibuprofen, ripped the sling off, careful not to pop his stitches, and squeezed himself into the wetsuit. Or tried to.

It didn't fit. He used his knife to cut a seam into the legs, and then tried again. Success ... until the whole thing ripped in half. So, the boxers.

He was a good swimmer. Normally, he'd freestyle his way across the lake to where Espy had started her climb, no problem. But considering that he only had the use of one arm at this point, he'd have to turn over onto his back. Flutter-kick his way across, with the little bag containing his clothes and his gun resting on his stomach.

He'd taken his first few steps into the water when he heard a thrumming noise in the distance. He looked up just in time to see a helicopter shoot past directly overhead—looked like a Bell Jet Ranger. It quickly disappeared out of sight. And the feeling in his gut—the feeling that had been there since Espy had disappeared up that trail—grew stronger.

This little dot on the map was exactly what Ferrone and Falconetti had been looking for.

And at that second, he saw the first explosion. A ball of fire, a plume of smoke high above, coming from the top of the mountain Espy had climbed.

A second, then a third, and fourth, and fifth explosion. Rocks began tumbling down toward the water. The rumbling beneath his feet increased. Changed in character, in sound…

A huge jet of water shot up out of the middle of the pool. A geyser. Just like Old Faithful. Like the fountains at the Bellagio, on steroids. A cloud of spray so vast, so thick, for a second it blotted out his view of the entire lake.

The initial spray lessened in intensity, and then stopped.

The lake was suddenly covered with debris—pieces of wood and metal sinking downward. And something else.

A person.

Espy.

"Sonofa…"

The water on the lake began to move. A circular motion. Slow at first, and then speeding up. A whirlpool. Coming from where the geyser had been.

Frederickson felt the water around him surge in that direction with unexpected force. Suddenly, he wasn't standing ankle-deep in the lake. In the time it had taken him to notice, the water had gone down two inches. The entire lake was disappearing, getting sucked back down into the ground, back to wherever it had come from.

Espy was going to get sucked down right along with it. And not just her. He saw another person now too. Another body.

Marcus Kleinman?

"HEY!" Frederickson yelled. "HEY!"

Espy's head moved. She looked up. Her eyes met his.

CHAPTER 62

"It's a whirlpool!" he yelled, gesturing frantically. "Swim!"

She looked around. He could see awareness of her predicament sinking in. The current carried Marcus toward her. She reached out, and for a second, got hold of him. Then the current ripped him away again.

"Swim!" Frederickson yelled again.

Espy rolled over, took long, powerful strokes toward the shore. Trying to break free of the whirlpool. She wasn't strong enough. The water held her in place and then swept her away, out of sight.

Frederickson took two quick steps forward and stopped. He could feel the power of the whirlpool even this far out from its center. Charging in after them—he'd just get himself sucked in too. It was like quicksand.

He needed to toss them a lifeline. Something to hold on to.

Ferrone's duffel. The rope.

He ran for it. Found the rope and ran back toward the water. Holding tight to one end of the rope with his left hand, he reared back and tossed the remaining coil with his right, ignoring the bolt of agony that came with it. Plenty of time for painkillers later.

The rope landed ten feet shy of Espy and a still-unmoving Marcus.

"Shit!" he yelled, and yanked it back toward him, just as another explosion shook the ground. A huge boulder tumbled down the canyon wall and landed in the water, sending up a cloud of mist and spray, momentarily obscuring his vision.

"Espy!" he yelled. "Espy!"

The spray cleared. The whirlpool brought Espy, then Marcus, back into view, then took them away. Frederickson gathered the rope and coiled it up again, focusing his attention on Espy, timing her motion as she spun round the center of the whirlpool, as she turned in place, trying to maintain eye contact with him.

He threw the rope again ... and missed again, the end landing a good dozen feet shy of Espy. Marcus suddenly lifted his head and plunged forward with two powerful strokes, snaking out a hand to try and grab the rope.

He missed too.

And then a third hand shot out of the water and seized hold.

Frederickson barely had time to absorb that shock—another survivor?—when the rope suddenly yanked him forward, cutting into his right palm. Yanking with sudden, painful force on his shoulder. He bit back a scream and grabbed hold of that rope with his left hand as well, easing the strain on his right. A man's head broke the surface of the water. The whirlpool slammed Marcus into the newcomer. He grabbed hold of the man. A second later, the current brought Espy around. She caught on to the rope too.

Frederickson managed to maneuver the rope over his left shoulder, easing pressure on his right further, letting him use the full power of his legs to brace himself.

He was being dragged forward, into the whirlpool.

He tightened his grip on the rope. Both hands now. Both shoulders. Felt the rope digging deep into his palm, felt his fingers growing numb. The roar of the whirlpool increased. Something popped in his right shoulder. The stitches? A muscle? His hand and shoulder grew slick. Sweat? Or blood? Both probably. He didn't care to look.

He closed his eyes, and held on.

How long, he had no idea. Ten seconds? Twenty? A minute?

But at last, the pressure on his hand slackened, then stopped. He dropped the rope.

His fingers were white where the circulation had been cut off. His palm was soaked in blood. He glanced down at his shoulder and saw that the stitches had held. The blood he'd felt was from

CHAPTER 62

lacerations made by the rope, digging into his skin.

Espy, Marcus, and the other survivor were sitting in a rapidly draining pool of water. Coughing. Recovering. He walked toward them.

"Espy. You blew up the whole freaking mountain, didn't you?" He smiled, shook his head. "Who's this?" He gestured to the other man, who looked up at him at the same instant. He was tall and thin, Frederickson saw now.

And all at once, very familiar.

"Holy shit," Frederickson said, "Nemkov?"

The man scrambled backward and drew a gun from a holster strapped to his side. He pointed it at Frederickson and fired. Missed.

A dart stuck in the ground next to him.

Marcus was moving already. Launching himself at the third man, catching him with an elbow right to the forehead. The man reeled; Marcus ripped the weapon out of the man's grasp, turned it on him.

"Nemkov," Frederickson repeated. "Shit. That's Nemkov, right? But how—"

"Blanks," she said. "Fake blood."

"The dossier's a fake too," Marcus said.

"Jesus Christ." Frederickson's eyes widened. He shook his head. "A fake. Of course it's a fake. Why didn't I—"

"None of us did." Espy took a deep breath and got to her feet. With a final, enormous sucking sound, the last of the water disappeared into the lake floor, leaving a field of perfectly flat stone behind.

"So what's this all about?" Frederickson asked. "That place up there."

"Water," she said. "Ferrone and Talbot working together to—"

"Talbot? CIA Talbot?"

"Yes. He's behind it. He's—"

"Gone. In the wind," Marcus said.

"I saw a helicopter."

"That was him." Espy nodded. "The question is where he went. What he's planning."

"I think our friend here might be able to help us figure that out." Marcus gestured toward Jann.

Espy studied the man. The decision to follow Jann off the platform had been a spontaneous one. An instinctual one. They'd lucked out, had been sucked through a narrow tunnel—out of control, spinning past Jann as they went—that had brought them back to her starting point: the little pool, and Frederickson.

Jann snorted. "I have no intention of telling you anything else."

"Yeah, well, lucky we have this." Marcus held up Jann's weapon—and fired it.

"Thank you." Espy knelt down next to Jann, who stared at the dart in his arm. "Now tell me. Talbot. What's he up to? What's his plan?"

Jann shook his head.

"Never," he said. "I have been trained to resist—"

Espy gestured, and Marcus shot him again.

"Training versus drugs. Let's see which one gives first, shall we?" She leaned closer. "Talbot. Where has he gone? What are his plans?"

Jann just smiled. Kept shaking his head.

Espy frowned. Did the man really have some sort of specialized training? Should they risk a third dart? He was big, but given what she knew, that might just knock him out.

Just then, the back-and-forth motion—Jann shaking his head—became a roll, his head swaying from right to left. He

CHAPTER 62

blinked. His eyes lost focus.

"Talbot," Espy said. "Where is he?"

"Where is he? Right now?" Jann looked her in the eye, then looked down at her wrist. "Ah. That is a very nice watch."

"What does that matter? Where's Talbot?"

He looked down at her wrist again and then back up.

"Five thirty. Yes. Okay. So right now, he is still getting ready."

"Getting ready? For what?"

Jann's eyelids fluttered.

Espy grabbed his chin. Shook his head back and forth. "Jann. Getting ready for what?"

He blinked. "Phase Two, of course. Now that Mr. Ferrone is dead … now that Mr. Talbot has sole control of the most valuable resource on the planet … it is time for Phase Two."

"And what's Phase Two?" she asked.

His eyes closed.

"Jann!" Espy shook his shoulders. "What's Phase Two?"

He started snoring.

"Phase Two," Frederickson said. "That doesn't sound good."

"No, it doesn't." Marcus looked at him and frowned. "Why are you in your underwear, by the way?"

Frederickson growled.

"Wardrobe is the least of our concerns right now." Espy stood. "We need to get hold of Stuart. Let him know what's really going on here."

"Actually…" Marcus cleared his throat. "There's a good chance Stuart knows what's going on already. Some of it, at least."

Espy turned to him. "How's that?"

"Well, when you reached out—sent the drone—you said not to contact you directly. To find another way to keep in touch. So I did."

"I meant stay under the radar." She glared. "So let me get this straight. Instead of sending me updates, you've been sending them to Stuart?"

"Of course not. What do you think I am, stupid?"

"Can I answer that?" Frederickson put in.

Espy ignored him. "Okay. So if you haven't been in contact with him, then who?"

"Well, I had to think out of the box," Marcus said. "I had to make sure it was somebody off the grid. I mean way off."

"Oh, this oughta be good," Frederickson said, putting his shirt back on.

"Please," Espy said.

Frederickson smiled and waved a hand at Marcus. "Continue, please. Somebody off the grid."

"Yeah. But somebody I could trust. Somebody who knew about us. Somebody maybe who'd even worked with us before. Somebody who knew about you, Espy—somebody I could say your name to and they'd know instantly that I was on the level."

"Oh my god." Espy shook her head. She had a sudden, sinking feeling in her stomach. A feeling that she knew exactly who Marcus had reached out to. "You didn't."

"Hey." He met her gaze. "He was the perfect choice. The logical choice, when you think about it. He's been off the grid now for a while. Way off the grid. So when I reached out, my messages—what I suggested he do, in a roundabout way, was go to your mother, and let her be the one—"

Frederickson started laughing. "Oh, this is perfect."

"Matt." Espy shut her eyes and sighed heavily. "You went to Matt."

Marcus nodded. "I did indeed."

Matt. Boys and their toys.

CHAPTER 62

Matt.

You know how I feel, Espy. But you and me ... it doesn't work. You're too intense. Too keyed up about everything.

"Well, this ought to be interesting," Frederickson said. "Don't you think?"

Espy glared. "Please finish getting dressed," she said. "And then let's get out of here."

The End... for Now.

Espy Harper and the Cincinnati will return in

CATARACT

Coming soon from Ternary Publishing
Please turn to Page 515 for a Special Preview!

CAST OF CHARACTERS

IN WASHINGTON, DC

The Society of the Cincinnati, Woodhull Chapter
Garrett Crandall—former chapter head and United States senator, deceased
Neil Frederickson—field operative and FBI agent
Esperanza "Espy" Harper—provisional chapter head and DOJ official
Li Min-Jing—chief of computer operations
Doug Rivers—field operative and actor

DC Metro Police
Detective Michael Cockerell
Lieutenant Dominic Colitti
Captain Rebecca Jorgensen

Minnesota Avenue
Showtime, a.k.a. Michael Cochrane
DeWayne
Wallet
Z (Rondell Zachary)

Others
John Bamberger—SEC official
George Casserly—retired DC police officer
Alice Crandall—Garrett Crandall's widow
Stuart Crane—president-general of the Society of the Cincinnati
Penelope Harper—Espy's mother
Yuri Nemkov—hired assassin
Mike Pritchett—DOJ senior official, Espy's boss
Perrin Talbot—CIA, department chief, Document Retrieval and Reconstruction

CAST OF CHARACTERS

AT THE GREENBRIER, WEST VIRGINIA

Ramon Cabral—data technician, Pyramid Technologies

Daniel Josephson

Raymond Lish—attorney for the Desert View Real Estate Corporation

Donna Pickering—Greenbrier employee

OTHERS

Sally Bartolo

Lynn Beck

Jackson "Doc" Kelley—retired CIA operative

Marcus Aurelius Kleinman—CIA agent and Society operative, Culper Chapter

Zerya Moradi—Doc's adopted daughter

IN LAS VEGAS

In 1962

James Averill—CIA, head of Special Projects Division

Frank Ferrone Sr.—manager, Peacock Hotel and Casino

Stephen Guidry—geologist and chief scientist, CIA Special Projects Division

Present-day

C.C. Brody—Frank Ferrone's stepmother

Vincent Falconetti—Ferrone's right-hand man

Frank Ferrone Jr.—CEO, Desert View Real Estate Corporation

Michael Fishman—president, Silver City Real Estate

Joseph Guidry—Stephen Guidry's son

Benjamin Kingsleigh—board member, Desert View Real Estate Corporation

Johnny Romano—vice president, Desert View Real Estate Corporation

Laura Sonores—board member, Desert View Real Estate Corporation

Kurt Vogelsang—private investigator and ex-CIA operative

David Whitestone—Las Vegas planning official

ACKNOWLEDGMENTS

A book this long and this long in the making does not come into existence through the work of only two people. We'd like to thank the following for their considerable assistance.

For their help in honing the manuscript:

Our omsbudsperson Emily Hitchcock, our editor Heather Shaw, our designer and typesetter Craig Ramsdell, Jean Zimmer, Pete Nelson, and Dr. Amy McClure.

Thanks also to all who read early drafts and commented: Haley and Kaci Roby - Betsy, Caleb, Jill, Larry, Maddy and Mike Stern— (the real) Mikey Cockerell, Renee Kauffman, Bill Koeblitz. T.J. Merker, Todd Mulliken, Yvette Bush, Tom and Susan Ricketts. Dick and Susan Haines, Fred Erfurt, John Huston, Fred Bernstein, and Jeff Scheinman.

For making the dossier come to life (in our novel):

Steve Campbell, Kate 'Nan' Benson, Rob 'that's what it was like in 1985' Kimmel, and Sparkie Allison.

For bringing those 16 pages (and the rest of our novel) out into the real world:

Pat Latham and Linda May at BR Printers.

For contributing their considerable talents to Espy Harper and her story, equally gifted artists Tim Parker and Nick Stull.

(Another tip of the hat to Steve Campbell for his work with the 1960s-era Washington DC police reports and the Sagas of the Cincinnati logo).

Special thanks to Emily Woo Zeller, whose voice talents brought our Sagas of the Cincinnati to life in audiobook form.

ACKNOWLEDGMENTS

A talented team of Baker Hostetler attorneys—notably Gary Wadman, Debra Wilcox, Megan Mischler and Scott Simpkins—protected our intellectual property and guided us through the many challenges our manuscript presented.

The Greenbrier Bunker tour staff and resort historian Bob Conte provided insights for our Greenbrier Hotel Segment, as did congressional staff members (NAMES?) who explained the ramifications of the Sarbanes-Oxley act to us.

During the course of our writing, we relied on many, many books and newspaper articles, but worth specific mention are:

The Death of A President by William Manchester. *The Case Against LBJ* by Roger Stone. *The Manchester Affair* by John Corry. *Hamilton*—and *Washington*—both by Ron Chernow.

Multiple visits to the JFK Library in Boston, and to Olin Library at Wesleyan University in Middletown, Connecticut, were necessary, and we'd like to thank the staff at both locations for their assistance. The staff at the Bloomberg Library at Harvard Business School also provided invaluable research material and insight.

Thanks are also due to Larry Abbott at Columbus' Aquatic Adventures, whose personal aquarium helped inspire Espy's Nemo habitat. Thanks also to Larry's management team for teaching us the basics of scuba diving and deep sea photography.

Andy Johnson provided us great insights into the luxury watch world.

Andy Graf gave us a crash-course in artificial intelligence, and how large language models really work. Sherman tells us he did pretty well ... for a human.

Thanks also to Jeremy Brennan, Josh Ferraira, Cristyn Mingo, Traci Olsen, and Aileen Schiro.

For assistance in the navigation of matters financial, military, and governmental, thanks go to Chris DeFrancis, Joe Ferrara, and David Grudberg.

For spiritual guidance and prayers—thanks to Don Doerr, Sheila Miller, Marvin Fowler and Jim Lillibridge.

Lastly, for special inspiration, we thank the Society of the Cincinnati, Henry Knox, members of the real Woodhull Spy Network, and three special generals—Arthur St. Clair, Cincinnatus, and George Washington.

ABOUT THE AUTHORS

Rusty McClure holds an M. Divinity from Emory and an M.B.A. from Harvard. He teaches an entrepreneur course at his undergraduate alma mater, Ohio Wesleyan. An advisor and investor in multiple entrepreneurial projects, he resides in Dublin, Ohio

Dave Stern is the author of over two dozen fiction and non-fiction titles including *The Blair Witch Project Dossier* and *Shadows in the Asylum*.

www.ternarypublishing.com

Now, a Special Preview of

CATARACT

Coming soon from Ternary Publishing

CATARACT

PROLOGUE

LAKE MEAD NATIONAL RECREATION AREA
LAS VEGAS, NEVADA

His name was Howard Jeffrey Newton, but everybody called him Fig.

Everybody: his friends, his students, the other professors, even the physical plant guys and the admin staff. When he'd first arrived at the college last year, he hadn't minded; it wasn't like he hadn't heard the nickname before. But lately, he was getting tired of it. Lately, it pissed him off. He'd tried to get people to stop, but not too hard. You didn't want to let anyone see how you really felt, because people were like sharks when it came to that kind of thing—they smelled blood in the water, they would pounce, do something nasty. Pull some prank like changing the nameplate on his door:

Fig Newton
Biological Sciences
Assistant Professor

Though the nameplate was going to change anyway. The *assistant* part was going to disappear. Nobody at the university knew it yet, but they were about to give him tenure. They were about to give him a little respect. They were going to stop calling him Fig and start calling him Professor. Stop making him teach the freshmen survey courses and give him some quality lab time.

All thanks to the bright green fish swimming in the pool of water in front of him.

He pressed the record button on the phone screen, kneeling down awkwardly to get the fish in the shot (he still had on the life vest the guy at the marina had insisted he wear), then began to speak. "This is Doctor Howard Jeffrey Newton. It is 13:25 Mountain Standard Time on May 16, and I am in a cave in the Lake Mead National Recreation Area, off the…" Damn, what was the name of the little side stream here? He'd just looked at it on the map a minute ago—something strange. That's right. "The Mariella Wash, where I have made an amazing discovery, this…" *Fish right here*, he was about to say, but as he turned the phone's lens toward the water, the fish moved away.

Moved was not a strong enough word—the fish shot away from him faster than Newton would have believed possible. Shot in a completely straight line right for a pile of rocks at the center of the little pool, then disappeared behind them. As if it was trying to hide. As if it didn't want to be seen or have its picture taken, which was impossible for a number of reasons, not the least of which was that the little fish was blind.

It was an *Amblyopsidae*—a cavefish. It had looked to be a couple inches long, which, if Newton was remembering right, was on the large side for the species. He didn't know all that much about cavefish, but the fact that they were all blind—that was a definite. They had evolved to function in near total darkness. Some people thought they navigated by sensing changes in pressure in the water currents around them; others thought that maybe they'd developed their sense of hearing to compensate for their loss of sight. Whatever. The point was, they couldn't see. So no way this one had seen him and darted off. And yet…

There it was, just barely visible behind the rocks at the center of the little pool. In fact, it wouldn't have been visible at all were it not for the fact that it was glowing. His little glow-in-the-dark cavefish. He had to have a shot of it—a video, some still captures—to go along with the article that was going to get him tenure and cement his career. He had a title for that article already: "Bioluminescence in the Amblyopsidae." By Howard J. Newton, PhD, Professor of Biological Sciences at the University of Nevada. Now all he needed were the images.

Oh, and the fish itself. He'd have to have that too. A sample to work with. Sorry, little guy. Though catching this little bugger would be tricky, he thought, remembering the way it had moved a moment ago, how quick it was. He was going to have to get his feet wet, so to speak. His hands dirty. He was going to have to get in the pool and corner it—and kill it.

Newton walked back to the boat. (Well, it wasn't really a boat, more like an oversized Jet Ski. A personal watercraft, the guy at the marina had called it. It had handlebars like a motorcycle and two seats, one behind the other.) He sat on the edge and pulled off his shoes and socks. He laid them on the rear seat next to the book he'd brought with him, some spy novel a friend of his had recommended. Mindless entertainment. That's what today had been intended as—mindless entertainment, some well-deserved R and R at semester's end, the academic year done, summer school waiting to start, and him sick and tired of being cooped up in his little office. He'd headed north out of the city, up through Henderson and then east into the National Recreation Area, out to the marina one of his TAs had told him about. Only that one was closed because of the drought, because of the water in the lake being down so low, so he'd had to go another ten minutes further up the road to another, which was where he'd rented the little watercraft. Hopped on board, got out on the lake, and gunned it. When he'd gotten out of sight of everyone, he'd just drifted for a while. Got a couple hundred pages into the book, got bored of the scenery, and headed off down the Mariella here, past some neat little rock formations and right into this neat little cave. Which was good timing, because he'd had a couple iced teas out on the lake and had to piss pretty badly, and there was something about peeing in reservoir water that he objected to. So he'd beached the boat and gotten out, intending to find some corner of the cave, and then he saw the pool, maybe twenty feet across at its widest point. Piss in there just as soon as anywhere else, he thought, but when he reached the edge he stopped short because there it was. The fish. The glowing cavefish, a kind of Amblyopsidae that no one had ever seen before, which meant he was going to get to name it, wasn't he?

Hah. Amblyopsidae Fig? Maybe so. He'd get it back to the lab, dissect it, and see. Maybe he should dash back home to grab his Nikon and get some help, someone else from the department to assist him in capturing the specimen. But who? Mayberry? Gomez? Holloway? They were all bureaucrats not teachers. They spent more time carrying around their coffee cups from meeting to useless meeting than they did in the classroom. Forming committees, subcommittees, issuing recommendations, reports. When was the last time they did any real science? When was the last time they really taught anybody? Not in this decade, he bet.

Maybe he didn't want tenure after all. Maybe private industry was the way to go. Time to decide all that later, he supposed. He took out his phone again and stepped into the little pool.

Surprise. The water was warm. Much warmer than the water on the lake. And it was moving too—there was a current running over his feet. Not much of one, but still, it was there. A hot springs of some sort? He wasn't aware of any hot springs in this area, though. Well. He'd focus on that part of the puzzle later.

He took a few hesitant steps toward the center of the little pool, wincing as he went because the bottom was littered with sharp stones. That meant the pool hadn't been there very long, that it was a relatively new formation. Though relatively new in geological terms could mean anything from a few weeks to a thousand years.

Newton recalled then that there had been a tremor a few days back, in the middle of exam week. He hadn't paid too much attention to it. An earthquake, the headlines had said, albeit a very minor one. But maybe that tremor had ruptured some of the formations out here, caused the hot springs—and maybe the fish?—to bubble up to the surface. Maybe. Time enough to figure that out later, too.

He took another step closer and raised the phone, focused the lens on the part of the fish he could see—its glowing green head darting in and out from behind the pile of rock at the center of the pool. Only now that he was closer, Newton realized there was something strange about that rock. In fact, he wasn't sure that it was a rock at all. Looked like a section of pipe, in fact, pushed up out of the ground. What was a pipe doing out here? Strange, and stranger.

And then, just as he was about to press the shutter button, the strangest thing of all happened.

The little fish attacked him.

It shot out from behind the rock, heading right at him, moving even faster than it had before, and before he could react it nipped at his foot and then darted away.

"Ow," Newton said, more surprised than hurt, surprised that a fish that size would go after something so much bigger than itself.

And then it did it again. Came at him a second time, and this time it went for his ankle. And bit harder. Much harder. Hard enough to really hurt.

"Sonuvabitch," Newton said, and reached down to slap the little fish away with his free hand. He got water instead. The sudden movement briefly unbalanced him—he stumbled and stepped on something. A rock, razor sharp, the tip of it just barely visible beneath the water's surface.

He cursed and lifted his foot, wobbling, nearly losing his balance, and threw his hands out to the side to steady himself.

The phone slipped from his grasp and fell. Not just into the water. Onto that same damn rock.

"Shit!" Even as he heard it hit, even as it splashed into the pool, his hand was there, snatching it out of the water, picking it up. He took one look at it and felt his heart sink.

The glass was cracked. Shattered, in fact.

Damn it. Why hadn't he gotten one of those full-enclosure, military-grade cases for it? He brought it with him everywhere, he should have—

The display flickered in his hand and went dark.

Newton stared at it in disbelief for a second.

There went his picture.

There went his video.

"Argh!" he yelled and, without thinking, threw the phone against the far wall of the cave. It clattered to the ground and lay there.

The fish darted out from behind the rock, back into the center of the pool, and held its position. Almost like a fighter beckoning him forward.

What the hell, he thought and started to laugh. He was in a fight with a two-inch fish, and he was losing.

Not for long, though.

"All right, you little bastard. It's on." Newton took a step forward, then stopped.

From out of the pipe at the center of the pool came a half-dozen more little glowing green fish, all identical to the first. They lined up in a row, one next to the other. A formation. Not like any formation Newton had ever seen or read about before, though.

Definitely going to get the Nikon, he thought then. The Nikon and some help. He lifted one foot out of the water, started to take a step backward…

And the fish moved. All of them moved, all at once.

Newton saw that and turned to run, he only had maybe two, three steps, seven, eight feet to go before he was out of the little pool of water, but he didn't make it. Not even close.

He felt the first bite on his ankle just as he turned, and goddamn, it hurt, and then the second bite came on his shin. How was that possible? The fish jumped out of the water to bite him? And that hurt even more than the one on his ankle, and then he could feel them digging their teeth in one after the other like little piranha. Jesus Christ were they trying to eat him? He was stumbling and running and cursing and then, finally—he was out of the pool.

He threw himself to the ground and lay there a moment, trying to catch his breath, to make sense of what had just happened. Killer cavefish? This was crazy, and yet, it had happened for sure. His feet, his ankles, the back of his right leg, they were all on fire. Little bastards. Jesus.

He rolled over and saw blood dripping down the back of his calf. He saw one of the little green fish, its teeth still firmly fastened to his ankle.

"Shit!" He reached down and grabbed hold of the little fish. It was scaly and hard. Hard as steel. Goddamn. He had been bitten by a lab rat once, and that hadn't hurt half as much as this. He yanked the damn thing out and threw it into the water behind him.

Then he looked at the wound it had left. Better disinfect it and get a band-aid on it, get back to the marina. Come back with a gun and shoot these things.

He got to his feet and hobbled over to his little watercraft, feeling lightheaded from all the excitement. So much for my day of mindless entertainment, he thought, getting out the first aid kit. There was a little flashlight in the kit; he leaned against the side of the watercraft, lifted his right leg up, and shone it on the bite.

There was a nasty-looking welt there. A quarter-size welt of reddish, inflamed skin. There were other smaller, similar welts on his ankles and feet. He tried to focus and count them, then his vision blurred for a second, and he gave up. But that wasn't what bothered him.

What bothered him was the little something still stuck in the wound. Hard to see in this light, probably one of their teeth, he supposed. There was a little smear of green next to that little something—the fish's blood? No, blood was red, no matter what species, but what else…

Venom.

What kind of fish had venom? For the first time, he felt a little tingle of fear.

Then he felt a wave of dizziness. He stood up and got both feet on the ground. His right leg buckled beneath him. He staggered backward, stumbled forward, and then—he couldn't stop himself, he couldn't do anything but watch it happen in slow motion, like he was a spectator not a participant—he began to fall. Face first, into the lake.

The water was ice-cold; the shock felt like it stopped his heart for a second.

Then he was floating. Floating away with the current. It carried him away from the entrance, toward the back of the cave. He tried to swim against it, but his arms weren't working right. Or his legs. It was the venom. Messing with his motor function. Jesus. He was paralyzed. He couldn't swim, couldn't make his limbs do what he was telling them to. He could barely think straight.

But he didn't need to do a lot of thinking to realize that if he didn't manage to turn himself over, he was going to drown.

So that's what he did. With the last of his strength, he pushed and twisted and turned and then…he was facing up and breathing air once more, the life vest holding him up in the water. He took in air for a second and third deep, deep breath.

He managed a faint smile. Thank god the guy at the marina made him put the vest on. It had lived up to its name, for sure. Life jacket. He blinked and smiled a second time.

This was actually going to work out just fine.

Those little fish. Those crazy little fish. What they'd done to him—this would be an even better article than he'd thought. "Aggressive Behavior in Bioluminescent Amblyopsidae." He could tell the story of what happened to him, how he'd almost drowned. Once the venom wore off. Once he got back in the boat—

He felt something tugging on his side. He looked down to his right and saw a little green fish swimming next to him.

It was chewing on the life-vest strap.

No, Newton thought. No. This is not happening.

But it was.

The little fish was gnawing through the strap. Like it was trying to kill him. Of course that was ridiculous, and yet…

"Stop it, goddamn it! Stop!" He'd meant to yell, but the words came out more like a mumble. As if, he thought, yelling would have done any good.

The fish kept sawing away. Newton tried to move his hand, to grab hold of it, but he couldn't. He had no motor function still. No control over anything. All he could do was watch.

The strap gave way. He felt the lifejacket loosen.

Water splashed on his face, and he started to cry.

The vest came loose, and he began to sink. He took a deep breath, the deepest breath he could, but it wasn't very deep at all. He didn't have the strength for it.

The water closed over his eyes. The light began to fade.

The little fish swam toward him again, hovering directly over his face. Watching him try to hold his breath. Watching him die.

The last thing Newton saw was its eyes, blinking and blinking, opening and closing as he sank. Almost like a camera shutter, he thought.

And then, in those final few seconds of his life, awareness came to him at last.

He recalled the way the fish had moved when he had first startled it, the speed of its reactions, its unnaturally aggressive behavior, as if it were aware not only of his presence but his purpose. The way it had hid and attacked, the formation it and the others had assumed, the way they had struck as one. The way it had not only come back to finish the job its venom had started, but was watching to make certain that job was done.

All those things which, taken together, led him now to the final realization that the little green glowing thing watching him was not an Amblyopsidae.

In fact, it wasn't a fish at all.

CATARACT

Coming soon from Ternary Publishing

Don't Miss The First Thrilling
SAGA OF THE CINCINNATI

Espy Harper, a young district attorney, stumbles across a secret society hidden in the very heart of the nation's capitol. Now, with the aid of her father—a highly-decorated FBI agent—and a washed-up onetime PGA golfer named Matt Thurman—Espy races across the country to thwart a group of terrorists intent on starting World War III.

Available now from Ternary Publishing

The New York Times Bestseller

"... sheds welcome light on the lives of two important but under appreciated figures of American business."
—*The Wall Street Journal*

CROSLEY

Two Brothers and a Business Empire That Transformed The Nation

Here is one of the great untold tales of the twentieth century—the epic, decades-spanning saga of Powel and Lewis Crosley, brothers born in the late 1800s into a humble world of dirt roads and telegraphs who rose to become kings of a global business empire.

The Crosley brothers helped pioneer the development of the broadcasting industry, possessing at one point the most powerful radio station in the world. Their revolutionary inventions, from the first mass-produced economy car to night baseball to the refrigerator door shelf, helped usher in the American century—a period of unprecedented prosperity for everyday consumers across the nation.

Crosley allows Powel and Lewis—and the company they built—to take their rightful place in the annals of American history.

Available now from Ternary Publishing